SIBBY'S SPAWN

Sibby Series Book IV

E. SLATE

Tabula Rasa Publishing

Cover Art & Design: Bailey McGinn

For Shana

Disclaimer

No one was injured during any of Sibby's yoga classes.

Chapter 1

Mom Blog Entry:

Saw my OBGYN this morning. Told her that my sex life was in need of resuscitation. She wrote me a prescription for a bottle of wine and a copy of Indiana Bones and the Temple of Poon.

That's porn, by the way. In case that wasn't clear.

"Sibby? Sibby, are you awake?" Aidan whispered.

I moaned into the pillow. "No."

"Sibby, I need your breasts."

"Not tonight, honey, I have a headache."

"Not for me. For your spawn. They're hungry."

"I just fed them," I grumbled, finally sitting up. The lamp on my bedside lit the room and I grabbed my cellphone to check the time. I'd gone to bed not even an hour ago. Annie had left after a night of girl-talk, I'd let Jasper out for a quick pee break and took the baby monitor with me, and then I'd climbed into bed to get some much-needed sleep. The nights of waiting up for Aidan to get home from work were long gone.

Bleary-eyed, I rolled over onto my back. I grabbed the monstrous nursing pillow designed to hold two babies at once and took off my T-shirt.

Aidan handed me Oliver first and then went back to the nursery to fetch Sophie. Oliver was three minutes into sucking one of my boobs dry before Aidan returned with a freshly changed Sophie, whom he placed at my other breast.

"Do you mind if I take a quick shower?" Aidan asked. "I'll be back before you need to burp the babies."

"Yeah. Go ahead."

Jasper hadn't moved from Aidan's side of the bed. I shook my head. "You know, dog, if you could figure out how to pitch in, that would be great."

His response was to close his eyes and go back to sleep.

Rotten, ungrateful mutt.

I went into a nursing trance and only came out of it when Aidan strolled into the bedroom with a towel around his waist, hair damp. I somehow managed to forget that I had two entities attached to my body and took a moment to admire the long clean lines of my husband.

"What?" Aidan asked with a wry grin. He removed the towel and used it to dry his hair.

"I'm just thinking about how pretty you are." My gaze dipped even lower and I frowned.

"Please never make that face again when you stare at my junk. It makes me nervous."

"You're flaccid."

"Uh. Yeah. So?"

I arched an eyebrow, but he turned and walked to the dresser to grab a pair of boxers, giving me an unhindered view of his gorgeous back and muscular butt.

"So? I know what you did in there."

"What did I do in there?"

"You touched yourself. A lot!"

He looked at me over my shoulder and grinned. "I might've touched myself, but I was thinking of you."

"You didn't ask me if I wanted to service you…"

"Okay, first of all, do you really want to call it 'servicing' me? And second of all, you told me you had a headache when you thought I was trying to get some."

"Yeah, but now I'm awake. Well, my version of awake, I guess."

"Are we about to fight? I feel like we're about to fight," Aidan said. He pulled on his boxers and then came over to take Sophie.

"Not fight. More like a discussion."

"So no yelling is about to occur?"

I glared at him. "You have the energy and hormonal arousal to masturbate, but you don't have the wherewithal to touch me? It's my fault. And what I did last time we got busy. It was a turn off, wasn't it?"

He grinned. "Being sprayed in the face by your breast milk wasn't a turn off. It was falling off the bed because I was laughing so hard—thus stubbing my toe—which was the actual turn off."

"And now you won't even try to grope me."

"Let me get this straight. I try and have sex with you, and you get upset. So I stop trying to have sex with you, and you get upset. Do I have that correct?"

"Well, when you put it that way…"

"You know, there are a lot of species of insects that eat their mates after doing the nasty. I used to think that the males got the short end of the stick, but now I realize it's better that way. They don't have to experience all the ups and downs of their wives' mercurial moods."

I stuck out my tongue at him.

He grinned.

"Insect sex," I said slowly. "Is that what you call insectcoital?"

Sophie burped, but because it was Aidan, she didn't have the nerve to spit up all over him like she did to me at least two or three times during the day.

"You didn't even laugh at my joke. I'm not sexy or funny anymore," I said, hysteria bubbling up in my throat.

"You are the mother of my children," he said. "You are beautiful and I love you."

I sniffed, trying to hold in the tears. "Don't think that I didn't notice that you didn't disagree with me."

"What I wouldn't give to be a Praying Mantis right now," he muttered.

"Don't. Just don't."

We were two months post-spawn, and I was exhausted and emotional. Aidan was beat and at the end of his rope. We weren't having regular sex, and it was wearing on both of us.

"I know I'm crazy. But I look in the mirror and my post-baby body looks nothing like my pre-baby body. My emotions are being held hostage by my empty womb."

"What do I even say to that?"

"Please don't leave me," I blubbered.

"Where would I go?" he asked gently. "Seriously, Sibby. I'm not going anywhere."

"Even though I'm hormonal and insane? And I spray you with breast milk when we get busy?"

"Can I show you something?" he asked.

I sniffled but went for it, "Your erection?"

He laughed. "No." Aidan went to his bedside drawer and opened it and then took out a pair of chemistry goggles.

"You're not serious."

"Completely. The next time you want to have sex, I'm ready. Spray me all you want. I'm prepared."

The next morning, Aidan was at the park with Jasper when there was a knock on the door, followed by the sound of the key in the lock. Mrs. Nowacki filled the doorframe, carrying a white pastry box with a thin pink thread tied around it.

"Is that what I think it is?" I asked in excitement.

Mrs. Nowacki smiled and set the bakery box onto the kitchen table. She removed her coat—yes, the woman wore a coat in August—and hung it on the back of a chair.

"It is exactly what you think," she said with a grin as she headed to the coffee maker.

I ripped into the box of donuts from Peter Pan Bakery. I leaned over and sniffed. "They're still warm," I breathed. "Oh, man." I picked up a fresh blueberry buttermilk donut and dunked it into my coffee.

"You shouldn't have done this," I told her through a mouthful of decadent crumbs.

She set her mug down at the place setting next to me before heading to the corner of the room where the babies were sleeping in their bassinet. She cooed at them, said something in Polish, and then came back to the box of donuts and grabbed a toasted coconut.

"You say this every morning," she reminded me.

"Every morning you bring me some sort of baked good. This is not helping me diet."

"Diet? What diet?" Her eyes narrowed at me. "American women too obsessed with weight. You just have the *bubelas*. Sugar help skin heal. Sugar help womb go back to original shape. Trust me."

Though I trusted Mrs. Nowacki with the life of my children, I definitely didn't trust her when it came to dietary habits. Her people served lard with bread.

"I want to look reasonably attractive the night of Aidan's opening next week. Pictures will be taken. Social media posts will be made. The last thing I need is for people to call me a heifer."

Mrs. Nowacki shrugged and then polished off her donut. "When you get to my age, you will look back on your life and think 'I wish I had enjoyed myself a little more.'"

"Well," I sighed. "When you put it that way..." I reached for another donut and instantly felt like I needed to hire someone to follow me around just to smack baked goods out of my hands.

The front door opened and Jasper loped inside, tongue hanging out of the side of his mouth. He went immediately to his water bowl and slurped up half the liquid and then with dripping jowls, trotted over to Mrs. Nowacki and placed his head in her lap.

She gave him a sliver of toasted coconut that had fallen onto the table. Jasper licked his lips, including his nose, and silently begged for more.

"What did you do?" Aidan asked with a smile. He leaned over and brushed a kiss against Mrs. Nowacki's cheek, all the while his hand dove into the box and came out with a sour cream donut.

"I bring the happiness," she teased, her cheeks blushing like a schoolgirl.

Aidan had that effect on women of all ages.

Aidan pecked me on the lips. "Blueberry?"

I nodded.

"Damn, I was too late for it." He took a seat at the table and ate his donut. "A package came for you. I set it on the counter."

"Really?" I asked, getting up from the table and heading toward the cardboard box.

"What is it?" Aidan asked, intrigued.

"Um. There's something I have to tell you."

He raised his eyebrows and mouthed *sex toys*.

I rolled my eyes. "No."

"Too bad." He grinned. "One of those DNA dog testing kits? Are we going to finally find out what type of mutt Jasper is?"

"It's not a test kit…" I picked up the box and brought it to the kitchen counter.

"You're killing me here," he said. "Tell me."

"So, I might've been keeping a journal."

He frowned in confusion. "Okay?"

Mrs. Nowacki shot me a look and then got up from her seat. "Come, dog. Let's go see the babies." They didn't go very far—only to the other end of the room. Living in a loft with an open floor plan didn't allow for much privacy, and considering our home seemed to get more visitors than an 1800s whorehouse, we learned to make do.

I waved Aidan to me. He got up and brought my coffee, taking a sip as he walked to the counter.

"So, I've been keeping a journal. Online," I said, trying to explain again.

"An online journal," he repeated, his brows furrowed. All of a sudden his expression cleared. "You mean a blog?"

"Ah, yeah, a blog," I said. "Publicly, but anonymous— about pregnancy at first, and now about being a new mom. It's gotten a lot of traffic and positive comments. I've built a really nice community."

"That's pretty cool," he said. "That's great that you've found people to talk to." He scratched the back of his neck. "Sometimes I feel like I don't say the right things or give you what you need. I'm glad you've found people you can share with."

My insides melted. "You're the best guy in the world."

He flashed a grin. "Glad you think so. Is that all you wanted to tell me?"

"Ah, no." I touched the box. "I told you the blog is anonymous, right?"

"Right."

"Well, some companies have started emailing me, asking me if I'll use their products and endorse them so the other women can read about them."

"No way! That's so cool!" He reached for the box. "What's in here?"

"Aidan, wait," I said. "I have to take the blog public. I mean, I can't hide behind an avatar anymore."

"I fail to see why this is a problem."

I lowered my gaze to stare at the box. "I've mentioned you."

"Okay…"

"And our sex life both before the babies and our sex life after the babies…"

"What sex life post-babies?"

"Exactly. I know you don't like it that I'm all over Insta-gram and that you kind of got dragged along for the ride. I didn't mean to air our dirty laundry, and I never thought this would happen, you know? I didn't know women would relate to me or that companies would want me to test their products."

Oliver started to cry, and Mrs. Nowacki scooped him up to soothe him—good timing, kid, seriously.

"I'm a private person," he began slowly. "But I get that you're not. I'm okay with that. If this is something you want to do, if you really want to take this blog and run with it and test products, be a face that really offers the truth behind motherhood and what parenting looks like, then have at it."

I brightened. "Really?" I looked over his shoulder to see Mrs. Nowacki walking around with Oliver who'd calmed immediately once he'd been picked up.

"Yeah, really," Aidan said with a soft grin. "I love you. I want you to be happy. If this blog and your community of mothers can help you, then I'm all for it. I just have one favor to ask."

"Anything."

"If you mention my penis, then I'd really appreciate if you could talk it up. You know, give it a few more inches."

I pressed myself against him. "You don't need any more inches."

He kissed the top of my hair. "That's what I was hoping you'd say. Now open this box, I want to see what's inside."

I was dozing on the couch with the sugared remains of donuts in the corners of my mouth, when my cell phone woke me with a soft buzz.

Jasper shot up from the couch and woofed.

"It's just my phone," I told him. "Don't be so weird." I answered my cell when I saw Em's name. "Bob's Roadkill Diner. You kill 'em, we grill 'em."

Em's vivacious laughter graced my ear. "You're ridiculous."

"Thank you. What's up?"

"What does your tomorrow look like?"

"Oh, let's see. Sleepy with a one hundred percent chance of spit up and baby poop. Why?"

She chuckled. "I won a couple's massage from that new spa that opened up in Williamsburg. When I asked Caleb if he wanted to go, he said no stranger was going to touch him. Though truth be told, he's so tightly wound right now that he could use a massage."

"Caleb? Tightly wound? That seems so out of character—even with this expansion, he's been remarkably even keeled."

"Has Aidan mentioned anything to you?" she asked.

"In passing last week. He did say Caleb was acting weird."

"Oh, God, I really hope…"

"What? Oh shit, you don't think he's going to break up with you do you?" I paused. "Insensitive, sleep deprived asshole, party of one! Sorry, Em. That was a little too blunt even for me. God these hormones…"

She sighed. "I appreciate the candor actually. It doesn't feel like a breakup is coming though. Usually I can tell."

"You guys are still getting frisky then, eh?"

"Yeah, like twice a day."

"Bitch. Sorry. Only, not really. I've been out of my groove with Aidan and it's getting to us both."

"Sorry," she muttered. "I didn't mean to make it sound like I was rubbing it in your face."

"You know you just set me up for a really good penis joke, right?"

"You're such a frat guy." She chuckled, but then sobered when she said, "Something's off and I can't put my finger on it. It's so bizarre. I've asked him what's wrong and he shrugs it off, tells me it's nothing or that I'm imagining stuff."

"You don't think, well, he might ask you to move in with him?"

She paused. "I didn't even think about that."

"That's probably what's going to happen."

"You don't think it's too soon?"

"Who cares what I think—which by the way I don't think is too soon. Aidan and I moved fast. Way faster than I was ready for, but *he* was ready, and he made sure I knew it. We actually got engaged before we lived together. I don't recommend that, by the way. Then again, I did live with a boyfriend before Aidan who turned out to be gay. So, who can say what's right or wrong? Sorry, what were we talking about?"

"Caleb acting funny. But I think you're probably right. I think he's gonna ask me to move in with him." She sounded excited and I knew what her answer would be. "Oh, and I actually called about the couple's massage, remember?"

"And Caleb won't go."

"Right, so do you want to go with me tomorrow afternoon?"

"Only if it's a Swedish man named Sven giving me the massage."

I heard the ruffle of a paper and a slight pause and then, "Helga and Janice are our masseurs."

"Dibs on Helga. I can pretend she's named Sven."

"Whatever floats your boat. I'll come by at two. Sound good?"

"Sounds perfect."

We hung up just as I heard the front door of the foyer and I went to open the apartment door. A moment later, Mrs. Nowacki appeared, pushing the stroller.

"They are hungry," she said in way of greeting.

I sighed. "When are they not hungry?"

"Little Sophella needs new diaper."

I reached into the stroller and lifted Sophie into my arms. "Ew. Gross. What the hell have you been eating, kid?" I took her into the nursery and set her down on the changing table, gently sliding her clenched fists through the arms of her onesie which I tossed in the hamper that was already overflowing. It was nearly impossible to keep up with the laundry of a new baby.

Twins? Forget about it.

"Ah, man," I moaned. Sophie had poop all up and down her back thanks to a diaper blowout. I ditched the diaper and cleaned her up as best I could with baby wipes, but she needed a bath.

Mrs. Nowacki was cradling Oliver in her arms and sitting on the couch. "You have poop all over your shirt."

"Yeah." I sighed. "Sophie's bowels exploded. There's enough breast milk in the refrigerator for Oliver to have a bottle. Do you mind? I need to get her into a bath."

"I take care of it," Mrs. Nowacki stated with a hand wave.

I took Sophie into the bathroom, cradling her while I drew a bath. She was screaming at the top of her lungs, her face angry and red.

I stared tiredly at the faucet, waiting for the tub to fill. When I felt something wet at the front of my shirt, I looked down to find that Sophie had used her naked time to urinate on me and was now hiccoughing. I attempted to calm her.

"This is a thankless job," I muttered.

I shut off the faucet. The water was warm but not hot. We were both covered in Sophie's pee and excrement, so I decided to kill two birds with one stone. I set her on the floor on a clean towel and got out of my soiled clothes.

I climbed into the bath with Sophie and the water soothed her instantly. I placed her against my breast. She sounded like a greedy little beaver; her eyes were closed, her cheeks were fat, and all the annoyance I felt suddenly melted away as I looked down at her face.

I let her have her fill, but when I tried to switch her to the other breast, she was no longer hungry. I gently washed her, hoping she would refrain from letting it rip all over again.

When I was done bathing her I tried to stand, but immediately realized there was no safe way to do it without the risk of slipping, and there was no one to hand Sophie off to.

I called out, "Help!"

A moment later the bathroom door opened and Mrs. Nowacki stepped inside. She grabbed a clean towel from the linen closet and gently lifted Sophie from my arms.

Without the hindrance of a baby, I was able to stand up. Water sluiced down my body. I tried not to look at myself in the mirror as I reached for the towel hanging on the rack on the wall, but it was inevitable. My lower stomach was loose, my body not having bounced back as fast as I would've liked. My breasts sagged, heavy with milk. My hair, which had grown thick and shiny with the pregnancy hormones now looked dull and lifeless.

I looked like a shell of my former self and unfortunately—unlike husbands—mirrors didn't lie.

I wrapped the towel around my shoulders, using it as a shield to protect myself from having to see the truth. I tilted my head down, hair falling over my eyes as tears cascaded down my cheeks.

A sob tore from my throat as I stepped out of the tub, mindful of not slipping. My toes curled into the blue bathmat and it felt like I was shaking from the inside out.

"Ah, *cukierku*. You're going to be fine. I promise," Mrs. Nowacki said as she slowly swayed with Sophie.

"People keep telling me that," I sniffed. "But I don't know if I believe them."

I looked at the sleeping face of my daughter and wished I didn't feel like I was drowning in emotion. Even with the help of Mrs. Nowacki, even with the calls to Nat, my good friend in Houston who'd already had a kid, I wondered why it felt like I was on the journey of raising two children alone. Maybe it was because my husband was consumed with the bar expansion and hadn't been home a lot.

I felt lost and in the dark, completely terrified that I was doing it all wrong, screwing up whenever I let exhaustion get the best of me. I had the most resentful angry thoughts that were directed at two infants who needed me to live—and I loathed myself for blaming them for taking my time and patience, my solitude.

Between the hormone dumps, lack of sleep, and the few and far between intimate moments with Aidan, I felt like I was in survival mode and I was barely hanging on.

"You need to get outside the home," Mrs. Nowacki said. "Take a nice long walk. Go to park. Stop at German beer hall at the end of block and have big pint."

I raised my eyebrows. "You're recommending the German beer hall? You?"

She shrugged. "They have better selection."

"I'm getting a massage with Em tomorrow," I said. "That will get me out of the house."

"Good. Good. You also need to talk to your *mąż*."

"He knows how I'm feeling."

She shook her head. "No, you need to tell him he needs to be here more."

"But he's working," I explained.

Mrs. Nowacki looked down at Sophie's sleeping face and then back at me. "You are working too."

"He'll be around more after next week," I said.

"You think this, but trust me. You have good man, but sometimes he does not know how you need help. You have to tell him. He will give it to you."

No one liked to admit they needed help, but I couldn't go on this way. Something had to change and soon.

"I come from time where woman raises children alone. She may have husband, but husband just provides money and falls asleep in chair after long day of work." She shook her head. "Not the way of things anymore."

"Yeah." I nodded.

"He is missing things," she said softly. "Not just baby things, but wife things."

I'd been missing Aidan's presence before the babies were born. He was already preoccupied with the bar and trying to reach the next level of success. Recently, it felt like we were roommates more than husband and wife. I knew he was working hard to provide for our family, but at what cost? I needed him. Our family needed him.

I'd have to try harder with Aidan. And not just emote all over him and hope he still spoke the language of crazy Sibby, but really try and explain to him what I'd been feeling. It wasn't fair to him unless I gave him that chance. I had to try and make him understand.

To do that, I needed time with my husband. Just the two of us. We needed to date each other again. We needed to sit across the table from one another and have a conversation that didn't focus on the bar or the babies.

It needed to just be us.

"How does one go about dating their own husband again after babies?" I asked, following Mrs. Nowacki out of the bathroom.

"You cook nice meal for him. And you wear black lace underneath the clothes."

"I can barely boil water. And black lace is itchy." I went to my underwear drawer and tried not to be upset about the high-waisted granny panties that I slid up my legs.

"You put Sophie to bed and then I need your help."

"My help?" I asked in confusion.

She nodded. "Yes. I pick your ear about something."

"Do you mean pick my brain, or bend my ear?"

"Yes."

"Okay." I nodded. I pulled on a pair of yoga pants and then took Sophie from her arms. Fifteen minutes later, I left the door of the nursery cracked in case Jasper wanted to leave, but he slept on the floor of their room a lot, preferring the twins over anyone else.

"What is it you want to talk about?" I asked as I took a seat on the couch next to Mrs. Nowacki.

"I am ready."

I nodded, encouraging her to go on.

"I am ready," she said again, "to start the dating."

I blinked. "Er, that's good. Dating is good. But—ah—how can I help you?"

"Internet is good for many things, yes?" Her eyes gleamed.

"Online dating? You want to try online dating?"

She nodded. "I hear good things about Z-Harmony."

"E-Harmony," I corrected.

She waved her hand in a dismissive manner. "Will you help me?"

I smiled, feeling my heart lift. "I'd love to help you."

Mom Blog Entry:

I've been impregnated by a Greek god. Now I look like a heffalump, and he looks like Apollo.

Not fair.

Aidan winced. "Jeez. That looks painful."

I looked down at the breast pump. "Not so much anymore. I'm pretty sure I've lost all

feeling in my nipples."

He sighed. "That's so sad."

"This pump is the new one I got to test out," I remarked. "So far I like it better than all the others, actually."

"Hmm. That's good."

Mrs. Nowacki was long gone, and Aidan had gotten home a little after seven. He was sitting on the couch, looking at his phone and drinking a bottled microbrew. They all tasted like crap to me. Too hoppy.

"Hey, can I talk to you for a second?" I asked.

"Sure," he said. "Hold on." He typed out something on his phone and then set it aside. "What's up?"

Maybe it wasn't such a grand idea to talk to my husband while I had a milk sucking apparatus attached to me, but the twins were still asleep, somehow, and I didn't know how long we'd have.

"Em won a couples' massage and Caleb doesn't want to go. She asked me instead."

"That's great," he said with a smile. "You deserve to be pampered."

"It's tomorrow afternoon and she's coming by at two to pick me up. Mrs. Nowacki will be here, but—"

His phone buzzed, pulling his attention away from me again. "Sorry. Last minute details. I need to make sure there's an updated list for the doorman."

Anger bubbled up inside of me, but I held my tongue and took a deep breath. And then another.

"I need you, Aidan."

"I know, honey, just give me a—"

"No," I said, my voice emphatic. "I *really* need you."

Something about my tone made him look up from his phone. His expression was perplexed. "Okay, I'm listening."

"You're not though. You're focused on the bar expansion. When you're here, you're not really here. Your mind is somewhere else."

"I'm trying, Sibby," he said, his face tight.

"I need more from you," I said, my voice cracking. "I broke down today, Aidan. I feel like… I'm alone in all of this."

"That's not fair."

"Maybe it is, maybe it isn't, but I feel the way I feel. You don't know what it's like. You've got chiseled abs and dimples and something to keep you busy. You might be tired, but your brain is clear and free of hormones. You don't look like you're being pulled under from sheer exhaustion, never to come up again. It's not like that for me. Everything is different."

His gaze softened. "Tell me, then."

I swallowed. "I don't look like me anymore. I don't *think* like me. I'm exhausted all the time and it's a miracle if my hair gets brushed or I leave the house not covered in baby fluids. I feel like…like I'm slipping away. Like *we* are slipping away."

He scooted closer to me, close enough that he could put his hand on my knee. "I love you. You know that, right?"

"It's not about love," I said, searching for the right words. "I know you love me. I know you love the twins, but there's something missing here. We don't talk anymore. Not like we used to. We've forgotten how to be a couple. And I think it started before the twins were even born, you know? Everything changed so fast and now it feels even harder to get back to us. We need to try a little harder to— I don't know—consider each other. I know I'm not at my most attractive. I know I'm not firing on all cylinders. Just know that I love you. I miss talking to you, and I need you."

He leaned over and kissed me on the lips. "God, Sibby. Do you know what a shit I feel like right now?"

"I don't want you to feel like a shit."

"But I do. I knew it was going to be hard," he admitted. "The bar expansion with two newborns. I just didn't know how hard. And maybe I was little arrogant in thinking because we're Sibby and Aidan we could handle it."

"We are handling it," I said. "Just not as well as I would like. You know?"

He sighed. "Yeah."

"Listen, I know your time is really pressed from now until next week, but I'd really like to have a date night. We can do it here. I'll cook."

"You're going to cook?" he asked in amusement.

"Yes, you dink, I'm gonna cook," I said with a grin.

"Only if you let me bring home a nice bottle of wine. Will you let me do that?"

"Yeah, honey, I'll let you do that."

It felt like a burden had been lifted off my shoulders. Mrs. Nowacki had been right; I'd needed to talk to Aidan. And maybe things wouldn't magically fix themselves overnight, but we were both aware of what we needed.

"I'm kind of jealous of those cultures where they actually had a village to help raise a kid," I said, removing the breast pump from my nipples.

Aidan helped screw the lids on the two bottles of milk I managed to pump.

I kept talking. "You could just drop your infant off with an aunt or grandmother. Someone was always there to watch your baby."

"Well, to be fair, those villages needed everyone in it to roast the wild boar and all the women were stuck doing laundry by hand," he pointed out. "Your parents live far away. My parents live far away. We have Mrs. Nowacki, but it's not really enough, you know? Most people move closer to their parents and that way they have help. We made a choice by being Brooklynites."

He put the milk in the fridge and then we locked up the apartment and turned off the lights. We headed into the bathroom to get ready for bed.

"Yeah, you make a valid point. Can't have it both ways, I guess," I murmured. I doused my toothbrush with toothpaste. "I have a theory on why Caleb has been acting weird. I think he's going to ask Em to move in with him."

"Care to make a wager on that?"

"Do you know something I don't?"

He shook his head. "I don't think he's gonna ask her to move in with him."

"You think they're going to break up?"

"Maybe. I don't know."

"Then we can't really bet, can we?"

We finished brushing our teeth and just as I crawled beneath the covers, a cry sounded through the baby monitor. "Rock paper scissors?" I asked.

"What if we both go?" he asked.

I smiled up at him and leaned in to press a kiss to his lips. "I'd like that."

Mom Blog Entry:

I used be a super hot, day-drinking hipster with zero responsibili-ties. Now I'm lucky to leave the house without baby vomit on my shirt.

What the hell happened to my life?

"Do you have anything less—I don't know—*turtle-necky*? You know, for your online dating picture?" I asked, looking at the screen and then back at Mrs. Nowacki.

She frowned and touched her collar. "I get the draft."

"I know," I said, "I just think it might look nice if we updated your look. Less Warsaw 1940, more Brooklyn modern."

"I have sweater I bring tomorrow."

"Good. Okay." I looked at my computer again. "It's asking about hobbies and what you like to do in your spare time."

"I bring you donuts and take care of your babies in my spare time."

I wrinkled my nose. "Caregiver doesn't have any sex appeal. Do you like to garden? Go for walks? Travel?"

"Okay."

I blinked. "What does that mean?"

"It means, you make up something for me. You the writer. I trust you. Oh, maybe you mention I have cat."

"Eh, I don't think mentioning Aiko is a good idea. You don't want to be labeled a crazy cat lady."

"What's crazy cat lady? What is wrong with cat?"

"Just trust me on this one. How is Aiko enjoying his new home, by the way? How are you, for that matter?"

Mrs. Nowacki had moved in with her widowed friend across the street when our building had gotten bed bugs. Even though the building was now bed bug free, she'd decided to stay with Dorota. It turned out Mrs. Nowacki enjoyed living with a roommate.

"It is nice," she admitted. "I miss the sound of people in a home. We are good friends. We have a lot in common."

"Then why not have her introduce you to someone? You don't need to do *this*." I waved my hand at the browser window open on the webpage StillSchtupin.com, a matchmaking website catering to the octogenarian crowd.

"I want someone adventurous. All the men Dorota knows have the dysfunction."

I got the idea that she wasn't talking about mental dysfunction, but about dysfunction south of the border of the pantular region.

"You still want it? At your age?" I blurted out.

She stared me down. "If it weren't for my left hip, I'd want it all the time."

Okay. Moving right along…

"I'll write your profile tonight and we'll deal with your wardrobe later. Sound good?"

"Yes."

I closed my laptop. "Em should be here any minute. Aidan will be home in about an hour. Are you good if I leave you for a bit?"

She nodded. "Yes. You left enough milk in fridge?"

"Yup. That new breast pump works like a champ." I shook my head. "I wonder when there will be a day that I don't have to talk about my milk supply."

The buzzer sounded.

"That would be Em." I briefly hugged Mrs. Nowacki and then looked in on the twins who were sleeping soundly. I smushed Jasper's face between my hands in an affectionate goodbye.

I met Em on the sidewalk outside the front of the apartment building. She wore a big smile and looked adorable in her black halter sundress and sunglasses perched on her nose. The woman was classy and elegant in an understated way.

"You look great!" she said with a hug.

I made a noise of disbelief. "Thanks."

"You clearly don't believe me," she said with a laugh. "Listen, I might've lied to you, just a little."

"What do you mean?" I dug around the bottom of

my purse for my sunglasses. I found them, along with a yellow peanut M & M and a guitar pick. How a guitar pick found its way into the bottom of my bag, I'd never know.

"I gave you the wrong appointment time." She grinned. "I thought we could have a drink together first."

"You what? Okay, one tiny drink," I said with a smile. "And what a *stellar* idea."

Fifteen minutes later we were at a bar around the corner from the spa. We grabbed two glasses of Prosecco and took them out to the back patio. It was quiet at this time of day, despite the fact that Brooklynites loved their day-drinking excursions.

"How are you doing?" she asked.

"I'm okay. How are you doing?" I diverted.

She shook her head. "Nah, don't do that."

"Do what?"

"Not be a straight shooter with me. Aren't we at that level yet? We've had how many dinners and girl hangouts? You can talk to me."

I sat back in my chair and stared at her behind my sunglasses. "Aidan confided to Caleb about what we were going through, and Caleb told you."

She admitted the truth with a nod. "Don't be mad at him."

"I'm not. I'm just…well, feeling a bit raw about it all. And sort of embarrassed."

"Why?"

"It's dirty laundry," I explained. "No one likes to admit when they're struggling in their relationship."

"Okay, point blank? You and Aidan are total relation-ship goals. Like, so much so that it's kind of disgusting," she smiled, "but don't you think sixty-year marriages have ups and downs? It's inevitable. And the fact that you introduced two babies into the mix? Forget it. I think you're amazing."

I wiped the spot underneath my eye. "You know I cry at the drop of a hat now, don't you? Like, worse than I did when I was pregnant."

"Sibby? Can I ask you something? Seriously ask you something?"

I nodded and then took a sip of Prosecco to steady my nerves.

"Do you think you might have postpartum?"

"I don't know," I answered truthfully. "I knew I'd feel overwhelmed and exhausted, but I love my babies. I just feel kinda…disconnected. Like everything is sort of hazy and everyone is on the other side of a curtain and I'm trying to reach them, but I can't."

"My best friend from when we were kids went through it; that's the only reason I'm asking. It's not a big deal if you are, you know? It's just that it can become a big deal if you feel like you can't talk about it."

I frowned and tapped the stem of the flute glass in front of me while I thought. "What did your friend do? How did she get through it?"

"She went on medication for a little while. It helped." She shrugged. "I'm not saying that's your course of action, but I'm not a doctor, you know?" She took a long draught of her drink. "I didn't mean to make you uncomfortable when I brought it up, I just wanted you to know that you can talk to me."

"I really appreciate that," I said. "I wonder why Aidan talked to Caleb, though, I guess I shouldn't be surprised that Caleb told you. Nothing is a secret in a relationship."

"I imagine Aidan told Caleb because he's worried about you and he's not sure who else he can talk to. They're best friends. Even guys need people to talk to sometimes, and talking to family can be challenging—and from what I've heard of your mother…"

"Yeah, no way would I want her to know how I'm feeling. Her anxiety would become my anxiety and I have enough on my plate."

"But she *is* your mom," she pointed out. "She might have some insight."

"My mother and I have a unique relationship. She's an over-reactor. I don't want to send her into a tizzy."

"Huh," Em said. "An over-reactor, you say? I wondered where you got that from."

"Oh, shut up," I said with a laugh. "Plus, she'd tell everyone in my family about my personal battle. So if I'm a little embarrassed that Caleb knows, think how I'd feel if my mom's entire family knew." I shook my head. "Thanks, Em. I really do appreciate your candor. Please don't think I'm ungrateful."

She waved away my apology. "I just wanted to mention it. Now we can move on and talk about other things."

I blew out a puff of air and nodded. "Yes, please, let's talk about something that doesn't include my hormones or breasts."

"Which, if I do say so, look fantastic."

I stuck my chest forward. "Thank you."

"How's the book?" she asked.

"Let's not talk about that either." My tone was dry. "Tell me how things are going with you."

"I'm about to get promoted," she said shyly. "My boss is thinking of stepping back just a bit to have more time with her family and she wants me to manage our accounts in Greenpoint and Williamsburg."

"That's awesome!"

"Yeah, it is." She bit her lip. "There's just one issue."

"What's that?"

"My promotion is contingent on locking down Mother Shucker as a client..."

"*Annie's* restaurant?" My eyes widened. "No way."

She nodded. "Annie's already been written about in a few foodie magazines, and Mother Shucker is one of the most anticipated restaurant openings of the year. Aria doesn't want our competition to be on Annie's wine menu."

"You sneaky wench," I said with a laugh. "You want me to talk to Annie for you, don't you?"

"God, Sibby, I hate asking you this. I really do, but I don't know how I'm supposed to go in there, put a smile on my face, and pitch myself and our wines to my boyfriend's ex."

I lifted my glasses so I could rub my tired eyes. "All right. I'll ask."

"Oh my God, really?"

I nodded. "Yeah. I'll do it. But you owe me another drink." I stared at her. "This massage... was it really a couples' massage?"

Em nodded. "I swear. This wasn't a setup, just a coincidence."

"Does Caleb know about this? About Annie's restaurant, I mean?"

She looked uncomfortable. "Not yet. I don't want to tell him until after I secure the deal."

"Who needs enemies with friends like these," I muttered. Her face fell and I reached across the table to grab her hand. "I'm kidding. I told you I'd talk to her, but we know Aidan and Caleb can't keep secrets, so please tell Caleb before he finds out from Aidan by way of me. If you do that, I'll talk to her."

"I'll tell him after the expansion," she promised. "I didn't want to give him something else to worry about, you know?"

"Yeah, timing with this is a big deal. I'll keep my yap shut until after the party. I promise."

"You know this is cheating, right?" Annie asked in amusement as she snapped the end off a green bean and set it in the bowl.

I poured a glass of Chianti and set it down on the counter.

"I'm doing the heavy lifting," I told her. I slid the cutting board set with two filet steaks in front of me.

"How do you figure? I'm basically giving you a private cooking lesson and then you're going to use the spoils to feed your husband."

"You don't think Aidan deserves filet mignon?"

"I think your best friend in the entire world who is working her nuts off deserves a filet mignon." She let out a laugh. "Why did you promise him you'd cook, anyway?"

"I wanted him to know how much I love and adore him and miss him."

My muscles and mood still felt soft like melted butter from the massage yesterday. "Do you know he actually bought chemistry goggles to wear during our next sexy time? Which I anticipate will be later tonight, because hello filet mignon."

"Why chemistry goggles?"

"So if I spray him with milk, he's protected."

"Some things, Sibby. Some things I don't need to know."

"The goggles are a joke. He's not *actually* going to use them."

"You guys have a weird collective sense of humor." She shook her head. "You should spice things up a bit one night. You know, get a babysitter, check into a hotel and then pretend to be strangers who meet at a bar and have a hot one-night stand."

"Maybe one day we'll try that. Right now, it takes enough effort just to get naked in front of him."

She rinsed the beans in the colander and set them aside. "Do you need help with those steaks?"

"I've got it." I began to massage the meat, letting my fingers get all up in the olive oil and meat juice.

"What are you doing?" Annie asked.

"Tenderizing the meat."

"They have this thing called a meat tenderizer."

"Yeah, but I don't own one of those, and even if I did, I still think this is a better way to cook steaks."

"I beg to differ."

"I did it before," I commented. "And Aidan said they were the best steaks he'd ever had."

"Was that before or after you went down on him?"

I paused. "After."

"Uh huh. Okay, those look tender enough to me. The crème brûlée needs about another hour to fully set, but the sugar is already sprinkled on top. When you're ready for dessert, you use this thing." She lifted a kitchen torch. "Let me show you how to use it."

After a few demonstrations, I had it down.

"What do you plan on wearing?" she asked.

"A post maternity dress with an empire waist. Stops at the knee."

She nodded. "Shoes? Heels?"

I sighed. "My feet are still swollen, and I can't fit them into heels."

"Sibby…"

"I'm not lying, I swear," I said.

She peered at me and then took her glass of water to the couch. I followed at a much slower pace.

"Okay, out with it," she said.

"Out with what?"

"Don't do the big-eyed innocent thing. You don't pull it off well."

"Rats. I don't?"

"Nope."

"Okay." I paused again.

"Sibby? I'm not getting any younger."

"Sorry," I muttered. "It's about the wine menu for Mother Shucker."

"I'm listening."

"Em asked me if I'd ask you if you'd let her bring you some samples."

She blinked. "I'm gonna need you to repeat that."

I did, and then I went on to explain, "Her boss is stepping back. If Em can get wines into your restaurant, she'll get a promotion."

"And she asked you to talk to me," Annie said slowly, "because of my past with Caleb."

"She just thought it would be easier coming from me. You know, instead of her cold-calling and pitching you."

Annie thought for a long moment. "All right," she said finally.

I blinked. "Seriously? You're saying yes?"

"I'm saying yes…with one condition."

"You guys and your conditions," I muttered under my breath.

Annie heard, and her eyes narrowed. "*You* taste the wine samples, and then you tell me what to buy. I'll do business with her because the company she works for happens to actually have stellar wines, but I don't drink anymore, and I need someone to vet the wines for me."

"You're not over Caleb," I accused.

"This has nothing to do with Caleb. If it did then I wouldn't let his new girlfriend anywhere near my restaurant. But she's good at what she does, her company is good, and the wines at Veritas are some of the best I've ever had. I'm not going to cut my nose off to spite my face."

"You trust me enough with your restaurant's wine menu? Why not entrust this to Mills? You said he was going to help with the drink menu."

"He's a mixologist."

I sniggered at that word.

"He's a mixologist," she repeated. "He's not a wine drinker, much less a sommelier."

"I'm not a sommelier either," I said, gesturing to the Chianti. "That was a ten-buck wine."

"You have a habit of choosing really good things based on the packaging and taste combo and ignoring the price. You've done it for years. I trust your gut."

"You're a class above the rest," I told her. "Will you finish the beans? I want to feed the beasts before Aidan comes home."

"You do know if I put the beans in now, you'll be eating at five o'clock. The sun won't even be set yet."

"Knowing how I am these days, I'll be asleep by seven."

I stood at the counter, wearing some sort of frilly apron I'd once found in a vintage shop and had thought was too cute to pass up.

All traces of Annie were gone, and I had even lit a scented candle to hide the aroma of her perfume. Aidan would never know that I'd called my best friend to aid in the seduction of my own husband.

"What smells so good?" Aidan asked the moment he walked through the front door. Jasper got up from the couch to greet Aidan who bent down to give the dog a hearty scratch.

"Those would be the steaks that I sautéed in butter for you." I grinned. "Along with warm French bread and blanched green beans with a lemon garlic aioli."

"You did all that?"

"I did," I lied easily.

He looked me up and down like I looked at steak. "You look really good, Sib. No, you look *great*."

I was wearing the dress I'd told Annie about and had

paired it with my pearl necklace and matching earrings, feeling very June Cleaver.

"You look really good too," I said, appreciating the way the gray trousers fit his butt and the white button down rolled up to show off his forearms.

"Nothing fancy."

"Reminds me of when you used to manage Antonio's and I was just the waitress who wanted to get it on with you in the wine room."

"Wine room. Wine. Crap. I was supposed to supply the wine, wasn't I?" He ran a hand through his hair, looking harried and harassed. "I'll go back out and grab a bottle."

"Don't. The food will get cold," I said. I served the two steaks onto the plates using a pair of tongs and then brought them to the table that I'd set with legit place mats and cloth napkins. I'd even pulled out the candlestick holders my great aunt Lily had given us for our wedding.

"Why don't you light those candles," I said. "I already opened a bottle of Chianti."

"Hey," he said, reaching out to grasp me by the waist to pull me close.

"I'm really sorry I forgot the wine," he said. His blue eyes peered into mine. "You did a really nice thing for us tonight and like an idiot, my mind wasn't on it. And I failed."

"Can I tell you something?"

"Yeah, of course." His brow furrowed as he waited.

"Annie cooked all this. She came over this afternoon and prepped with me. I did the steaks, that was it."

"You mean it?"

"Yup. You're off the hook."

His shoulders slumped. "Thank God. Is it wrong that I like you barefoot and wearing an apron and pearls?"

"Your children are asleep in the nursery. They won't be up for a while," I said as I batted my eyelashes.

He hoisted me up against him. His lips covered mine and when he stepped back, I stared at him, feeling just a little bit wistful and very much in love with my gorgeous husband.

"That will get you out of a lot of trouble, you know that, right?" I asked, my cheeks heating.

"Maybe next time I should try that when I get pulled over. You think a cop will let me go with just a warning?"

I laughed. "Maybe if you slip him some tongue."

"What? No! In my scenario, the cop is a woman."

"You didn't specify." I shrugged and grinned. "Sit down. I'll get the wine. Eat before it gets cold."

"Let me wash my hands and check on the babies first." After a quick peck to my lips, he left the room.

I poured two glasses of wine and brought them to the table. Mine was considerably smaller than Aidan's, for obvious reasons.

Aidan returned to the kitchen. "They're sleeping like two angels, but we know the truth…"

"They're demon-spawn, I'm sure of it."

"Sometimes I swear they're changelings. One minute they're perfect, the next it's like they're holding us hostage at scream-point."

After taking our seats, Aidan reached for his glass, lifting it in the air. "To the mother of my children, the most amazing woman in the world, who took pity on me and married me."

"Cheers," I said with a grin and then took a sip of wine.

We spent a few minutes carving into our steaks. After we'd enjoyed a few bites, I said, "Your toast is just a toast, right? Like you're not trying to butter me up and ask me for something else. Like you don't want to open another bar?"

He laughed. "No. The toast was just a toast. Though I do have something for you." Aidan reached under the table and pulled out a black velvet jewelry box.

"What is this?" I asked in excitement.

"Something you've been wanting for a very long time."

"You didn't."

"I did."

"Are you sure you want to play this card now? You don't want to hold onto these until you screw up royally and this is the only way to claw your way out?"

"I've already screwed up," he said. "I've made you feel alone and lost, and I'm ashamed of it, Sibby. I thought I could handle the expansion of the bar and the growth of our family. But it turns out I don't multitask well." He gave me a wry grin. "Will you forgive me?"

"Yes." I kissed him to let him know I meant it. Now was not the time to bring up what Em and I had discussed about postpartum—and frankly, ever since I'd spoken to Aidan, my feelings had lightened. Maybe it had just been a dark spell and we were back to being us.

I flipped open the jewelry box and my breath caught in the back of my throat when I saw the diamond earrings. They were about the same size as my engagement ring and similar in style.

"You're unbelievable," I breathed, my eyes misting. "Thank you. These are gorgeous."

"Will you wear them to the party?" he asked, gaze hopeful.

"I'd love to." I cleared my throat. "So…do you want to put dinner on pause and go into the bedroom?"

Aidan jumped up so fast he knocked over his chair.

"Guess that answers that."

Aidan grasped my hand, hauled me up, and dragged me toward the bedroom. The moment we got to our room he was on me.

"Are you in the mood?" he asked between kisses and getting naked. "What can I do to get you in the mood?"

"Can we role play?"

"Just when I think I know everything about you, you surprise me." He grinned. "Yeah, we can role play. I really love that idea. Tell me your fantasy."

"I don't have a fantasy. What's *your* fantasy?"

"No, this is the Sibby show. Come on, you just said you wanted to role play. Tell me what you want."

"Well, I do have this one idea…"

"I'm listening."

"I want you to pretend to be an alien overlord and fantasize that I'm your human sex slave."

He paused like he wasn't sure what to say and then, "This is a testament to how much I love you. I'm sincerely entertaining this scenario."

"Testament to loving me? Please. I feel your erection on my leg. You're into this. Go on," I prodded. "Say something in your alien war language."

Aidan blinked and then made a noise like a yak.

"I don't have yeti fantasies, Aidan. Try again."

"I'm Shrau. From Planet Meaton."

…

"You know what? Silence is golden. Why don't you just climb on top of me?"

"I thought you'd never ask."

Chapter 4

Mom Blog Entry:

Had to go to the DMV to renew my license. During the renewal process they asked how much I weighed…

Oh, hell no.

After a very pleasurable few minutes, we got up and tended to the family. The babies had woken up and were demanding milk. Aidan took Jasper out while I fed and changed the twins. And then Sophie spit up on my beautiful dress.

"You changed," Aidan said in way of greeting as he came back into the apartment. He detached Jasper from the leash. The dog bounded toward the couch and curled up with his butt on one of the throw pillows. At this point it was too hard to break him of the habit, so I let it be.

"Your daughter," I said in way of explanation. "Is it wrong that I want to jump right to dessert?"

"I support this decision. We can eat the steaks later tonight." He hung up the leash and came back to the table. "Do you want some help with the crème brûlée?

"No, I've got it. Annie showed me how to use this thing." Both ceramic custard dishes rested on the counter and I grabbed the doohickey that would caramelize the hell out of the top layer of sugar.

Only when I turned on the contraption, the flame was four inches bigger than I was expecting.

"Whoa!" I fiddled with the knob to turn it down, but then the flame went out completely. "Ah, man, come on. I just wanted to make a nice dessert for my husband. Cooking god, do not fail me now!"

The flame flickered back to life and then whooshed out of the canister.

"Yeehaw!" I yelled.

"Sibby, be careful," Aidan warned.

"I'm good." I turned the flame toward the first custard dish and torched the sugar.

The sugar caramelized and then quickly started bubbling and then whooshed into a fire.

"Ahhh!" I yelled, dropping the canister as I felt heat on my forehead.

"Sibby!" Aidan cried.

A flood of water shot me in the face.

"Don't move," he ordered. I heard him shuffling around and then he said, "Okay, I've turned off the torch. Are you okay? Look at me, let me see the damage."

I finally opened my eyes and turned to him. My face was dripping with water and the spray nozzle from the sink was leaking all over the counter. In a bemused sort of detachment, I leaned over and shut off the faucet.

"That was quick thinking," I said.

A moment later, the smoke alarm went off, its high-pitched beep causing Jasper to woof.

"Ignore it," Aidan said as I made a move to open a window. "Let me see you." He touched my chin and turned my head around.

"How bad is it?" I asked when I saw his gaze.

And then the bastard's lip twitched.

"How bad? Come on, tell me," I pleaded.

"You're going to be okay, only your hair is burnt."

"My hair! How bad is it?"

"You don't have any eyebrows."

Instinctively, my fingers went up to touch the spot where my eyebrows had once been.

He pulled me to him.

The smoke alarm stopped beeping almost as quickly as it had started, but Jasper was sitting up, ears perked, and I heard the terrified screams of my children.

"Holy cow," I murmured. "I almost became Sibby flambé."

Aidan was no longer able to contain his laughter. He stepped away so he could grip the edge of the counter and then he bent over and laughed so hard he could barely breathe.

Then he kept laughing until tears streamed down his face.

Somehow, I found a well of laughter bubbling up

inside of me and it escaped. The sound of our mingled chuckles echoing off the walls warmed my heart.

We were a team again.

I had screwed up, and Aidan was there to clean up the mess.

All was right in my world.

Even if I had to sacrifice my eyebrows to make it so.

We calmed the babies quickly and then Aidan led me into our bathroom so I could look in the mirror.

Yup. No hair above my occipital bones. Just two bare arches and a lone hair or two where my brows used to be.

"Can I ask you something?" Aidan said.

"Ya."

"Why aren't you freaking out?"

"I don't want to tell you because you're going to think I'm cray."

"Sibby, you're a mother of two and almost thirty. You're not allowed to use the word cray."

"Jerk," I huffed. "Me accidentally setting my own hair on fire made me feel more like myself than I've felt in a *long* time."

"You mean you totally had a Sibby's Law moment and now you feel like you again?"

"Yeah."

"You're right," he said, blue eyes twinkling in humor. "I do think you're cray."

"Stop," I said with a laugh. "I'm serious. And if I can't say cray, then you *definitely* can't say it."

"Well, I guess it makes sense." He scratched his jaw, which was rife with two days of stubble. It was nice to see him without a beard again; it reminded me of when we'd first gotten together.

I hadn't known at the time that he was going to be the man I'd end up marrying. Years later he was still a source of constant surprise by being so honestly himself. He owned his mistakes. He apologized for them. He tried to do better. That's what surprised me. In a world stuffed with people who were full of crap, Aidan was steadfastly genuine and real.

"Why are you looking at me that way?" he asked.

"Because I realize how much I love you."

"It took you singeing off your eyebrows to remember that? Honey, there must be an easier way."

"It was the diamond earrings," I teased. "Okay, legit question for you."

"Hit me with it."

"Do you think I can grow new eyebrows by next Friday?"

"You have a lot of superpowers, Sibby. Destroying technology, setting things on fire, taking down waiters. But re-sprouting a full set of eyebrows in a week?" He shook his head. "I don't think it's possible."

"Better get creative then. I'm not showing up in your social media posts for the bar without eyebrows."

"You could wear a hat and a veil."

"Like an Edwardian widow? No thanks. Keep brainstorming though, we're bound to come up with a good idea."

I heard the front door shut and Annie called, "Sibby? I came over as soon as I got your message! Where are you?"

"Bedroom!" I called back.

Her steps were swift across the wooden floor, but I didn't turn around. I needed a moment to prepare myself for her reaction. Because knowing Annie, she wasn't going to be at all sympathetic. In fact, I expected full on heckling. It was her right as my best friend.

"Where are the twins?"

"Mrs. Nowacki took them to the park. I think she's using them to pick up men."

"How? Men run from babies."

"Not grandfather-aged men," I said.

"Okay, why am I having a conversation with your back? How did last night's dinner date go?"

"Are you sitting down?"

"No."

"Sit down."

She sighed. "Okay. I'm sitting on the bed."

I slowly turned my body and swiveled my head.

Her eyes widened. "No."

"Yes."

"You didn't."

"I did."

"You—you—"

"Have no eyebrows." I grimaced. "I know."

"But, how?"

"Your torch was defective."

"I've had that thing for five years. It's never once done something like this. I blame it on operator error."

She closed her eyes and stuck her fist in her mouth. I watched her silently convulse and I waited. Annie didn't disappoint, and soon her guffaws filled the room.

"Oh, God," she gasped. "Make it stop. Can't breathe." She panted a few more breaths and then finally managed to gain control of herself.

"You and Aidan basically had the same reaction."

"What did Mrs. Nowacki do when she saw you this morning?"

I sighed. "She just handed me a donut and patted me on the shoulder."

"Why isn't this all over social media? Your fans live for this kind of stuff."

"There's humor at me being a dingus, and then there's just ammunition for the total annihilation of my soul. And frankly, I'm too fragile to alert them to this SNAFU."

Her face suddenly looked stricken. "What are you going to do about the party? You're going to be in pictures."

"I feel like one of those hairless cats!" I wailed. "An eyebrow pencil will look *ridiculous*."

"Hold on, let me think." She got up off the bed and began to pace. "I've got it. What about a costume store?"

"You want me to buy a slutty costume and wear it to Aidan's opening so when the media takes a photo of me, they'll ask, 'Hey, who's that eyebrowless pirate wench married to Aidan Kincaid?'"

"They have wigs and stuff," Annie said, not even bothering to berate me for my snark. "We can find you something, a black beard maybe, cut it and glue it to your eyebrows. Voila!"

"You're a genius!"

She looked smug. "I know."

"I don't want to leave the house looking like this," I said. "I can't go out in public yet."

"Amazon!"

I brightened. "Two-day shipping!"

She nodded. "There you go. Don't take this the wrong way, but have you considered taking a vitamin or supplement to help clear your mind? It's supposed to help with brain function, and the Sibby of old would've come up with this idea without my help so it can't hurt. And frankly, my mind is completely on my restaurant opening. So I can't think for you *and* me. I can barely think for one. And I need my best friend back if we're going to get into a bunch of capers."

"Capers? We're getting into capers?"

"When you can stand to leave the twins for longer than two hours, you and I will be up to our necks in capers."

"I prefer the term shenanigans. Up to our necks in shenanigans."

"Bonnie and Clyde did not get up to their necks in shenanigans. They got up to their necks in capers."

"Bonnie and Clyde were lovers," I pointed out. "And they died together in a shootout with police."

"Relationship goals, perhaps?"

"Hmm. Hard pass."

"Get out of here. Go be a productive member of society."

"You know," she began as I walked her to the door. "Bald women were in fashion a few years ago. I think you have enough social standing to make brow-less women a thing."

"Seriously, leave. I finally have twenty pounds on you, and I know I can take you down."

She looked down at her chest. "And yet, I still somehow beat you in the cleavage department."

"As of this day, Stacy is my new best friend."

"You. Bitch."

"You know I could never replace you." I hugged her. "You came when I was in crisis. You will always have the best friend badge of honor."

"You mean best friend badge of courage," she quipped. "Pretty sure it takes a whole lot of courage to be your best friend. After all, everyone knows that your super villain power is setting stuff on fire."

"Oh, wow, time flies when you're being shoved out the door."

"I want photos of the brow wig." She saluted me and then was gone.

Jasper let out a whine and pawed at the door. "Do you miss her? Or do you need a walk?"

He whined again.

"Are you really going to make me go out in public looking this way? Seriously?"

I pulled my hair up into a ponytail and put on a hat with a brim. I found a pair of Aidan's sunglasses that were too big for my face, but at least they concealed my lack of eyebrows.

I clipped Jasper to his leash and took him for a walk to Transmitter Park. Kids playing soccer stopped to pet him. I breathed a sigh of relief when none of them noticed my eyebrows, and I took a moment to enjoy some time outside of the apartment. I had gotten away with being brow-less, but I hoped no one would recognize who I was since I was trying to be incognito.

By the time I made it back to the apartment, Mrs. Nowacki had returned with the babies.

"They are asleep. They've eaten and had diapers changed. Big poops for both of them," she said from her spot on the couch.

"Er—great. Thanks. You're like a Polish Mary Poppins, you know that?"

"Who?"

"She's a—never mind." I gestured with my chin as I took off the ball cap and sunglasses. "What are you reading?"

"*People* magazine."

"Where did you get that? I don't subscribe to *People*."

She shook her head. "I buy at bodega on way home. Want the ideas for clothes." She looked me up and down. "Maybe you look at magazine with me?"

Okay, I could take a hint.

My wardrobe of late had consisted of Aidan's T-shirts and exercise pants—despite the fact that I was doing no exercising.

"New dress that show off the boom-booms and no one will see that you don't have eyebrows. And make sure to wear the glasses. Your glasses make you look smart."

"I have a dress I wore the other night when I flambéed myself."

"Bad luck to wear that dress again. Who knows what will happen if you wear it to husband's big night."

"You have a good point." I sighed. "I'm really

depressed, Mrs. Nowacki. I look in the mirror—and, eyebrow-less face aside—I don't like the way I look."

"So. You change it."

"How?"

"You try. You make effort. Even if you are tired. You get your once tight bottom out the door."

Her words weren't cruel, just honest—but they still made me tear up. It was just the sort of kick in my—ah— non-tight rear-end that I needed.

"Book an appointment at favorite salon. Get haircut— it will make you feel better." She leaned close and dragged a finger across my furry upper lip. "Might want to take care of that, too."

"You have no eyebrows," Mama Goldstein stated. It came out like an accusation.

I sighed. "Yes. I'm aware."

"Do you know how I had to find out you had no eyebrows?" Her frowning face filled the screen as we commenced our bi-weekly Face Time chat.

"No. I have no idea how you found out."

"Mrs. Nowacki Skyped with *Bubbe*. *Bubbe* called me. Why didn't you call me?"

"You're mad because I didn't tell you myself that I didn't have eyebrows?" I closed my eyes. "It's a wee bit humiliating, okay?"

"Of course it is. But you're Sibby. You think, therefore you set things on fire. Only this time you did it to yourself," she said. "I think we need to take a trip to New Orleans."

"I'm confused by the abrupt subject change."

"In New Orleans, there are people there who can talk to spirits, channel energy, and cleanse auras. I think you need an aura cleanse."

"Okay, what the heck are you talking about?"

"Becca and I went on a girls' weekend," she explained. "Your aunt dragged me into a tarot reading shop. The woman had crystals and feathers in jars. It was really weird, but I let her read my cards and then I let her clean my aura. And you know what? I felt better. Lighter. Like I had gotten rid of something I'd been psychically carrying around."

I had no idea what to say to her.

"Anyway, I think you need to do something like that. Maybe then the fire department can rest easy."

"Har-har. How's the business doing?" I asked, switching gears.

"Fine," she said. "Busier than ever. People always want to find love, and I'm glad I can help. Actually, I need to jump off and tackle some last minute things. Don't forget, we're flying in Thursday and leaving Monday."

"I have it on my calendar."

"We want to take a cab straight to you and the babies. Check in at the hotel later. We're staying in Greenpoint instead of Manhattan. We booked the hotel that used to be a pillow factory."

I nodded. "You told me already. I still remember."

"I just wanted to remind you, that's all. New mom brain and all."

"Okay, love you. Bye," I said pointedly.

"Bye." She blew a kiss and then clicked off, my screen going dark.

The front door opened and I managed to hoist myself off the bed. Jasper and I padded out of the bedroom.

"Hey," Aidan said with a smile as he wrapped me in a hug.

I buried my face against him.

"What's wrong?"

"Nothing. Just missed you. And I just talked to my mother…"

"Ah," he said.

I stepped away. "She's acting weird."

He raised his eyebrows. "Weirder than normal?"

I nodded. "Yeah. I don't know what's going on, but she just suggested I go to New Orleans to get my aura cleansed so I stop setting things on fire."

"The idea does have merit," he said with a wry grin.

"I'm serious, Aidan. She's acting strange. She's flightier than usual."

"Here's an idea. Why don't you call your dad and ask him? He lives with her. I'm sure he has some insight."

"He's hard to pin down. I'll ask him when they're up here next week."

Aidan went to the fridge and pulled out a bottle of iced tea. "How has the rest of your day been? The twins?"

"Twins are fine. They went down for a nap about thirty minutes ago." I paused. "Mrs. Nowacki kind of mentally kicked my ass."

"What do you mean?" He headed over to the couch and plopped down. Jasper jumped up next to him and nuzzled his snoot into Aidan's neck in the exact place I liked to put my own face.

"Sibby?" he prodded.

"Huh?"

"What were you saying about Mrs. Nowacki?"

"Oh. She just gave me some very honest advice about getting my groove back. Haircut, new dress for the party, exercise…waxing my upper lip."

"Hmm." His eyes were bleary, like he was trying to listen to me, but exhaustion was taking its toll. I knew he was burning the candle at both ends and with newborns he didn't stand a chance. The twins had been up four times the night before.

I crouched down in front of him to take off his shoes and gently pushed his shoulder to get him to lie down. I tucked a pillow under his head and then covered him with a blanket.

"Rest."

"Are you sure?" he asked, even as he set his iced tea on the coffee table.

I nodded. "I'm going to sit at my computer and see if I can get some work done."

"You want to work? Now?"

"It's the one thing I can control in my life right now, so I'm going to try." I pressed a kiss to his forehead. His eyes were already drooping shut.

I grabbed my laptop and took it to the kitchen table. I opened the document with my manuscript—the one with all the notes from my editor.

The cursor blinked in rapid-fire succession as I began to read through the words I'd written. After twenty minutes of staring at the same paragraph, I realized it all looked like gibberish.

With a labored sigh, I closed my laptop. Maybe it was

foolish to think I could jump back into who I used to be just because I willed it. Even though the twins hadn't made a peep, my mind was with them. Were they warm enough? Had Sophie soiled her diaper and was she about to scream her head off to let me know she needed changing? Had Oliver scratched his cheek with his tiny, adorable fingernails? I swore he was part werewolf, because his little baby nails grew so fast.

Opening my laptop again, I navigated to the blog I was keeping and poured out my thoughts into a post. I wrote that I was no longer the screw up hipster girl trying to find her way in Manhattan. I'd fallen in love, I'd built a life with Aidan, I'd had his children. I was a writer, but lately, all I felt like was a mother.

I took my cell phone into the bedroom and called to make an appointment to get my hair cut. Even though it was last minute, my stylist had an opening the following morning.

It was time to take back what control I could.

And then I willed myself to cook grilled chicken and broccoli for dinner when all I wanted was a pizza.

Chapter 5

Mom Blog Entry:
  I have found an intruder in my pants. I have named him Earl.
  Earl is a hemorrhoid.
  Fuck my life.

"Aidan?" I asked, moving Tupperware and bottles of condiments around in the fridge, searching for the breast milk I knew I'd defrosted for the twins.

"Yeah?"

"Where's the breast milk? It was here last night before I went to bed."

"I don't know," he said, a little too quickly.

I stood up and looked over my shoulder at him. He had Oliver cradled in one arm while he ate his cold fried eggs and toast with the other hand, taking bites in between wrangling our son.

"You know you're a terrible liar, right?"

He scrunched his face up. "I'm a great liar."

"Um, maybe as a husband you shouldn't brag about that. My overactive hormonal mom- brain might read into that. You feel me?"

"What are you? A low-level gangster?" he asked with a chuckle.

"Don't change the subject. And for the record, a hormonal new mother is scarier than any gangster. The milk, Aidan. What happened to the milk?"

"Promise not to get mad? I know how much you loathe the breast pump."

I waved my hand at him. "I'm listening."

"I made coffee this morning. And I realized we were out of half-and-half. And I didn't want to get dressed and go to the corner bodega. So—"

"No."

"Yes."

"You didn't."

"I did."

"You put breast milk in your coffee?"

"Maybe."

"The whole thing? There was like, six ounces."

He cleared his throat. "I kinda, maybe, put it into a saucepan and frothed it."

"You made a breast milk café au lait?"

"I prefer the term café con leche."

I leaned against the counter. "How was it?"

"Sweet."

I shook my head and couldn't stop the laughter that escaped. It was so utterly ridiculous.

Like something I would do.

"You're not mad?" he asked.

"Do I look mad?"

"No."

"I needed that laugh. It burned like five calories, which is a total win. The only issue, though, is *that* breast milk was supposed to be enough to get the twins through my salon appointment."

"And now you have to take them with you. Crap. I'm sorry."

"Yeah, I don't know how this is going to work," I admitted. "I guess I could feed them right before I leave?"

The buzzer to the apartment went off.

"Are you expecting a package from one of your product sponsors?"

"Why, are you jealous?"

"Of devices that arrive in the mail that attach to your nipples? Kinda, yeah."

I laughed and went to answer the door. I pressed the button that worked the camera. All I saw was a big smile and a head of purple hair.

"Oh my God," I said in excitement, buzzing Stacy in.

"What? Who is it?"

I opened the door and a moment later, the stylish form of my unofficial PR rep and personal assistant appeared.

"You weren't supposed to be here until next week!" I said, embracing Stacy.

She set aside her wheelie suitcase. "Change of plans. I missed the city too much. And I have to see the munchkins." Stacy stared at me and paused for a moment. "You have no eyebrows."

"I know."

"What's that about?"

"Sibby's Law."

"Say no more." She grimaced. Jasper came to greet Stacy and then dogged her heels as she walked over to Aidan.

"Hey," he greeted with a sincere smile.

"Hi," she said, wrapping him in a side hug while she peered down at Oliver's sleeping face. "He's huge."

"I know."

"Did he like, double in size?"

"Looks that way, doesn't it? I swear they grow overnight."

"Where's Sophie?"

"Sleeping in the bassinet in the corner," I gestured with my chin.

She darted over to the bassinet and looked in on Sophie. "What an angel."

I snorted. "I'm pretty sure if she wasn't mine, I'd demand a refund. That one is a handful."

"Oooh, the teenage years will be so fun with her." Stacy grinned.

I looked at the clock on the stove. "I have a hair appointment in an hour. I have to bring the twins with me due to a milk supply situation." I glanced at Aidan, whose cheeks had gone a dusky rose color. "You want to come with me and help be a twin wrangler? We can catch up. Unless you have somewhere else to be."

She shook her head. "I'll come with you. And what do you mean by a milk supply situation?"

"You know what? It's not really important," Aidan interjected.

"I'm gonna go change," I said with an evil smile. "You two have fun."

A few minutes later, there was a knock on the bedroom door. "Come in!" I called out.

Stacy entered and plopped down on the bed. "Sorry to show up out of the blue."

"Please. You know this place is bedlam. I should just give you a key so you can come and go as you please."

"Wouldn't that be weird for you?"

"Mrs. Nowacki, Annie, Caleb, Zeb, Nat—they all have keys."

"Annie *and* Caleb both have keys?"

I made a face. "Yeah, they used to come and go as they wanted, but now it's all sorts of screwed up."

"I feel so out of the loop."

"Tell me about it. Between the twins and my lack of eyebrows, I've basically been a shut in. I can't wait to get my hair cut for this event. Oh, hey, will you go shopping with me? I need to find a dress that makes me feel sexy and hides my pierogi pouch."

"Your what?"

I placed a hand on my lower abdomen. "I called the babies pierogis when they were in utero. Now I have a pierogi pouch."

She smiled suddenly. "I missed you. Like, a lot."

"I missed you, too." I gestured to the yoga pants and one of Aidan's old button downs. "Does this look terrible?"

She shook her head. "You're going to the salon. No one will care."

"Good, because at some point I'm gonna need to find a way to whip a boob out and the button down makes it so much easier."

Thirty minutes later, both babies were fed and changed and hanging out in their double stroller. Aidan and Jasper were supine on the couch watching some sporting event that involved balls.

Ha ha. Balls. Never gets old.

"Caleb's coming over," he said. "Is that okay? We need a day to chill and drink beer and not move from the couch."

"Sounds like a pretty good day," I admitted. "Mrs. Nowacki might still come by even though I told her you'd be home with the babies."

"Cool. Text Annie, yeah? Let her know about Caleb being here."

"You do know we're having brunch the morning after the soft launch. They're both invited. They're going to have to find a way to be in the same room as each other at some point or else this is going to suck, forever."

"Ten bucks says Annie finds an excuse to bail," Aidan said.

"I'm with Aidan on that one," Stacy agreed, grabbing her shoulder bag. "She's not going to the party, right? Even though she was invited?"

I shook my head. "She weighed the pros and cons and decided it would be a lot less awkward if she didn't attend."

I scrunched my face together toward the center of my nose.

"What are you doing?" Stacy asked.

"I'm using all my mental energy to wish my eyebrows back into existence."

Aidan grinned. "It's not going very well."

"Bite me."

His smile widened. "Better get going, love. You're going to be late."

After a quick kiss to his lips, I grabbed a hold of the stroller and left the apartment with Stacy at my side.

"What are you planning on doing for the night of Aidan's event?" Stacy asked when we were out on the sidewalk. "I'm going to be taking dozens of photos and posting them all over social."

"I've got a plan."

"Are you going to share it with me?"

"Nope."

She raised one of her perfectly waxed eyebrows and then changed the subject, "You should see the dress I have planned for the event. Strapless. Black. *Tight*."

"I'm sure Joe's mouth will drop open when he sees you."

"Yeah, about Joe." She sighed. "He's not coming."

"Did the band book a last-minute gig somewhere?" I asked.

"Joe and I broke up," she said without any inflection. "I'm moving back to New York. Permanently."

My head whipped around so fast I nearly toppled over. "What? When did this happen?"

"About three days ago."

"About three days ago? Why didn't you text me? What happened? And I'm so sorry!"

She shrugged, looking resolute, but not angry or even that sad. "He was cheating on me. I kind of suspected it about a month ago. An incriminating text proved it. I should've known, right? I mean, he's a musician and his band started doing well. It's not that surprising really."

"It's okay to be upset about it," I told her as we approached the salon.

"I'm just kind of embarrassed, you know? Like, my mom wasn't even surprised."

I didn't have the heart to tell her that Zeb and I had taken bets on when her relationship would fall apart. Not because we wanted it to, but because we were older and could see it for what it was.

"Hey, don't feel that way. I walked in on my live-in boyfriend in bed with another man. Trust me, you do not have the market cornered on feeling embarrassed."

She smiled slightly. "I'm just glad I didn't throw my entire career away for him. I'm glad I can come back here. The Veritas party is just what I need to get back in the swing of things."

Aidan and Caleb had hired Stacy for the evening. With her social media presence and her huge Instagram following, she could definitely make the night a success. Between Stacy and the magazines coming to do write-ups about the event, the launch was poised to put the boys on the map. They'd done very well for themselves, but getting to that next level of success took a lot of time, effort, and frankly, the right connections.

Stacy opened the salon door for me and I managed to maneuver the huge stroller inside. The receptionist hung up the phone and then jumped up when she saw the twins sleeping in their stroller. Ladies who were waiting to get their hair cut came over to see the twins, too.

When a woman reached into the stroller about to touch Oliver, I lost my shit.

"You look with your eyes, not your hands, lady," I snapped.

The salon went quiet and even the hair dryer blowing somewhere in the back of the room shut off. My voice echoed in the expansive room.

"I'm sorry," the woman said, her chin wobbling.

It was my first inclination to tell her it was okay, but it wasn't okay. I didn't know this woman; I didn't know where her hands had been.

Everyone was holding their collective breath as they

waited to see what I was going to do. I couldn't let this woman off the hook, but I could soften the blow.

"Come talk to me. Away from everyone," I said to her.

She followed me to the room off the main floor that had all the hair products stored, along with tubs of hard wax and linen strips. It was like the salon gods were telling me to get my lip waxed.

I turned to the woman who looked like she was about a decade older than me. Her hair was cut into a chic brunette bob and she was long and willowy, like one of those people who wore out treadmills. In another time and in another place, I would've been really jealous of her body.

Scratch that, the time and place was now, and I was *definitely* jealous of her body.

"I'm really sorry," she blurted out before I could even open my mouth. "I didn't even think—I just—"

"*I'm* sorry," I interjected. "Not for what I said, but how I said it."

She shook her head. "No, you were totally right. I was in the wrong. You don't know me, you don't know if I've washed my hands." Her fair face was suddenly blotchy with embarrassment. "I'll ask before I reach out a touch a stranger's baby. I just," she swallowed, "can't have kids of my own and I—"

I grabbed her hand and gave it a squeeze. "Say no more. Please. I feel like a giant ass now."

"You shouldn't. Not at all. I didn't tell you to make you feel guilty, I was just trying to explain myself."

"Thank you," I said. I dropped her hand and looked down at Oliver and Sophie.

Rita, my stylist, popped her head through the semi-closed door.

"Hey," she said with a smile and then she tilted her head to the side. "Wait, what happened to your eyebrows?"

"For the love of," I muttered. "Excuse me a minute, would you?" I asked the woman who I'd been speaking to.

"Sure thing."

Rita opened the door so I could push the stroller out onto the salon's main floor. "Hey!" I called out to the people in the waiting area.

Eyes turned to me. Some were curious. Some were confused. One woman looked scared.

"I have no eyebrows, okay? Let's all move along."

Stacy muffled a laugh behind her hand, but my addressing the issue on its head diffused the curiosity.

"Well, that took care of that," Stacy said as I pushed the stroller to Rita's station.

"I'm afraid to ask you what happened with that customer," Rita said in her thick, Staten Island accent. "You nearly bit her head off."

"Rita, you've been part of my life for a long time. You get a free pass to ask all the things."

She lifted my lack-luster locks and wrinkled her nose. "What are we doing with this mess?"

"Um. Ouch."

"I have an idea, if you're interested," Stacy said, standing next to the stroller like a purple-haired protective goddess.

"Who are you?" Rita asked as she looked at Stacy, her stance pugnacious. Rita had grown up with three older brothers. She was barely five feet tall, but packed more attitude than most people a foot taller than her.

Stacy held out her hand. "I'm Stacy. I'm Sibby's friend, PR rep, personal assistant, and make-up tutorial YouTube guru."

Rita blinked and slowly took Stacy's hand. "I like your style. What's your idea?"

"Hey!" I interjected. "Don't I get a say in what's happening."

"Hush, you," Rita said, patting my shoulder. "Let us talk."

I looked at my eyebrowless reflection, noting the bags of exhaustion under my eyes, the limpness of my hair, and the general malaise I seemed to carry around me like a blanket.

"You're gonna need magic to fix this," I stated. "I hope you've got elves and unicorn glitter somewhere around here. Have at it."

Three hours later, after a haircut and a color change, two screaming babies who'd needed feeding while I was getting my hair dyed, three diaper changes that I had to manage, and a lip wax, I was finally looking at myself in the mirror and marveling at the woman staring back at me.

"Do we know our shit, or do we know our shit?" Rita asked, high-fiving Stacy.

I turned my head from side to side, enjoying the lightness of my hair that had been chopped a good four inches, now gracing the tops of my shoulders. Combined with the red dye, I could almost ignore that fact that my eyebrows were gone.

"I don't even look like me," I said.

"That's the point," Stacy said and then immediately retracted. "I mean, don't you like it?"

"I do actually, yeah. I've never been a redhead before. I feel exotic for the first time in my entire life. It's like I'm a different person. I almost feel like I need a new name to go with my new identity."

"You have enough identities," Stacy stated. "You don't need any new ones."

I hugged Rita goodbye after paying and then Stacy and I were out in the sunshine. The twins were conked out thanks to my soporific milk.

"Do we have time to go to one of my favorite boutiques?" she asked. "Or does Aidan want you home?"

"Aidan and Caleb are probably sitting on the couch, scratching their stomachs and drinking beer while watching some sporting event. Trust me, he doesn't care."

She laughed. "You're totally wrong. He's already texted me three times asking why you haven't answered his texts."

"Really?" I whipped out my phone from my purse. Sure enough, Aidan had texted me a dozen times. His messages brought a smile to my face.

Stacy's expression went sour and she said, "Ugh, if you weren't such a good person, I'd punch you in your throat. Stupid hot husband who loves you…"

"Guess you're not as fine with the Joe thing as you claimed, huh?" I asked with a commiserating smile.

She shrugged. "It comes in waves. One minute, I'm totally Zen. The next, I want to bash him on my YouTube channel and then high five him…in the face…with a chair. But I don't want to be *that girl*. You know, the angry bitter one who rants on social. That's like career suicide. Plus no one will want to date me because I'll have been labeled psycho. Damn the high road!"

"Don't take this the wrong way, but you could really use a drink."

"No kidding."

We walked the few blocks to Stacy's favorite boutique and awkwardly got the stroller inside the really tiny store. Thankfully, no one decided to reach out and try to touch my children. I was a redhead now and I was feeling spunky.

I wondered how Aidan would feel about my new look.

"Aidan is going to want to have sex with me," I said to Stacy.

At full volume.

In front of everyone.

Stacy rolled her eyes. "Forgive Sibby, she knows not what she's done with her filter."

The boutique assistant laughed and embraced Stacy. "I didn't think I'd see you back here for a while."

"Joe and I split up," Stacy said with a wave of her hand. "But I'm doing great."

"Glad to hear it." She looked to me and said, "I'm Lauren."

"Sorry, I forgot to introduce you guys."

"It's okay," I said with a smile. "I'm Sibby."

"Love your hair."

I beamed.

"Sibby's husband owns Veritas," Stacy explained.

"I love that bar!" Lauren exclaimed in genuine excitement.

Stacy nodded. "The party for the expansion is happening next week, and Sibby needs a new outfit to go with her new hair. Something sexy."

"Something that hides my stomach and doesn't make me feel like I gave birth only a few months ago." I gestured to the stroller with my chin.

"Yeah, fair." She looked me up and down. "Are you comfortable showing off a bit of cleavage?"

"A little." I sighed. "But I also have to wear a thick nursing bra because, well, yeah."

She nodded. "I think I have something that will work really well actually. Wait here."

When Lauren disappeared into the back, I leaned in to whisper to Stacy, "She didn't even comment on my lack of eyebrows."

"I texted her on the way over to prepare her," she whispered back.

"You're a good friend."

"I try." She cocked her head to the side. "You took theater classes in college, didn't you?"

"Yeah."

"Stage makeup class?"

"Yep."

"Then how is it you didn't think to get creative with your eyebrows?"

"I can make a good bruise or gash using stage makeup and that's about it. And really? Aren't *you* the makeup guru? Where are your suggestions?"

"I've got a brow pencil."

"Thanks, genius. I already thought of that. I've got a plan and it's better than a brow pencil."

"Why won't you tell me? I helped Rita with your new look. You don't think that warrants taking me into your confidence?"

"Don't take this the wrong way, but you blab."

She looked affronted. "I do not *blab*."

"You kinda do. Remember when we met in Rite Aid?"

"That was an accident," she defended.

"I know."

"Then why are you still holding it over me? Tell me! I want to know how you're going to manufacture eyebrows."

"I'm a mom now," I said, straightening my spine. "And I don't have to tell you if I don't want to."

"Mature, Sibby, real mature. Fine, I'll text Annie. She'll tell me."

"She will not."

Stacy looked smug. "She will when I tell her I met Gregory Roubideaux at his Las Vegas restaurant and he would be honored to come to Mother Shucker's opening. If only she will tell me what you have planned for your eyebrows…"

"You're going to hold Gregory Roubideaux over her head?"

"Of course not, I've already asked him." She grinned. "He's coming."

I laughed. "Fine, I'll tell you. But it's embarrassing."

"More embarrassing than setting singeing off your own eyebrows using a crème brûlée torch?"

"How did you know that?" I demanded.

"I asked Aidan while you were getting ready."

"It's impossible to have any secrets where my friends are concerned," I muttered. "No loyalty. Not even from my own husband, the father of my children."

"Yeah, yeah. Spill it."

"Oh my God," Aidan said.

"You hate it," I said, hand going to my hair.

He shook his head. "No. I don't hate it at all. I *love it* actually. I just—you didn't tell me you were going to dye it."

Aidan got up off the couch, looking alert and coherent despite the fact that Sophie's wail had jarred him out of a doze. Caleb was gazing around, trying to figure out what was going on. Both of them were utterly exhausted, and when Stacy and I had walked into the apartment, we'd caught them in the act of sleeping in front of the television.

Stacy set the boutique bag down on the kitchen table. "It was my idea."

Aidan gripped me by the shoulders, completely ignoring the screeching twins for a moment while he looked me over.

He leaned in to kiss me passionately for a moment and then said, "I've always had a thing for redheads."

I laughed. "You and every other man alive."

"I like your hair too," Caleb said, standing up and stretching his arms over his head. He was wearing a Red Sox T-shirt, along with a matching hat, and it made me think of Annie, who was a die-hard Sox fan. That had been one of the things they'd had in common. They were fanatical about the Sox.

"How was your afternoon?" I asked, shaking off the somber change in my thoughts.

"Good. I'm hungry, though," Aidan said.

"Me too," Caleb added.

"So am I," Stacy voiced.

"So are the twins." Aidan looked down at the strollers. "Tag team?"

"Let's do it."

"I'm gonna head home," Caleb announced, swiping his keys, wallet, and cell from the coffee table.

"Yeah, I should go too," Stacy said.

"I have a better idea," I announced. "Why don't you both stay for dinner. Caleb, call Em and have her come over."

"That's a great idea," Aidan said.

"You guys figure out dinner. We're going to tend to our offspring," I said.

Caleb winced when Oliver let out a high-pitched scream. "Don't take this the wrong way, but even though he's my godson, that noise makes me want to jump out a window."

"Same. Uncool," Stacy agreed.

"My babies' cries make my milk let down and my nipples leak," I said.

Stacy made a face. Caleb looked wide-eyed and uncomfortable.

"And on that note, if you'll excuse us," Aidan said with a laugh.

We headed into the nursery with our squawking infants. "Give them both to me."

"You sure? Should we change them first?"

"Why? They're just gonna poop more. I'd rather have my eardrums intact right now. Quiet them down, you know?"

I sat down in the rocking chair and grabbed the nursing pillow. It had only been a couple of months, but exhaustion was a powerful teacher and Aidan and I had this down to a science. A few minutes later the room was quiet.

"You got some more packages today," he said.

"Did I?" I grinned. "Have you opened any of them?"

"In front of Caleb? No way."

"Why not?" I asked with a laugh.

"I don't know. I have no idea what to expect when it comes to baby stuff. It could've been something really embarrassing."

"Pretty sure the most embarrassing thing to see would be a breast pump or nipple cream for chapped nipples. Aside from that, I don't know what else there could be that would embarrass the hell out of you."

I leaned my head back against the chair and rocked, feeling sleepy and ready for a nap of my own.

"You were gone a long time today," he said softly. "Missed you guys."

"It felt good to get out," I admitted. "I feel sexy and sleek. Sorta. I bought a new outfit for the party."

"You gonna show it to me?"

"Nope. You're just going to have to wait and see me in it. But trust me, it's gonna make you shriek like Shrau."

<hr>

Chapter 6

<hr>

Mom Blog Entry:
  Raising a dog isn't anything like raising a human.
  Except the poop.
  There's a lot of poop with both of them.

"I need your man tool," I said the next morning.

"Oh, Sibby, I thought you'd never ask," Aidan said, going for the belt on his khaki shorts.

I held up a hand. "Easy there. I was referring to the *actual* man tool you carry in your pocket."

"That would be called a pocketknife, not a man tool. And way to get my hopes up."

"I'm ignoring you now."

"I'm not letting you use my pocketknife. I'm afraid you'll cut off a finger." He flicked open the knife. "What is it you want me to do with this?"

"Please open all the packages on the counter."

"Using my sexy man tool?"

I grinned. "I love watching you work, baby."

He laughed and went to the biggest box on the counter. Aidan sliced through the tape and got the box open. "What do we think this is? Care to guess?"

"Just give me the goods."

Aidan pulled out a high-end canvas diaper bag. "No way."

"Way," I said. "Look at all the pockets!"

"Pockets? Who cares about pockets? Look at this zipper. That piece of crap we're using is history! Okay! Next box."

Even though all the boxes were addressed to me, I let Aidan open them because I wanted to involve him, and he was excited.

"Are these what I think they are?" he asked, holding up nursing pads.

"Yes. Though I'm not sure why those are any different than the ones I already have."

He read the product description that came in the box. "These are made of bamboo. And reusable."

"Fancy pants."

Aidan set aside the nursing pads. "We've come to the final box of our program." He sliced the tape, opened the box...and pulled out a massive tube of lube.

He held it up. "Something you want to tell me, Sib?"

"Such as?" I filched the tube of lube to examine it. "Made in Canada. Vanilla scented." I looked at him. "I did not order this, nor did I ask for it."

"So, when you said mom blog, you really meant sex blog, right?"

"No!"

He grinned.

"You jerk," I said with a laugh.

"Why would this company send you lube?" he asked, reaching for his phone.

"What are you doing?"

"Googling the company. Obviously."

"Obviously."

"Ah. Okay," he said. He held out the phone to me. "The lube is supposed to help with dryness."

"Dryness? Are you calling me dry?"

"No! That's not what I…no." Aidan cleared his throat. "Apparently they have a whole line of products designed to, ah, help new moms get back in the swing of things."

I peered closer at the screen and tapped on a picture. "Speaking of swings… How does one even get into that?"

"You have to lift your leg and then—"

I raised my nonexistent eyebrows. "You've been holding out on me, Kincaid."

He pointed a finger at the lube. "You're not going to actually write about it, are you? That would mean you're going to be writing about our sex life."

"For the good of womankind—and motherhood," I stated.

The front door opened and Mrs. Nowacki strolled in carrying three garment bags over her arm. Her eyes immediately went to the open boxes and the lube tube in my hand.

"I'm interrupting."

"No," I said at the exact same time Aidan said, "Yes."

"What do you have with you?" I asked her.

"Clothes for online dating profile photo."

"Ah. Why don't you change in our room?"

She nodded and looked again at the lube. "I hear good things about this company."

Aidan and I exchanged a glance.

Don't you dare, he mouthed silently.

Oh, I'm daring, I mouthed back.

"Mrs. Nowacki?" I asked.

"Ya?"

"How have you heard about this company?"

"Your *Bubbe* and *Zayde* recommend it to me when I told them I wanted to start dating again." She smiled sweetly and then clopped off to the bedroom.

Aidan opened his mouth to say something, but I held up a hand. "Don't. If you have any love for me, you'll close your mouth and pretend you weren't right."

Smiling, he closed his mouth.

I couldn't stop the wrinkling of my nose as I took in Mrs. Nowacki's dress. It was black. Collared. It looked like the last time it had been worn was to a funeral…in the 1970s.

All she needed was a broom and a hat and she had one easy Halloween costume.

"Er, what else have you got?" I asked from my spot on the bed.

All hail Aidan, king of the fathers. He was watching the twins while I helped Mrs. Nowacki find the perfect outfit to entrap a man on the internet.

Mrs. Nowacki looked down at herself. "What is wrong with this dress? It is high quality."

"Yes, it is…"

How was the woman not sweating? Her neck was concealed. Her wrists were covered. And she hadn't taken off her stockings.

"Listen. I know we're from different generations," I began. "And we have different ideas about what is acceptable to show off, but can I ask you a serious question?"

"Yes."

"Why are you dressing like a widow?"

"I *am* a widow."

"Yes, I know." I felt a pang in my heart and thought carefully how to proceed. "But don't you want to give off a different vibe when you start to date again?"

She sighed. "I'm scared."

"Of what?"

"It has been so long since I have had male companionship. What if no one finds me attractive? What if I hate all men, and I should just get more cats?"

"You looked up the definition of 'cat lady', didn't you?"

She nodded.

I scooted on the bed so that I was closer to her and reached for her hand. "You are an amazing woman. You've raised children, had a family. You're strong and independent, choosing to live in Brooklyn despite your children attempting to get you to move to Florida. You have become invaluable to me and to Aidan, and frankly you're part of the family now. Don't tell my mother this, because I'm sure it would send her into a fit, but I'm pretty sure Oliver likes you best."

She laughed and hastily wiped the corner of her eye. "Sometimes I feel like a burden."

"You? Dear Lord, woman. If it weren't for you, I'd know half as much about raising those babies."

"Thank you," she whispered. She cleared her throat and straightened her spine, shoving all emotion away so she could focus on the present. "Should I show you the other two outfits I bring?"

"Are they like the dress you're currently wearing?"

"Yes."

"Then I think, no." I patted her hand and then climbed off the bed. "I have some things in my closet that I think will fit you. Pre-pregnancy clothes."

I went into the walk-in closet I shared with Aidan and starting riffling through the hangers. I pulled out an A-line black skirt and a plum colored, short-sleeved turtleneck sweater.

"What do you think?" I asked, showing her the outfit I put together.

"I like the color of the sweater. Do you think it will look good on me?"

"With your complexion? Definitely."

Sure enough, she looked like dynamite. Unfortunately, Mrs. Nowacki wouldn't let me do anything with her hair or makeup.

We went out into the living room to show Aidan the final result and he was very complimentary and even helped us take the photo since I knew next to nothing about lighting or photography.

An hour later, Mrs. Nowacki's profile was complete, the photo was uploaded, and she was searchable. The browser pinged almost immediately.

"What was that?" Mrs. Nowacki asked.

"Your profile has been liked."

"Already?"

"Already," I repeated.

It pinged again.

"You're a hot commodity, Mrs. Nowacki," Aidan said with a devilish wink.

She waved her hand away and leaned in close to the computer. "You show me how to check to see who liked my picture?"

I nodded. "See the little heart in the corner of your profile photo? Click that." I clicked the heart and the page opened up and there was already a list of at least ten men who'd liked her profile.

"Sit," I told her, gesturing to the kitchen chair. "Look at some of these gentlemen and see what you think."

She took a seat and I went back to Aidan who had plopped down on the couch.

"The woman has ten guys interested in her already," I marveled.

"Don't get any ideas," he said.

I snorted. "What? Make a fake online dating profile to try and make myself feel better? What would that profile read? Eyebrowless, overweight mother of two newborns looking for love…and a donut?"

He grinned. "You want a donut?"

"No, I don't want a donut. I want five." I sighed. "This is why I have to wear Spanx with my party outfit."

"You're really not going to let me see you in it before that night?"

"I want to knock your socks off."

"Still trying to impress me, after all these years?"

"All these years?" I repeated. "It's not like we're anywhere close to our golden anniversary."

"Oh, this one is good-looking!" Mrs. Nowacki called from the kitchen table.

"Let me see," I said, coming to her side. I leaned over her shoulder to read the screen. "Oh, run away from that guy. Trust me."

"Why? What's wrong with him?" Aidan asked in curiosity.

"The first three paragraphs of his profile are a list of all his ailments." I wrinkled my nose. "Do old people really introduce themselves that way? Like, 'Hi, I'm Phil, and I have cataracts and angina.'"

"I have cataracts," Mrs. Nowacki voiced. "You think maybe I should tell them that?"

"No, I really don't."

She shrugged. "I thought about the laser eye surgery when I turned seventy-five. I didn't think I'd get to eighty-five so what was the point?"

"This conversation just turned really depressing," Aidan muttered.

"Nothing is wrong with my hearing, *moje serce*." She tossed a smile over her shoulder at him.

"I like this guy," I said, pointing to a photo of a man who had no ear hair or nose hair peeking out to make an appearance. His smile was wide and from what I could tell, all his teeth looked like the originals. Clearly, hygiene was important.

"He is wearing plaid jacket."

"So?"

"So, he has no fashion sense."

I looked at Aidan. *Help me.*

He grinned. "Nothing wrong with plaid. I've got a pair of boxers that are plaid. Sibby always gets very handsy when I wear them. Isn't that right, sweetums?"

I made a face. "Cut the cutesy, sugar britches." To Mrs. Nowacki, I said, "No harm in chatting with him, you know?"

"He looks like goody-goody."

"Why, Mrs. Nowacki. Are you into the bad boys?"

I'd never seen the woman blush before, but sure enough, color suffused her cheeks while she tried to appear nonchalant.

"We all have a type, Sibby," she informed me loftily. "You like man who clean up your messes. I like men who wear leather and spank—"

"Oh wow, I totally hear Sophie crying," I said as I got up and practically ran from the room, darting into the nursery.

It just so happened that I caught Sophie right before she let out a howl. I quickly picked her up and took her to the changing table. Just as I finished putting Sophie in a new diaper, the door to the nursery opened and Aidan slipped inside. He immediately went to Oliver who'd started fussing.

"You left me to drown out there," Aidan accused. "She just told me things I wish I never knew."

"Sexual things?" I picked up Sophie so Aidan could use the changing table.

"Positions. What she and her husband used to do to get *it* back after they had a baby..." He shuddered. "I now have visuals of two old people going at it."

"They weren't old when they had a baby."

"Whatever. I never knew Mrs. Nowacki when she was

young, so in my head they're old."

I grinned.

"What?"

"You totally want to try something she suggested, don't you?"

He sighed. "I'm eighty percent curious, twenty percent ashamed."

"I like adventure," I told him. "After all, you indulged my alien warlord fantasy. Next date night, you get to pick the fantasy."

Aidan laughed. "Hallelujah."

"Go for a run," I commanded. "You're driving me insane."

"It's the heat of the day," Aidan complained. "I'm not going to run in this."

"Then go hang out with Caleb."

"He's occupied," he growled.

"With what?"

"Em."

"Oh. Afternoon delight, perhaps?"

"Don't know, didn't ask."

"You've got to figure something out. My parents are

due here any moment, and I'm pretty sure my mother will find a way to push you over the edge."

He grimaced. "Yeah, you're right. Fine. I'll go to the gym."

I shook my head as Aidan changed into exercise clothes. I still carried twenty-five pounds of baby weight, and yet my husband had somehow gotten hotter. Better body, drool worthy abs.

"Will you be okay for an hour or two while I'm gone?" he asked, his eyes worried. "I'm not sure it's a good idea to leave you and your mother to your own devices."

"We'll be fine. If she gets unruly I'm gonna spike her coffee with Kahlúa. It's like my mother's Benadryl. It will knock her out and then my dad can take her back to the hotel."

"You've known this for how long? And you're just now telling me this information? Why? Not that I'd use that trick," he hastened to add.

I grinned. "Ah, so there are still things you don't know about me. Fantastic."

"It has nothing to do with not knowing *you*, Sibby, but about your mother. Although…"

"Although what?"

"I've never seen you drink Kahlúa. Like mother like daughter perhaps?"

"Don't get any ideas."

His smile widened. "See you in a bit." He grabbed his gym bag, leaned down to kiss me, and then quickly left the apartment.

I picked up my phone to text Annie: *Is Mills coming to brunch at our house the morning after the party?*

After a few minutes, Annie replied with: *Yup.*

What type of bagel does he like?

Sesame.

The weekend was going to be mayhem. All week, Mrs. Nowacki and I had been running errands in preparation for my family visiting, including going to the Costco in Queens. I had more lox than I knew what to do with, but my parents were coming to town, so lox was a necessity.

Mrs. Nowacki and I had started the baking days ago and now my counter was covered in Polish pastries with names I couldn't pronounce.

I looked around the apartment. It was relatively clean. I sniffed the air. Smelled like lemon, which was a lot better than baby feces. The laundry was under control, and even Jasper had gotten a bath.

I didn't want to give my mother any reason to think that I wasn't able to handle it all because then she'd insist on coming up and staying with us for the foreseeable future.

I felt more stable after a week of taking control over my life and I was sure with the regrowth of my eyebrows, I'd have the pep in my step back in no time. The red hair was really doing wonders. I'd missed my last two Face Time chats with my mother, so this would be a fun surprise.

I heard the buzzer and the front door in the foyer open. Grinning, I looked at Jasper and said, "Who's that?"

He lifted his head off his paws and cocked his head to the side. Jasper stood up, his tail wagging as I repeated, "Who's that?"

My father's face appeared in the doorway first. A heart surgeon with a full head of salt and pepper hair and an easy smile, he reminded me of an old school soap opera star. In a good way.

Jasper jumped off the couch and went to greet my father, who crouched down to scratch the dog's ears.

"Move on in," came my mother's muffled voice from somewhere behind my father.

My dad stepped inside the apartment and headed to the kitchen area. "Hiya, Wapa," he greeted, using the favored childhood nickname I could never get him to forget. He'd even said it in his father of the bride speech at my wedding.

We hugged and Dad pulled back to get a look at me. "You have red hair. When did that happen?"

I grinned. "Last week. I just wanted something different, you know?"

His thumb brushed across my brow ridge. "No fuzzies yet, huh?"

I rolled my eyes. "What? Did you think the power of the Russian DNA would finally be on my side and I'd sprout new eyebrows into existence in time for the party?"

"Yeah, kind of," he admitted with a grin.

"Sibby! Your hair!" Mom exclaimed, finally pulling my attention away from my father.

I looked at her and my mouth dropped open. "*My* hair? What about *your* hair?"

She gestured to her locks that were nearly identical in shade to mine. "What do you think?"

"I think it looks *great*. And that we might be telepathically linked. I mean come on, how did we both wind up with the same color?" I laughed and went to her. "Why didn't you send me a text with a photo?"

"I wanted it to be a surprise." She smiled. "You really like it?"

"I love it." The red in her hair brought out the pink in her cheeks, and at that moment I realized how beautiful my mother truly was.

"Yours looks fantastic, too," she said. She cradled my face and looked into my eyes. Mom's gaze scanned me, looking for changes, taking stock.

"You're not mad, are you?" she asked quietly.

"Mad? About what?"

"That I dyed my hair. I don't want you to think I'm trying to upstage you."

"You look great. And changing your look is always fun, right?"

"Right," she agreed with a smile. "Now where are my adorable grandchildren?"

"The demon spawn are sleeping in the nursery."

"Mind if I go have a peek?"

"Go for it. If Sophie wakes up, it's all you."

My mother smiled and then headed off to the nursery.

"She didn't even ask where Aidan was," I said to my father with a chuckle.

"She'll remember him once she's had her fill of the twins," Dad said. "Where is he, anyway?"

"I told him to go to the gym. He's got a lot of nervous energy about tomorrow night."

"Ah."

"You want to see the twins?" I asked, gesturing to the nursery.

"In a moment. I love my grandchildren, but I'm not into babies the way your mother is."

"No one is into babies the way Mama Goldstein is."

He smiled. "That's true."

"What's up, Dad? You're being weird."

"I'm not being weird."

"Hmmm. Okay. How's work?"

"Busy. Always busy. There's always someone eating too much terrible food and I have to remedy it."

"You sound tired."

"Not tired, per se. But I think I might be ready for semi-retirement."

I raised my non-existent eyebrows. "Semi-retirement. What does that mean?"

"I'm thinking about giving up my position as head of the department."

I blinked. My father had been head of cardiothoracic surgery at Atlanta Memorial for as long as I could remember. Most of my childhood, for sure. There were many nights that he didn't make it home for dinner because of a last-minute emergency surgery or because he had to catch up on paperwork or research.

"What are you going to do with your free time?"

"Travel with your mother. Golf. Tinker."

"Tinker?" I frowned. "Tinker with what?"

"I like old cars."

"You're not seriously thinking about entering semi-retirement just so you can get your hands greasy, are you?"

He shrugged.

"How long have you been thinking about this?"

"A while."

"What does mom say?"

"She ignores me."

"She does?"

"She chooses not to hear," he corrected. "I don't think she can process that I want something else."

"You don't even know what you want," I pointed out. "I mean, you have a vague idea of what you think you want your life to look like, but what happens when you're done traveling or you get sick of golf, or you realize that you're not good at working on old cars?"

"I thought you of all people would understand," he said.

"Me of all people? What does that mean?"

"You changed your entire life not that long ago. You became a YouTube sensation of whatever."

"Instagram," I corrected. "And that was by accident—I

actually became an author. A full-time, make real money, legit author."

"Well, look how it all paid off."

"Okay, first of all," I began, "I didn't change because I wanted to. I changed because I had to. Matt cheated on me, my job imploded, I had no choice but to figure something else out and discover what would make me happy. Plus, I was in my mid-twenties. It's different for you."

"Why? Because I'm older? Am I not allowed to change and grow? Have I grown too old to be allowed to want something else?"

"No. It's just—well, you're at the top of your field. People fly from all over the world to Atlanta for *you* and your skills. Why are you willing to walk away from that?"

"Because I'm not sure it makes me happy anymore, Sibby."

My dad wasn't *happy*? The man who'd been the stable parent my entire childhood, the one who was steadfast and never given to dramatics, a master of business and medical excellence, wasn't happy. And now he was talking about changing his entire life. Which would coincide with changing my mother's entire life.

"This isn't a mid-life life crisis, is it?" I pitched my voice lower so Mom wouldn't overhear what we were discussing. "You're not unhappy with Mom, are you?"

"No," he hastened to assure me. "This has very little to do with your mother."

I didn't know if that made me feel better or worse.

I suddenly had a vision of Aidan and me, thirty years from now. Aidan was the steadfast one in our relationship. Was this time in a man's life inevitable? Would Aidan want to reevaluate everything?

"Sibby?" Dad pressed.

"Huh? What?" I came back to the present.

"I asked if I'm not allowed to want something different?"

"Sibby!" Mom called from the nursery. "Oliver is hungry!"

Jasper had been patiently sitting by my father's leg, but at the sound of my mother's voice, he rushed to the nursery, slipping through the slit between the cracked door and wall.

"My baby needs me," I said woodenly.

Dad nodded and then headed for the front door.

"Where are you going?"

"I need some air," he said.

"You going to the roof?"

"I'm going to All Star."

All Star was the sports bar around the corner. Beer wasn't air, but I nodded anyway. I watched my father leave the apartment, suddenly looking a little more defeated than I had ever seen him before.

The door clicked shut with finality.

I went to tend to my infants.

Chapter 7

Mom Blog Entry:
   Aggghhhhhhhhhhhhhhhhh!

"Where's your father?" Mom asked the moment I entered the nursery. She pulled a tab on Oliver's diaper and then lightly touched his belly before handing him to me.

I whipped out a breast with ease. "He went to All Star."

"He didn't even come in to see the babies."

I looked down at Oliver, who'd latched onto me like an algae sucker fish on glass. "He says he wants to semi-retire."

Mom went to the crib and picked up Sophie, gently cradling her head. "He doesn't know what he wants, Sibby."

Though I was inclined to agree with her, I couldn't bring myself to vocalize it. In what normal scenario was my mother the one who sounded rational?

"He seems pretty adamant about it," I said slowly. "When did all this start?"

"About a month ago." She shook her head. "I'm not even sure what set him off exactly, but ever since he's just been *sulluzen*. Downright mopey."

"Maybe it's a hormone imbalance."

She laughed. "Your father still gets an erection every morning and puts it to good use. No, it's not hormonal."

Why? Just why?

"You ready for Sophie?" she asked.

"In a moment. God, I feel like an 18th century wet nurse. Do you know how much time I waste putting my breasts away? If we didn't have people in and out of the apartment constantly, I swear I'd just walk around with a boob out permanently."

"It would make things easier," Mom agreed. She put a burp rag over her shoulder and held out her hands. Oliver had detached from my body, milk dribbling out of his mouth.

"Whoops," I said. "I think he's got milk in his choddle."

She frowned. "Choddle? What's a choddle? Is it Yiddish?"

"Choddle is a word I made up a few days after they

were born. When I'd discovered breast milk in the fat folds of their baby necks. You know, the *choddle*. Given enough time, I'm pretty sure the twins could make their own breast milk cheese."

Mom stared at me. "Sometimes, I have no idea how you come up with any of this stuff. Anyway, your father is acting all *kerflewy*. And I'm not sure what to do about it."

"Maybe it's one of those situations where you let him do it. You know? Give him what he thinks he wants. The travel, and the time for golf, and working on vintage cars." I rolled my eyes. "That last idea really threw me for a loop de loop."

"Tell me about it. He bought us tickets to the antique car show in Nashville. And he expects me to go with him."

I shook my head. "Doesn't he know husbands and wives are supposed to have separate hobbies? It's the only way to stay interested in your spouse."

"Speaking of spouses," Mom said, smiling as Oliver let out a raging burp. "How's yours holding up?"

"He's ready for this party to be over. So am I, actually. Then I'll get Aidan back."

"Thank you for inviting us," she said with sincerity.

I frowned. "Why wouldn't I invite you?"

"I don't know. Sometimes I think, well, never mind."

"No. Not never mind. What is it, Mom?"

"Are you embarrassed by me?"

I blinked. "How can you even ask that? And what the hell is going on? Dad isn't acting like himself. You're not acting like yourself."

"Not acting like myself how, exactly?"

"Usually you storm in here and take over. You're usually all over the place and—" I winced. "Sorry for the honesty."

"Don't be." She sighed. "Your father isn't the only one going through some changes."

"I thought you already went through menopause."

She mock glared at me as she paced across the nursery floor. "My business is doing well."

"I've heard."

She shook her head. "No, like, *really* well. The local news wants to do a spotlight on me for their morning show. They like to highlight community businesses, that kind of thing."

"That's great."

Mom nodded. "Yeah, I think it is."

"So, what's the problem?"

"The problem is your father. When I started Rent-a-Yenta, he was supportive, but I don't think he really believed it would turn into anything, you know? I mean, what the heck do I know about running a business? I've been a cardiac surgeon's wife most of my adult life. A stay-at-home mother. I used to be there when he got home. Talk to him about his day. Now, I'm out of the house at night. I'm successfully organizing dating events. I'm not—well, I guess I'm not the woman he married and he's not dealing well with the change."

"People change. That's okay."

"That's not the only thing," Mom continued.

"Okay?"

"I'm going through a sexual revolution."

"Um. Please don't say things like that to me. Ever."

"You're not the slightest bit curious about my sexual awakening?"

"Not even a little bit."

I heard the front door open and thanked Moses for the arrival of another human being.

Mrs. Nowacki popped her head into the nursery. "Sorry to interrupt—your *pierś* is out. I come back."

"No, please, come in," I rushed to say as I lowered Sophie onto my lap so I could conceal myself.

Mrs. Nowacki stepped into the nursery and reached for Sophie, placing her against her shoulder.

"You and Mrs. Nowacki should talk," I said, turning my attention back to my mother.

"About what?" Mom asked.

"About what you were trying to tell me. I'm sure Mrs. Nowacki has some great insight."

Mom looked uncomfortable and part of me took great delight in that.

Mrs. Nowacki was best friends with my grandmother, and it would be like Mom talking to her own mother about sex.

"I've started online dating," Mrs. Nowacki began.

"I've started a personal sexual revolution," my mother stated.

Exit stage right.

While Mrs. Nowacki and my mother chatted and burped babies, I took Jasper for a walk to clear my head.

My phone vibrated in my bright pink fanny pack—yes, a fanny pack, because I didn't wear clothes with pockets since I couldn't fit into any of them.

I saw Aidan's name flashing across the screen. "Boy, do I have some funky news. Are you on your way home from the gym?"

"I just left the gym," he said. "I just got a call from Caleb about our caterer for the launch party."

I didn't like his tone. "What's wrong?"

"They had an electrical failure at their catering sight. All the refrigerators and freezers went down. Our trays of food are completely spoiled. Why is New Jersey going through a heat wave? Why is this happening right before the most stressful moment of my life?"

I let out a litany of curses that made a mother carrying her adorable blond toddler glare at me.

"Emergency," I told her. "And try to relax, they don't learn that quickly. It's not like she's going to learn 'fuck' in five seconds."

"Fuck!" the toddler yelled at the top of her lungs.

"Thanks a lot, asshole," the thin, willowy woman muttered, loud enough for me to hear. "And your fanny pack is stupid."

"It's vintage," I sassed.

"Sibby? Sibby, you there?"

"Yeah, I'm here. I just almost had a rumble with another mother. She insulted my fanny pack. I should've taken her down."

"Focus, for the love of God, focus. We don't have time to talk about you rumbling. I'm panicking here."

"Yeah, I can hear that. Where are you now?" I asked. "I'm at Transmitter Park with Jasper."

"I was headed home, but I'm changing course. I'll meet you there."

"Meet me on the pier, yeah?"

"Okay." He sighed and hung up. I stuck my phone back into my righteous fanny pack and took Jasper out onto the pier. A pigeon teased him by flying in front of his face and cooing.

He went into the red zone and I had to wrangle him. Finally, I was able to get Jasper under control and he lay down at my feet while I sat on a bench. About ten minutes later, Aidan showed up. He was in clean clothes since he'd showered at the gym, but he looked sweaty.

"Did you run here?"

He nodded and sighed. "What do I do? Why can't I think of a solution? Usually exercise clears my head, but I've got nothing."

"As a panicker of the highest order, I know what it's like to go completely brain dead." I patted his knee. "The solution is staring you right in the face."

He looked blank.

I sighed. "Who is my best friend? Who happens to be a chef?"

"Annie."

"Ding, ding, ding! We have a winner."

"Save the snark, please." He shook his head. "Do you think she would do it?"

"Of course she'd do it."

"What about Caleb?"

"What about him? Do you really think he'd toss away this opportunity? You guys have been working for months. *Months*. He's not going to let asking his ex for help be the thing that stands in his way of success. Besides, he's not asking. I'm asking."

I gave Aidan Jasper's leash and then went into my fanny pack. I pulled out my phone and speed dialed Annie.

"What up, Mother Shucker?" she asked after answering on the first ring.

"I'm in a cucumber."

"You mean you're in a pickle?"

"Pickles are gross, so I'm going with cucumber."

"All righty then. What can I do for you and your cucumber?" she asked.

"Why did you make that sound sexual?"

"Sibby," Aidan growled next to me.

"Oops, sorry." I shot him an apologetic glance. "I'm gonna cut straight to the chase before Aidan's head explodes in epic cartoon fashion."

"I'm listening."

"The boys have a problem with the catering. As in, the food all spoiled, and they've got no hors d'oeuvres to serve tomorrow night."

She paused. "Are you asking what I think you're asking?"

"Yes. Will you fly in with your white apron and save the day? We'll pay you."

"How many trays do they need? How many people are showing up? What—"

"Talk to Aidan." I shoved my phone at my husband's ear.

Aidan gave her a quick rundown of the situation. "You sure you don't mind saving the day? I'd owe you forever." He looked at me, worry creasing his brow. "No, I'll tell him. Yeah. Oh, one more thing. I don't have servers. Do you have anyone who—three? I really wanted six on the floor. Okay, see you in an hour. I owe you my firstborn. Yeah, Oliver. You can have him."

"Hey!" I slapped his arm.

"Just kidding. Sibby's rather attached to our spawn. You'll have to settle for my undying gratitude for now."

He hung up and tilted his head all the way back and closed his eyes. "So, here's the deal. We're going to her restaurant. We're to bring everyone and anyone willing to peel, chop, wrap, whatever."

"Her restaurant? She doesn't have a restaurant," I pointed out.

"She's got a working kitchen. They finished it this week. There was an issue with the cooling vent in the walk-in, but they finally got the part in and replaced it."

"No wonder I haven't seen her."

He nodded. "Wells drove down from Montauk two days ago with a fresh seafood delivery and he left the van."

Annie's uncle had owned a seafood restaurant in Montauk, but it was closing for good. He'd sold the delivery van to Annie for next to nothing. Her cousin Wells owned a fishing boat and he would supply Annie her seafood deliveries.

"Why did they drive down with their catch?"

Aidan made a face. "She was supposed to be cooking for a private anniversary dinner for two. I feel bad coming to her in a crisis, but we are paying her, so I guess it's okay."

We got up from the bench and booked it home. On our way, Aidan called Caleb.

"How'd he take it?" I asked, after Aidan had hung up.

"He was silent. Resigned. And then totally grateful. He's going to meet us at Mother Shucker."

"He's going to help? Really?" I swallowed. "Should we bring a bottle of booze?"

"God no. We'll all get drunk to ignore the awkwardness and then nothing will get done."

When we walked into the apartment, Mom and Mrs. Nowacki were sitting on the couch, holding the twins. Dad had wandered back from the bar, looking just a trifle glassy-eyed as he watched TV.

I glanced at Aidan to see if he saw what I was seeing. But he was too absorbed in his own immediate concern. Not that I blamed him, but I wondered when I'd have the spare time to talk to him about my strange new parental dynamic.

"What's wrong?" Mom asked when she took in Aidan's harried appearance.

"Issue with the catering company," he said.

"We've got it figured out, though. Annie is going to save the day. But it's an all hands on deck situation. Aidan and I are heading to Mother Shucker to pitch in."

"What can I do?" Mom asked.

"Exactly what you're doing. Will you and Dad stay with Mrs. Nowacki and take care of the twins?"

"Yes. Sure." She looked at my dad who still hadn't reacted to anything we'd said.

"You pump?" Mrs. Nowacki asked.

I grimaced. "No. I haven't." My breasts would be rock hard in a few hours if I didn't pump.

"I'm going to head to Mother Shucker now," Aidan said. "You can meet me there. Do your thing."

He kissed me goodbye and with a wave, left the apartment.

I sighed and then grabbed my breast pump, feeling like a farm animal that was only good for one thing.

"What did you do? Call in the cavalry?" I asked in amazement when I walked through Mother Shucker's front door.

Aidan grinned. "It takes a village."

"You owe me a manicure for this," Zeb called. "I can't believe you're going to have me doing manual labor."

"Oh, shut up," Zeb's fiancé teased, and then leaned over and kissed him.

"Food violation!" Stacy called out, snapping a photo of the two of them.

"What happened to your eyebrows?" Terry asked me.

"I sacrificed them to the crème brûlée gods," I said. "Don't worry, I have a plan for tomorrow."

"What do you mean you sacrificed them?" Zeb asked. "You know what? Never mind. I don't think I want to know."

"I can't wait for these suckers to grow back," I muttered. I made the rounds, hugging Zeb, Terry, and then Stacy.

Annie appeared from the back kitchen, her arms loaded with butter, flour, and vanilla extract. Mills was behind her with the eggs.

"You made it," Annie said with a grin. "How are the boobs?"

I put a hand to them. "So far so good. Hey, Mills. Thanks for aiding our cause."

"Happy to do it," Annie's boyfriend said.

I exchanged a glance with Annie, whose expression clearly said he was lying. He just didn't want to leave Annie in the same room as her ex-boyfriend.

Speaking of which…

"Where's Caleb?" I asked.

Aidan cleared his throat. "He and Em are on their way over."

I watched Annie out of the corner of my eye, but she didn't even blanch.

She laid out all the ingredients on the counter in front of her.

"The restaurant is really coming together," I said.

She'd found a spot in Greenpoint with excellent foot traffic. The storefront had huge windows, and she had plans to use the area as a fish market. The restaurant itself would only have five tables along the back wall and the counter had stools on the floor so that customers could sit and watch her cook. It was an open kitchen floor plan. She wanted transparency so people could see their meals come to fruition.

"It's still a bit of a mess, but yeah." She laughed. "The chalkboards above the stove," she pointed over her head to the area she was talking about, "will be put in next week."

Caleb and Em entered through the front door and for a moment everyone stopped talking. But Em flashed a smile and said, "Why are we all standing around? Annie, put me to work."

Two hours later Stacy said, "People are really loving these behind the scenes photos. Don't worry, I've managed to avoid snapping photos of your face."

"Thank goodness," I said with a laugh as I rolled out the pastry dough. "It was a stellar idea to get photos and videos of all of us helping."

"Anything to help build buzz." She grinned. "I'm just glad there are no fires to put out, so to speak."

I felt like she was referring to the Caleb-Em-Annie-Mills square of weirdness going on at the counter. They were all laughing and joking, having a grand old time. There were no side-glances, no awkward pauses. And as far as I could tell, no one had been sneaking sips from flasks or mini bottles of booze.

"It's going better than I could've expected," I admitted.

Aidan was in the back kitchen with Terry and Zeb, but I could hear them laughing all the way up front.

My phone rang.

"Do me a favor and answer my mother's call. Put it on speaker." My hands were covered in flour and I didn't want to get the screen dirty.

Stacy pressed a button and scooted my phone closer to me. "Hello? Mom?"

"Sibby?"

"Yes, Mom. It's me." I looked at Stacy and rolled my eyes. She'd called me. Who else did she think was on the other end of the phone?

I heard screaming in the background and my nipples tingled immediately.

"What's wrong?" I asked immediately.

"Nothing, nothing," Mom assured me.

"Then why does it sound like Sophie is being tortured for government secrets?"

"How did you know it was Sophie and not Oliver?"

"Mother, please."

"Fine. Sorry." She sighed. "She's hungry, but she won't take the bottle from me or Mrs. Nowacki."

I sighed. "So, you need me and my breasts to come home?"

"Well, your breasts go where you go, so yes, that's what I'm saying."

"Okay, I'm leaving now."

"Hurry. Please, God, hurry. She's been screaming for ages and I can't take it anymore."

"Welcome to my life story, Ma," I remarked dryly.

The phone went dark and I realized everyone was silent. I glanced around. Annie looked amused, but Caleb and Mills appeared uncomfortable.

"What?" I snapped. "Have you never heard a mother talk about her breasts before?"

"Ah, Sibby?" Annie said, pointing to me. "Look down."

Two wet splotches where my nipples were had appeared on my red T-shirt. "My milk just let down. Wonderful. Back to business!"

I clapped my hands together and then went to find my husband to explain the situation.

"Well, I guess if we run out of milk for the biscuit dough I know where we can find some," Zeb said.

"Maybe you don't say everything that comes to your mind," I snapped.

"You're right. That's really more your style."

I reached around his neck and pulled him close so I could give him a noogie.

"Hey, no roughhousing!" Annie called.

I let Zeb go. He ran a hand through his hair. "Did she ruin it?"

Terry rolled his eyes. "Your hair is fine."

"I have to go home," I told Aidan. "Sophie won't take a bottle."

"All right." He cupped his hands around my face and gave me a kiss. "You should just stay home."

"Why? I want to come back and help."

"Knowing our children, the moment you get back here, you'll just have to turn around and leave."

"Two grandparents and a Mrs. Nowacki all of a sudden can't handle our infants?" I shook my head. "I wonder why Sophie refuses to take the bottle."

"Because she's your daughter."

"She's also *your* daughter."

"Yeah, but I don't have the difficult gene." He smiled teasingly.

"And you're saying she got the difficult gene from me?"

"That's what I'm sayin', yeah." He kissed the end of my nose. Someone behind him made a faux gagging noise.

"Call me if you have trouble," Aidan said.

"I'll walk you out," Annie said, wiping her hands on her apron.

When the front door to Mother Shucker was closed and we stood on the sidewalk facing each other, I asked her, "Are you doing okay? Like, seriously?"

"Yeah, I'm fine. It's all fine."

"Hmm. Yeah."

"What?"

"You know when Aidan asks if I'm fine and I say yeah and then he passes me the box of tissues because he knows I'm really about to cry?"

Amusement washed across her face. "Yeah, but I really mean I'm fine. It's nice to talk to him in a public setting and not feel like I'm going to die. It's even better that Mills is so fantastic and not being weird. And Em? She's so great."

She'd said the word *so* twice, and I knew her well enough to know that she wasn't as fine as she pretended to be. But now was not the time to talk about it. She was in the middle of saving Caleb and Aidan's launch party and emotion did not have a place here. Everything needed to be put on hold until Monday.

"Your husband is paying me a small fortune, you know," she said with a smile. "Thanks."

"We're not moochers. Thanks for coming to our rescue."

"I'll see if I can find a few more cater waiters, okay?"

"Thanks." I hugged her quickly. "Okay, gotta jet."

There were no cabs out front and I was only about a twenty-minute amble from the house, so I decided to hoof it. I was out of breath by the time I made it to the apartment and my breasts were throbbing in pain.

"Dad!" I called out. "Cover your eyes!" I stripped off my shirt as I got into the apartment.

Sophie was wailing. Oliver was fussing. My mother had earplugs in her ears. My father was asleep on the couch and hadn't moved. I doubted he'd heard me at all. And Mrs. Nowacki looked like she had everything under control.

I took Sophie from my mother and immediately placed her at my breast. She latched on and went about sucking me dry.

My mother reached into her ears and pulled out the earplugs—no, wait, scratch that. She pulled out two cloves of garlic.

"Really?" I asked, gesturing with my chin as she set them on the coffee table.

"I couldn't find cotton balls," she said defensively.

I rolled my eyes. "You don't think she suddenly has abandonment issues, do you?" I asked worriedly.

"I don't think so."

I took Sophie into the nursery and sat down in the rocking chair. A few minutes later, Mom knocked on the door and said, "I'm taking your father back to the hotel. He needs a real bed and I need a Melatonin, a bubble bath, and a white wine spritzer. Don't judge me."

"I wasn't judging you."

"I can see the snark thought bubble forming over your head. Right now, it's something I can do without, thank you very much."

"Ma, I was just thinking I'd love a Melatonin with a white wine spritzer." I grinned. "A bubble bath sounds like a luxury I won't get for a very long time. So please enjoy it for both of us. Okay?"

She rubbed her third eye. "Will do. You know I love my granddaughter, right?"

"Uh, yeah, you've made that pretty clear."

"I love my granddaughter," she repeated, "but that girl tried to break me."

"A lesser woman would've broken. Thank you for your service." I saluted her.

"You're a champion, Sibby," she said, her tone completely serious. "I'm proud of you."

"You're proud of me? Why?"

"You're doing a really good job with the babies."

My throat tightened with emotion and I was three point two seconds away from ugly crying. "Thanks, Mom. I really needed to hear that."

She leaned over and brushed her cheek against mine. "We'll see you tomorrow night at the party, okay?"

"You're not coming over during the day tomorrow?" I sniffed. "Sophie did break you emotionally, didn't she?"

Mom laughed. "No. Not really. I just decided to be melodramatic."

Well, it was clear who I'd gotten my theatrics from.

"Tomorrow Aidan is going to be a nervous nelly. He doesn't need his in-laws adding to the fray. We'll see you at Veritas tomorrow night."

Chapter 8

Mom Blog Entry:
 A few months down, twenty-five years to go…

"No. No, no, no, no!" I moaned.

"What? What, what, what, what?" Mrs. Nowacki's already wrinkled forehead wrinkled even more with a frown.

"I don't have any clean nursing pads. I thought I did,

but I don't. And I don't have time to wash any. I was supposed to be out the door fifteen minutes ago."

"Do not move your face. Your eyebrows need time to set."

I hastily patted the dyed wig fur on my face to make sure they were still stuck to my skin. They were shellacked on, but it had taken me longer to make them look realistic than I thought it would and I was late.

I was standing in my robe, my bright red jumpsuit hung up on the door of the closet mocking me with its sexy neckline. It had thick enough straps that I could wear a bra with it—because there was no way at this time in my life I could get away without a bra.

Nor could I get away with a bra without nursing pads.

The color of the jumpsuit should've clashed with my newly dyed hair, but Stacy had assured me it worked.

"What about the new ones from that company?" Mrs. Nowacki asked.

"New ones, what?" I asked in distraction.

"You got box of new nursing pads to try. So, try them tonight."

"Oh my God, yes! I'd completely forgotten about them!" I kissed her cheek in my exuberance, leaving a red lip print on her skin. "What would I do without you?"

"Not be able to tell if your eyebrows were on straight." Her eyes twinkled. "They are, by the way."

"Don't scare me." I laughed and then ran out into the living room, tearing through open boxes of products that needed to be tested and written about. I found the nursing pads and silently thanked the breast gods for looking out for me.

I dug through my lingerie drawer and pulled out a bra I could wear with the jumpsuit, gave it a cursory sniff, hastily put it on, and then inserted the nursing pads.

"Oh, they're comfortable."

I slipped into the jumpsuit, had Mrs. Nowacki zip me up, and then I was running to the closet to find the nude peep-toe sandals with a kitten heel.

"Okay," I said. "How do I look?"

Mrs. Nowacki smiled. "You look like woman who will surprise husband. It's good. Very good."

"Thank you." I sighed in relief as I looked into the full-length mirror one last time to make sure everything was tucked and sucked in, but I got misty-eyed when I saw myself.

"No crying," Mrs. Nowacki warned. "You ruin the mascara."

I nodded. "You're right. I've got this." I grabbed my nude clutch from the nightstand and made sure I had my keys, ID, and cell phone.

"Okay. The dog walker will be here at nine to let Jasper out. He should be good for the rest of the evening. I've pumped enough to feed an army of baby goats, and I plan on being back before midnight."

She waved. "I've got it handled. Go have fun. Bring me plate of Annie's appetizers."

I grinned and gave Jasper an ear rub and then I was out of the apartment. The night was hot and sticky. We needed a good rain to clear it all out and wash the filth from the streets, but I didn't care.

I was baby free, wearing my version of high heels, and I was about to join my husband for a career making night. I caught a cab and soon I was standing on the sidewalk outside of Veritas. I took just a moment to stare at the sign and then looked through the front window to see the bar swarming with guests.

I heard the click of a phone camera and whirled. Stacy

was peeking out from behind the corner of the bar, grinning at me.

"What are you doing back there? You're skulking like paparazzi in the bushes."

"That's the idea," she said with a huge grin. The strapless tight dress and black stockings made her look like a vintage pinup girl.

"What gives?" I asked, gesturing with my chin to her hiding place.

"I wanted some candid shots of people before they entered the throng. Aidan told me to get a photo of you, too. Want to see it?"

"Maybe. Depends on whether or not you'll delete it if it's crappy. I don't always photograph well. And who knows with these things…" I pointed to my eyebrows.

She peered at me. "I seriously forgot those weren't real."

"Really?"

"Really." She showed me the photo. "I think you look dynamite."

She'd caught me looking up at the sign, slightly off kilter with the angle of the camera, but my lips looked full, my gaze was soft, and my body's flaws were marvelously hidden by the pair of Spanx and the jumpsuit.

"Please let me post it," she said.

I nodded.

After her fingers flew across the screen for a few moments, she finally looked back at me. "Ready to go inside?"

"Yes."

The party had already been going for a full hour. I'd wanted to be there the moment we opened the doors to greet the magazine writers and PR people, to say hello to

Annie and ask if she needed my help, but the faux eyebrows and the babies waylaid all my grand plans.

Stacy linked her arm with mine and we strode to the front door. She held it open for me and I stepped inside the main room of Veritas. Caleb was behind the bar, talking to one of the two bartenders who were in charge of making drinks and pouring wine.

People gave Stacy and I cursory looks as we approached.

"Don't look now, but you're totally drawing the attention of some suits," Stacy said, handing me a drink menu that rested on the bar.

"Really?" I asked, whipping my head around to find the men in question.

"I told you not to look," she hissed.

"What do I care?" I held up my ring finger. "I'm married. And wearing a nursing bra for crying out loud. I want to check out the guys checking me out. It's been so long since I've gotten a good ego boost."

She rolled her eyes.

"Besides, you're the one who's single. Shouldn't you be, like, prowling?"

"I'm working," she reminded me. "Social media tag artist or whatever."

"Is that your official title?" I asked with a wry grin.

"Sibby!" Caleb called from the other end of the bar.

More heads turned in my direction and I felt a blush stain my cheeks.

Caleb maneuvered his way around his bartenders to come talk to me. "Hiya," he greeted with a smile. He looked happy and relaxed, totally in his element. He was wearing a tie for the first time in forever and I was proud of him.

"Looks like a smash," I said. "Congratulations."

He smiled. "We're doing okay. Aidan is around here schmoozing."

"And where's Em?"

"Last I knew, the restroom." His eyes twinkled with happiness at the mention of his girlfriend. He gestured to the cocktail menu. "What are you drinking? Club soda for you, Stacy?"

"With lime, please," she said, gaze on her phone as she typed something.

"I'll have the Muddled Berry Madness. But half the amount of tequila. I can't drink like I used to."

"Coming right up." He filled a rocks glass with club soda and a lime and slid it to Stacy.

She grasped her drink and took a sip. "If you'll excuse me, I need to mingle."

"Make good choices," I called after her.

She blew me a kiss. "Never."

I turned my attention back to Caleb. "You're not seriously going to make my drink. It looks messy and you're wearing a white shirt."

He grinned. "Ma'am, I've been in this business a long time." He spoke in an over the top Southern drawl. "Besides, I don't think Sibby's Law is transferable."

"Six degrees of Sibby's Law. And trust me, it's transferable."

He muddled the berries, added the rest of the ingredients to the cocktail shaker, and then poured it over ice into a rocks glass.

"What a pretty pink color." I lifted the glass in a silent toast and then took a sip. "Oh, hello tequila. I've missed you."

I felt someone big and tall press up against me from behind. I smelled the familiar scent of Aidan's cologne, and decided to have some fun by leaning back against him. His breath hitched.

"You look amazing," he whispered huskily in my ear.

I looked at him over my shoulder. He was wearing a three-piece gray suit, something he hadn't done since our wedding. He had two days' worth of stubble on his jaw and for the first time in far too long I felt sexy. And I wanted my husband like I did when we'd first gotten together.

I was hornified.

"You look pretty good yourself," I said as I grinned at him.

We got lost staring at each other. There, in that moment, there was no bar opening, no children at home, no body issues between us, nothing. We looked at each other like it was still new, like we were still new. Like the honeymoon phase hadn't really disappeared, it had just been clobbered by life.

"Dude," Caleb muttered. "Stop eye groping your wife."

Aidan reluctantly pulled his gaze away from me, but placed his hand on my hip in a show of possession that I really, *really* liked.

"Dude," Aidan said back in the same drawl tone. "You got berry stains on your shirt."

"What?" Caleb looked down. "Ah, man!"

I chuckled. "I warned you that Sibby's Law is completely, one hundred percent transferable. It's like an STD which has no cure. In fact, you might be doomed. Good luck."

Caleb cursed, filled a glass with club soda and grabbed a clean bar rag. He didn't even say goodbye as he dashed off the floor to tend to the mess on his shirt.

"Sorry I'm late," I said looking back up at Aidan.

Maybe it was the little bit of tequila or maybe it was his adorable smile, but I reached up and pressed a finger to his dimple.

"It's okay. You're here now."

"How's everything going?"

"Aidan!" someone called, turning my husband's attention.

"No rest for the wicked," he said with a wry grin. "Do you mind?"

I shook my head. "Go be part of Team Awesome."

"Hmm. Veto the Team Awesome thing."

"Okay, fine. Love you."

"Zeb is around here somewhere. So are my parents and your parents, but I haven't seen them in a while." He kissed me briefly. "I'll find you later. There are people I want you to meet, but right now I'm still dealing with party stuff."

I nodded. "Go, go. I can entertain myself."

He kissed me again and then disappeared into the crowd. I took my drink and wandered into the store part of Veritas. The room was divided into two sections: liquor and wine. Aidan and Caleb had decided to supply high quality off-brands, giving both the companies they represented and themselves a chance to stand out in the trendiest neighborhood in the country. They carried local Brooklyn craft liquors, along with wines and ciders that were made Upstate. Anyone could carry Grey Goose or Hendrick's. But Veritas wanted to be the bar and liquor store that had unusual stock, highlighting companies that were still heavily invested in the success of their products from start to finish.

Mason jar light fixtures illuminated the liquor room. The oak shelves had been stained by hand. The whiskey barrels had sign stands on them, so there was no confusion about what you'd find heading down any given aisle.

"Sibby!" Em called, waving her hand. She was currently standing in the liqueur aisle, drinking something clear with a mango garnish.

"Hi!" I wrapped her in a hug and then stood back so I could check out her outfit. An off the shoulder purple dress with a tulle skirt. Her glossy brown hair had been styled in a top bun.

"You look like Tinkerbell's cousin. I love it!"

She grinned. "Thanks. I'm in love with that jumpsuit."

"Stacy. She's the only reason I could be talked into this thing. It's *so* not my style, but I'm really into it actually. I kind of feel like a hotter version of myself. Is that weird? That's weird."

"It's not weird. I get it." The humor stayed on her lips as she glanced around the room. "It looks like the boys will have nothing to worry about. Judging by the amount of people who showed up."

"I think you're right." We talked for a few more minutes about nothing of importance and just when I was about to ask her if Caleb was still acting funny, my phone buzzed.

I sighed. "Sorry. I need to grab this. I just hope it's not Mrs. Nowacki with some issue with the twins."

She waved away my apology. "Go for it."

It wasn't Mrs. Nowacki, and it wasn't a phone call. It was a text from Annie: *SOS.*

"Rats," I muttered. "It's Annie. I need to get outside so I can call her."

"Find me later?"

I nodded and then headed for the exit. I was waylaid by Aidan's parents, who looked decidedly out of place. Aidan's sisters hadn't been able to come, which might've made his parents more comfortable. This wasn't their scene at all, but they were supportive of their son. Aidan's dad was drinking a pint of beer and his mother had a lemony concoction in a martini glass.

"Hey!" I said, giving them each a hug. "I'm so sorry. I have to make a phone call. I'll be back in a bit, okay?"

Nancy smiled. "No rush."

"Have you seen my parents?" I added as an afterthought.

"Not for a half an hour or more," Bud answered. "If you see your father, tell him we weren't done with our conversation and I need someone to keep me entertained at this thing."

Nancy looked at her husband. "What do you think I'm doing here?"

Realizing they were about to get into a loveable bickering match, I high-tailed it out of there. As soon as I got out onto the sidewalk, I dialed Annie.

"It's a disaster," Annie said, her tone bleak.

"What is? The food?"

"No. The food is amazing. The food is stellar. The food is a shining beacon of—"

"Okay, move it along."

"Mills just projectile vomited in the trashcan outside the bakery. And he was supposed to serve for me to tonight. Which means—"

"Which means you're one server down," I said with a sigh. "I'll be there in two minutes."

"Run."

"I can't run. If I run, then my breasts will flop. Flopping breast are bad."

"Pretend it's an episode of *Baywatch*. Please hurry."

"I'm pretty sure there's a whale joke somewhere in there, but I'm too brain dead to come up with it." I hung up on her and made my way to the bakery that was three doors down from Veritas. Aidan and Caleb had asked the owner if they could rent the space for the evening, since the bakery wasn't open at night. A wad of cash and a handshake later and the owner had readily agreed.

Annie was just taking a tray of cranberry brie pastries out of the oven when I opened the front door. I smiled at the five waiting servers who were all wearing black pants and white button downs rolled up to the elbows. On their feet were different colored Converse sneakers.

"Testing out the Mother Shucker uniform?" I wondered aloud.

Annie didn't bother replying to me. "Guys, as soon as I pull out the hot food, load it onto the serving trays, and then haul ass to Veritas. I'll stagger the food so it won't get cold, but Caleb texted that people are already a few cocktails in. The food will keep them from getting sloppy."

They all sprung into action and before I knew it, the five servers were out the door with their trays and chafing dishes.

"What can I do?" I asked her, not bothering to address the fact that Caleb and Annie were texting each other. It might've been about work stuff, but that still triggered a red flag.

"You can take the cheese crackers and the homemade peanut butter and chocolate party mix. I'm putting them in bowls—just leave them around the bar and the liquor room. They're meant to be eaten at room temperature. Hopefully it's not too hot in there or the chocolate will melt."

"What are you doing?" Zeb asked from behind me.

I jumped and then felt something cold splash down the back of my jumpsuit.

"Jeez, Sib. Way to make me wear my drink," Zeb growled.

"I'm also wearing your drink." I grabbed a stack of bar napkins. "You know not to sneak up on me." I turned and surveyed the damage. The front of his suit jacket was wet, but luckily he was drinking something clear. "I'll clean you up if you clean me up."

We spent the next few moments tending to our clothes and then chucked the soiled napkins in the trashcan behind the bar.

"You never did answer my question." He gestured to the bowl of cheese crackers. "What are you doing with those?"

I quickly explained about Mills. "Where's Terry?"

"Client emergency." He rolled his eyes. "I'm dateless."

"I'm dateless, too. My husband is gallivanting around his bar and talking to people. I haven't seen him for almost an hour."

"Do you mind if I cut out after they make their 'thank you so much for your support speeches'? Those will no doubt be happening in the next hour or so. It's not any fun at a party without your partner."

I patted his shoulder. "I get it. And no, I don't mind if you cut out. Do me a favor?"

"Sure."

I gave him my clutch. "Hold this for me? I have to grab another tray of food."

I tweaked his nose and then somehow managed to slip through the crowd. Every now and again, I saw Annie's servers winding their way through the clusters of people.

I walked out onto the sidewalk and breathed a sigh of relief. I hadn't had this much social stimulation in months, and I felt a headache coming on. I started down the street toward the bakery but stopped when I heard my mother's voice. She and my father were facing off in the side alley.

"You're being absolutely ridiculous," Mama Goldstein said, crossing her arms over her chest.

"Me? You're the one that insists on this Rent-a-Yenta business." My father's stance was combative and though he was a good foot taller than my mother, she wasn't intimidated by him.

"You were supportive of it. What's changed? The fact that it's actually starting to do something?"

My father was silent, and my mother verbally pounced.

"You ungrateful—my entire adult life I've been nothing but *your* wife. I stood by you while you were in med school. I stood by you when you became a resident and then a doctor. I moved where you needed to move to become a world-renowned surgeon. And for the first time in *my* life, I've got something that's just for *me*, and you're trying to belittle that. It's unfair and it's unkind!"

My parents had never fought growing up. They were sickeningly in love and always presented a united front. To see them facing off against each other sent shock waves vibrating through my body.

I knew my parents. My mother was usually the one who couldn't be reasoned with, who was dramatic on a good day. But it felt like they'd gone through a *Freaky Friday* moment, switching bodies as well as personalities.

I made myself keep walking and pretended I didn't hear them because I couldn't do anything about it at the moment. I had to help Annie. That was my priority. The next day at brunch I'd pull them both aside and talk to them, but for now, I kept walking, head down.

"Where the hell have you been?" Annie yelled when I opened the door.

"Don't take this the wrong way, but during your restaurant opening week, you might not see me. Like at all."

That gave her pause and she checked herself. "I'm sorry."

"Okay."

"How's the food going? I wish I was on site to witness it first-hand."

"I imagine it's going like gangbusters. I wasn't able to check."

"Next time, lie."

I laughed. "How many more trays of food do you have left to bake?"

"Three. The spinach artichoke squares, the crab puff bites, and the roasted edamame. Everything else is room temperature appropriate."

"So, do you want to give me more of the room temperature stuff or a round of hot stuff."

"Hot stuff."

"I love it when you call me hot stuff."

She rolled her eyes. The timer on the oven went off and she pulled out a tray of spinach artichoke squares.

With her snazzy chef spatula, she slid them off the cookie sheet onto a tray with a doily.

Three of the five servers who were working the party entered the bakery. "We need more food," one of them said. He had slicked back hair and resembled Don Draper.

"*A lot* more food," a woman added.

"I'm baking it as fast as I can," she said. "Take these."

They swapped out their trays and then quickly left again.

She bit her lip.

"We prepped enough food," I assured her. "It'll slow down."

Fifteen minutes later, I was carting the last of the hot food into Veritas, trying to hold in my curses. Annie's food was just too good, and combined with Caleb's cocktails, people were devouring crab puffs at an alarming rate.

It seemed even more people had showed up to the bar from the time I'd been gone. Sweat beaded on my upper lip; the heat in the room had gotten completely out of control.

I walked around the bar, offering up puffs to people, all the while trying to look for Aidan or Caleb so one of them could lower the thermostat.

"Ah, miss?"

"Hmm?" My gaze swung around to meet the scrutiny of a very attractive older man. If I'd been in the market for a second husband, he would've been exactly the type I'd have gone for.

He leaned in close, his mouth moving toward my cheek. My hands went up to fend him off, but I forgot I was holding a tray of food. Crab puffs rained down like confetti. I leapt for the tray, which was just out of my reach and twisted an ankle, consequently knocking me off balance and propelling me into the gentleman who was getting fresh.

"Gah!" I grabbed onto his arms, but he was going down. He hit the ground with a soft thud. I landed on top of him, the sound of air whooshing from his lungs. The man emitted a low groan when I struggled to get off him.

He propped one eyelid open and said, "I was just trying to tell you your eyebrow was loose."

Mom Blog Entry:
    I totally get mom jeans now.
    AKA pouch hiders.

"Sibby!" Aidan exclaimed. "Are you okay? I saw you go down and—oh, shit."

I didn't like the sound of his *oh, shit.* Nor did I like the fact that my milky breasts were squashed against the chest of a man I didn't know. Not that I'd be okay with my milky breasts being squashed up against anyone except Aidan.

I scrambled off the man, making a face when I realized one of my eyebrows had fallen off my face and landed on the man's upper lip, giving him a faux mustache. I quickly snatched the piece off his face before Aidan had a chance to haul me up.

Damn skin glue and miserable heat from a crowded room.

The gentleman, whose flushed face was slowly returning to a normal color, took Aidan's offered hand and got up off the floor.

"Felix McCallister, I'd like to introduce you to my wife. Sibby, this is Felix McCallister. He writes for the magazine, Brooklyn Hype."

"Er, pleased to meet you," I said with what I hoped was a winning smile.

Felix grunted. He tried to say something, but only a wheeze came out. He pounded his chest, cleared his throat, and said, "Nice to meet you too."

"I'm really sorry about what just happened. I thought you were trying to kiss me."

"Why would you think that?" Aidan interjected.

I looked at him, abashed, and held up the eyebrow piece. "Felix was just trying to tell me my eyebrow was about to come off. I mistook his movement as an advance. Hence the crab-puff fiasco."

"Felix," Aidan said with a sigh, "if you knew my wife, you'd understand this is nothing out of the ordinary. I know that sounds crazy, but we're talking about a woman whose eyebrow just fell off, so…"

"Why are you wearing a fake eyebrow?" he asked me pointedly. "Inquiring minds want to know."

"Do you want to tell him while I find some rubber cement and re-glue this thing to my face?" I asked Aidan.

"I think it would be better coming from you," he replied. His lips were twitching, which told me he was holding in his laughter, but it was one hell of a struggle.

"Mr. McCallister," I began.

"Felix, please. I think we're past formalities." His smile was wide and genuine, and I hoped like hell it meant the man had forgiven me and wouldn't dog Veritas for my SNAFU.

"Felix," I said with a nod. "I attempted to caramelize sugar for a crème brûlée I made to seduce my husband, and the torch turned against me and took my eyebrows."

Felix let out a hearty and robust laugh.

"If it makes you feel any better, I absolutely thought you were a silver fox and if I wasn't married, I'd attempt to flirt with you."

I looked at the tray of crab puffs strewn about the floor. "Annie is gonna kill me. That was the last of those."

"Who's Annie?" Felix asked.

"The chef who catered the event tonight," Aidan said. "And Sibby's best friend."

"The food is absolutely incredible," Felix said. "I'd love to meet her and give her my regards."

"She's opening her own restaurant in the next few months. Maybe you've heard of it? Mother Shucker?"

"That's her place? Well, well, well. I hope I score an invite to the opening."

"You're on the list," I assured him.

"Then all is forgiven between us." He winked.

Someone clinked a champagne flute lightly with a fork and the entire bar fell silent. I turned toward the noise and saw Caleb jump up onto the bar, holding a cocktail. His tie was gone, his shirt was unbuttoned, and he looked relaxed but happy. "Aidan and I want to say a few words."

"We do?" Aidan asked in droll amusement.

Everyone laughed at his response and then there was a round of applause. He kissed me and then headed toward his best friend and business partner. He climbed up onto the bar and stood next to Caleb. The two of them were a striking pair and I was suddenly transported back in time to the night Annie and I had met them. Upper East Side bar. Totally wasted, trying to drink away the pain of walking in on my ex with another man.

Fun times.

Little did I know that night would be the beginning of something amazing.

I looked around the bar. Stacy was in the corner and her phone was held up high. No doubt she was getting all of this on video. Zeb stood next to her. I caught his eye and waved.

My gaze continued to roam around the room. My parents stood by the door, both looking extremely uncomfortable, but trying to smile. Nancy and Bud were next to them.

"As many of you guys know," Aidan began, pulling my attention back to him, "Veritas has been a dream of mine and Caleb's for a long time. I want to thank my wife, Sibby, for her unwavering support."

People glanced at me, but I looked down to the ground so my hair would conceal my face. I only had one eyebrow, after all.

"We couldn't have gotten this far without you all and the support of this neighborhood. You guys took us in, let us become part of your lives. So, while we're celebrating us, I want to celebrate you. Thanks for being here—and we'll see you at the ten-year anniversary party."

People laughed and clapped, enjoying Aidan's honesty and candor. Aidan slapped Caleb on the back. "I think my partner wants to say a few words now."

"Thanks, dude," Caleb said with an eye roll. "Aidan is right. It takes a village to make something like this happen. He said all I wanted to say. Emmie? Where are you?" He searched the crowd for his girlfriend and when his eyes landed on her, he waved her forward.

He jumped down from the bar, landing in front of her. "Without this woman, I wouldn't have gotten through these last few months. Emmie, I love you." He pulled out a jewelry box from his pocket. "Will you marry me?"

A collective hush settled over the crowd. Em's eyes were wide with surprise, but then quickly morphed into elation as she cried out, "Yes!"

The room erupted into cheers and applause. My gaze met Aidan's and I was pretty sure we wore the same stupefied expression. Caleb was now embracing Em as well-wishers swarmed them and people began to drink and talk amongst themselves again. Someone turned on jazz, which filtered through the sound system, and the party roared back to life.

Aidan climbed down from the bar and immediately came toward me.

"Did you have any idea that was going to happen?" I asked him.

He shook his head. "I swear I didn't."

"Your launch party just turned into an engagement party." Felix grinned. "If you'll excuse me, I think I'll grab myself a glass of champagne and talk to the happy couple."

Felix wandered off, leaving Aidan and I alone. Aidan wrapped his arm around me. "Wow. I just—wow."

"On the list of wow stuff for this evening, this takes the cake," I agreed.

"On the list? What else is on the list?"

"You know what? I'll spare you until tomorrow. This is your night."

"Technically this just became Caleb and Em's night," he said with a wry grin. "What a sneaky bastard. He managed to keep this from me. How did he manage that?"

I looked around the room as I answered, "However he did it, it's a good thing. He was probably worried about you telling me, who'd then tell Em…"

"You wouldn't have spoiled it for him, would you?"

"Hard to say," I admitted. "I was never a good secret keeper. Now that I'm habitually sleep deprived and hormonal, who knows what I'm liable to spill. So, it was probably a good idea that Caleb kept it to himself."

Caleb's parents were talking to him and Em. Caleb's mom hugged Em, her excitement just as great as her son's.

Zeb was waving me down from the corner of the room. "I need to talk to Zeb for a second. You good if I leave you?"

"Yup. You might want to remember to fix your eyebrow," he said.

My hand went to my face. "Ah, screw it. Stacy got her good photos. I already clobbered one magazine critic after making an incorrect assumption and mashing him to the ground with my ginormous breasts. I'm pretty sure I'm done for the night."

"Never say never. This is you we're talking about."

"Be nice to me or I'll head home. Oh, wait, what time is it?"

Aidan looked at his watch. "Just past eleven."

I nodded. "Yeah, I need to get home. I told Mrs.

Nowacki I'd be back no later than midnight. And my boobs feel hot."

"Can I feel?"

I waved away his roving hand. "I'll be back in a minute." Before he could feel me up in public, I headed to Zeb. He held out my clutch to me.

"Thanks for holding that. I'm sorry that took so long."

"What happened to you?" He pointed to my eyebrow.

"Costume glue failed me." I sighed. "I took a magazine writer down. We made amends, all is well in the kingdom."

"M'kay. So, Annie might've seen Caleb propose to Em."

"Shit, really?"

He nodded. "She came in here with a stack of business cards and was just going to leave them on the bar. But she —ah—saw what was going down and left. By the way, usually the host of a party thanks the catering staff. What's up with that? They didn't mention her at all."

"Annie asked them not to," she said. "Thought it would be weird for everyone."

"You mean weird for her?"

I nodded. "Caleb's parents are here and they're not Annie's biggest fan." I sighed. "Do you mind if I ditch you to go find her?"

He shook his head. "I'm going to walk out with you and catch a cab home. I swear, since the moment I hit thirty I have no stamina to party."

"You just want to go home and get into your matching pajamas with your monogrammed initials."

"And a snifter of brandy."

Thankfully mine and Aidan's parents had moved away from the door, so I didn't get waylaid with having to stop and chat. Zeb hugged me and then hailed a cab. One came almost immediately.

"You guys are still coming to brunch tomorrow, right?" I asked.

"Yup. Need us to bring anything?"

"Mimosa fixings are always welcome."

"Done and done."

"Text me that you got home safe."

"Will do." He waved and then climbed into the cab. I watched it zoom off and then I was reaching into my clutch for my cell phone. I had a text from my mother, one from my father, a few from Aidan's sister Janet who lived Upstate, but none from Annie.

I called her.

"Hello?" she answered.

"Hey, where are you?"

"Cleaning up the bakery."

"I'll be right there."

I hung up. Before I went to her, I stopped in the bodega along the way and bought a bag of Mint Milanos. I walked into the bakery joint and without saying a word, I slid the bag in her direction.

She stared at it for a moment and then said, "I'm good. You're missing an eyebrow and it looks really weird."

"Weirder than no eyebrows? You know what? Don't answer that." I ripped into the bag of cookies. "I don't have long. It's getting on close to midnight and I told Mrs. Nowacki I'd be home before then."

"So, you're Brooklynella?" she asked with a slight smile.

"Clever. Really clever. So clever that I should've thought of it, actually." I sighed. "I think my funny bone has been temporarily broken. Fractured at least."

"Your funny bone isn't in charge of your humor."

"Don't get off topic."

"What is the topic?" she asked.

"You saw."

She nodded. "Yeah. I saw."

"How do you feel?"

"I'm not sure."

"You're not sure?" I repeated. "How can you not be sure? Your ex, who begged you to marry him multiple times, just proposed to the girl he got serious with not that long ago."

She pinned me with a stare.

"I've never had a filter, so I can't blame that on the twins," I said.

"I don't know, Sibby. I really don't. I want him to be happy."

"I know that."

"And she's great to him. I saw that when they were together yesterday. I really do think they're right for each other."

"You know when we saw Avenue Q and the puppets would talk, but the humans' mouths would be moving? And I couldn't stop watching the humans who were literally pulling the puppet strings?"

"You're rambling and I have no idea where you're going with this. What's your point?"

"My point is you're the puppet and some human is opening your mouth and saying these lines—these lines you're supposed to say because you've memorized them. And you've convinced yourself it's the truth."

"Sibby?"

"Yeah?"

"Please, let it go. I need you to let it go. Okay?"

I looked into her eyes. There was clear resolve in them, but something else too.

"Tell Mills I hope he feels better," I mumbled. "Guess

this means I won't be seeing you guys tomorrow for brunch?"

She shook her head.

"Okay." I took a deep breath. "Thank you for what you did tonight. You made the party a ten."

Her smile was just a bit sad when she said, "No. I think Caleb and Em's engagement did that."

"You forget my appetizers," Mrs. Nowacki said the moment I walked through the front door. "And you're missing an eyebrow."

"I'd like that as my epitaph."

"Epi what?"

"On my tombstone. I'd like that engraved on my tombstone. *Here lies Sibby Goldstein-Kincaid, sans eyebrows*. There were no appetizers left over, but I brought you a half-eaten bag of Mint Milanos." I set it down on the kitchen counter. "How are the twins?"

Jasper was bumping my leg with his nose and I crouched down to pet him. I buried my face in his neck and just breathed him in for a moment, trying to corral my thoughts. Nothing like the love of a good dog.

"Asleep. Due to wake up any moment." She got up off

the couch and padded toward me. "You need tea? I make tea and you tell me why you look like you want to eat entire cheesecake."

"I'm going to change real fast, okay? Do you want to stay the night? The couch folds out."

She grinned and nodded.

I grabbed my phone out of my clutch and shot off texts to my parents, apologizing for having to bail and not being able to spend any time with them since I'd gotten roped into cater waitering. I sent Nancy a text, too, telling her that I'd see them in the morning for bagels.

My Instagram notifications were going nuts; Stacy had tagged me in a bunch of photos on Veritas's account. She'd uploaded the video of Caleb and Aidan's speech, which included the proposal.

As I washed the makeup off my face, I thought about the insanity of the night. I hadn't even been the focal point of it, which left me feeling very odd, but also relieved.

I was just throwing my hair into a ponytail when one of the twins belted out a cry.

Jasper followed me into the nursery and plopped down in the corner. Mrs. Nowacki came in just as I was finishing changing Sophie.

"I feel like all I do is change diapers and feed them," I said to her. "When does it get funner?"

"You want truth or lie?"

I grimaced. "Can you do a mix of both?"

Mrs. Nowacki paused in thought and then nodded. She held out her arms for the clean twin and then I went for Oliver.

"Right now, your world is very small," she began. "And instead of one baby at a time, you got two. There will come a time when the twins are older that you wish you could go back to these moments."

"You're saying I should suck it up and relish these moments with them because one day all too soon they'll be bigger and won't need me?"

"Oh, they'll need you." She closed one eye as she stared at me. "They will need your money and your car. They will need constant monitoring so Oliver doesn't get a girl pregnant, and Sophie doesn't get pregnant. You will feel like prison warden, psychologist, and foreigner in your own home—one who does not speak the same language as your children. And then, finally, there will be that moment where you've given everything, and then they want to move you to retirement community in Florida and take your house."

"Yeah," I said with a sigh. "I was hoping for more of a lie."

It was a little past four in the morning and it felt like I'd only just fallen asleep when Aidan's curse, followed by Jasper's yelp woke me up.

"Sorry," Aidan muttered.

"Are you apologizing to me or the dog?" I asked, yawning, my jaw cracking. I leaned over the turn on the bedside lamp so Aidan wouldn't hurt himself further.

"Both." Still in his three-piece suit, Aidan collapsed onto the bed. "I'm so exhausted."

"And tipsy?"

"And tipsy," he admitted. "I didn't mean to get tipsy. But Caleb kept pushing shots at me. He called me an old man when I refused."

"So of course, you downed the"—I rolled over and sniffed his breath—"bourbon."

"Yup." He sighed. "I'm going to be utterly useless tomorrow."

I hated to be the one to remind him that we were hosting brunch and that people would start arriving around ten.

"You didn't wake Mrs. Nowacki up as you stumbled to our bedroom, did you?"

"Mrs. Nowacki slept over?"

"I didn't want her to go home so late at night. And besides, she wanted my opinion on some of the men who've been emailing her."

"Hmm."

"Do not fall asleep," I warned. I snapped my fingers and Jasper jumped up on the bed and settled between us. "This is the first time I've gotten to talk to you all day."

"Talk fast, I'm fading."

"What do you think about Caleb and Em's engagement?"

"If he's happy, I'm happy."

"What a dude response."

"Is there anything else you want to talk about, or can I roll over and go to sleep?"

"I caught my parents fighting in the alley."

"I don't believe you."

"It's true. Remember how I said Mom was acting weird?"

"Yes."

"Well, it turns out, she and my dad have done a complete one-eighty. My mom's matchmaking business is doing well, and my father wants to semi retire."

When Aidan didn't reply, I gently nudged him. "Aidan?"

His light snore greeted me.

Just as I was about to drift off again, I heard a whimper through the baby monitor and knew it was only a matter of time before it escalated into a full-on scream.

Somehow, I managed to hoist my exhausted body out of bed. On my way to the nursery, my other eyebrow fell off.

Pretty sure the universe was laughing at me.

Chapter 10

Mom Blog Entry:
    I'm supposed to write a sex scene for my new book, but I've never felt less sexy than I do right now.
    I just sniffed myself to see if I had baby poop on me.
    I did.
    Sexy has left the building.

Everyone canceled on brunch.
Every last stinking one of them.

I knew Annie wasn't coming because she'd told me she wasn't. Mills and Annie were a thing so I didn't expect Mills, and besides he was busy vomiting from being ill.

Caleb and Em didn't come because *they* were vomiting, but that had to do with celebrating their engagement the previous evening.

Terry had surprised Zeb with a trip to Vermont last minute, so they bailed.

Stacy was MIA and not answering her texts.

Nancy and Bud had a pipe burst at their house, and they left for Upstate.

My parents had gotten an earlier flight and went to the airport.

Even Mrs. Nowacki—who'd left before the twins had even woken up—had gone home. She had a date that afternoon and wanted time to prepare.

"We're left with twenty pounds of lox," I stated. "Twenty pounds of locks and no bagels."

"Why did we think lox would be a good hangover food?" Aidan said, looking chalky white as he sat at the kitchen table, nursing coffee and toying with two Aspirin.

"I feel great, all things considering," I stated. "I'm exhausted, but that's normal."

"Our first free day in months and all I want to do is go back to bed."

"You should go back to bed," I said.

"And what are you going to do?" he asked.

"Cook myself breakfast and then work."

"Work."

"Yes. Work. That little thing called book edits. I'm forcing my brain into work mode. I'm a fan of calling myself an author. Authors have to do the authoring in order to be an author. Plus, another book, equals paycheck. I'm a fan of paychecks."

He slowly rose from the table and steadied himself. "Wow."

"What?"

"I'm in my thirties," he said, like he couldn't believe it. "I still think I'm in my twenties until moments like these."

"You're so cute when you're going through a weird life crisis." I brushed a kiss across his lips. "Take a nap. See you when you're human again."

He needed no further urging. He headed to the bedroom, Jasper following him.

I made myself scrambled eggs and lox, then shoved most of the fish into the freezer. Maybe Annie could use it, I mused.

While I ate breakfast, I scrolled through Instagram. The photos from the previous night were great. Stacy had caught people laughing and smiling. Others had tagged Veritas from their own accounts. And then as I scrolled, I noticed that someone had caught Annie unaware in the background, her face crestfallen after Caleb's proposal.

I knew she was feeling things about Caleb and Em that she wasn't telling me.

My thoughts of Annie were conflicted; I wanted to send Caleb and Em a gift and invite them over for dinner to celebrate, but damn, my best friend was so hurt by what was going on. And I realized that it was her fault, and that thought alone bothered me to no end. Everything was all out of whack. My best friend and Aidan's best friend weren't together. Caleb was going to marry someone else —someone I *really* liked—but this would change things forever. Holidays were never going to be the same.

I'd been deluding myself into thinking Caleb and Annie were going to get back together. They were both dating other people, and now Caleb was engaged.

When I saw a photo of Caleb and Em on Instagram,

their smiles and eyes bright, the ring on her finger sparkling in the dim lighting of Veritas, I knew it was meant to be. Annie had missed her shot, and that was that.

After finishing breakfast, I realized I didn't want to work on my book, but instead wanted to focus on my Mom blog. I wrote about the nursing pads I'd worn to the bar and after considering that they kept me dry and leak-free I gave them ten out of ten nipples.

Win.

My phone vibrated with a text from Stacy: *Is brunch over?*

I texted back: *It never happened. Everyone bailed.*
If I bring a bottle of Prosecco, can I come over?
I'd prefer it if you brought bagels.

Two nights later, Caleb and Em were sitting on our living room floor, sharing a plate of pizza.

Yes, they shared.

The twins were in their bassinet and I thanked the world for the not so small miracle that neither of them were hungry, cranky, or smelly.

"Your eyebrows are sprouting," Caleb said.

"Yeah? Good. I'm manifesting them into existence."

"I don't think that's how that works," Em teased. "But yeah, I see the fuzz too."

I sighed. "Thank goodness."

"You guys want beer?" Aidan asked, opening the fridge.

"Em and I will share one," Caleb said. "Do you know it took me two days to recover from my hangover?"

"Dude," Aidan said in agreement. "Same here."

"Not me. I was fine later that day," Em said.

"Youngin," I said with a grin.

"Not *that* young. Not Stacy young." Em took the bottle of beer Aidan had brought over and thanked him with a smile.

"Speaking of Stacy," Caleb added after taking a sip of beer, "she's going to take over the rest of Em's lease, and Em is moving in with me."

"That's great," I said. "Everyone wins, and she really wants to get off her friend's couch."

"We did offer her our couch," Aidan reminded me. "But she totally didn't want to stay here with two newborns. Not that I blame her."

"*I* don't even want to stay here, and I own the newborns."

"Do you really own your children?" Em asked with a laugh.

"Absolutely."

Caleb and Em exchanged a look.

"What's that look for?" I asked, noting the way they were speaking without speaking. "You're not pregnant, are you?"

Em held up the bottle of beer. "Really?"

"Yeah, not everyone is dying to procreate, Sibby," Caleb said with an amused grin.

I had to stop my frown. That hadn't been the case

when he'd been dating Annie. He'd wanted a kid almost as much as he wanted to put a ring on her finger.

"We want kids," Em interjected. "Just not for a few more years. We set a wedding date."

"You guys just got engaged," I stated.

Aidan had taken a seat next to me on the couch and he slid his hand onto my thigh to give it a warning squeeze.

"My cousin manages a wedding venue Upstate," Caleb said. "And she said they had a cancellation for March."

"March," I repeated. "Wow. March Upstate is going to be beautiful."

"And cold," Em said with a wry grin. "But we're thinking somewhere tropical for our honeymoon."

"That gives me seven months to lose the baby weight," I said.

"You should work out with me, Sibby," Em said. "I go to the gym four times a week."

I blinked, and then without realizing what I was doing I reached for another piece of pizza.

Dammit.

"Maybe having a gym buddy is the only way I'll go," I muttered. "What time do you work out?"

"I take a spin class twice a week in the mornings and then do a Pilates and meditation class twice a week in the evenings."

"I hate you. I mean, no I don't. But I kind of do."

She grinned. "Next spinning class is tomorrow. Are you in?"

I looked at Aidan. "Can you be on twin detail?"

"Sure thing," he said as he grabbed the piece of pizza I'd reluctantly put back.

I glared at him.

"So the other night your parents left in a hurry, what

happened? Sib said it's something to do with their house, right?" Caleb asked.

"It's bad. The contractor that remodeled their bathroom upstairs used plastic fittings instead of soldered brass and a pipe burst. The house flooded, and the hardwood floors hadn't yet been sealed so they soaked up too much water and split and are ruined. The entire house has the floor ripped up to prevent mold, so they're staying in their RV while they do repairs."

"That sucks," Caleb said.

"I didn't get a chance to meet your parents," Em said to me. "I'm bummed they had to fly home early."

"Yeah, me too."

I'd only gotten a brief text from my parents that they'd made it home safely, but since then it had been radio silence.

Of all the people we knew, somehow Aidan and I had become the stable adults. It was weird.

And I wasn't sure I liked it.

The next morning, I left the twins with Mrs. Nowacki and Aidan. I was wearing yoga pants and one of Aidan's

T-shirts, my red hair was in a ponytail and my eyebrows were growing back.

Life was pretty swell.

I breathed in the hot air, grateful that I was out and about. My boobs hardly hurt, and even though I was headed for the gym to meet Em for a spinning class, I was in good spirits.

She'd given me a guest pass the night before, and so I walked into the gym, showed them my pass and was then directed toward the spinning room. Em was already there and she was perched on a bike, looking like a high-energy sprite, all sexy and vibrant.

"Hey!" she greeted.

"Hey, back!" I set my keys and water bottle into one of the bike's cup holders and then awkwardly climbed onto the seat. "Oh, that's painful."

"You can adjust it. Here." She hopped nimbly off her bike and helped me get comfortable on mine.

"Thanks."

"Have you ever taken a spinning class before?" she asked.

I shook my head.

"Don't feel like you have to keep up with my speed, okay? Just go at your own pace."

"Cool."

Three minutes before the hour, the instructor came in. Her ponytail was blond and high on her head, her arms were toned, and she wore only a black sports bra and black spandex shorts. She had a headset attached to her ear and an Apple watch on her wrist.

She slung her leg over the bike that was in the front of the class, her gaze intense as she looked at every person in the room.

"You are ready to feel the burn, ya?" she asked in a Norwegian accent.

"Oh no," I murmured.

"That's Astrid," Em said. "She's amazing."

Astrid looked like she was ready to torture me. She touched her watch and all of a sudden the lights dimmed, the screen behind her lit up with a bucolic scene, and high-energy dance music better suited for a club in Europe a decade ago came on the surround speakers.

"Begin!" Astrid yelled.

Everyone began pedaling at breakneck speed. I looked around and immediately felt left out so I started to pedal as fast as my legs would move.

The scene on the screen changed to show a road and a bend.

"Ah yeah! We go 'round the curve!" the instructor barked.

Everyone stood up to pedal. Everyone except me, who struggled to even move.

"You!" Astrid pinned me with her blue eyes. "You are not working hard enough! You want legs that can crush a man's neck? Then you work harder!"

I didn't want legs that were powerful enough to crush a man's neck—I had no desire to be an assassin. But I didn't want to get yelled at again, either.

Someone on a bike behind me started to cry.

"No," I moaned, "No, please don't cry."

I felt my nipples tingle.

"Yes!" Astrid yelled.

"Stop screaming at us!" I yelled back. "You're making someone cry! And their tears are making my milk let down! You should be ashamed of yourself!"

Astrid hopped off the bike mid pedal and strutted

toward me until she was standing in front of my bike. "Get out of my class."

The heavy bass of the music drummed in my ears, pulsed in my blood, and made me feel bold. Or maybe it was the red hair. Or maybe it was the twenty-five extra pounds I was dying to lose in seven months before Em's wedding.

"I have a guest pass for an hour of spinning, and damnit, I'm not leaving until I get it."

Her blue eyes bored into me, trying to intimidate me. Sibby of old might've cowered or awkwardly fallen off a bike to get out of the way of her death stare, but the new Sibby—Mama Bear Sibby—wasn't going to back down from a toned AF hot blonde that could easily kick her ass.

"All right, you can stay," Astrid allowed. "But you will work hard the last thirty minutes. You will suffer and be better for it."

True to her word, Astrid made me suffer. By the end, my legs were jelly, I had two wet spots on my shirt, and I was in danger of throwing up.

"Well?" Em asked, grabbing the towel that rested on her handlebars as she wiped her brow. "What did you think?"

"Let's get the hell out of here before she makes me get back on that bike."

"So, I guess it's safe to say you're not coming back to Astrid's class," Em gathered.

"Listen, my morale is already pretty low, and my ego is basically in the toilet. I don't need to give Astrid any more ammo."

Mom Blog Entry:

I'm pretty sure caffeine no longer affects me. I look like a zombie, which seems to be my general state these days.

"You…what?" I demanded.

"Got married. Terry and I got married in Vermont! That was the surprise," Zeb said.

"Well, do you have any pictures?" I asked, setting my

phone down and pressing the speaker button so that I could feed Sophie and talk at the same time.

"Of course we have pictures! I'll send them to your email."

"Why did you guys elope? You asked me to be matron of honor. I've never been matron of honor, and now I'll never get to be matron of honor."

"What about Annie?" Zeb asked.

I looked at my best friend who was sitting at my kitchen table, eyebrows raised. "Yeah, what about Annie?"

"Er."

"You don't think I'll ever get married, do you?" Annie demanded.

"Oh, wow, gotta go," Zeb said quickly. "Fuck. Why didn't you tell me I was on speaker?"

"Pictures, Zeb. I want pictures," I growled.

"Yeah, yeah. I promise."

"Did you guys have cake?" I asked.

He paused. "We had cake."

"What kind?"

"Chocolate with butter cream frosting."

My neurons blasted around my skull at the mention of sugar. "That sounds amazing."

"Nah. It tasted like utter shit."

"Are you lying?"

"Yup."

I sighed. "Diets suck."

"You're the one who said you needed to lose weight for Caleb and Em's—"

"Byyyyyyye!"

I hung up on Zeb and quickly glanced at Annie who was drinking a mug of tea.

"I'm aware that Caleb and Em are getting married,"

Annie said. "I was there the night he proposed to her, remember?"

I swallowed. "They set a date."

"Did they?"

"March."

"March," she repeated. "Wow. That's fast."

I looked back down at Sophie who was done nursing. I fixed my shirt and then placed her to my shoulder.

Just as I was about to change the subject, the front door opened and Aidan walked in... followed by Caleb.

Caleb had a basketball underneath his arm and both of them looked sweaty and attractive.

My gaze darted to Annie who was staring at Caleb— and the shirt stuck to his chest.

"Hey," Caleb said.

"Hey," Annie replied.

"Hello, wife," Aidan greeted, coming over to me. He looked down at Sophie. "Hello, spawn."

She let out a belch that put truckers to shame.

"How's Mills feeling?" Caleb asked suddenly.

"A lot better," Annie said. "Thanks for asking."

There was a long pause where no one said anything.

"Zeb and Terry eloped," I said to Aidan, pretending like there wasn't a ginormous pink hippopotamus in the room no one was talking about.

"Get out," Aidan said, heading to the fridge. "That's amazing. I wish we'd eloped."

"You can elope with your second wife," I quipped.

He shook his head. "Are you kidding? No doubt my second wife will think I'm a silver fox and a cash cow and demand a beach wedding at sunset or something."

"Just don't marry a blonde," I said. "I can handle being replaced by another brunette or even a redhead, but not a blonde."

"Are they really discussing Aidan's second wife like she's a real possibility?" Annie asked, directing the question at Caleb.

"It looks that way, yeah." He rubbed the back of his neck, like he wanted to leave but didn't know how to be polite about it.

"Ah, rats," I muttered.

"What?" Annie asked.

"I just heard Sophie expel into her diaper. Gotta change her." I stood up and so did Annie.

"I've got to get going. Thanks for the hang out and chat about weird mom stuff," Annie said.

"Anytime."

"You know, if you're committed to this working out thing, I run every morning," Annie said.

"You run every morning?" Caleb's eyes widened in surprise.

She nodded. "Yeah. I got into the habit when I was in Montauk. I really wanted to stick with it, and I have."

Aidan and I exchanged a look.

Weird, Aidan mouthed.

I nodded in agreement.

"Are you out of here too?" I asked Caleb.

"Are you trying to kick me out, but being polite about it?" Caleb asked with a grin.

I laughed. "If I wanted you to leave, I would tell you. You're welcome to stay for dinner, if you want. We're having leftover lasagna and discussing new mom and baby products for my blog. It's going to be a hoot and a half."

"Pass," Caleb said. "Em and I have dinner plans anyway, but thank you."

"Right," Annie murmured. "Okay. I'm out. Sibby, see you later."

I wanted to remind her that I was coming by Mother

Shucker with wines to try out in the next few days, but the last thing I wanted to do was pile on more awkwardness.

"I'm out too," Caleb said with a bro handshake to Aidan.

And then Annie and Caleb walked out together, keeping up a steady stream of polite conversation. When the door shut, I could no longer hear them.

"Was that like, the oddest thing in the world?" I asked Aidan.

Aidan took a drink from his bottle of water and then nodded. "The oddest."

"Do you think this means we can have everyone over for Thanksgiving this year and it won't devolve into a drunken screaming fest?"

"That remains to be seen. I'm begging you though. Please don't offer our home up for Thanksgiving. We should go to my parents' house. Or yours."

"Traveling with the twins in November is out of the question." I headed toward the nursery to change Sophie. "It's hard enough with them in our own home where we have all our own stuff and a double crib. Besides, you know if we go to your parents' house, my mother will guilt trip me until she dies. Scratch that, she'll die, remain a ghost and haunt me just so she can guilt me."

I set Sophie onto the changing table and pulled off her clothes.

"If anyone is capable of posthumously Jewish guilt-tripping a person, it would be your mother. How are your parents doing, anyway?"

"I have no idea," I said. "My mom has only called once since they've gotten back to Atlanta. She's being interviewed by a local news station about her matchmaking business sometime next week, though. I called Dad, but he hasn't called me back."

"Your family is so weird."

I got Sophie's diaper off, and in the middle of cleaning her up, she let out a giant shart. Glancing at Aidan, I raised an eyebrow and gestured to his child. "*Your* family is so weird."

"Jesus, your phone is blowing up," Stacy said, sipping on a latte.

My phone in question was lit with dozens of notifications, but none of them had anything to do with me. I pushed the double stroller with one hand to keep the twins lulled into a state of rocking while I glanced at my screen that rested on the sidewalk café table.

"Mrs. Nowacki is online dating," I said in explanation. "But since technology eludes her, guess who is fielding all the responses."

Stacy's eyebrows nearly shot up to her hairline. "And she's gotten *that* many responses?"

"Today. She's gotten this many today."

She laughed. "This is a full-time job."

"Tell me about it," I muttered and shook my head. "How are the new digs?"

"Good," she said. "Em's roommate is really nice and

only there about half the time. I'm just glad I have my own room and a door to close." She tapped the rim of her coffee mug and looked thoughtful.

"What?" I asked. "What's that look for?"

"Just thinking. About all the stuff."

"Life stuff?"

"Yeah." She nodded. "Can we talk about you?"

"I'd really rather not. We always talk about me."

"Not lately. We talk about the twins. That's not the same."

"They're an extension of me. And if we talk about the twins, it means I don't have to be pinned by the stare you're giving me right now."

"You know what I'm going to say," she said.

"I don't want to hear it."

"Sibby."

"Can't hear you." I put a finger to my ear and sang, "La, la, la."

"Book, Sibby. When do I get to read this book that has been in the editing stage for God knows how many months?"

"Ah, you get to read it when my brain actually starts to function again."

She shook her head. "Yeah, I thought you'd say that." Stacy reached down to her sassy leather bag with fringe, riffled around for a moment, and then pulled out a medicine bottle and set it in front of me.

"I'm not taking stimulants to get work done," I said, offended. "How can you even offer me that? I'm breast-feeding!"

With a smirk she held up the bottle and shoved it in my face, so I was forced to read the label.

"Krill pills? You take krill pills?"

"Yup. I started taking them a few months ago and I

swear I can tell a difference in my cognitive function. It's just concentrated krill oil, like fish oil but better, and I'm gifting this bottle to you."

"Thanks."

"One condition, though. You get me this book. I want to read it. I *have* to read it."

"I don't know if it's any good. I wrote it on preggo brain."

"What did your editor say about it?"

"I don't know. I'm too scared to get to the end of the book and read her notes."

"Sibby."

"Stacy."

"You have to read her notes."

I sighed. "After the flop of my last book, I'm trying not to let self-doubt creep in. But it's hard, you know?"

"You want to talk self-doubt? I'm in a man hating 'I can't believe I let Joe get away with treating me like crap after I followed him across the country' mentality."

"You need to have a fling," I said. "Clear the sexual palate."

"Is that what you did after your ex cheated on you?"

"I tried." I gestured to the stroller. "My fling gave me those."

Stacy laughed.

"Is there anyone you're remotely interested in? If not, I think I can scrounge someone up. Though, everyone I know has already paired off, so actually, if I think about it, it's not looking great for your prospects."

"I'm good. Really. I'm taking time to myself. Focusing on my work. Wrangling my client to get me a book that I know is stellar."

I smiled. "Selfishly, I'm glad you're back in New York full-time."

"I'm glad to be back here, too. This is my place." She finished off her latte and set it down on the table. "Oh, I totally forgot to tell you! Caleb and Em hired me to orchestrate their wedding."

"I don't get it. Orchestrate? Like a wedding planner?"

She shook her head. "No, I mean, the pictures and videos. I get to hire a real team."

"Wow. That's cool."

"I know. They were so happy with what I got the night they got engaged—I mean, I did get the proposal on video—they trust me enough to handle their wedding."

My phone pinged again with another notification from StillSchtupin.com. "Mrs. Nowacki is one hot commodity."

"I can't believe they make online dating sites for people in her age bracket."

"Oxygenarians, yeah, sure. Why not?" I asked.

"Don't you mean *octogenarians*?"

"Most of the men hitting her up walk around carting oxygen tanks. Hence oxygenarians."

"Wow. That's—wow."

"You know what's insane? She's having better luck with men at her age than I ever had when I was in my twenties."

"Better luck than what?" She laughed. "Have you seen your husband? I think you're pretty freakin' lucky."

I grinned. "Yeah. You're right about that."

The server came with our check and we paid quickly. I got up, made sure I had everything that belonged to me, and then hugged Stacy goodbye.

I pushed the stroller to Veritas. Aidan was working behind the counter of the liquor store, handing off a brown bag to a customer.

"Thanks, Aidan," the guy said.

"I'm sure your wife is going to love that gin. Come back and let me know how it goes, yeah?"

"I'll do that. Take care."

The man smiled at me as he walked to the exit.

When the door closed and Aidan and I were alone, I said, "Were you this sexy this morning?"

"Nah." He grinned. "I get sexier as the day goes on."

"Must have something to do with the five o'clock shadow."

Aidan came out from behind the cash register to greet me. He leaned down and pecked my lips. "This is a nice surprise."

"I was in the hood. What are you doing later?" I asked, pitching my voice low.

"Later when? Later this afternoon or later this evening?"

"Later this evening when the twins are in bed, I'd very much like to take a ride on your love rocket."

He blinked. "Does that mean what I think it means?"

"Yes. I'll even shave my legs for the occasion."

"Above the knee?"

I grinned. "Come on, now. Who do you think I am?"

Chapter 12

Mom Blog Entry:

I put my underwear on inside out this morning. But it was clean, so I consider it a win.

"What about this one?" I asked Mrs. Nowacki the next morning, showing her my phone screen.

"Too old," she said.

I sighed and swiped. "What about this one?"

"Too hairy."

I lifted her hand and placed my phone in her palm. "You're up, chief. I'm out. I've got too many things on my plate. And you're being really picky."

Her gaze narrowed. "When was last time you eat?"

"What does that have to do with anything?"

"You are grouch."

"Sorry. I stepped on the scale this morning and somehow I've gained a pound."

"You can't go to gym once and expect anything to change."

"Well, I'm not going back there," I said. "The spinning instructor made people cry. I don't need that kind of negativity in my life."

She frowned. "Spinning? You spin in circles and call that exercise?"

I briefly explained the actual mechanics of what constituted a spinning class.

"Why you want to ride stationary bike with fake scenery?" she asked in confusion.

"I don't," I said. "Which is why I'm not going back."

"So, what will you do instead?"

"Wish away the pounds?" I asked with a false sense of hope.

She shook her head. "You come with me when I do the exercise."

Mrs. Nowacki held up a hand before I could say no, so I nodded.

I got up from the couch and went to the kitchen to grab myself a glass of water and a krill pill. Stacy swore by them, and after asking my OBGYN if they were safe to take while breastfeeding, I'd taken one the previous night before Aidan had gotten home. I wasn't sure if it did anything for my brain function, but it sure made me receptive to Aidan's advances.

If one was good, two was better, so I decided to pop a handful of krill pills. They were small—way smaller than regular fish oil—and I wanted to get some work done before I met Em to discuss wines for Annie's restaurant.

"The babies are conked out," I said after I downed the pills and finished my glass of water. "I'm gonna dive into my edits."

She waved her hand at me. "Go. I need to reject some men."

"Let me get you set up on Aidan's computer. It will be easier than using my phone."

She nodded. "But I still keep your phone. No distractions while you are in office. You get it back when baby needs boobie."

I got her situated with Aidan's laptop and then headed to my office. I closed the door and leaned against it, breathing in the scent of a cinnamon candle that still hung in the air.

Maybe it was the krill pills, maybe it was my own excitement, but my fingers itched for the keyboard. With a clear mind, I sat down at my desk and opened the document that had all my editor's notes.

I cheated and scrolled all the way to the end to finally read what she'd had to say.

Her words had me punching the air in excitement.

I went back to the beginning and lost myself in the work.

Three chapters in and there was a knock on my office door.

I sighed but called out, "Come in."

Mrs. Nowacki popped her head in and held up my phone. "Your mother."

"Will you answer it, please? She probably just wants to Face Time and see the babies."

Mrs. Nowacki shrugged and then answered the phone, turning it to face her.

"Mrs. Nowacki," Mama Goldstein greeted. "Hello."

"Hullo," Mrs. Nowacki stated. "Sibby is working. I take you to see the twins."

Just as the door was about to shut, I heard my mother say, "I actually need to speak to Sibby. It's important."

I pulled my gaze away from the computer screen and held out my hand. Mrs. Nowacki came back into my office, handed me the cell, and then left.

"Hi," I said. "Is everything okay? Is it *Bubbe*?"

"Sibby—"

"It's *Zayde*, isn't it? He fell and broke his hip. I knew we shouldn't have gotten him that mini trampoline—"

"Sibby!"

I blinked. "What?"

"*Bubbe* and *Zayde* are fine." She took a deep breath. "It's about me. And your father. I've left him."

I paused. "What's that now?"

"I left your father. I'm staying with Aunt Becca and Uncle Michael in their spare guest room."

My mother was unusually calm and put together.

"Did aliens abduct you and give you a new personality?" I demanded.

"No. Not that I'm aware of."

"You can't leave Dad."

"Yes, I can."

"But you *love* him. He loves you."

"Sometimes love isn't enough, Sibby."

"Don't say that! If you say that then every 1980s rom-com is a damn dirty lie."

"They're all lies. It's not natural for human beings to stay with the same person for thirty years. Biologically, we aren't designed for that."

I snapped my finger as a light bulb moment went off in my head. "You're just having a mid-wife crisis. Take some time. Don't do anything drastic."

"I signed up for an amateur burlesque class."

"I said *don't* do anything drastic!"

"Burlesque isn't drastic," she continued, still cool and calm. "I'd originally wanted to take a pole dancing class, but I thought of my reputation."

I removed my glasses and pinched the bridge of my nose. "What did Dad say, when you left him?"

"He doesn't know yet."

"Huh?"

"I packed a suitcase, left a note. When he comes home from work, he'll find out."

"You can't leave your husband of over thirty years a note. You owe him a face to face conversation."

"I owe him nothing. He doesn't respect me or understand me. So, let him fend for himself and find out what it's like not having me around."

She looked off to the side and shook her head and then nodded.

"Who are you nodding at?" I demanded.

"Becca. She held up a bottle of white wine and then a bottle of red. Got to go. Kiss the twins for me."

She disconnected and the screen went black. I slowly set my phone down, trying to process the calm delivery from my mother. My mother invented the word *theatric*, and this wasn't my mom being true to herself. Or so I thought.

"Burlesque?" I murmured. "Is she high?"

She was leaving my dad after thirty plus years of marriage. If she wasn't high, then she was definitely off her rocker.

I stood up from the desk and left my office. Mrs.

Nowacki sat on the couch, laptop on her lap, her eyes tracking me.

Without saying a word, I went to the fridge and pulled out a bottle of Kombucha and took a shot.

Sure, it was only four percent alcohol, and the carbonation did more to my brain than the actual alcohol, but it was the ritual of the matter.

"Sibby?" Mrs. Nowacki pressed.

"My mom left my father. She's staying with my Aunt Becca."

"Ah." Mrs. Nowacki nodded and then went back to looking at the screen. "Too bald."

"Did you hear what I just said?"

"Yes. I hear. It's not a big concern."

"My parents' marriage is on the rocks, and you don't think it's a big concern? She left my dad *a note*. She didn't even wait around to tell him face to face."

"Your mother didn't really leave your father," she said. "She thinks she did, but she is only doing it to prove point and to get attention. She go back when he apologizes. Trust me. You have nothing to worry about."

"What if you're wrong?" I demanded. "My mother didn't sound like herself. She was calm and didn't resemble a screeching hyena. I think he really hurt her feelings."

"Of course he did. He is man. This is what men do. They hurt feelings because they have the testosterone and do not know how to speak the woman language. Once he realize how empty his life is without her, he realizes he made mistake, he make amends, she forgives, then they have the sex."

"Ew."

"Not ew. It is part of life. That's all life is about anyway." Her gaze went back to the screen and she lifted her pointer finger. "Ah, now this…this is a man I want to meet. Hair only on head, no list of prescription medications." She leaned in closer. "What is angina?"

"Sibby?" Aidan called quietly. "Sibby are you awake?"

I removed the couch pillow from my face and looked at my husband. "You're home early."

He grinned. "I was thinking about you…and my love rocket."

"I'm not in the mood," I stated without preamble. "My mother left my father."

He took a seat next to me. "What happened?"

I spent a few minutes filling him in.

"I'm waiting on a call from my father. He clearly hasn't gotten the note she left for him yet, otherwise my phone would be ringing."

He shook his head. "That's rough."

I touched a finger to my face. "I'm in total shock. I can't even process it." I sat up quickly, the pillow falling to the floor. "Crap. What time is it?"

Aidan looked at his watch. "Five."

I moaned. "Where's my phone?" I asked the question just as I remembered that I'd left it in my office.

"Yup, three missed calls and a dozen text messages," I

said as I came back into the living room. "I was supposed to meet Em an hour ago to taste wines."

I kissed him. "Hi, by the way."

"Hiya."

I dialed Em's number and she answered immediately.

"What happened to you?" she asked.

"Life."

"Do you still want to meet? Or—"

"I'm so sorry, Em. Can you come over here? I can pay for your cab. Is that too much trouble? Mrs. Nowacki left to meet a man for pastry and tea, the twins are about to wake up from their nap and I'm gonna have to feed them, and my parents are separated and I just—"

"Sibby, calm down," she said. "Seriously? Your parents? What happened?"

"Bring the wine and come over."

"Can I bring Caleb?"

I looked at Aidan. "You want to hang with your dude while Em and I try wines?"

He gave me a thumbs up.

"Yeah, bring him."

"Cool, see you in about twenty."

We hung up and then I looked at Aidan. "This is the part where you tell me not to order carbohydrates for dinner and eat my feelings."

"I have a better idea," he said, leaning over and kissing my nose. "When Caleb gets here, I'll enlist his help. We'll grill."

"We don't have any defrosted steaks."

"You've heard of this thing called a store?" He patted his pants pocket for his wallet and then swiped his keys from the counter.

"Dog, come," Aidan said.

Jasper's nose peaked through the crack of the doorway of the nursery and he trotted into the room, tail wagging.

"Jasper's riding shot gun in the Subaru. See you in a bit."

No sooner had he left than the twins bellowed their angry demands. Shoving all thoughts of my parents' marriage away, I went to tend to my needy children.

"This is a White Bordeaux," Em said, uncorking a bottle of white and pouring me a taste.

I sniffed and sipped as she blathered on about the notes and what region the wine was from. None of that ever mattered to me. If I liked it, that was enough. And I liked this wine. A lot.

"That's a win, too." I dumped the rest of the taste into a waste glass, lamenting the fact that I couldn't finish it. Em had brought over fifteen wines and if drank all the tiny samples I would've been conked out before dinner.

"So out of the fifteen you liked thirteen." She grinned. "That's a pretty good percentage."

"I don't think we need that many, though. Annie said she wanted to keep the wine menu small."

The thirteen bottles of wine that I liked were lined up on the island counter.

"My suggestion?" she posited. "Seafood menu. You don't need three big reds."

"Yeah, you're right." I immediately removed two bottles and Em stashed them back in her traveling wine carrier. "That still leaves eleven."

"You have to have both chardonnays. One California oaky, one European and crisp."

"Right you are." I left the chardonnays alone. "I think we can get rid of the Sauvignon Blanc. We've got the Sancerre. That's overkill."

She pulled the Sauv Blanc and put it away. "So, these are what you're left with. Is she going to try them?"

I shook my head. "She doesn't drink anymore. She's relying on my taste buds."

"Huh."

"What?"

"Her boyfriend is a bar manager."

"Guess she trusts me more." I mentally smacked my forehead. Why did I say that? The last thing I wanted to do was make it look like Mills and Annie weren't serious. Then again, I wasn't sure they were. He wanted her to move in with him, but she was adamantly refusing.

And come to think of it, I hadn't seen Mills since before Veritas's party and I'd been too preoccupied with my own family drama to even ask Annie about Mills.

"Sibby?"

"Yeah?" I looked at Em.

She grinned. "Do you want a glass from one of these bottles?"

"I'd like a glass from all the bottles," I said with a laugh. "How about a small glass of the big red. Our men should be coming down from the roof in a few."

The apartment building had a communal grill on the roof, which the boys made regular use of.

"Can I talk to you about something?" Em asked.

"Nothing serious, I hope," I said, reaching for a bottle of Cab. "I don't have the bandwidth for something serious."

"It's about my wedding."

"Shoot."

"I've asked my best friend since we were kids to be my maid of honor."

I nodded. "That makes sense."

"And my two younger sisters. I've asked them to be part of my bridal party, too."

"Uh huh." I nodded and took a sip of wine.

"Sibby?"

"Yeah?"

"This is me trying to ask you if you'll be in my wedding party."

I blinked. "Are you sure? We haven't been friends that long."

"I know." She bit her lip. "But Aidan is going to be Caleb's best man. And—well—we're going to be in each other's lives for, like, ever."

"Ah, so I'm stuck with you." I grinned. "That's what you're saying?"

"Kinda, yeah." She smiled. "Listen, if it's too weird because of Annie, I totally understand. I'm not like, trying to steal you away from her or anything. I just— it's a really special day, you know? It's not just mine and Caleb's families that are blending, but you're becoming part of my family too. I kind of friend people for life."

The front door opened and Aidan walked in holding the tongs and a cutting board, complete with our sizzling steaks. Caleb was behind him carting a pan of grilled asparagus.

"Men bring meat," Aidan said in his best Neanderthal voice.

"How did men bring meat?" I asked. "Medium rare?"

Aidan looked at Caleb. "Told you she'd give me shit if it wasn't cooked right."

"You did tell me," Caleb said with a grin. He set the asparagus down on the kitchen table that was already set with place settings and napkins. "What have you guys been up to?"

"Wine tasting, and Em just asked me to be a bridesmaid. I was about to tell her yes when you guys walked in."

"Really?" Em asked with a wide smile.

"Really," I said with an equally happy grin, and then it slipped from my face.

Em's expression fell. "What? You've changed your mind already?"

"No, I just realized that I'm actually going to have to get serious about exercise if I want to look good standing up there next to your waify butt."

"I'm not waify," she protested. "And the bridesmaid dresses are going to be black. Everyone looks good in black."

I stared at her with dreamy eyes. "I heart you."

Chapter 13

Mom Blog Entry:

My husband and I left our children with our nanny so we could enjoy a kid-free date night.

Date night consisted of checking into a hotel, ordering room service, and passing out at 7 PM.

Most expensive nap ever.

Aidan and I were in the middle of giving Oliver his

pre-bedtime bath when my husband asked, "You sure this is a good idea?"

I frowned in confusion. "Bathing our child? Yeah, he was starting to smell."

"No, not that."

I dribbled warm water across Oliver's chest. "Then what are you talking about?"

"I'm talking about you being in Em's bridal party."

"I knew it. You don't think I'll look hot in seven months."

"Sibby, you look hot now. I'm hot for you all the time. I'm constantly trying to get into your pants. That hasn't changed."

"You mean it?" I asked, feeling vulnerable.

He rolled his eyes. "Of course I mean it. But I don't want this conversation to get away from us. You're Annie's best friend."

"Yes."

"Her ex-boyfriend is engaged to someone else. His fiancée just asked you to be part of one of the most important days in a woman's life. You don't think this is… Well, what is this going to do to you and Annie?"

"Nothing. It will do nothing," I said. "Because I plan on telling her tomorrow when I swing by Mother Shucker and give her a list of the wines I chose for her restaurant."

"This is going to blow up in your face. You know that, right? Annie already feels left out."

"Was I supposed to turn down Em's offer of solidifying our friendship? She did point out that we're going to be in each other's lives for a good long time, you know?"

"I know. Caleb is my best friend and business partner. It makes sense. Rationally. But I'm a dude."

"And you're saying women are emotional and Annie's going to flip out."

"Yes."

"She didn't flip out when Caleb and Em got engaged. She was stoic, calm. And didn't drink. Same goes for when she found out they set a wedding date."

"You're not going to be her maid of honor first. Don't you see? If she were getting married before Em and Caleb, and she'd already called dibs on you as her maid of honor, then you'd have some leverage. Some pull. But this?" He shook his head. "No good can come of this."

"Matron of Honor."

"What?"

"I'm not a maid of honor, I'd be a matron of honor. Because I'm married. Here, take your son. He's clean as a colon before a colonoscopy."

"Veto on that visual."

I gently handed Oliver to Aidan who already had a towel ready and waiting.

"This will hurt her," Aidan said. "And she means more to you than anyone. Maybe even more than me."

I sighed. "Okay. I'll be really, really sensitive when I tell her. Did you know Em was going to ask me to be a bridesmaid?"

"How would I know that?"

"You and Caleb don't talk about the wedding?"

"Did you and I even talk about *our* wedding when were the two main characters?"

"No, but that's because my mom orchestrated—sorry, commandeered everything. She basically just told us when to show up."

"Yeah, that's true. We picked a day and location. That was it. I didn't even have final approval on my tux."

"Kosher wedding food. Yuck. I think for our ten-year wedding anniversary party it needs to be a Renaissance Festival theme."

"You wouldn't by any chance be trying to distract me by making me think of super large turkey legs, would you?"

"I knew it. I knew you thought my legs were fat."

"Really?" Aidan demanded.

I grinned.

He grinned.

"You want to get these pierogis down for the night and then we can play ride the dragon?"

"I like where your head's at, Kincaid."

He arched a brow. "I won't even make the dirty joke. Even though you set me up perfectly."

"I aim to please."

"Hold on to that sentiment, would you?"

"Your mother is insane," Dad said.

I held in a sigh as I struggled into a pair of yoga pants.

"Sibby? Are you there?"

"Yeah, Dad, I'm here. I have to put you on speaker phone now, okay?"

"Is Aidan around?"

"He's in the living room with the twins. Why?"

"Just curious," he said. "Did you know she left me a note?"

"Yeah, I knew," I said. "I tried to talk her out of it. I swear I did." I set the cellphone down and pressed the speaker button so I could open my chest of drawers and pull out a sports bra and a T-shirt.

"I can't believe—what is she thinking?"

"She's thinking you don't understand or support her and that's why she's staying with Aunt Becca."

He was silent for a moment and then he said, "What do you think I should do?"

"Seriously, Dad?" I asked, my tone abrupt. "Are you really asking me how to fix your marriage? No offense, but can't we have some boundaries? I'm not your therapist. I'm not a marriage counselor. I'm drowning under the weight of my own responsibilities as I try to figure out how to raise twins with my husband."

There was a knock on the bedroom door and then Aidan popped his head in. "Mrs. Nowacki is here."

I nodded. "I'll be right there." I pointed to my phone and mouthed *Dad*.

Aidan grimaced and then gently shut the door.

"Dad? I have to go," I muttered.

"I understand."

He sounded broken and defeated—and I'd just yelled at him over the implosion of his marriage.

"I can't fathom a world where you and Mom aren't together," I said softly. "It's not fair of me to school you over it. But I think, if it were me, and Aidan and I were going through this kind of thing, I'd want him to remember what it was like in the beginning, when he was trying to win me over. I'd want him to remember why he fell in love with me in the first place. But I guess, the bigger question you've got to ask is, do you *want* her to come home? And if you do, are you willing to try and understand where she's coming from?"

He paused. "Thanks, Sibby. I'll talk to you later."

"Love you," I muttered and then we disconnected.

I wasn't a miracle worker. I was their daughter, and both of them were talking to me instead of talking to each other. It wasn't fair to me. I had my own issues to sort out.

Somehow, I managed to wrangle my boobs into a sports bra. My nipples were chafed due to the twins thinking my nubs were sucking candies.

I grabbed my phone and a pair of athletic socks and headed out of the bedroom. A smile spread across my face when I saw Mrs. Nowacki—and her attire. She was wearing a pair of bright red athletic shorts, a white T-shirt…and a 1980s sweatband around her head.

"Mrs. Nowacki, I'm shocked," I said. "I can see your knees. I didn't think you had knees."

"You can't work out in a skirt and tortoise neck."

"Tortoise neck?" Aidan asked in amusement.

"She means turtleneck," I said with a wry grin.

I slipped on my socks and tennis shoes and then kissed Aidan goodbye. I looked at the twins sleeping in their bassinet and then patted Jasper's head.

"I'll be home in a couple of hours," I said to him. "There's extra milk in the freezer."

"Have fun," Aidan said with a wave.

I grabbed my bag and cell and then Mrs. Nowacki and I left.

"Where are you taking me? Please not to the gym."

"No. We go to senior center up north a few blocks. We take the Zumba."

"Zumba? You do a Zumba class?"

"Yes. I go three days a week," she said. "It keep joints loose."

"How did I not know about this?" I asked.

"You never ask."

"Well, you have me there."

Ten minutes later, we were walking into the senior center that didn't know the meaning of the word air conditioner. I started to sweat immediately, but Mrs. Nowacki didn't appear at all bothered by the heat.

She took my hand and led me to a room with a wooden floor and no mirrors. I was already a fan.

"Where do we stand?" I asked.

"I like middle row."

A flood of women in Mrs. Nowacki's age bracket entered the room. They jabbered away in Polish and a few called greetings to Mrs. Nowacki, who kindly replied. She gestured to me.

"Sibby, meet Zuzanna, Lena, and Beatrice."

I waved a hello and then Lena moved to stand next to me on my left side and Mrs. Nowacki on my right. The instructor came in—and I was glad to see that she in no way resembled Astrid from the spinning class. I doubted I'd leave senior center Zumba crying.

The instructor bellowed something in Polish and then a woman in the front row ran to the sound system and pressed a button. Latin music pumped through the speakers as the instructor led us through a warmup.

I didn't know the steps, but it was easy enough to follow along and for the first time in a long time, I didn't worry about how I looked, I just had fun as all the women in the room danced and exercised in a way that didn't really feel like exercise.

Three songs later, Mrs. Nowacki huffed, "Your shoe is untied."

I crouched down in the middle of the routine to tie my shoelace. Unfortunately, I didn't count on Lena's exuberance and the force with which she was swinging her leg. Somehow, she kicked me in the shoulder, bumping me off balance.

"Ah!" I yelled, falling over onto my back, which coincided with the dance routine stepping forward.

I rolled like a bowling ball into the woman behind me, who went down like a bowling pin.

The music stopped almost instantly, and the instructor ran to the woman behind me to assess the damage.

All eyes looked to me and before I could figure out what was happening, someone threw a silver sneaker at me —which hit my other shoulder.

"Run!" Mrs. Nowacki screeched.

I scrambled up from my spot on the floor and dashed after her, all the while covering my head as more silver sneakers worn by the octogenarian crowd were thrown at me. I remembered to grab my small bag that rested in the corner.

Once we were out of the street, I bent over to breathe in the fresh air.

"It is not safe here," Mrs. Nowacki said, looking around like an army sniper. "Come. We walk at power speed back to apartment."

She took off without even waiting for me, leaving me to scramble after her once again.

"What was that back there?" I demanded. "Lena was the one who kicked me, causing me to knock someone else over."

"That group," she began, "take the Zumba very seriously. I must pay restitution to ensure good will."

"Restitution? Why do you sound like you're in the mafia?"

Mrs. Nowacki ground to a halt and turned to stare at me. "Some things, Sibby Goldstein-Kincaid, we do not discuss in the open. Ever. Nod if you understand, and then keep walk."

I nodded, no doubt looking like a demented chicken.

She grabbed my hand and gave it a squeeze. "Go see your *bubelas* and husband. I must think about how best to proceed."

Mrs. Nowacki left me on the stoop of my apartment building and then continued on her way home.

I got out my keys as my gaze surveyed the neighborhood, wondering if any of Mrs. Nowacki's powerful Zumba friends were coming after me.

When I walked into the apartment, Aidan looked up from the TV, surprise on his face. "You're home way earlier than I expected."

I shut the door. "I might've run into some trouble at Zumba."

"What did you do?"

"Me? It wasn't my fault." I paused. "Okay, it was a little my fault. I took down a senior citizen. But it was purely accidental!"

"Is she okay?" Aidan asked, trying for concern, but failing when his lips devolved into a huge shit-eating grin.

"I think so." I set my bag down on the counter. "There's a bigger issue we need to discuss."

"Bigger than taking down a senior citizen? She might've broken a hip."

"Yes. Bigger than that," I snapped. "I'm pretty sure our nanny is in the mafia."

Three hours later, I left the house again and walked to Annie's restaurant. I couldn't wait to tell her about my failed attempt at Zumba.

I arrived at Mother Shucker and opened the heavy glass door. I didn't see Annie or anyone else, but I came in and perched at one of the stools on the counter.

Annie appeared from the back kitchen, holding a cardboard box full of Brussels sprouts.

She grinned. "Hey."

"Hey."

"Did you just get here?" She slid the box onto the counter and wiped her hands on her chef pants.

"Yeah, about two minutes ago."

"You just missed Mills."

"How *is* Mills?"

"Good." She grinned. "He's taking me to Amish country this weekend for a romantic getaway."

"Two things. One, can you really be romantic in Amish country. And B, how did he manage to get you to take the time off?"

"He convinced me by doing this thing with his hips—"

"*And* you're done."

She laughed. "Nah, I'm just kidding. We have both

been working every hour of every day, we don't see each other, and it will only get worse after Mother Shucker opens. So, yeah. Romantic weekend to nakedly hang out with the guy I'm dating."

"Ah, naked hang out time." I sighed. "I miss that."

"You have sex with Aidan. Successfully, if I recall."

"Yes, but it's like a race to the finish line. I'm always worried one of the twins will scream into the baby monitor and totally disrupt my sexual flow."

She shook her head in feigned disgust. "So, tell me all the things? It's been a while since I've seen you."

"Yeah, where should I start?"

"Oh, hold on. Have you had lunch? I want to try out a few recipes."

"I'll guinea pig for you. Sure. Thanks." I grinned.

Annie snapped her fingers and then got to prepping in front of me.

"I did see Em the other day. I've tasted wines and I have a list."

She reached underneath the bar and grabbed a cutting board and set it on the counter.

I riffled around in my bag for my phone. I opened the screen and swiped through the photos. I sent Annie pictures of the wines I'd chosen along with an actual list.

"I stayed true to what you wanted." I set my phone down.

"I trust you," she said.

"Yay. So, what are you making me?"

"Deep fried Brussels sprouts and homemade buttermilk ranch dressing."

I blinked. "You do know I'm on a diet, right?"

"I do."

"And you do know I'm trying to actually burn the calories I get from stalks of celery."

She grinned. "How's that working out for you?"

I told her about spinning and Zumba.

"You went spinning?" Annie dropped the vegetables into the deep fryer and they sizzled.

"Yeah."

"Alone? I know you. You need a buddy for those things."

"I went to Zumba with Mrs. Nowacki. And I went to Em's spinning class."

"Ah." She kept her head down, gaze on the fryer.

I cleared my throat. "I have to tell you something."

"I'm listening."

I inhaled a deep breath and channeled my inner Zen. "Em asked me to be one of her bridesmaids. I said yes."

"You said yes?"

"Yeah."

She fell silent. She lifted the fryer basket and checked the Brussels sprouts, but they weren't done so she stuck them back under the oil.

"Annie? Can you say something, please?"

"I'm trying to come up with something that isn't a bunch of curse words."

I winced. "Maybe cursing at me might make you feel better."

"The nerve of that wench."

"It's not Em's fault."

"It's not? You're right. It's yours. Don't you see? She's trying to steal you away from me. She already got Caleb."

"I thought you were over Caleb," I said in confusion.

"This isn't about Caleb," she snapped.

"Then what's it about?"

"She's marrying the guy who wanted me first," she yelled, finally letting the emotion that had been bottled up for months burst free. "She's marrying the *perfect guy* and she gets *you* as a bridesmaid and Aidan by proxy, and before you know it you'll be spending Hanukkah with them. And where will I be?"

I had no idea how to handle her rant. She hadn't raved in so long, and I thought she'd had a grip on reality, on life.

"You didn't want him," I said gently.

She swallowed.

"*You* didn't want the perfect guy. *You* didn't want the same life he did. You didn't want kids or a house and mortgage. You wanted *this*." I gestured around Mother Shucker. "You wanted freedom. You wanted space to figure yourself out. And you know what, you got it."

Annie nodded. "Yeah. You're right about all of that. But I never thought you'd betray me this way."

"Betray? How am I—"

"You chose her."

"I did no such thing," I huffed.

"You're about to be a part of the most special day of her life—up until the moment she becomes a mom. But, hey, you'll probably be there for that too. Your kids and their kids will all grow up together. You'll vacation together. In forty years, you'll be sitting around a restaurant table shooting the shit with the waitress and telling her that you've been friends for more than half your life. And where will I be?"

She pinned me with a stare.

"Oh, are you actually asking or is this a rhetorical question?"

"Get out, Sibby."

"Annie, come on—"

"No. You don't get to—just go."

I felt my throat clog with emotion. "I know you're mad. You have every right to be. But you said it yourself. It's not about Caleb, and it's not even really about me. This is about you. This is about you getting everything you wanted and you're still not happy. So, I gotta ask you: What *will* make you happy? Do you even know anymore? Did you ever know?"

I grabbed my purse and left.

My best friend in the world didn't try to stop me.

Mom Blog Entry:

I hate vegetables, but as a mom, I'm supposed to make my kids eat them. How is this going to work?

"I need a drinking buddy," I said into the phone.

"Ah, now is a really bad time," Stacy said.

"You're right. It is a bad time. And I need a drink."

"Hold on."

I heard the sound of muffled conversation for a few beats and then she was back. "Where am I meeting you?"

I told her.

"Great. I'll catch a cab and be there in a few."

We hung up and then I shot Aidan a text, telling him that my plans with Annie had gone awry, and that I was meeting Stacy for a drink.

Aidan: *She flipped her shit, didn't she?*

Me: *Yeah.*

Aidan: *Sorry.*

Me: *Why? You warned me. Do you have enough breast milk?*

Aidan: *We're good for a few more hours at least.*

Me: *I'll only have a beer. I really just need to talk to another girl.*

Aidan: *Understood. Love you.*

Me: *Love you, too.*

I went into the bar where I was meeting Stacy and ordered a beer—and then because I was trying to be a rational adult, I changed my mind and switched to a club soda.

Stacy blew in ten minutes later, looking flushed as she perched her huge bag onto the seat across from me.

I cocked my head to the side. "You look great."

She grinned. "Let me grab a drink real fast." She went to the bar and ordered a vodka tonic and then came back with it in hand.

"I'm sorry I dragged you away from whatever you were doing."

"Not a what. A who."

I paused. "You're having a rebound?"

"Yes."

"Well, who is it?" I demanded. "You can't keep me in suspense."

"Can you keep a secret?"

"Ehm, sure?"

"I mean it. This *can't* get out."

"Cross my heart."

"That's not good enough. Pinky swear."

She held up her pinky finger and we locked appendages.

"Do you want blood or my first-born child?"

"Blood makes me squeamish and so do babies. Yours are cute though."

"Stacy, out with it. My gray hairs are growing gray hairs here, the suspense is killing me."

She took a deep breath. "Gregory Roubideaux. I'm sleeping with Gregory Roubideaux."

"The famous British chef who lives in Las Vegas?" I asked.

She nodded.

"The one who has a reality TV show that makes amateur chefs cook in really weird places with not a lot of ingredients?"

She nodded.

"The one who is separated but not divorced?"

"Divorced. He's been divorced for about a year."

My mind whirled. "Oh, good, that's good. But I thought he was still in Las Vegas! And how did you guys meet? Spill it."

She looked into her cocktail glass. "Joe's band had dinner at Pound, and Gregory came out to see how we all liked the food. We—ah—locked eyes and…"

"Oh my god, you cheated on Joe first!"

"What? No!" She shook her head adamantly. "But I might've," she swallowed, "run to him after I caught Joe cheating on me. *Then* I slept with him. And snuck out the next morning before he woke up…and then I got on a plane immediately and came here."

"Okay, so then what's he doing here?"

"Looking at commercial spaces."

"Why do I feel like I'm unravelling a ball of yarn? Gimme the rest!"

"He's opening a new restaurant in Manhattan. He was going to do that before we met," she assured me. "And it's not like we're even really together. We're having fun. Casual. He just got out of a ten-year marriage. I just got out of a three-year relationship. Neither one of us is looking for anything serious."

I leaned back in my seat. "You've already caught feelings."

"What? No!"

"Thou doth protest too much."

She took a big swallow of her drink. "Anyway. He's coming to Mother Shucker's opening in October. We'll see where we are then."

My mood instantly plummeted when Stacy reminded me of Annie.

"Now you. What's happened?"

"Will you be honest with me?"

"About what? I mean, yes, of course."

"You'll tell me if I'm an insensitive dingus?"

"Absolutely."

"Em asked me to be one of her bridesmaids and I said yes. Annie's feelings are really hurt. Am I a shit friend?"

"Oh, moral ambiguity." She sighed. "I think this is a tricky situation."

I waited for her to say more, but when it was clear nothing else was forthcoming, I said, "That's it? You're leaving me with moral ambiguity?"

"Let's do a little role reversal, shall we? What if you and Aidan broke up?"

My eyes instantly began to water.

"No, it's not real! Come back, come back!"

I wiped my eyes. "I'm fine. Go on with your parallel universe story."

"You and Aidan broke up and Annie and Caleb were together. And Aidan got a new awesome girlfriend who compliments him like, super well, and she asks Annie to be her maid of honor. How would you feel?"

"Left out. Left behind. Like my entire world was imploding—oh. Oh, I see." I sighed. "I just thought because this is Caleb, this is Aidan's best friend in the world and Em is going to be his wife, our lives are going to be intertwined forever and I just thought—oh, shit I *am* an insensitive dingus."

"No. This is one of those terrible choices where you'd hurt someone no matter what you decided. If you told Em no, she would understand, but part of her would always wonder if you'd wished Annie and Caleb had gotten back together. She would've remained the odd man out. Always. But Annie is the odd man out now by default because Em orchestrated you being part of her wedding party, you know?"

"I should've been friends with all dudes."

She shook her head. "Then you'd have to go to locker rooms and compare junk size. They have their problems too."

"Yeah that doesn't sound fun either." I paused. "How do I make this right?"

"Is being in Em's bridal party worth jeopardizing your entire relationship with Annie over?"

"I have to back out, don't I?" I said.

"Yeah. I think you do."

"Fuck a muck a duck."

"You can say that again." She threw back the rest of her drink. "Another?"

I shrugged. "Why not."

"What are you drinking?"

"Club soda."

Stacy shook her head and rose from the table. "I need younger friends."

"Hey, watch it."

She grinned. "Just kidding."

"Thanks for your advice," I said. "I mean it."

"Aidan didn't walk you through this one?"

"He tried. But as a wife, I'm conditioned not to hear anything he says until it's too late."

Annie wouldn't pick up my phone calls or answer my texts. And I knew she kept odd hours because it was the last few months before opening Mother Shucker, so I knew there was no excuse for her not picking up at three in the morning when I had a twin on each breast.

I really didn't have the energy to be going through an epic fight with my best friend. My parents were separated and I had lost my mojo. I had two tiny humans who belonged to me—it wasn't like I could return them to the store where I'd bought them, you know?

On top of my monumental struggle of not feeling like a failure of a mother, I was worried I was failing as a wife.

After what transpired between me and Annie, I had finally toppled the Jenga pile of life.

I finished feeding the twins and enlisted Aidan's help in burping and changing them.

"Why do I suck at life?" I asked as I climbed into bed. Jasper waited until I was comfortable, and then he wormed his way underneath the covers to snuggle at my feet. Our sheets smelled like dog-meat sweat, but I felt guilty over Jasper too. I had been ignoring the poor guy a lot recently to take care of the twins, and myself.

"You don't suck at life."

"Yes, I do. Let's go down the list."

"Let's not. I'm not going to let you shame spiral."

He lifted his arm and I rolled into his side.

"Something's wet," Aidan said.

"Is it Jasper's nose on your knee?"

"No."

"Then it's probably my leaking breasts." I closed my eyes. "I feel like I'm juggling all these balls and I'm constantly afraid I'll drop one. Or all of them."

"Okay, go down the list. What can we fix? You and me, together," Aidan said.

"Well, with your help, I'm pretty sure the kids will make it to toddlerdom."

"Something to look forward to. Good. What else?"

"I have to find an exercise routine that I enjoy and that doesn't make me cry or make other people cry. And it has to work. I need this."

"Okay, that's trial and error, so you'll tackle that and you'll eventually find something."

"My parents. I can't help with that."

"Can't or won't?"

"They call me to complain about each other instead of talking to one another. I can't be the go between. I live in

New York. They live in Atlanta and my parents are behaving like children. I have two kids. I can't handle any more."

"Duly noted." He laughed. "What else?"

I paused. "I have to tell Em I can't be in her bridal party. I have to hurt her feelings when I don't want to—all for the sake of my best friend, who might not even be my best friend anymore because she's not speaking to me."

"She'll speak to you. Just give her some time to cool off."

"You warned me."

"I did."

"I was kind of hoping for a different outcome, but everything just got all…messy."

He yawned. "Welcome to life."

"What's that smell?" Mrs. Nowacki asked the next morning.

I stared at her bleary eyed. "I have two infants. I'm pretty sure it's coming from one of them."

She sniffed again, raising her nose to the air in my direction, reminding me of Jasper when he went to the park. "No. It is most definitely coming from you. Why do I smell…fish? You eat all that lox by yourself in middle of night, didn't you?"

"As fond as I am of lox…and my ability to pack it away, no. I didn't eat all twenty pounds of lox in my freezer."

"But you smell like the fish."

"I hung out at Mother Shucker the other day. Seafood smell clings to clothing," I said quickly.

Her eyes bored into mine. "You tell the truth. Now."

"That is the truth, I…" My jaw slackened. "No. No, no, no, no. It's not possible." I darted over to the trashcan, opened it, and pulled out an empty plastic bottle.

"What is that?" Mrs. Nowacki asked.

"I was attempting to jumpstart my brain function by downing a bottle of krill pills."

Mrs. Nowacki's lips twitched. "What is end result? Is your brain function better?"

My shoulders slumped "No. No higher brain function. And apparently my odor is less than stellar. What's wrong with me?"

"How do you mean?"

"My life is a joke," I stated. "I smell like krill, I have baby fluids on my shirt, I lose my train of thought halfway through a conversation, I take out senior citizens at Zumba. My parents are having a mid-life marriage crisis and my best friend won't talk to me. Oh, and my eyebrows still haven't fully grown back."

"Hilda is fine." Mrs. Nowacki said with a wave of her hand. "She has been taking her calcium so no problem with the fall on her leg."

I ran my hands through my hair. "I'd kill for Bailey's in my coffee right now."

"I wouldn't tell," Mrs. Nowacki said with a wink. "As far as your parents, that is their issue. Let them work it out.

Your eyebrows will eventually grow back, but it will take a while. The baby fluid will not be over for years, so best to make your peace with that. Explain to me what happened with Annie."

"Where do we stand on the Bailey's and coffee?" I asked.

"I told you I wouldn't judge."

I thought about it for a moment before shaking my head. "No. I have to be strong. And I have to fit into a bridesmaid dress in March. I don't need empty calories."

"Ah, so this is why Annie is upset. You are bridesmaid to Em."

I nodded. "Aidan told me not to do it because it would hurt Annie's feelings. Stacy told me it was a gray area, but didn't really give me much direction to go on. What do you think?"

"I think you're screwed either way."

I blinked. "Thanks a lot."

"You plan on being friends with Em, yes? Good friends? Confiding friends?"

I nodded.

"And you plan on keeping Annie as your best friend?"

I nodded.

"Yes, then you're screwed. You cannot have them both."

I paused and then walked over to the cabinet where I grabbed a bottle of Bailey's. "Screw the empty calories. Mama needs a drink."

Chapter 15

Mom Blog Entry:
   Make the crying stop.
   Make.
   The.
   Crying.
   Stop.

The front door opened and I waited.
Waited like a spider for a bug to fly into my web.

Aidan flipped on the light in the kitchen. He set his keys and cellphone down on the counter and then his eyes landed on me.

He stilled. "How long have you been sitting there?"

"Long enough."

"In the dark? It's only seven…"

"I needed the element of theatrics."

"Well, mission accomplished."

I slowly rose from the couch and walked toward him, stopping when I was right in front of him. "I know where you've been." I traced the front of his gray T-shirt with my finger.

"You don't know where I've been," he denied.

I leaned forward and sniffed. "I know *exactly* where you've been. I can smell it on you." I inhaled deeply. "You're covered in sin, Aidan…"

"It's not what you think—"

I gently pushed against his chest. "Don't deny it. You were at the strip club!"

"I wasn't!"

"You were! You were at the chicken strip club and you ordered the chicken deluxe sandwich with extra special sauce!" I sniffed him again. "And a chocolate shake. I can't believe you went to our place without me!"

"I know how hard you're working to get your body back. I didn't want to be your downfall."

"You coming in smelling like fried chicken is the equivalent of waving a donut in front of a diabetic." I paused. "Oh. A donut—"

"Sibby…"

The front door opened and Caleb and Em walked in with Jasper. They'd had him all day so I could attempt to get work done.

Jasper ran over to me, but quickly diverted his direction and launched himself into Aidan's arms.

Aidan swiped at his face and grimaced as he lowered Jasper to the floor. "Jasper just snuck one in and licked the roof of my mouth."

"Karma," I muttered.

"What did we walk into?" Em asked. "I'm sensing some tension."

"My husband is a chicken clucker," I stated with a glare at Aidan who rolled his eyes.

"Don't you mean a—what's a chicken clucker?" Caleb asked, going to the fridge and helping himself to a beer.

"It's a person who eats fried chicken, lies about it, and then doesn't even bring home a doggy bag for his wife," I huffed.

Em nodded. "Total chicken clucker."

"Of the highest order!" I looked at Em. "How was Jasper today?"

"Adorable. Perfect. I want a puppy."

"Not tonight, honey. I have a headache," Caleb said.

She shot him a grin. Em turned her attention back to me. "Did you get any work done?"

"A bit. Not as much as I would've liked. Mrs. Nowacki still needed me to use my breasts to feed the twins, so I was kind of at their mercy off and on all day."

"Riiiight."

I glanced at the boys who were shooting the shit and I looked at Em.

"Hey, can we talk a second?" I asked her softly.

We headed to the corner of the living room, which wasn't exactly private. I waved Em down to the couch. She perched her pixie body onto the cushions and looked up at me and waited.

"I need you to know two things," I began. "One. I'm so

happy you and Caleb are getting married. Two. Even though I think you're marvelous, and I know we're going to be friends *forever*, I can't be in your wedding party."

She stared at me for a long moment. "Annie?"

I nodded. I didn't go into details. The details weren't necessary.

"I understand."

"You do?"

"Well, sure," she said with a smile. "I'm not surprised, Sibby. Women are territorial."

"She's not in love with Caleb," I hastened to add. "So, I don't want you to think it's about him."

"I know it's not about him. I never really—well, I guess in the beginning, I was worried about them. His feelings for her." Her brow furrowed in pensive thought. "But it's about you. She thinks I'm stealing you from her. Combined with the fact that I'm going to marry her ex." She shrugged. "I get it. That's all I'm saying."

"You're not mad?" I asked. "That I have to back out of the wedding party?"

"I'm not mad at all," she assured me. "Disappointed? Yes. But I get it."

"You're like, the most understanding person in the entire world. How are you so even keeled?"

She looked over her shoulder at Caleb and smiled. "I'm happy, you know? I got what everyone hopes they find. He's wonderful. And I can't—I'm not going to get caught up in something that's not really even about me. You know?"

"I do."

"You're still coming to the bachelorette party, right? I mean, it's not for a few months yet, but you're in?"

"I'm in. Unless it's a strip joint. I can't get excited about penis straws and chlamydia."

"I don't know anyone that would get excited about chlamydia," she said with a laugh. "I told my best friend under no circumstances am I wearing a tiara or sucking from a penis straw." Her eyes twinkled with humor. "She's in brainstorming mode, so she's running ideas past me. I have full approval and there will be no surprises. I don't do surprises."

"I sometimes think my life is one giant surprise after another." I shook my head. "Are you hungry? Have you guys eaten?"

"Yeah, we've eaten."

I pressed a hand to my chests. "My boobs are hot."

"Er—yeah, they are. I guess?"

I laughed. "The twins will be awake soon and then I'll have to feed them. That's what I meant."

"Oh, I see." She smiled. "How are you doing? I mean, since we last talked. Really talked."

I nodded slowly. We hadn't discussed my mental state since we'd gone for drinks and a couple's massage.

"I think I'm doing okay," I admitted. "Having Aidan not constantly at the bar has helped. Mrs. Nowacki has been a lifesaver with the twins. But I've also been doing more *me* stuff. Today I got through five whole pages of edits. It's slow going, but it's going. I really can't thank you guys enough for taking Jasper for the day. I don't want him to feel neglected."

I looked at Jasper who was asleep on the couch. He made me smile.

"You're juggling a lot."

"Yeah, but I think I'm getting a handle on it. Yet I do feel like I'm one disaster away from it all imploding."

Em laughed. "I feel that way and I don't even have kids."

"Everyone said my life was going to change once the

babies came. And I heard them. At least I thought I heard them," I amended. "But knowing and doing are sometimes very different."

"Would you go back?" she asked. "I mean, knowing how hard it is now, do you ever think, well, what would your life look like if you'd decided not to have kids?"

"Since I got knocked up by accident, I don't think the choice was really mine. Not in the end." My gaze drifted to the nursery where my children slept. "They are the hardest thing I've ever done, and it's not going to get easier. Sure, they'll get older and at some point they'll both be in school and take care of themselves to some extent, but I'll worry about other things because I love them."

I exhaled. "No. I don't wish for my old life. I mean, yes, part of me still mourns the loss of my ability to be able to do what I wanted when I wanted. But I don't know, Em. I feel like having kids is more than just providing for them. It also forced me to become an adult."

"You weren't an adult before?" she asked in confusion.

"Technically, yes. I had a career. I was married, and my checking account was never overdrawn. Those are all wins." I grinned. "I guess, becoming a mom made me level up, you know? What I want is now secondary to their needs. It's taught me patience. It's taught me how to exist in this weird sleep deprived state of love and loathing. What that's done to me is—well, no words really.

"I didn't know if I even wanted kids," I told her. "But it was like the universe knew better—and so it made sure a condom failure would result in the two best things I've ever done."

"You're kind of awesome. You know that?"

I snorted. "I'm just taking it one day at a time."

"What's that smell?" Caleb asked, pulling my attention.

"What smell?" Aidan asked.

Caleb's brow furrowed. "I don't know, it smells like…
salmon. Your whole apartment has the faintest aroma of
salmon."

I moaned. "It's krill, and—stop laughing, Aidan."

I climbed the stairs to Annie's apartment. My steps
were slow but resolute. I'd come armed with something she
couldn't say no to. The chocolate raspberry soufflé from
Baked. It was Annie's favorite. It would surely get her to
talk to me. If not, I'd shove a forkful of the chocolaty
goodness into her mouth and then talk to her while she
chewed.

I stood outside her door and raised my hand to knock,
but the sound of heated voices compelled me to stop.

The door was thin, and I could make out the muffled
fight fairly easily.

"Why won't you move in with me?" Mills demanded.

"I told you why," Annie said. "I have to dedicate my
time to my career right now."

"And moving in with me would be a detriment to that?
How do you figure?"

"Your apartment is too far away," she said. "I don't
want to spend all my time commuting from Manhattan

when I know I'll have to be at Mother Shucker at five in the morning most mornings."

"So, I'll move in here. Problem solved. I don't mind commuting into the city."

"This place is too small."

"Then we'll get a bigger place."

"Mills. No. I like it here. I like my life the way it is. Why are you trying to force me to change it?"

"I'm not trying to force you to change it. I just want to take our relationship to the next level, but you keep putting on the brakes."

"I'm just not ready," she said. "I'm sorry, Mills. I really am, but I told you I had to take it slow. And now I feel like I'm being pressured into something that I'm not ready for. Maybe in a few months, after Mother Shucker opens…"

"You'll find an excuse then, too," he said, his tone sounding defeated. "A few months won't make a difference. You either want to live with me or you don't."

His statement hung in the air as he waited for her to reply.

"I don't," she said softly. "I don't want to live with you."

"Why? Because of Caleb?"

"What does he have to do with anything?"

I should've knocked on the door and alerted them to my presence, but I couldn't. I wanted to hear what Annie had to say more than I wanted to practice the common decency of not eavesdropping.

"This has *nothing* to do with Caleb."

He laughed, but it wasn't in amusement. "Like hell it doesn't."

"Mills," she began. "If this had anything to do with Caleb, the Annie of old would've moved in with you the first time you asked. She would've dived into a relationship with you in hopes of trying to forget that she caused someone she cared about a great deal of pain. The Annie of old would have gotten lost in you because that would've been easy. Don't you see? I want this to work. I want *us* to work. But I can't do something before I'm ready. I won't make the same mistake with you that I made with Caleb."

Point for Annie, she actually sounded mature. She sounded like she wasn't spewing bullshit. But I knew her better than anyone—and even I knew there was something she wasn't saying.

"I can't keep having this same fight with you. You're ready for something and I'm just not."

"He's getting married, you know."

"I know."

"Will your answer change after he ties the knot?"

She didn't reply to his statement. Instead she said, "You should sleep at your place tonight."

"Gladly."

The door opened before I had a chance to pretend I hadn't just heard them air their dirty laundry.

"Sibby," Mills said in surprise. "Hello."

"Hey," I said, holding up the bakery box. "I came with dessert."

Mills looked at Annie over his shoulder. She was standing in the doorframe, a T-shirt slipping off her shoulder, her blond hair in a messy bun. She looked exhausted, and not just because she'd been burning the candle at both ends.

"I've got to go," Mills muttered. He hadn't even bothered trying to come up with a decent lie.

He brushed past me and took the stairs quickly.

Annie's hand was on the propped open doorway. "You're here."

"Yup."

"How much did you hear?" Her blue eyes were curious but not hostile. If anything, they looked sad.

"Pretty much all of it," I admitted. "Listen, I don't have endless amounts of time. I've left the twins full and in clean diapers with Aidan, but they're gonna have to feed in approximately two hours. I've already pumped six ounces. I tried a prepackaged boobie smoothie recipe for my mom blog to see if I could get myself to produce more milk for the nuggets and it's turned me into a leaking milk volcano. If my kids don't eat from me, I'm gonna explode."

"You're really dramatic. You know that?"

I held up the bakery box. "I brought your favorite."

She paused, looking like she was weighing letting me in. Finally, she moved away from the door, and I walked inside.

Annie took the bakery box and went to the kitchen. "I'm not bothering with plates."

"Preach."

"And we're using plastic forks."

"I'm down."

She opened a cabinet and pulled out two glasses. "We have a problem."

"What?" I asked, setting my purse down.

Annie glanced at me over her shoulder a grinned. "I'm all out of milk. Fill her up?" She held out a glass toward me.

I laughed. "Shut up."

She grinned and set the glasses down. "Just kidding. I've got some milk in here."

Once we were seated at her tiny kitchen table, the pastry box between us, I asked, "Where do we start?"

She handed me a plastic fork. "You start on one side, I'll start at the other, and we'll stop when we reach the center."

"No." I shook my head. "I meant, what do we tackle first? Oh, I know. How about the fact that it's been days and you haven't returned my calls or texts?"

"I needed some time."

"You don't get time. Not away from me."

"Okay, psycho." She smiled slightly and then dove into the raspberry soufflé. "Hmm. It tastes different this time."

"Really?" I tried my own bite. "Tastes the way it always tastes."

"Nope." She shook her head. "It tastes like guilt and an apology."

"You!" I flung a piece of chocolate at her. It landed on the table with a splat because I couldn't have actually done it well enough to hit her. She wasted no time scooping it up and shoving it into her mouth.

"I'm sorry," I said with sincerity. "I didn't mean to hurt you."

"I know. But you did."

I nodded. "Yeah."

"But I don't think I was fair to you, either. I reacted—well, emotionally. I just felt like she was stealing you away. Sure, it starts with being a bridesmaid, but that's just an entry point."

"I backed out. Told her I couldn't do it. She understood."

"Okay, now I feel even worse." She groaned. "I don't want it to be a me or her thing. And I know I made it into that. But she already has *everything*, you know? Caleb—and a life with him. Shiny hair. Perfect teeth. I couldn't handle her taking you away from me."

"Okay, first of all. You broke up with Caleb. You didn't want a life with him. Not in the end. Right?"

"Right."

"You have shiny hair, too."

"Not lately. I haven't had time to go to the salon."

I rolled my eyes. "You have perfect teeth. It's actually stupid how white and straight and pearly your teeth are."

She beamed at me, showing off said white teeth.

"And me?" I said softly. "No one will ever come between us. No one will ever steal me away. It's not possible. You're my family. You were in my life before Aidan, and when I inevitably drive him away with my theatrics and inability to quit eating sweets and the resulting four-hundred-pound heifer I'll become, then you'll be there for me."

"That man will never leave you. He worships you."

"I have no idea why."

"Because, he, too, likes to play alien warlord in the bedroom. Even though he claims it's just for you." She winked.

We ate in silence for a few moments and then she asked, "Do you mean what you said?"

"Every bit of it."

"Family?"

"Until the bitter end."

She laughed and nodded. "Thanks. It's so hard sometimes. I don't talk to my parents, my uncle is a good guy, but we're not super close. I have Wells, but he likes to fish and lives in Montauk."

"What about Mills?" I asked gently. "He seems like he wants to be your family. If you let him."

She nodded. "Yeah."

"Are you self-sabotaging?"

Annie paused in thought for a moment and then said matter-of-factly, "No."

"If you're not self-sabotaging, then what's the real reason you don't want to move in with Mills?"

"The real reason is because I'm too focused on my career to take that next step. I feel like if I moved in with Mills now, then I'd start to feel guilty about not being home all the time."

My face screwed up into a picture of confusion. "But you don't feel guilty now because you live by yourself?"

"Yeah."

"That's weird logic."

"Not really." She sighed. "If I moved in with Mills, I'd have to check in with him constantly. When are you gonna be home? What's your day look like tomorrow? I want to see you for dinner."

"You sound like the same old version of yourself. Commitment-phobe."

"It blew up, okay?" Annie lashed out. "It all blew up with Caleb. Where would we be right now if I hadn't moved in and we'd left space to miss each other?"

"What's the name of your therapist?"

"Dr. Shufflebarger. Why?"

"Yeah. Give me his number. I want to call him and tell him to up your dosage."

She rolled her eyes.

"You're not doing yourself any favors by being gun shy."

"I'm not gun shy!"

"Then what are you?"

"Not in love with Mills!"

She dropped that bomb at the same moment she smacked the table, the edge of her hand hitting the bakery box, which in turn sent the remainder of the chocolate soufflé flying into my lap.

I stared at it for a moment and then looked at her. "Did we switch bodies?"

Annie groaned and then hopped up. "Don't move. I'll get a plate."

"And do what?"

"Scrape it off onto the plate. I'm not throwing this thing away. I don't care if it does have cotton fuzz and Jasper fur on it."

Once we got me sort of cleaned up, I looked at her. "Let's go back to that last thing I got you to finally admit."

She sighed. "I feel like a grade A asshole."

"You are."

"Hey!"

"For not telling him," I said gently.

"Mills is the hottest and sweetest guy I've ever dated. You want me to break his spirit by telling him I don't love him?"

"No. I want you to tell him that you care for him too much to fake a relationship that you don't see having a future."

"You heard him. You heard how he gets. He won't let me off the hook."

"I thought Annie 2.0 owned her shit," I pointed out.

"Annie 3.0 needs to be a cold ruthless bitch and smother Annie 2.0's tender heart."

"Annie 1.0 was a cold ruthless bitch who needed to grow into a mature Annie 2.0."

"Annie 2.0 is fucking confused about which version of herself she's supposed to be," she replied.

"Tell Mills," I said. "Be truthful, but kind."

"I'm not sure that's in my DNA."

"Try," I said. "Rats."

"What?"

"I think I've sprung a leak. I gotta go." I got up from the table and headed to the front door. "Are we okay?"

"Yeah, of course we're okay." She blew out a breath air and followed me to the door. "This adulting thing…"

"Yeah?"

"Whose idea was it? Because I'm not sure I'm a fan."

Chapter 16

Mom Blog Entry:
    Some species eat their young.
    Just sayin'.

I opened the front door and was immediately pounced on by Jasper. I gently pushed him away when he attempted to lick the chocolate off the hem of my shirt.

"Down, mutt. Chocolate isn't good for you." I closed

the door and walked into the kitchen and set my bag on the counter.

Aidan muted the TV and got up from the couch to greet me. After he kissed me hello, he stood back and glanced down at me and grinned.

"I didn't do this," I said. "It was Annie."

"That's low, Sibby. Blaming your best friend for your clumsiness."

"I'm serious," I said with a laugh. "She caused this accident."

"Hmmm." He leaned in to kiss me again. "I missed you."

"Yeah?"

"Yeah."

He started getting handsy and I couldn't say I hated it. "Let me check on the babies first. I feel like I've been away from them for a month."

"It's been two hours."

"And yet part of me feels like it's missing." I shook my head and we headed toward the nursery. Jasper nosed his way through the crack of the door and settled down onto his dog bed and closed his eyes.

Sophie and Oliver were asleep on their backs, fists clenched. Oliver was bigger than Sophie. They were only a few months old and already my heart was in danger of breaking—they were growing too fast.

I must've made a noise because Aidan was gently leading me out of the nursery so we wouldn't wake them up.

He closed the door. "What's wrong?"

"I'm missing everything," I blurted out, my eyes stinging with tears.

He frowned. "I'm not following. You're with them twenty-four seven."

"And yet I still feel like I'm missing things."

"I have a solution."

"What?"

"We're going to ignore work and careers, goal aspirations, friends, and just stare at our kids. How's that?"

I gave a watery grin.

He smiled back and then wrapped an arm around me. "You're doing everything you're supposed to be doing. Okay? Don't feel guilty about wanting time away, or time to yourself, or time to work on your book, or time with your best friend. How is Annie? Are you guys okay?"

I nodded. "Yeah. We're okay." I bit my lip so I wouldn't say more.

"What? What's that look for?"

"Nothing."

"I don't believe you."

My brow furrowed. "I don't know if I should tell you."

"Oh, well, now you *have* to tell me. Unless she swore you to secrecy with your secret handshake?"

"No. There was no secret handshake this time." I paused.

"Well? You can't keep me in suspense."

"You're such a gossip whore," I teased.

"I admit to no such thing."

"Uh huh. The other day at the grocery store you weren't casually browsing the headlines of *US Weekly*?"

"It was *People,* and we're getting off topic," Aidan said. "Come back to me. Tell me what you're not sure you want to tell me."

"Annie is breaking up with Mills."

Aidan shrugged. "Oh, that."

"What do you mean, *oh that? Oh, that* is not common knowledge. It just became *my* knowledge."

"Uh huh. What reason did she give you for wanting to break up with Mills?"

"Because she's not in love with him."

"Right. Because she's in love with Caleb."

"What? No! She's over him."

Aidan set his hands on my shoulders and stared into my eyes. "She bailed us out the night of our soft launch. Why?"

"Because you're my husband, and I'm her best friend, and she didn't want you to fail. And because we paid her. A lot."

"And? Because she's still in love with him."

"She's not. She swears she's not."

"Then why did she get so upset about you being part of Em's bridal party?"

"Because she's a woman! And we have emotions that run wild. Wild emotions. Me being in Em's bridal party had nothing to do with her feelings for Caleb—which she doesn't have, because she's over him!"

"You really believe she's over him?"

"Yes."

"Why? Because she told you?"

"Well, yeah."

"She's not over him. You're naive if you think that."

"Watch it. You may be the father of my children, but you do not get to call me naive."

He chuckled. "I'm not trying to pick a fight with you, but I am trying to get you to realize that she's *not* over him. Even if she says she is."

"Okay, let's play a game. Let's say she's not over him. So what?" I demanded. "She's not interfering in Caleb and Em's relationship. Em is her wine distributer. She's not causing any waves."

"Yet."

I rolled my eyes. "I thought you wanted to have sex with me."

"Are you trying to distract me from this conversation?"

"Yes. Is it working?"

"Absolutely."

"Then you better hurry up and climb on top of me before the children wake up and demand our full attention."

"For a romance author, you're not so good with the seduction."

"I just offered to get naked and do dirty things with you. How much seducing do you need?"

"Why am I always coming to Brooklyn?" Zeb asked the moment I let him into my apartment. "You never come to Manhattan." He set his gym bag down by the door.

"Manhattan is so far away. And Brooklyn is cool. In fact, I think you and Terry need to buy a place in Greenpoint."

"Is your goal to have all your friends live within a five-block radius of you?"

"Uh, yeah. Now we just need to get Nat to move back and my life will be complete."

He shook his head. "Nat is strangely fond of Texas. I don't know why."

"They have good barbecue."

"Do they?"

"And cowboys. They wear tight pants."

Zeb paused. "Maybe we should take a trip to see her."

"Or I could make Aidan dress up in chaps and we could pretend we went to Texas."

"Better. Think he'd be a good sport and do it?"

I had to bite my tongue so I didn't spill the beans that Aidan was more adventurous than people knew. Not everyone needed to know about Shrau.

"Yeah, I think he'd do it."

"Are you going to tell me why you harassed me into coming to Greenpoint? With my gym bag?" he asked.

"We're going to a yoga class."

"You're kidding."

"You do yoga."

"Yeah, *I* do yoga." He grinned. "But *you* don't do yoga."

"I'm going to do this brand of yoga. I downloaded the local gym app and looked at the schedule and it said Fondue Yoga. I've never heard of that type of yoga, but anything that involves cheese is a win in my book."

He looked at me curiously. "Show me this class on the app."

I went to my cell phone, which rested on the kitchen table. I swiped it open and got to the app in question and showed him the screen.

His lips twitched. "Sibby?"

"Yeah?"

"This doesn't say fondue yoga."

"What? Are you serious?"

"It says *Fun, Do Yoga*. How the hell did you mistake that as fondue yoga?"

"I don't know," I murmured. "I think—I think I was projecting that I wanted to combine something I loved with something I hated. It's probably the epic sleep deprivation that caused this."

I glared at the fresh bottle of krill pills on the counter. I marched over to it, swiped it off the counter, and dumped it into the garbage. The first bottle had gotten me into trouble.

"What was that about?"

"Krill pills. Not only did they make me smell like salmon, but they've done nothing for my brain function."

"I'm so lost."

I closed my eyes and held in a sob.

I'd really, really wanted to eat cheese and lie on the floor and stretch.

"We should still go to the class. You might actually enjoy it," he said with a wry grin.

"I'm losing my mind. I swear I am."

"Yoga will help with clarity. Trust me."

"Fine. I'll change and then we can go. Where do we stand on the cheese situation?"

"Cheese after. With a glass of wine?"

"Now you're speaking my language."

I went to the bedroom and quickly threw on my yoga clothes before coming back into the living room.

"Your house is obscenely quiet. Where is everyone?"

"Mrs. Nowacki and Aidan took Jasper and the twins to the park. I was working for a while before you came over."

He grabbed his gym bag and we left the apartment. The back of summer had broken, and it was nearly Autumn. The leaves on the trees had yet to turn, and I wondered when they did, if Aidan and I could spare a few days and drive Upstate and see the fall colors.

"Speaking of husbands," I said. "How is yours? I still haven't seen your wedding photos."

"The photographer still has them," Zeb said. "And Terry will kill me if I show them to you before they're doctored. He's good though…"

"Spit it out," I said when I realized he'd trailed off.

"My husband is ready for a baby. He's full steam ahead on adopt a cute Asian baby."

"And you're not ready?" I guessed.

"We like, just got married. His uterus is in overdrive."

"Why is this a theme in my life?" I asked with a laugh.

"What?"

"My friends. Who are all married or committed. One is ready for something and the other is digging in their heels."

"What other friends are you talking about? Stacy is an infant and just broke up with her musician boyfriend."

My lips were sealed on that situation, so I just said, "True."

"Annie? What's she disagreeing about in her relationship?"

My lips were sealed on the truth of that, too. "Oh, just that Mills wants her to move in, but she's not ready."

"Hmmm."

"Don't say it. Don't even think it."

"Say or think what?" He looked at me with his eyebrows raised.

"You know."

"Do I?"

"You're Zeb. You know all there is to know, all the time."

"Is it what I think it is?"

"No. It's not about Caleb," I said.

"Okay. Good. Because aye yai yai. I don't have the energy for these youngins and their relationship ups and downs."

I smirked at him. "I think you might be ready for a baby, even if you say you aren't, because right now, you just sounded old."

"Take it back, Sibby Goldstein-Kincaid."

"No. I stand by my assessment. Plus, I need a friend with a kid. I'm dying here."

We got to the gym and I opened the door, letting Zeb enter first. It was a nice gym and didn't even have that sweaty rubber mat smell most gyms seemed to have. I checked us in at the front desk and presented two guest passes to the desk attendant.

"Why don't you have a monthly membership?" Zeb asked as we headed to the back toward the yoga rooms.

"Because that would mean I'd be committed, and if I commit to a membership then I'm obligated to go."

"You and Aidan should work out together. Buddy system."

"He works out with Caleb."

"Then drag Stacy or Em to be your buddy."

"Em is into hardcore S&M."

"TMI, Sib."

"I meant, she's into Spinning and Meditation."

We entered the yoga studio. The lights were dim and there was a sign that asked us to take off our shoes. Mats were in the corner. We each grabbed one and set up shop on the far side of the room.

A few minutes later, the door was shut and we were all lying flat on our backs and instructed to take deep, calming breaths.

Everything in yoga was tied to our breath, apparently.

Zeb was a limber yogi, but I struggled with balance and a new center of gravity.

"Now, we're going to do what's called a pigeon move," the super hippie yogi instructor said, her voice as calm as a summer breeze. She demonstrated the position and we all followed suit.

"We're going to hold this pose for a few minutes. Some of you may experience emotion bubble from within you like water from a natural spring. This is more than a stretch, it's a good way to release emotion buried deep within you. Don't fight your feelings, just breathe."

I bowed my head until it touched the floor and breathed for a few minutes. I was so comfortable with the position that I almost didn't hear the instructor tell us to switch to the left side.

Then I started to cry.

Loud, ugly tears.

"Sibby? What's wrong?" Zeb asked, suddenly at my side. "Is it the position? Are you feeling through some things?"

I shook my head. "I'm crying because I can't get myself *out* of the position!"

"How is that possible?" Zeb demanded.

"My leg cramped and I can't move!"

It took Zeb on one side and the yogi instructor on the other to lift me off the ground. Once they were sure I had my footing, they released me.

"I could really go for that fondue and glass of wine now," I said to Zeb, rubbing feeling back into my leg.

"We have a very nice juice bar," the yogi instructor said.

"Wine is juice," Zeb said. "Well, at least that's how Sibby and I categorize it."

The yogi girl blinked and then awkwardly left us alone

so she could get back to tending to her flock of limber pigeons.

"Let's go," I mumbled.

We returned our mats to the corner and then we grabbed our stuff and shoes and got out of there.

"I need you to be honest with me," I said when we were in the main area, sitting on couches to put on our shoes.

"Your eyebrows are growing in, but they look like that fuzz from a leafy plant you find in the forest."

"Yeah, okay, not the direction I was going, but sure." I took a deep breath. "Am I a loser?"

"What?"

"A loser. An L-7 weenie? An Oscar dog?"

"Did you just quote *The Sandlot* to me?"

"Maybe."

"If you can do *The Mighty Ducks*, I'm pretty sure I'll turn straight and beg for your hand in marriage."

"Quack, quack, quack, Mr. Ducksworth."

He grinned.

I grinned.

"Why do you think you're a loser?" he asked.

"I don't think I'm a loser."

"Then why did you ask?"

I paused. "No, I lied. I do think I'm a loser."

"Explain and expand."

"I can't even do yoga right."

"Okay, I'm gonna let you in on a secret. No one knows how to do yoga. Not really, we all say we're breathing the right way, but who the fuck knows."

"I hate kale."

"Then congrats, you have taste buds."

"I thought we were doing fondue yoga. Did I really

think that was a thing? Am I dumb? Did having kids make me dumber?"

"You graduated college, right?"

"Like that proves anything. You pay for the degree, you get a piece of paper."

"Don't tell that to people who went to Harvard Med School."

"We're getting off topic."

"What's really going on here?"

We picked up our bags and left the gym, hitting the sidewalk and breathing in the air. I lifted my nose and turned.

"There's a taco truck, one point two blocks away," I stated, hoofing it in the direction of the aroma.

"How do you know that?" he demanded, scrambling to keep up with my sudden brisk pace.

"One, my nose totally changed when I got pregnant. I feel like a ferret who can sniff out a single cube of cheese in a football field."

"Exaggeration, maybe?"

"No, really. The other day, I found a cube of cheese between the couch cushions."

"Please tell me you didn't eat it."

"I didn't eat it. I have limits."

"Sexual or food related?"

"Moving on," I said with a glare. "Two, I'm pretty sure since I'm at a calorie deficit, my nose is working overtime." I sniffed the air again. "Yup—there's five *carne asada* tacos with my name on them. It's not cheese and wine, but it might be better for my diet."

Sure enough, we found the taco truck right across the street from a brewery. It was late afternoon on a weekday, so it wasn't busy, and we ate our food at a picnic table.

"You never did explain to me what this loser talk is all about."

I swallowed and then took a drink of my water.

And all I could think about was having an ice-cold soda.

"I don't—I want to take a break from writing romance." The moment the words were out, I wanted to shove them back inside my mind.

"I don't see why that would spawn ideas of loserdom."

"I want to write a children's book," I admitted. "And I want Nat to illustrate it."

He blinked at me for a few minutes. "I think that would be amazing."

"Yeah? Even though I've got this great momentum with romance?"

"Is your soul dying?" he asked. "I mean, when you think of writing romance?"

"No. I just—I want to try something else. I feel like," I paused, "I had children and it opened up this weird new creative avenue. I write in my mom blog daily. I'm testing products. I'm loving this new part of my life and frankly, I was terrified I wouldn't."

I looked at his last taco. "Are you going to eat that?"

"Buzz off. This beef is mine."

"Rats." I sighed. "I wonder if it's bad form to get another taco."

"I say do it. They're small anyway. Besides, I'm pretty sure Aidan doesn't mind your curves if that's what you're worried about."

"I was actually worried about going to the grocery store and having a woman ask me when I'm due."

"Why would you worry about that?"

"Because it already happened."

"Oh." He made a face. "Then maybe you shouldn't get a sixth taco."

"My heart wants another taco." I sighed. "But yeah, you're right. You're so lucky."

"How so?"

"When you have a baby, you won't lose your figure."

He grinned. "Perks of being a sexy gay man."

"You really don't think I'm a loser?"

"You're Sibby," he said. "You're hilarious and sometimes destructive, but you're the light in a sea of darkness."

I screwed up my face and felt my eyes prick with tears. "You bastard. You're making me cry in public."

His gaze dipped. "I also seem to be making you leak. Why is that? Is it time to feed?"

"No." I touched my breast and weighed it in my hand.

No. Shame.

None.

"I pumped earlier."

"Then what's the deal?"

"When someone cries, my milk lets down."

"But you were the one doing the crying."

I paused in thought. "What the fuck is in those boobie smoothies?"

"Boobie what?"

"Don't you read my Mom blog?"

"Not if I can help it."

"I value you for your honesty. Do you mind giving me another compliment? I'm still feeling fragile."

Mom Blog Entry:

My children have now pooped on me, peed on me and vomited on me.

Maybe we need some space.

"How do I look?" Mrs. Nowacki asked.

"For?" I prodded, taking in her appearance. For once she wasn't wearing a turtleneck, but her hair was still in a tight bun and her makeup looked like a showgirl in Vegas had done it.

"I have date with midwife."

I frowned. "I don't understand—you have a date with a midwife?"

"I have date with man who is midwife. He helps deliver babies."

"Yes. I know what a midwife is. So, you're going on a date with a man who is a midwife? Do I have that right?"

"Right."

"What time is your date?"

"Three. We are going for the coffee and pastry."

I didn't have the heart to tell Mrs. Nowacki that her look was better slated for an evening in a dim restaurant, but she was putting herself out there and meeting people, and I wasn't going to stop her.

"Well, you look nice. What's his name?" I asked.

"Jesse."

Jesse the midwife. Okay then.

"You going to the gym?" she asked, taking in my appearance.

Yoga pants and two sports bras underneath one of Aidan's gray T-shirts.

And a fanny pack.

"No. I found this Greenpoint mom group that power walks with their strollers. I'm meeting up with them in a few minutes."

"How you find out about this group?"

"A meet-up app. We'll see. I'm not cut out for Zumba, spinning, or yoga. That leaves walking. Hopefully I can do that without tripping over my own two feet."

I wouldn't let Mrs. Nowacki help me wrangle the twins into the double stroller. She was dressed for her date and I knew the twins were liable to mess up her outfit. They'd already both thrown up on me once this morning, but they were fed, changed, and ready to embark on a Brooklyn power walk.

I said goodbye to Jasper who looked sad that he wasn't coming along. "You're not well behaved enough on the leash for me to take you. I can't handle you and the twins alone."

He whined but then lowered his head to his paws and lay down.

"I want to hear everything about your date later tonight," I told Mrs. Nowacki.

She nodded and smiled. "I will need girl talk."

With a wave, I left the apartment and began maneuvering the stroller through the foyer of the apartment building. I got out to the sidewalk and slid my sunglasses onto my nose.

I meandered my way down the tree-lined street, enjoying the fall air. Maybe after I went on my power walk with the moms I was about to meet, I could swing by Veritas and see if could convince Aidan to take an early dinner.

I got to the park and found the group of moms congregating by the north fence. They all looked svelte and sleek, with full faces of makeup, matching Gucci sunglasses, designer leather fanny packs, and Venti Starbucks cups.

They reminded me of the popular girls' clique from my high school.

The thought made me falter, but I had to remind myself that I was a successful author who, at one point, had been considered hot. Sure, I sometimes had issues with my hair, but otherwise, there was no reason to be nervous.

Shoulders back, push forward, and strut!

"Hi," I greeted with a smile. "I'm Sibby."

The woman standing at the front of the hoard lowered her sunglasses to the bridge of her nose and took me in.

She pushed the sunglasses back up into position and said, "I'm Anya." Anya pointed to the woman next to her. "This is Angelika. With a K."

Angelika with a K waved and then pointed to the twiggy brunette next to her. "Avonlea."

"Like Anne of Green Gables? That Avonlea?"

"I'm Canadian," Avonlea said with a sniff.

"Cool." My eyes went to the last woman.

"I'm Trish."

My eyebrows rose, but I said nothing. I felt like I'd found my way into an alternate reality.

Brooklyn, meet Stepford.

"Your shoe is untied," Avonlea said.

"Oh, thanks."

I immediately dropped to the ground and tied my shoe. When I stood up, I was alone. I blinked and looked around. Four women with strollers were suddenly nowhere in sight.

It was like they'd poofed out of existence.

"Wow," I said to Sophie and Oliver. "We just got Mean Girl-ed."

I pushed their stroller along the pavement through the park, determined to enjoy the day and my walk, regardless of the moms who'd clearly ditched me.

About twenty feet deeper into the park I saw three women sitting underneath a tree, babies in front of them on a checkered blanket.

One of the women with a messy black top bun smiled at me and waved. "Hey!"

I stopped, unsure that she was talking to me. "Hi?"

"We saw what happened," she said with a commiserating smile.

I grimaced. "How stupid did I look?"

"Not stupid at all. They're the ones that were stupid,"

said a boisterous red head with a baby in a sailor outfit sitting in front of her.

"Those were nannies—not moms," the blonde explained as she rubbed the back of the baby at her shoulder.

"Oh, thank God!" I breathed. "They were all so skinny I should've known something was wrong with them."

The brunette laughed and held up a graham cracker to me. "You want to join us?"

"I don't want to intrude," I hedged.

"No, sit," the redhead commanded.

"Okay, thanks." I pushed the stroller onto the grass and left the sleeping twins in their carriage. "I'm Sibby," I introduced.

The brunette's baby was on its back and let out a shriek. She didn't miss a beat; she whipped out a boob, shoved her kid against her chest, and it was quiet once again.

"Ow." The brunette grimaced. "Teeth. I'm Kelsey. The bubbly blonde is Shay, and the angry redhead is Jill."

"I'm not angry," Jill snapped.

"Yes, you are," Shay said with a teasing grin.

Jill sighed and shot me a look. "Apparently my post-partum has resulted in a lot of rage."

"Ah," I said in understanding. "Mine resulted in a lot of tears and not looking at my reflection in the mirror."

"Sibby," the blonde said. "Why does that name sound familiar?"

"Maybe you've heard of me," I said shyly. "I've been known to injure serving staff at most of Greenpoint's restaurants."

Kelsey laughed. "No, I don't think that's it. Your name sounds familiar though."

I scrunched my face up. "I have a blog?"

"Yes!" The redhead snapped her fingers. "You write about maternity products!"

"Oh my god, I love that blog!" Kelsey said. "It's been so helpful. Your article on the boobie smoothies changed my life."

I smiled. "I'm glad I could help."

"Do you want any snacks?" Shay asked. "If you don't want graham crackers, I've got other things. Like Bugles and Funyons."

"I think you guys just became my tribe."

On my way home from the park, my cell phone rang. My mother's name flashed across the screen. Mama Goldstein was ready to Face Time.

I grimaced and then reluctantly answered it, setting the phone down in the stroller's cup holder so I could see the screen.

"Hi," I said.

"Your father is driving me crazy," she stated.

"How can he drive you crazy? You moved out."

"He sends me gifts every day. Two days ago it was a Harry and David gift basket. Yesterday was a dozen red roses. Today? Diamond earrings. The nerve of that man!"

"I fail to see the issue, Ma. You're a Jewess. Diamond earrings are like a cure-all for marriage ailments."

"Don't be glib," she snapped. Her color was high, and for the first time in forever, I noticed that her makeup wasn't perfect and her hair…

"Ma? Is your hair in a messy top bun?"

She stuck her head forward to give me a better angle. "How'd I do?"

"Really well."

"Your eyebrows look like they're growing in."

"Don't change the subject. Let's talk about you and Dad."

"Sending gifts means he thinks I can be bribed into coming home."

"And you're upset because you want words, not presents."

"Yes."

"Did you tell him that?"

She paused.

"Ma," I said with a sigh. "Call Dad. Talk to him."

"No. If he doesn't know how to fix things this late in the game, then I'm not going to tell him."

I suddenly felt teleported back to junior high.

"You look like you're wearing exercise clothes," she said.

"I am."

"You finally joined a gym."

"No, I finally met up with some other hip Brooklyn moms in the park."

I wasn't going to mention that my top lip still tasted of salt and vinegar from the bag of potato chips I'd eaten.

"It's good you're meeting other moms," she said. "It's important to have a group of friends you can drink with once you're done breastfeeding."

"Speaking of breastfeeding. I thought that was a sure-fire way to lose the baby weight."

"I didn't lose the weight until after you were weaned."

"You're kidding. Please tell me you're kidding."

"Nope."

"How did I not know that?"

"I don't know, I'm sure I've mentioned it before."

I shook my head. "How's the business?"

"Booming. Honey, listen I gotta go. And if you talk to your father, don't tell him what I told you."

I counted to three Mississippi before I said, "Okay. Love you."

"Talk to you later."

She hung up just as I got back to the apartment. I maneuvered the massive stroller into the foyer and parked it for a second. I pressed a button and let the phone ring on the other end. I got voicemail.

"Stop sending your wife gifts and actually talk to her." I hung up and shook my head. If my parents didn't get it together soon, I was going to have to do something drastic. Like re-watch all my old favorite rom-coms as research and find a way to force my parents to interact.

I mentally made a note to text Aunt Becca to see if I could get her involved in the shenanigans.

I unlocked the door just as Sophie let out a squawk.

Mrs. Nowacki sprang apart from the man sitting next to her. They were on my couch—and they'd been in the middle of a lip lock.

"Sibby," she greeted with a flushed face. "You're home."

"I live here," I said, momentarily tuning out the fact that I now had two wailing children who needed my attention.

Jasper trotted out of the nursery to greet me and then nose the twins.

Mrs. Nowacki stood up and the man by her side rose as well. His silver hair was pulled back into a ponytail, his beard was long, more Dumbledore, less Gandalf. He wore gold-rimmed spectacles and his bellbottoms were faded and worn.

"Hi," he said with a wide smile, coming toward me, hand outstretched. "I'm Jesse. Nice to meet you."

"You're the midwife," I blurted out, taking his hand and shaking it.

"I am." He beamed.

"I thought you guys were having coffee?" I asked.

"We drink it fast," Mrs. Nowacki said.

I nodded, still unclear about why she'd brought her date back to *my* apartment. Didn't she know anything about men on the internet? And then I realized I'd been the one to set up her online dating profile. I had no one to blame but myself.

"They sound hungry," Jesse said, looking into the stroller. "Do you want me to make them bottles?"

I blinked, and suddenly I didn't care if he was a sociopath that wanted to wear my skin as a coat. At the moment he was a freakin' godsend.

"Sure. That would be really nice."

"I help him," Mrs. Nowacki said. "While you change the *bubelas*."

"Okay."

Mrs. Nowacki grasped Jesse's burly forearm and led him to the kitchen, looking up at him with infatuation.

"You're such a help, Ada," he cooed, pressing a kiss to her nose.

Ugh. I suddenly had sympathy for people who saw Aidan and I together.

I got the twins changed into clean diapers, but Sophie was still shrieking like a spoiled cheerleader at a football game.

Mrs. Nowacki came into the nursery and grabbed her from me and all but shoved a bottle into her mouth. I followed her out into the living room with Oliver in my arms.

Jesse held up another bottle. "I made him this. Here."

"Thank you," I said, taking the bottle and pushing the nipple into Oliver's open mouth.

"How was time in park?" Mrs. Nowacki asked. "Did you do all the walking?"

"Uh. Sure."

In the middle of feeding Oliver, I heard a vibrating noise. I looked around, wondering where I'd left my phone.

"That's me—my pager," Jesse said calmly. "I have to go deliver a baby now."

He leaned over to kiss Mrs. Nowacki's cheek. "I'll call you. Dinner this week?"

She nodded, looking like an excited schoolgirl.

"Sibby, it was a pleasure meeting you."

"Er—yeah. Nice to meet you to," I murmured.

Jasper hopped down from the couch and walked with Jesse to the front door.

"Bye, lad," he said with a stroke to Jasper's head.

The front door shut and Jasper let out a whine.

I looked at Mrs. Nowacki. "You guys hit it off pretty fast."

"Yes." She nodded, continuously patting Sophie.

"We need to establish some ground rules," I said.

"I promise we use protection."

I blinked. "No. I mean—oh God. That is not what I wanted to talk about."

"Then what?"

"You can't bring your internet dates back to my home. Take them to Dorota's."

She shook her head. "That no work. Dorota make amazing pot roast and potatoes. She is also a widow. A black widow."

"She's your best friend."

"Still, I know what she is." Mrs. Nowacki closed one eye as she looked at me. "She is sneaky. And I have no plans to bring back any more internet dates to your home. Jesse is the one."

"The one. The one what?"

"The one who will become second husband."

"Okay, let's dial it back a second. You can't get serious with the first guy you go out with."

"He is not the first man I go out with. I went out with three others before him."

"You need to date around."

She shook her head. "Sibby. You are young so you don't know the ways of the world. What if Aidan died and you were dating again? Eh? Would you date around? Or would you latch on to a man you knew was another good one as soon as you found him? They are so rare."

"That's never gonna happen because I'm going to find a way to make us immortal." I blinked back the threat of tears. "Besides, I can't stomach the idea of living without him. I have to die first."

"Women live longer than men," she pointed out.

I burst into tears. And then Oliver burst into tears. And because Sophie didn't want to be left out, she burst into tears too.

The front door opened and Aidan walked in, his face slackened in shock.

"Oh good!" I blubbered. "You're not dead."

Chapter 18

Mom Blog Entry:

I watched kid shows for four hours the other day. Part of me wanted to see what I was in for once the kids started watching that stuff.

Part of it was I lost the remote and didn't have the energy to get up to change the channel.

"Your mother hasn't driven me this crazy since we

were teenagers," Aunt Becca bemoaned. "You have to help me get rid of her."

"Okay, you just sounded like a mob boss trying to dispose of a body."

"Well…"

"Aunt Becca!"

"I'm sorry! But it's been a nightmare. Your Uncle Michael and I can't ever be alone. Our routine is totally thrown off."

"You don't have to entertain her. She can take care of herself."

"She's a Jewish woman, Sibby. Do you know what that means?"

"I'm a Jewish woman," I pointed out.

"You're a New York Jewish woman. It's not the same."

"I'm so confused where you're going with this." Phone on speaker, resting on the coffee table, I got back to folding baby clothes. There were two mismatching socks that were missing mates, so I mated them together. I didn't care anymore. As long as the kids were wearing clean clothes, I could feel good about motherhood.

"Are you listening to me?" my aunt demanded.

"I'm really trying not to," I said.

"Sibyl Ruth!"

"Rebecca Irene."

"You can't middle name me. I'm your elder."

"I have an idea on how to get Mom and Dad back together."

"I'm all ears."

"I'm going to invite Mom up for a visit. I'm going to book her a suite at The Rex in Manhattan. A day later, I'll have my dad fly up and tell him I booked him a suite at The Rex. Accidentally on purpose, there will be a clerical error where the hotel 'made a mistake' and booked the same room twice. Ooopsie. I'll get my parents in the same place, pay off the hotel, and ask them to lock the door from the outside so they can't get out. Hence, they will be forced to communicate, and then fornicate."

"Did you just say what I think you said?"

"Yes."

"You do realize you just said fornicate…about your parents."

"Hey, Mom is apparently going through a sexual revolution. No doubt she's still hot for my dad even though she's mad at him."

"I've heard hate sex is a thing."

"Yeah, it's a thing. We'll use it. If the hate sex idea fails, we still have the Goldstein charm to fall back on. Mom won't be able to resist the Goldstein charm. I'm pretty sure that's the only reason Aidan married me. Because of my Goldstein charm."

"The Goldsteins have charm?" she quipped.

"I'm hanging up now."

"Sorry, sorry! Yes, I think your idea is oddly solid. Do you think the hotel will aid you in your quest?"

"Oh yes. Annie knows someone who used to work there. She catered his wedding. She'll hook me up."

"Okay. Great."

"Don't spill the beans, okay?"

"Okay. Go team Reunite-the-Goldsteins!"

I didn't say anything.

"We can think of another team name later."

"Sounds good. Bye, Aunt Becca."

I hung up with her and paused, listening for any sounds coming from the nursery, but all was quiet.

I dialed Annie who answered immediately. "I broke up with Mills last night."

"Oh."

"Isn't that why you were calling? To see if I'd done it yet?"

"No. That's not why I was calling. Did you tell me already that you broke up with Mills and I forgot?"

"No. I didn't tell you. I thought about sending a text, but it was two in the morning…"

"I was awake."

"I'll know for next time."

"Are you okay?"

She paused. "Yeah. I think I am. Which tells me I did the right thing."

"How'd he take it?"

"Not well."

"Huh. Poor guy."

"Yeah. Poor guy is right. Honestly, that's one of the reasons I put it off for so long. I knew it was going to break his heart." She sighed. "I'm glad it's off my plate, you know? Like it was weighing on me, but I didn't know how much. And I think this is better for him in the long run."

"Were you kind, at least?"

"Tried to be, but is there ever a good way to tell someone you're not in love with them when they're in love with you?"

"You make a surprisingly rational sort of sense."

"It's what I do now. So, you called. What's up?"

"I need your help getting my parents back together."

"What, do you want me to make oysters as an aphrodisiac?"

"No. They don't need help in that department. Do you remember the wedding you catered for that couple who used to work at The Rex?"

"Alia and Jake? Yeah, what about them?"

"Do you mind giving them a buzz. I have this plan and in order for it to work, I need their connections…"

"You're pretty," I murmured, looking across the restaurant table at my husband.

He grinned. "You're drunk, Kincaid."

"Not drunk. Tipsy."

"Drunk." He laughed. "Because whenever you call me pretty, that's how I know. Men are handsome, rugged. Did you call me those things? No."

"You have nice forearms."

"Yeah, definitely drunk."

"Would you both like to see a dessert menu?" the server asked as he approached, holding out a menu.

"Yes, please," I said, filching it from him. "And will you tell the chef, I thought the areola was delish."

The server blinked.

"She means aioli," Aidan said, his grin so wide I thought it would stretch off his face.

"Ah, right. The aioli. I'll just give you guys a moment…" He walked away, leaving us alone.

"You're fun," Aidan said. "I can't believe I let you convince me to leave our twins with Mrs. Nowacki and her new boyfriend. Aren't we in danger of being the worst parents ever?"

"Well, after what I saw at Zumba I'm pretty sure Mrs.

Nowacki is a closeted bad ass, so I don't think we have anything to worry about. He had a really nice calming presence about him. If he wasn't already a full-time midwife, I would definitely put him on payroll."

"As what? Baby wrangler?"

"Yes. Absolutely."

"Mrs. Nowacki would be out of a job," he pointed out.

"We don't even pay her."

"We've tried, but she refuses to take the money." He grinned. "She's family."

"Did you guys decide on dessert?" the server asked. His presence made me jump.

"Actually," I said. "I'm gonna pass."

"Same." Aidan handed the menu back to the server who then discreetly dropped the check at our table.

"You passed on dessert," Aidan commented. "That's… unusual."

"I've lost five pounds. I've got twenty to go before the wedding. I'm determined, Aidan."

He reached across the table and stroked my jaw. "You're amazing. You know that? Any time you ever put your mind to something, you achieve it."

"I am pretty awesome, huh?" I said with a grin.

He laughed.

"I'm determined to lose weight before the wedding, and I'm determined to get my parents back together. Hanukkah just won't be the same if they're not living together."

"Your plan seems—"

"Genius?"

"I was going to say screwball, but we can use your word."

"I put The Rex Hotel suite on our American Express.

We got a lot of points which I used to buy a Kitchen Aid Mixer."

"We already have a Kitchen Aid Mixer."

"Do Caleb and Em have a Kitchen Aid Mixer?" I asked pointedly. "Two pigeons, one roll."

He grinned. "Pretty sure that's not how the saying goes."

"I made it my own," I said with a wave of my hand. "How are your parents? Please tell me they're still together and happy."

"They're good. Janet called me yesterday to tell me the plumbing has been fixed in Mom and Dad's house, so everything is fine. All the damage has been repaired. And they're visiting Kara in Kentucky."

"Kara is in Kentucky? Why?"

"Apparently, she wanted to learn how to make bourbon."

"I really admire that about Kara. You know? Like, she doesn't do anything the way anyone does it and she just goes for what she wants."

I picked at the paper napkin until it was in tiny pieces. Aidan reached for the check, opened it, and pulled out his credit card.

The server had been waiting for the check presenter to hit the table before swooping in and scooping it up.

"Okay, what's going on with you?" Aidan asked, taking my hands to still my nervous tick.

"What makes you think something's going on?"

"Sibby, you're a terrible actor, and your emotions play across your face. Something is on your mind and you're concerned about it. Is it me? Us?"

"What? No! We're great! I love you so hard."

He smiled slowly. "Then what is it? You can tell me."

"We just found a rhythm, you know? The bar expansion is done. You're back to working normal hours. I see you. The twins see you. We manage to go out, split a bottle of wine, slither against each other naked once in a while. Everything is good. It just feels good."

"You want to shake it up, don't you?"

"Not sexually."

"Thanks for dining with us tonight," the server said with a sigh, setting down the check presenter.

"Thank you!" I said with a grin.

The server left us alone again.

"You have the worst timing," Aidan said. "That poor guy, he has no idea—"

"I want to write children's books," I blurted out.

Aidan cocked his head to the side. "I don't get it. Why is that bad?"

"It's not. It's just—well, I've got this amazing momentum with my career. And I finished my first round of edits and sent the book to Stacy to read, but I don't know, Aidan. It doesn't," I paused, "light up my soul the same way. And if I write children's books, I'm going to have to start over, write under a pen name, and spend a lot of time building a new fan base. I'll be starting at the beginning."

"Is it money you're worried about? You know Veritas is doing very well."

"It's not money I'm worried about. Oddly enough." I shook my head. "Man that's so weird. In my early twenties, I sometimes wondered if I had enough money to order Chinese take-out. And now? You're telling me I can do this and not worry about money."

"Then what has you worried?"

"What if I suck at it?"

"Seriously?"

I nodded.

"You won't suck at it."

"I won't be able to use the power of my mom blog to help."

"Why not?"

"Because it's already linked to my real name, my real persona, the name I publish romance under. No one is going to read their kid a book by an author who writes porn."

I glanced up at the server who stood at the table with a pitcher of water. He sighed.

I sighed.

Aidan sighed.

"I—you know what? I am not ashamed of it," I said, sitting a little straighter in my chair.

"Do you really write porn?" the server asked.

"Porn for women. Sibby Goldstein," I held out my hand to him, "saving relationships one romance novel at a time."

He shook my hand. "My girlfriend loves romance novels. I'll tell her to look you up."

"Thanks. I appreciate that."

The server meandered away to fill water at another table.

"Speaking of porn," Aidan said, clearing his throat. "I found a book under your side of the bed the other day."

"Oh really." I leaned forward. "Did you thumb through it?"

"With a book titled *The Mamasutra,* you're damn right I thumbed through it."

"You want to go home and try the thing on page forty-six?"

"Did I ever tell you that I really like drunk Sibby?"

Aidan I were in the kitchen, the windows of the living room open, letting in the scent of the autumn air. Jasper was spinning in circles attempting to eat his tail. He needed to go to the dog park and burn some energy.

"Operation reunite the parents is a go," I said, hanging up with Annie. I bounced gently, my hand on Oliver's back. He was happy and asleep in his baby carrier. I felt like a kangaroo.

Aidan looked up from feeding Sophie a bottle. "What do you mean?"

"Annie came through for me. She got The Rex staff on board."

"Why haven't we ever stayed at The Rex?"

"Because it's eight hundred a night for a standard room and they don't do coupons."

"Eight hundred—"

"Desperate times," I stated. "And remember the American Express points are paying for a wedding gift. It's a win-win. The vein above your eye is twitching. Did you know that?"

He opened his mouth to say something and then shook his head. He tried again, "When does your mother get here?"

"As soon as I call her."

"And you think she'll come?"

"To get away from my father? Absolutely. To get time with her grand-pierogis, most definitely. She won't admit it outright, but she's jealous of Mrs. Nowacki."

"Mrs. Nowacki who's been arriving later and later in the mornings," Aidan stated with a wide grin. "If I had to guess I'd say she found a new hobby. One far more enjoyable than hanging out with babies."

I nodded. "She's been staying with Jesse. Who owns like, half of Kent Street. He bought a ton of Greenpoint real estate back in the early nineties when you did not go to Greenpoint unless you wanted to get shanked."

"Get out."

I shook my head. "He told her on their third date. The dude is super loaded."

"Third date? How many dates have they had? They just met."

"It's looking like full steam ahead." I shrugged. "Apparently I am my mother's daughter, for I know how to yenta with the best of them."

"I just hope she doesn't over-share their—"

The front door opened, and Mrs. Nowacki and Jesse strolled in. Jasper stopped chasing his tail to greet the both of them.

Mrs. Nowacki went to the coffee maker and poured two mugs full.

"I bought some hazelnut creamer," I said to Jesse. "Someone told me it's your favorite."

He grinned and then leaned down to brush a kiss across Mrs. Nowacki's wrinkled cheek.

Aidan looked at me and raised his eyebrows.

I shrugged.

"Dog needs play date," Mrs. Nowacki said after Jesse doctored his coffee. "I see his poodle girlfriend at dog park on way over. We take him for frolic."

"You don't have to do that," Aidan said. "I can do it."

"No, you sit, enjoy time together." Mrs. Nowacki smiled and looked at Jesse. "You want to go for walk?"

"Absolutely. Brooklyn in the fall is my favorite season." Jesse gazed at Mrs. Nowacki.

She gazed at him.

I choked down some vomit.

Jesse leashed Jasper and off they went, Mrs. Nowacki toting travel coffee mugs.

"Why did you buy him hazelnut creamer?" Aidan asked with a laugh.

"Because I assume he'll be spending a lot of time here. I want him to be able to have his coffee the way he likes it."

"Sibby," he began. "We have half-and-half, two percent milk, whole milk, goat milk, coconut milk, soy milk, and now we have hazelnut creamer. Who the hell is drinking all this stuff?"

"Have you forgotten the revolving door of people we have coming through here? I swear, our apartment gets more action that a gynecologist's office. Stacy drinks soy, Em drinks goat, I like coconut, half-and-half is for you, Caleb and Annie, whole milk is for Mrs. Nowacki, and two percent milk is for my parents. Oh, which reminds me, I need to call my mom and then my dad."

I looked down at Oliver and brushed my lips across his forehead.

"You keep saying your brain isn't firing on all cylinders, but you seem to have it all sorted. You're a regular mastermind, Sibby."

I bowed. "Thank you. Thank you."

After I tricked both my parents into a visit, I went into the nursery to change Oliver. Aidan was already done changing Sophie and sat with her in the rocking chair. He stared down at her with a googly-eyed expression.

"You're stupid over your daughter," I said to him with a wry grin.

"No stupider than you are over your son."

"Touché."

"Hey, do you want to have Caleb and Em over for dinner? It's been a while since we've seen them."

"Yeah, I think they're around. Haven't you been in contact with Em?"

"Not since I awkwardly backed out of her bridal party

after saying yes." I unfastened the tabs on Oliver's diaper and turned my head. "Oh God, that's making my eyes water."

"Sophie's diaper was the same. What did you feed him?"

"Breast milk," I said. "Duh."

"What was in said breast milk?"

I bit my lip to keep from answering.

"Sibby…"

"Okay, I might've cheated on you…with Indian food."

"When?" he accused. "And how dare you eat Indian without me."

"You don't get to be mad. You ate fried chicken without me!" I sighed. "I had saag paneer."

"Jeez, no wonder their poop is vile." He shook his head. "I miss the days of not talking about bodily fluids."

"Preach," I said. "Yikes!" I hadn't been paying attention to Oliver who decided to shoot a geyser of urine in my direction. I quickly covered him.

I glared at him. "We do not pee on the Mommy." I glanced at Aidan. "When did my life get so glamorous?"

Mom Blog Entry:

Date night with Aidan used to consist of bar hopping and groping each other in a cab on the way to fornicate like rabbits.

Date night post-spawn includes takeout, laundry, and a breast pump malfunction.

This is my new normal.

"There's no way you can pull this off," Caleb said, pushing back his empty plate.

Em stood up and reached for his setting. "You're a jerk."

"I am not." Caleb laughed.

"You really don't think I'll be able to trick my parents into getting back together?" I demanded.

"I mean, do I think your parents will get back together? Uh, yeah. Because when they're happy, they make my parents look like they're on the outs."

"Your parents are high school sweethearts," Em said with a chuckle.

"Why don't you think I'll be able to pull this off?" I asked, taking a sip of my glass of red wine.

"Because there are so many moving parts," Caleb said. He shot Aidan a look. "Dude, help me out."

Aidan shook his head and placed his arm around my chair. "Nope. I don't bet against the wife. Never have. Never will."

I leaned over to kiss him.

"That means you've been roped into this crazy plan." Caleb stood and helped Em clear the plates to the sink.

"Damn right," Aidan agreed. "My in-laws are in their weird version of a separation. I want them back together as much as Sibby. More actually."

"More? Why more?"

"Because who else would jump at the chance to babysit the twins when they're off the breast so we can go somewhere tropical for a few days?"

"Your parents?" I reminded him.

"Yeah, but they hate coming to the city. And they're traveling in their RV. Apparently they really like it." He shrugged. "I doubt we'll see them for a while."

"Em," I called out, "you don't have to load the dishwasher."

"You cooked," she reminded me.

"Actually, Aidan cooked." I grinned. "Besides you and Caleb brought the wine."

"The wine was a bottle we wanted to test out on you guys," Caleb said. "We want to serve it at our wedding."

"It's delicious," I said. "How's the planning going?"

"Good," Em said as she washed off the silverware and placed it in the dishwasher. "We've only gotten into two fights."

"You guys *fought*?" Aidan's jaw gaped. "This I do not believe."

"It would be like Tinkerbell fighting with Peter Pan. I don't believe it either," I said.

"I don't want to be likened to Peter Pan," Caleb said. He raised the brim of his Red Sox hat so that it rested on the top of his head.

"I like Tinkerbell. She has a good stylist." She winked at me. "Oh, my best friend is finalizing details for my bachelorette party. She's going to send out save the dates. It's in February."

"Let me check my calendar. Oh, right. I'm sure I can move around getting spit up on by the twins."

She chuckled. "We're going to a rage room."

"What's a rage room?"

"It's a place you go and break dishes. They set up all these tables with plates and glassware. You take a bat and you just start smashing stuff."

"Why are we going to a rage room when you're in love?" I asked curiously.

"Because it's fun to break stuff."

"Word. I'm in." I looked at Caleb. "What's your bachelor party going to look like? Atlantic City for the weekend? Coming home smelling like strippers and booze?"

Aidan interjected, "Sibby would prefer I come home smelling like strippers over smelling like fried chicken."

Caleb laughed. "You have strange lines in the sand, Sib. No. Not Atlantic City or strippers. We're going to go hang out in The Brandy Room in Tribeca. Smoke cigars. Play pool. Complain about getting shackled to you gorgeous women for life."

He looped his arms around Em's waist and pulled her to him. He kissed her quickly and then released her.

"Yeah, that sounds pretty fun, actually," I said.

There was a sound through the baby monitor and then a moment later, Jasper was at my side, nosing my leg.

"He comes to get me when the twins need something," I explained. "Who's the smartest boy in the world?"

Jasper's tail wagged and then he dashed back to the nursery.

"Excuse me, I'm needed in a meeting."

I stood up from the table and went to tend to the children.

"You want some help?" Em asked, drying her hands on a dishrag.

"I'm about to expose my breasticles. If you're not worried about going blind…"

Em grinned. "Nah. I'm good. I'll avert my gaze."

We went into the nursery and for the next few minutes, Em helped me. I changed the babies and then with her aid, put them both to my chest.

"I'm not going to lie, I had an ulterior motive for coming to help you," she said. She picked up the stuffed bear that rested in the crib.

"Go on."

"I wanted to ask about Annie."

"What about Annie?" I questioned. I rocked in the rocking chair, the movement soothing to the twins and myself.

"Is she nervous about Mother Shucker's opening next month?"

I let out a slow breath. "No. Actually, I think she's got a good handle on it."

"Are you excited for the friends and family night? I know it's just a test run, but it will tell her a lot about what the restaurant opening is going to look like," she said.

"I am. I love her food."

"She invited us."

"She did? Huh. She didn't tell me. Neither did Aidan."

"Yeah." She frowned. "I think she wanted to be polite, you know? Like her restaurant is carrying wines from my company. She probably just invited us to be nice."

"Annie's not really good at the polite thing. I mean, she wouldn't get hung up on obligation. That's what I meant. So, if she invited you and Caleb, she genuinely wants you to come."

"Then why didn't she tell you that she was inviting us?"

"Probably because mentioning it might sound like she was making it a big deal when it's not? I mean, don't come if you feel weird, but don't not come because you think Annie will feel weird."

Em looked at the ceiling. "I think I understand what you just said. I'll talk to Caleb. I'll let it be his decision."

"Did you know that Annie invited Caleb and Em to the friends and family night at Mother Shucker?" I asked, removing the throw pillow on the bed and setting it in the chair in the corner.

Aidan pulled back the covers and slid beneath them. "No. I had no idea. She didn't tell you?"

"No. He didn't tell you?"

"Nope."

I patted the mattress and Jasper hopped up and settled at Aidan's feet. I got into bed and let out a sigh of relief.

"What do you think it means?" I asked him.

He hit the base of the lamp on his bedside table and the room pitched into darkness.

"I think it means Caleb and Annie are both pretending they're fine but they're not fine."

"Caleb is engaged to another woman," I pointed out. "A really great woman. You don't think…"

"What?"

"He's having doubts?"

Aidan paused before replying. "I don't think he's having doubts. I think he's just suddenly very aware of what his future is going to look like."

"Were you scared to marry me? People say cold feet is normal, but I didn't have any cold feet where you were concerned. My feet were toasty warm. My pinky toe was cold though, when it thought of wearing the concoction my mother envisioned for me."

Aidan chuckled. I felt his arm move and curl around me. I rolled into him and snuggled against his chest.

"To answer your question, no I didn't have cold feet. I think it's bullshit, actually."

"What? Cold feet? That's a thing. Last minute nerves."

"Is it? Or is it your subconscious telling you you're about to make a huge mistake?"

I pressed a kiss to his chest. "Well, whatever it is, I'm glad you didn't feel that for me."

"Same." He ran his fingers through my tangled hair. "I didn't think this would be my life."

"Bad?"

"No, I mean—it's just, you have no idea what's in store for you when you're twenty-five. You know?"

"I'm still twenty-five," I lied. "Twenty-five with a bangin' body."

"Do you miss it? Our old life?"

"Truth?" I asked.

"Always."

I swallowed. "I really thought I knew what love was, and then the twins came and it…deepened my capacity for love; for empathy, for patience. Every day I find I bend a little more to their needs, I find that last little bit of strength I wasn't sure I had. I think I'm a better human because of them."

I fell silent.

"But?"

"But I miss the quiet." I smiled into his chest. "I miss it just being us and Jasper. I miss being able to go out to an impromptu dinner. I miss the ability to decide if we want to hop on a plane and travel somewhere and not have to plan for taking two children. Everything is new again because I'm watching them grow, but at the same time my freedom is curtailed. I can't be selfish, I can't ignore their needs in favor of mine."

"A new reality."

"Which changes every day. No two days are alike. No matter how much I wish for a routine, it's not in the cards."

"Are you feeling better? About us?"

"Yes. Are you?"

"Yes."

He hugged me tighter. "I don't know what I'd do without you, Sib. I really don't."

"Good, because you never have to worry about that. You're stuck with me. Now and forever."

Three days later, I attempted to save my eardrum as my mother screeched through the phone, "You rotten child!"

I winced and pulled it away from my ear. Mrs. Nowacki shot me a look with raised eyebrows.

"Mom—"

"You tricked me! You tricked me and the man I claim as your father—"

"I *am* her father!" Dad yelled in the background.

"You've somehow managed to lock us in this room with no way out! My blood sugar is dropping, and I need food."

"Mini bar," I said.

"Highway robbery!"

There was a muffled sound followed by my father getting on the line and saying, "Your mother is no longer available. Talk to you later."

He hung up on me and I stared at my phone.

"That sounded bad," Mrs. Nowacki said.

"Well, let's just say I know where Sophie gets her lung power." I pressed my ear with my hand and shook my head, trying fruitlessly to shake the ringing out of my ear.

"How long will hotel staff pretend knob is faulty?"

"An hour. Two at the most. Hopefully, my dad realizes he doesn't have a ton of time and gets back into my mother's good graces. I had the hotel overload the mini bar with fifteen-dollar bags of Peanut M&Ms—my mother's favorite. They have more than enough liquor from the mini bottles. Booze helps married people to remember they're in love, right?"

"Why won't you let them figure it out for themselves?" Mrs. Nowacki asked curiously. "Why you get involved?"

"Because my world doesn't make sense when my parents aren't a team."

Mrs. Nowacki nodded and then sipped her coffee and then took a bite of a rice cake smeared with peanut butter. She made a face and set it aside. "Cardboard, covered in peanut butter, is still cardboard," she muttered. "I do not think you are being honest with yourself about your parents, Sibbila."

"I am."

She shook her head. "If you focus on your parents, it means you don't focus on yourself."

"You think this is some avoidance tactic?"

"When was last time you took time for yourself? You have goals, yes? Career goals? Body goals? How do you accomplish them when you are focused on your parents?"

"Don't I owe it to them as their daughter to help?"

"They're adults, yes?"

"Debatable. Lately, they're acting like children."

"Yes. And as you pointed out you already have two of them. "You know what I think you should do?" Mrs. Nowacki asked.

"What?"

"I think you should go for massage. Go to salon. Get pampered."

"The salon?" I pressed.

"Your roots are showing." She shrugged.

"Add it to the list of things I need to take care of."

"Yes, but you need to take care of self. Self-care is important…" She shot me a look and widened her eyes.

"You're not saying what I think you're saying…"

"What do you think I'm saying?"

I cleared my throat. "Tell me about you and Jesse. How is that going?"

"He's a real *mensh.*"

I grinned. "You told *Bubbe* about him, didn't you?"

"Yes. They want to meet him. We are going to go down there. Probably for Hanukkah."

"You won't be in the city for the holiday season?"

"I don't weather the winter the same way I used to." She absently rubbed her left hip.

"What aren't you telling me, Mrs. Nowacki?" I pressed. "Because I feel like my life is about to change dramatically."

"My children are no longer here," she said slowly. "I live with Dorota. I love you and Aidan. The twins. Jasper. But I think I need to be living life for me."

"What are you saying?" I whispered.

"I am going to visit your grandparents this winter and I am going to look at buying a condo near them."

"You're leaving me?" I whispered, feeling like she'd taken a hammer to my head and knocked me numb.

"I am not leaving you, Sibbila."

"What about Jesse?" I blurted out. "You just met him? Are you breaking up? What's happening?"

She sighed. "I have lived many years alone. My late

husband—we did things the way he wanted them. I am from a different generation, yes? But I have been on my own for a very long time. I am not making choices based on a man."

"Didn't you say he is special?"

"Yes."

"Then why—"

"I will not sacrifice any more for a man. I am independent. I cook for myself. I take care of myself. I take care of others." She pinned me with a stare. "Have I not earned the right to enjoy my life the way I want?"

"No, of course you have."

"Do not wait, Sibbila. Do not wait until you are old to be a little selfish. A little selfish is good."

"You're not selfish. You're selfless." I paused. "Is that what this is? You're finally fed up with us? Why won't you take the money we've offered you?"

"Because it is not about money. I have enough money. I help you because we are family. I help you because I love you. But you are no longer a new mother who feels like she is drowning. You are capable. You have Aidan."

"You know it's really sunny in Atlanta. You're going to have to get a new wardrobe. Get rid of the turtlenecks."

She smiled. "You're not mad at me, are you? For wanting to go?"

I shook my head, feeling tears prick behind my eyes. "I never would've gotten through the twins' first few months without you. You know that, right?"

"I know." She winked. "But now you just have more of a reason to come down to Atlanta for visits."

"Who's going to talk sense into me or bring me pastries?"

"You get mad when I bring you pastries," she reminded me. "And I know Skype, yes? We can Skype."

I wasn't ready for my life to change so dramatically again. But that was the way of things, wasn't it?

Once you settled into a routine, the universe decided to take a wrecking ball to your stability.

"Go out into the sunshine, Sibbila," she said gently. "I'll stay with the babies."

"She's *what?*" Aidan asked from behind Veritas's liquor store counter.

I nodded and picked up a bottle of high-end vodka with a lemon peel on the label.

"Mrs. Nowacki is moving to Atlanta," I said, setting the vodka back on the shelf.

Aidan looked like I felt. Completely and utterly devastated.

"What are we going to do?" he demanded. "There's no way we can handle the twins on our own. They're going to break us. And what about Jasper? He doesn't do well with a change in routine."

I moaned. "He'll probably revert back to peeing in the house."

The door between the bar and the store opened and

Caleb came in. His ball cap was on backwards and his too long hair stuck out over his ears.

"Hey, Sib," he said, side hugging me.

"Hey."

"Whoa. Why do you sound like you need a big drink?"

"Because I do," I said morosely. "Mrs. Nowacki is moving to Atlanta."

"No way. I thought she was a die-hard New Yorker?"

I shrugged.

"What are you guys going to do for a nanny? Isn't she like, raising your children for you?" he teased.

I playfully smacked him.

"We wouldn't have survived this long without her," Aidan stated. "We're so screwed."

"I really could use a cocktail right now," I muttered. "Maybe I'll settle for a carbonated beverage."

"We just got Doctor Brown's Black Cherry in. I'm playing around with a new cocktail," Caleb announced. "You want to try it?"

I reached up and grabbed my breasts, which made Caleb's eyes widen.

"I've got to feed the beasts soon. I'll settle for a regular soda, though."

"Uh. Okay. Can you do me a favor though? And stop grabbing your boobs in my presence. It's just weird."

I sighed. "I keep forgetting that grown men are into breasts, because to me, right now they're just feeding machines."

"Yeah, on that note, maybe I don't want children," Caleb muttered. He turned and marched away, back to the bar.

Aidan laughed. "He's really fun to freak out."

"Small pleasures, right?" I sighed.

"What's going on in your head?" he asked softly, taking my hand and bringing it to his lips.

My finger traced his mouth, his cheek. "I don't know. It's a mess up there."

"Have you heard from your parents?"

"Not since my mother screeched into my ear," I admitted. "I'm empty, Aidan. I don't think I have anything left for anyone."

"What about me? Anything left for me?"

"I don't know," I stated.

"What if I take you to dinner tonight? Might as well make use of Mrs. Nowacki while we still have her."

His words made me burst into tears.

"Ah shit." He came out from behind the register and hugged me to him. "When did I become so insensitive?"

"You haven't," I assured him, sopping the front of his shirt. "I just cry at the drop of a hat. I thought that would go away after giving birth, but I think it's worse now."

"Yeah, it might be." He brushed the hair away from my cheeks and cupped my chin. "We'll get through it. You know that, right? We'll find a way to be stronger and better."

I sighed. "I'm so glad I married you."

He grinned. "So am I."

Two days later, there was a knock on the front door. I got up from the kitchen table and my laptop and went to answer the door.

My parents stood on the threshold of the doorway looking very much not like my parents. My father's button-down shirt was wrinkled and untucked from his jeans…yes, my father was wearing *jeans,* not his normal slacks.

And my mother?

My mother wore no makeup—well, mascara and lip gloss. She was Southern, but to a Southern woman, that was basically wearing next to nothing on her face. And her hair was in a messy top bun.

Both of them wore radiant smiles.

"Uh. Hi." I stepped back. "You guys want to come in? Unless you're going to yell? The twins are still asleep."

"We won't yell," Mom assured me.

Dad grinned at me as he took my mother's hand and crossed the threshold of the apartment. "You're a smart girl, Sibby. Faulty doorknob?"

I smiled. "How long did it take you to figure out?"

"Almost immediately," my mother said. "And by the time the hotel staff 'fixed' it, we were on speaking terms. Your father paid for an extra two nights at the hotel and we had a sexual reconciliation."

"And an emotional one," my father added.

"Oh." I swallowed my nausea. "That's good."

"It took a lot of tequila and a lot of discussion, but we're finally speaking the same language. We've decided to go on a three-month cruise through the Greek Islands. We were supposed to go there on our honeymoon, but your father's career got in the way. So, we're taking the honey-moon now."

"I'm retiring," Dad said. "Officially."

"Congratulations," I said numbly. "And the Rent-a-

Yenta business? What are you going to do while you're on the three-month cruise? What about the momentum?"

"Your aunt will run it while I'm gone," Mom said.

"That's…great."

"Why do you look so confused?" Mom wondered.

"Resting confused face," I said. "It's my norm."

First Mrs. Nowacki making a huge life change, and now my parents? What the hell was in the Kool-Aid?

The front door opened and Aidan strolled in.

He grinned. "Hello, parents." Aidan looked at my father and mother holding hands. "I see all is well in the Goldstein family?"

"Better than ever," Dad said. He looked lighter, happier. Was it because he and my mother had gotten back together? Or was it because he'd decided to retire?

Who cared? They were happy and my life was partly back to normal. Two parents, sickeningly in love.

Why did it feel like my life was still topsy-turvy?

Mom Blog Entry:

It's time to get my body back, so I went to the gym to use one of those large exercise balls to do crunches. I fell off the ball, made a loud thud, and then treated myself to an ice cream cone to make myself feel better.

I love the gym.

Aidan and I walked hand in hand down my favorite street in Brooklyn. The trees were completely immersed in

Autumn, there was a chill in the air, and I was wearing a cute new red sweater and ankle boots, courtesy of Stacy, who'd gotten them for being a fashion and social media influencer.

We were sans babies—they were at our apartment with Mrs. Nowacki and Jess, Since they refused money, I paid them in lasagna and a bottle of wine. They were only too happy to babysit for us.

The last couple of weeks had been a mental cluster-fuck. I hadn't been able to stop thinking about how dramatically my life was going to be impacted when Mrs. Nowacki left New York. Sure, some of that had to do with the help we were getting with the babies, but she had also been instrumental in helping me get back on my feet as far as my life went.

I'd started power walking with Jill, Kelsey, and Shay and our massive strollers. It had done a lot for feeling like I'd found a community, as well as helping me burn a few calories. I couldn't tell a huge difference in my body yet, but I could definitely tell a difference in my mental attitude.

"You're quiet," Aidan said, squeezing my hand. "What are you thinking about?"

"I'm thinking about how I can't wait to taste Annie's food," I said, which was only half the truth. "And I'm glad my pants have a stretchy waistline. Can you believe it? My best friend is having a restaurant opening?"

"I can," he said. "We're growing up, Sibby. All of us."

I shot him an amused grin and then it fell. "Caleb and Em really aren't going, are they?"

He shook his head. "No. He debated about it for a long time, but in the end, he said he didn't want Annie worrying about anything except serving food and talking to people. He didn't want her to have to put on a friendly face."

"Does he know she broke up with Mills?"

He shook his head. "I sure as hell didn't tell him."

"Smart."

After a few more blocks, we arrived at Mother Shucker. Aidan opened the heavy glass door for me and we stepped inside. There was a host behind the fish market counter holding an iPad.

He looked up and greeted us with a smile. "Good evening. May I have your name?"

"Sibby and Aidan Kincaid."

"Excellent," he said. "She wants you at the counter." He winked.

A few friends and family had already arrived, but we were part of the early crew. Annie's aunt, uncle, and cousin were sitting at the three-top in the corner. We went over to say hello before taking our seats at the end of the counter.

Annie was wearing a clean white chef coat and a ball cap with the Mother Shucker logo—all cooks and wait staff had to wear a hat of some sort.

The chalk board above the counter had all the fish she'd be serving that evening, all ranging in dishes from fish and chips to fish tacos.

"What are you drinking?" Annie asked.

Aidan took the paper menu and flipped it over. "Narragansett."

"Got it." Annie looked at me.

"Sancerre."

"I'll get those drinks for you," a female server said who'd been standing next to Annie.

Once she moved away, I said, "Are you nervous?"

"I'm too jacked up on coffee to be nervous," Annie said with a wide grin. "I feel like I've been waiting for this moment my entire life."

"You've *so* got this," I said, reaching for her hand and giving it a squeeze.

"You guys want to start with a selection of oysters?" Annie asked, once the female server had set our drinks down.

"That was rhetorical, right?" I quipped.

Annie grinned and then headed to the two oyster shuckers who were manning the shellfish station. She said something to them and then pointed to me.

I waved.

The restaurant started to fill up. Stacy walked in with a man who looked very familiar.

"Is that—no, it can't be," Aidan said.

"Gregory Roubideaux," I nodded, "It is."

Aidan's head whipped toward me. "You knew?"

I leaned closer to him and said, "Stacy swore me to secrecy, but now that they're walking in holding hands, I think it's safe to tell you…she's been sleeping with him."

His eyes widened. "I need the full story later."

I smothered my laugh as Stacy and Gregory approached. Gregory and Aidan shook hands and started talking after a brief introduction by Stacy.

Stacy came to stand by me. "Well?" She raised her eyebrows.

"Uh, he's so hot. Like way hot. Like, my DNA is tingling."

Stacy's grin was wide. "Right?"

"You guys wanna join us?" I asked. "Nobody has taken those stools yet."

"Sounds good to me," Gregory said. He looked at me. "Hi, we haven't met yet, but I've heard a lot about you."

"Ditto." I shook his hand.

Stacy took her phone and started snapping pictures of

the restaurant with Annie behind the counter and our massive oyster platter when it arrived.

"There's no way we can eat all this," Aidan said.

"We'll help," Stacy said with a laugh, reaching for an oyster and shooting it straight from the shell.

"My kind of woman," Gregory said as he reached for a sliver of the raw sea scallop.

Stacy grabbed my glass of wine and took a sip. "Oh, I *love* this. I want a glass."

"Why don't we just get a bottle?" Gregory asked.

"I'm in," I said. "I'm not pumping and feeding."

Gregory looked confused until Stacy explained, "They have four-month-old twins at home."

"Ah," Gregory said with a winsome smile.

I knew that kind of smile.

It was a smile that said he was hungry for a baby.

I glanced at Stacy to see if she realized what was going on—because Gregory was looking at her like she was a baby factory in waiting.

Nope. Totally oblivious in that young, still in her twenties, I've got my entire life before me way.

God, I envied her.

The server came and asked how things were. We ordered a bottle of Sancerre. Annie turned from the stove to finally greet Stacy and Gregory before getting back to frying fish.

Annie wasn't letting anyone order food from the menus —she was just cooking up batches in small servings and sending them to tables. The two servers on the floor were constantly running food and beverages, all the while the two hosts at the front of the restaurant were getting customers drinks while they waited for seats.

"I thought you said friends and family only," I called to

Annie when I saw a line starting to snake around the front sidewalk, down the side of the restaurant.

"Yeah, it was supposed to be that way," Annie said with a smile over her shoulder, "but there are some people from a few food magazines here doing write-ups—not to mention Stacy's new boyfriend. It's all over social by now. If not from her account, then from everyone else's, which is awesome. I thought that might happen and the kitchen has been stocked to the gills, but even then, I'm not sure how much longer this food will last."

She said something to her sous chef who was manning the other grill. He opened the bottom drawer below the stove and whipped out a bag of fresh tortillas and placed six of them on the plancha.

I listened to Gregory, Stacy and Aidan carry on a conversation in the background, but I was more interested watching Annie in her element. There wasn't a frazzled nerve in sight, and even though it was only friends and family and it was the first night, I knew Mother Shucker was going to be a huge success.

The evening wore on, and I checked my phone every once in a while. Mrs. Nowacki texted about the twins, but they were fine, and I was able to relax—as much as any new mother could relax when she left her children at home in the care of someone else.

"Aidan said your parents are back together," Stacy said, pulling me from my reverie.

Annie set down a bowl of wedge fries and three different dipping sauces. "Ketchup, wasabi mayo, and chipotle aioli."

"Be still my fattening waistline," I stated.

Annie grinned. "And speak louder so I can hear about your parents."

I laughed but gave my attention to Stacy. "They're

good. They just left for a cruise to Greece, so it'll be a little while before I get any postcards."

She shook her head. "I can't believe your rom-com inspired plan worked."

"No one has any faith in my plans. It went off without a hitch." I looked pensive. "Mrs. Nowacki is moving out of the city."

"No shit," Stacy commented. "Why? Where is she going?"

"She's moving to Atlanta to be close to my *bubbe*."

"What are you going to do?" Stacy asked.

"I have no idea," I commented. "Ask the Babies and Brews club if they know of any nannies for hire, I guess."

"What's the Babies and Brews club?" Annie called over her shoulder as she flipped a piece of grilled fish onto its other side.

"I told you about them—the three moms I met in the park. We power walk together now."

"Oh, right. Sorry, I've been forgetful of anything that doesn't involve the filleting of fish."

"Totally allowed," I quipped.

"Annie!" someone from the prep kitchen yelled.

"I'm being summoned." She set her spatula down and then rushed to the back.

Out of sheer curiosity, I leaned over the counter, wanting to see what was going on. My mouth dropped open when I saw Mills standing in the prep kitchen.

I quickly turned my attention back to Stacy and took a huge glug of wine. "So, you and Gregory. That looks like it's going well?"

She grinned. "It is. You and I need to have coffee though. And completely girl out."

"Name the time and the place. I'm there."

"Oh," she blinked, "I can't believe I forgot." She smacked my shoulder.

"Ow." I rubbed it. "What was that for?"

"For writing a book with a cliffhanger!"

"Oh, that." I grinned. "Aside from that, how do you feel about it?"

"That depends. When do I get the next book in the series?"

I paused.

"I do not like the look on your face right now."

"Can we save it for coffee? I have a lot of thoughts about a lot of things, and I just want to enjoy tonight."

"Fine." She glowered.

"But you did like the book, right?"

"No. I *loved* the book. It's old school Sibby, but grittier. Sharper."

"Thanks."

"It has a dark edge to it, you know?"

I nodded. "I know."

Annie came back onto the floor, looking flushed and purposefully not meeting my eyes.

"You guys ready for another round of food?" she asked the four of us.

"Whatever you want to throw out, we'll eat," Gregory announced.

She looked at him and blinked. "Wow. I still can't believe you came to Mother Shucker. This is surreal."

"How are you feeling? About all this?" Gregory asked with a wave of his hand at the restaurant.

"I'm pretty sure I'm high on adrenaline. I'll feel everything later, I think."

He nodded. "There's nothing like the first restaurant. You slave away working every hour of every day hoping and praying your restaurant doesn't fail, and if you're lucky enough to open a new place in a few years then you have a lot more to worry about. Your name, your reputation. It's almost easier to carve out your success with the first restaurant, but when you open that second or third, you have so much more riding on it. Make sense?"

"I wish I still drank." Her attention was diverted when one of the hosts manning the front door skipped behind the counter and came to her side.

"You're kidding," she said after a moment. "Seriously?"

He nodded.

"What's up?" I asked, taking a drink of wine.

"Apparently, I've sold out of Mother Shucker T-shirts."

"Don't you have more in the storeroom downstairs?" I asked in shock. "You had stacks and stacks of T-shirts."

"Gone," she said.

One of her prep chefs came onto the floor from the back kitchen and whispered in her ear. Her face was wreathed in a smile. "Thanks." Annie came out from around the counter. "Excuse me!" she called, addressing the room.

Conversation stilled and all eyes turned to her. "Thank you all so much for showing up with such amazing support and healthy appetites."

There was a smattering of chuckles moving throughout the restaurant before quieting down.

"We've run out of lobster, so take a crayon from the cup on your table, and cross it off the menu!"

"You're a seafood restaurant!" someone called. "How can you be out of lobster?"

Annie shot the speaker a smile. "All my food is freshly caught each day. If my delivery guy only has forty lobsters, he only has forty lobsters. You're getting the freshest of the fresh each and every day. Never frozen, never day-old anything. I'd rather run out than serve old shellfish. Enjoy!"

"Nice diplomacy," I said to Annie after she stepped back behind the counter.

By the end of the night, Annie had run out of three quarters of her supplies and had to close the doors before she was able to serve the entire line of customers snaking around the block.

Mother Shucker was already a huge success.

Three days later I was sipping on a cup of coffee, scrolling through Mother Shucker's latest write-ups. All the press had been positive. So positive in fact that I hadn't even heard from Annie since the night of her opening. She was so busy she hadn't even responded to my text about Mills showing up at her restaurant.

A cry from the nursery had me pulling my attention from the effusive praise of Mother Shucker's lobster roll.

With a belabored sigh, I set my coffee down and got up to tend to the children. Jasper was lying on his dog bed in the corner of the nursery, his ears flattened against his head. The moment he saw an escape, he took it.

"Traitor," I commented. "You're leaving me alone to deal with this?"

I walked to the crib. Sure enough, it was Sophie hollering up a storm. Her fists were clenched and her face was red.

Oliver was in the process of deciding on whether or not to scream, and then he committed fully, howling like a banshee.

My ears rang from the noise and I went through the routine of changing, feeding, and changing them again. Finally, they were quiet, my eardrums throbbing from the type of torture that could only be inflicted by tiny shrieking humans that had come out of my body.

I was just getting ready to set Sophie back in the crib when I noticed one of her eyes was slightly swollen. Though she'd stopped crying, her eye was still weepy.

Frowning, I looked around for my cell phone. I'd left it in the kitchen. I held her in one arm and called Aidan.

"Hey, love. Have you pulled all your hair out by the roots yet?" he asked in way of greeting.

"Getting there," I replied. "I'm noticing something with Sophie's eye."

"It's still in her head, right?"

"Leave the snarkiness to me," I said lightly. I looked back down at Sophie whose mouth was hanging open as she conked out.

"Talk to me about Sophie's eye," he said.

"It's red and puffy. And weepy."

"Call Janet. She's had enough kids to have seen it all by now. She'll know what to do."

"Oh, that's a good thought." I sighed. "If only Mrs. Nowacki was here."

"We have to learn to get along without her," he

reminded me. "Better start sooner rather than later, don't you think?"

"Yeah." I sighed. "You're right. Okay, let me call Janet. I'll give you a buzz back."

Four hours later, Aidan and I entered the apartment with a paper bag filled with eye ointment for Sophie and Oliver's pink eye.

Sophie transferred it to her brother.

Because, life.

"I want them to learn how to share," I moaned, "but maybe I should've been more specific. They don't need to share ailments and diseases."

"It could be worse," he said with a smile. "They could have chicken pox."

"Which they'll get at some point. How did this even happen?" I asked. I'd called Aidan's sister, sent her a photo of Sophie's eye, and because she was a veteran mother, she'd diagnosed the issue immediately. Nothing to be concerned about. Just annoying.

"My guess? Jasper butt on a pillow," Aidan said.

"Vile. Vile, vile, vile." I looked over at Jasper who was sitting, his tail wagging and brushing across the floor.

"Guess that means we have to sterilize everything and wash sheets constantly," I muttered.

"Do we have enough of those onesies that cover their hands so they can't rub their eyes and keep spreading germs everywhere?" Aidan asked.

"No idea."

I pushed the stroller further into the living room but didn't bother taking the twins out of it. They'd both fallen asleep and I was not about to disturb them.

The next morning, I woke up with pink eye.

And by the middle of the day, Aidan had pink eye, too.

"We are quarantined," I stated. "I'm not leaving this house until we're all healthy. I refuse to be the cause of the pink eye outbreak that takes out Brooklyn."

Aidan took the tube of ointment from my hand and went into the bathroom. "I think you overestimate the power of our children and their pink eyes."

"They felled us, didn't they?" I asked.

Finally, after a few days of endless loads of laundry and gunky eyes, we all healed. Life returned to normal. Aidan went back to work, Caleb and Em came over for dinner, but I still hadn't seen Annie. She only replied to my texts to tell me she was too busy to talk.

The girl was dodging me. No more.

I called her and she picked up.

"Where are you?" she asked.

"Where am I like, all the time?" I quipped.

"Are you alone?"

"I have the twins and Jasper."

"But your husband? He's gone?"

I frowned even though she couldn't see me. "Yes, he's gone. He's doing that thing that brings home the paycheck."

Annie paused. "I'm coming over."

She hung up before I could respond and then I set my phone aside. Not ten minutes later, the front door blew open and Annie stormed inside.

Jasper lifted his head from the couch and then jumped down to greet her. She absently pet him on the head before setting her large bag down on the counter.

"Uh. Hello, stranger," I said, crossing my arms over my chest.

"Don't give me that, you've been a shut in, what with your eye plague and all. I don't want to get too close to you in case you're still contagious."

"Not a weepy eye in sight." I held up my hand in the classic *scout's honor* hand sign. "Now are you going to tell me what the hell Mills was doing there the night of your restaurant opening? Which by the way, you totally killed and now your name rings out on the blogosphere."

She rolled her eyes. "Hardly. I've been written up in a few magazines and I'm grateful for that, but how about you keep my ego in check and maybe not say stuff like that."

"So, Mills?"

"I kind of accidentally slept with him the night of my opening," she admitted.

"How did you accidentally sleep with him? Were you drunk?"

"No." She rolled her eyes.

"Was your zipper on your pants caught and he was gracious enough to tug it down…with his teeth?"

"Does that really happen?"

"I don't know."

"You write romance novels. If you don't know, who does?"

"Annie."

"I was wearing chef pants. They were easy to get off. I

was feeling…excited and elated, and in disbelief. And he showed up and brought me a key lime pie."

"I thought you guys haven't been talking since you broke up with him."

"We haven't been talking—ah, but I wasn't totally honest with you."

"Go on."

"We broke up, but we were definitely still sleeping together."

"Okay…so opening night? You slept together again. Where? The walk-in?"

"No. In my apartment. And then we ate key lime pie in bed."

"That sounds kind of nice."

She nodded, and then pinned me with her blue gaze. "I'm four days late."

"Four days late for what?" I asked with a frown. "Oh. Oh, I see. Wait, what's the date?"

Annie told me.

My eyes widened. "Are you sure?"

She nodded.

"Oh lord."

"What?"

"I'm late, too. I've been so preoccupied with the mounds of laundry and the ointment squirting I haven't been keeping a close eye on it. I can't be pregnant!"

"*I* can't be pregnant!" she shouted. "You at least love the man who might've knocked you up!"

"I already have twins! I can't be this fertile, I just can't!" I rubbed the bridge of my nose. "That's it. Aidan's getting fixed. We used condoms, but clearly they are the devil's membrane and they don't work!"

"Hey, you stop freaking out. This was supposed to be

my freak out. I came over here so you could talk *me* down—and ask if you had a pregnancy test."

"Why would I have a pregnancy test?" I demanded. "Why didn't you grab one on your way over here? This is Brooklyn. There's basically a pharmacy and a Starbucks on every corner. You know, they should just combine the two and be done with it."

"You're getting off topic!"

"Stop panicking. Panicking doesn't do you any good."

"I'm not ready for this. Babies are hard even when you have a partner. I don't want a partner I'm shackled to just because of a fertilized zygote!"

"Oh! I saw this thing in a movie once! Jump up and down!" I immediately started hopping up and down and then winced as my milky breasts bounced around, almost smacking me in the eyes. I held them like a makeshift sports bra and then continued to jump.

"What are we doing?" Annie asked, but damn if she didn't hop to.

"We're jumping out our periods!"

"Does that really work?"

"Do you have any better ideas?"

We continued to jump, not stopping, not even when the front door opened and Aidan walked in.

He looked at me and then at Annie and then slowly retreated, closing the door to give us privacy.

After five minutes of jumping, I finally stopped. "Whoa. I think I have vertigo."

Annie quit moving and then bent over in half, breathing hard. "Do you really think you're pregnant? Or is this your way of trying to make me feel better?"

"I'm eighty percent sure I'm not pregnant. My period hasn't been regular at all, so there's a good chance it just forgot to RSVP to my womb's party."

Annie blinked and then grinned. "I just had a really weird vision of a pink uterus full of streamers and balloons." Her smile slipped. "I think I might actually be pregnant, Sibby."

"You've been stressed, hun. You've been burning the candle at both ends. I doubt you're pregnant."

"Even when I was fourteen you could tell the phase of the moon by my cycle."

I snorted. "Dark side of the moon curse." My eyes widened. "Did I just—my funny bone is working again! Yay!"

"Sibby," she whispered.

"I can run out and grab us a box of pregnancy tests. We can take them together."

"This is not something I ever wanted to have to take together." Her lip wobbled. "But I have to know. I have to know, like right now."

I nodded and grabbed my purse and phone. "The twins should be fine for the next twenty minutes while I'm gone."

"Okay."

I all but smacked into Aidan's chest when I dashed into the vestibule. His hands went to my shoulders. "Where's the fire?" He made a face. "Sorry, force of habit to ask."

I looked up at him and took a deep breath. "Do me a huge favor, okay?"

"Anything."

"Go hang out at Veritas for like an hour."

He frowned. "Sibby, what—"

"It's not about me," I fibbed. "It's about Annie and she needs a place to maybe fall apart. Okay?"

Aidan nodded slowly. "Okay." He leaned down and pecked me on the lips. "You'll tell me? Later?"

"If she doesn't make me do the handshake promise to keep her secret, then yes. I'll tell you."

We walked out together, but then I quickly diverted away from him and ran to the drugstore. My heart jumped into my throat when I located the pregnancy test aisle. I quickly grabbed a box without really looking at it, dumped it at the cashier, and swiped my card. I shoved the box into my purse and jogged home.

I was out of breath by the time I made it back to the apartment.

Annie was pacing back and forth across the living room floor, holding a glass of water. "I came over here with an empty bladder. I'm pretty sure I drank a gallon of water since you've left."

"Right, I'm empty too. The twins?"

"Didn't make a noise."

"Is it okay if I'm not like, in the bathroom with you shouting ready, set, pee?"

"I think that might give me stage fright." She set her glass of water down. "The box?"

"In my purse," I said as I headed toward the nursery.

A moment later she asked, "Why is the writing in Polish?"

"Because I went to the Polish pharmacy up north. No one knows me up there. If I'd gone south, I would've run into a bunch of people who might know me. I'm just gonna check on the twins and then I'll cheer you on. From out here."

She saluted me and then darted for the bathroom, the box of tests clutched against her chest.

The twins were fine, completely still milk drunk, so I quietly closed the nursery door and then went back to the living room.

Jasper was resting on the couch, his eyes watching me. I

patted my leg and he came to me immediately and then the both of us took up vigil outside the guest bathroom door.

"Annie? How's it going in there?" I asked.

"Going," she muttered.

"Do you mind sliding a test out to me when you're able?"

The door opened a sliver and a prepackaged stick was shoved through the slot.

"Why don't you seem more freaked out that you could be pregnant?" she asked.

"It's almost the new year," I said. "I'm trying to practice the art of not jumping to conclusions."

"We have two months until the end of the year," Annie stated.

"Like I said, I'm trying to practice."

She opened the door all the way. "Okay, I lied. I want you in here."

"Turn about is fair play, huh?" I asked. "After all, I ran to you when I thought I was pregnant, and it was up to you to talk me down."

"Yes, but you were in fact pregnant," Annie pointed out.

"Turn around, I have to pee."

Annie turned around to give me some semblance of privacy.

I shimmied my elastic banded jeans down my legs, grabbed the stick, and ripped into it.

"What's it like," she said quietly after I finished up and then set my stick next to hers on the sink counter.

I turned on the faucet to wash my hands. "What? Pregnancy? Motherhood?"

"Yes."

I thought about how to answer truthfully. "I wouldn't say I'm an expert on the subject."

"But you've done it. You *are* doing it. I'm terrified, Sibby."

"Of course you are. I'm terrified every moment of every day."

Jasper pawed at the bathroom door and Annie let him in.

"It's like having two strangers in your house," I admitted. "These two strangers who come between you and your partner, and you're not really sure what to do with them. You don't know what they like to eat. You don't know how they like to sleep. You don't really know them at all, really."

"Is it worth it?" she asked.

"I'm guessing it is," I said. "But that's not really the point, you know? I mean, it would be one thing if you were discussing the pros and cons, deciding yes or no to do this thing, this huge monumental thing of procreating, but when it's thrust upon you, it doesn't matter if it's worth it, because you suck it up and do it."

"Suck it up and do it," she repeated. "That's not exactly a billboard for parenthood."

"They don't do much right now, you know? They eat and sleep and make a lot of dirty diapers. This isn't *fun*. I'm waiting for it to get fun."

"What if it's never fun?"

The timer on her phone beeped. She whipped it out of her back pocket and turned it off. "My test is done."

I nodded.

"Will you look for me?"

I nodded again. "Close your eyes."

"Why?"

"Because you're going to visualize the outcome you want."

"That won't work against hormones."

"Annie."

"Sibby."

"Close your eyes."

I waited until she closed her eyes and then I leaned over the counter.

Her test was negative.

"Congratulations, your uterus is empty of seed."

She let out a deep breath and then she burst into tears, hugging me to her.

I was able to glance over her shoulder at my own test.

Also negative.

I let out a deep exhale and sent up a thought of gratitude.

"Come on," I said, pulling away. "Let's go eat our weight in ice cream cake."

"You have ice cream cake?"

I nodded. "You never know when you're going to need an ice cream cake."

Chapter 21

Mom Blog Entry:

Sometimes I use the babies as an excuse not to leave my house. It's easier than explaining to my friends that I'd rather sit at home and cry while watching Hallmark movies than I would go out to dinner or a bar.

"You thought you were pregnant?" Aidan asked, pulling the bed covers back. "And you didn't want me there with you while you took the test?"

"It seemed fortuitous that Annie also needed to take a pregnancy test."

He blinked. "Say that again."

"Annie thought she was pregnant."

"With whose baby?"

"Mills'."

"She and Mills are back together?"

"I don't know if they ever really broke up." I climbed into bed next to him. "There's a bigger issue we have yet to really discuss."

His hand sought mine even as Jasper jumped onto the bed and sidled up between us.

"What's that?"

"The additional kids thing," I said.

"You want to have this talk? Now? The twins are only four months old."

"I just had a really big scare, Aidan," I said slowly. "If we don't talk about this now, then when?"

"All right. I'm listening. You tell me what you want and then I'll tell you what I want."

"What if we don't want the same thing?"

"Then we'll find a way to meet in the middle like we always do."

I nodded. "Okay." I took a deep breath. "I think I'm done. We have two babies. One of each sex. I'm good. You know? I can't imagine doing this all over again. I'm not sure I want to. I already struggle enough trying to feel like I'm a good wife, a good mother, a good author. I'm slowly adjusting to our new normal. But Mrs. Nowacki is leaving. She's a huge part of why I felt like I could do this."

Aidan was silent for a long moment and with each passing breath, I grew more and more nervous.

"Crap. You want more, don't you? You want a big

brood. You want them to call you Papa and one can bring you your slippers and another can bring you a pipe."

"When did I become a father in the 50s?" he asked with a laugh. "And no. I don't think I want any more either."

"Really? You're not just saying that because I said that?"

"I'm really not. I think two is good. Perfect, actually."

"But there's something else you're not saying."

"You know me so well."

I smiled and looked over at him. "Go on."

"I've been thinking more and more about moving out of the city. And I know we talked about it a while back and shelved the whole idea for a bit, but I can't get the idea out of my mind."

"You want to move Upstate after you just expanded your business? Is that a good idea?"

"Probably not." He paused. "But there are ways around being an absent owner. I just keep thinking…"

"What?" I pressed gently.

"Mrs. Nowacki is leaving. Your parents don't live here. My entire family is Upstate. We need a support system, Sibby. It's only going to get harder with the twins."

"Harder?" I asked faintly. "Harder how?"

"I have nieces and nephews. I watched what my sisters went through. Right now is the easiest parenting is ever going to be."

"Oh great, now you tell me. When it's too late to give them back."

"Sibby," he said gently.

"Harder how?" I repeated.

"Harder like they're going to be mobile and into *every-thing*. You can't take your eyes off them for even a minute.

You want to get your writing groove back? You want to write children's books? We can't do this alone."

"We can hire a nanny—"

"I don't want some stranger taking care of our kids. I think it's time we really discuss what we want our lives to look like now that the twins are here."

"You want to move so we can be close to family."

"It's more than that." He sighed. "Do I think it would be better to have family close by to help? Yes. I miss the camaraderie that goes along with a big family."

"I have a big family. My mom's entire family is in Atlanta."

"You're an only child," he reminded me. "And no. I don't want to move to Atlanta."

"I don't really want to move to Atlanta either. I just wanted to throw it out as an option. You know, while we're talking about blowing up our entire life."

"You love where I grew up," he reminded me.

"In an idyllic, I-wish-I-knew-how-to-make-goat cheese, kind of way. But Aidan, I'm not a country girl. You know this. All my friends are here. Annie's here. Stacy's here."

"Is staying in a city for friends a big enough reason?" he asked gently. "It's not just about us anymore."

"Yeah. I know, but we just moved into this place. Are we really going to—we just got settled."

"Do you feel settled? Honestly."

"No. I don't feel settled. Isn't that normal, though?"

"I don't know what's normal and what's not. I just know, this itch I was feeling before the twins were born has gotten worse."

"It might be time to see a doctor."

He didn't laugh at my quip.

"I didn't work this hard and this long to keep having to

work this hard and this long. For what? Miss my kids growing up?"

"It sounds like you have city fatigue."

"I love our life here. I really do, but I think in the long run it would be better for us if we moved Upstate. Better for you and me, for Jasper. The twins."

"What about what I want? Does that matter?"

"What do you want, Sibby? Because I don't think even you know."

"That's not fair."

"No. I didn't mean it the way it sounded. I just meant I see your struggle."

"And you think to ease my struggle by taking me away from everything familiar. My favorite take-out places, my friends, my community…"

"Just think about it." He didn't rise to the bait, which told me that Aidan was serious, and he'd been thinking about this for a while. I'd put him off once about moving Upstate, but I wasn't sure I could push it again.

I was awake long after Aidan had fallen asleep, thinking about the future, thinking about the new direction I wasn't sure I was ready for my life to take.

Thanksgiving passed with minimal, non-arsonist fanfare. It was a quiet affair and we spent it by ourselves. We didn't have the energy to host or even travel with the twins to spend it with friends and family.

Jesse took Mrs. Nowacki to meet his children. Caleb and Em were with Caleb's family Upstate. Annie was MIA, but hadn't left the city because Mother Shucker was going to be open on Black Friday. Stacy had flown to Vegas with Gregory, and Zeb and Terry had decided to take an impromptu trip to Barbados.

My parents were still on their cruise—and I was getting postcards every few days from my mother about which ports she was sunbathing topless in. They seemed happy and even more in love than before their separation.

One early December day, I met Kelsey, Jill, and Shay for a beer at the German beer hall across from the park. There was a fire in the wood-burning fireplace, and a few of the long tables were commandeered by customers playing Jenga or card games. We'd all left our babies home with our husbands, and it felt good to be out of the house without having to worry about someone else's immediate needs.

"Is it wrong that I want the holiday season to be over?" Jill asked, pulling her dark red hair up into a bun.

"I'm exhausted already," Kelsey admitted, taking a small sip of beer from the stein in front of her.

"You didn't do anything for Thanksgiving, did you?" Shay asked, directing the question at me.

I shook my head. "We ate turkey sandwiches and watched the parade on TV. Pathetic? Maybe. Low key? Definitely."

Jill shook her head. "Smart, actually. I'm not sure I'm ready to travel with a six-month-old and I already have travel anxiety around the holidays."

"We're going to California for Christmas," Shay said. "To see my parents. It'll be…interesting."

"Yeah, but your kid is a dream." I grinned.

"Let's hope he stays a dream and doesn't become a monster."

"You need a beer," Kelsey said to me.

"And maybe a pretzel," I agreed, but I made no move to get up.

The three of them looked at each other.

"Out with it," Jill commanded.

"Aidan wants to move out of the city."

The three of them fell silent and waited for me to continue speaking.

"And it's not out of the blue or a shock. He's wanted to move Upstate for a while—it's where he's from."

"Do his parents still live there?" Kelsey asked.

I nodded. "And two of his three sisters. I adore his family. That isn't the issue."

"What's the issue then?" Shay asked in confusion. "You work from home, which is a blessing. You can do that from anywhere."

"I love the city," I admitted. "And my whole life is here. I'm not sure I'm ready to give it all up."

"What would you gain?" Kelsey asked.

"Well," my brow furrowed in thought, "I'd get more space. I'd have the help of Aidan's family to raise the babies. Jasper would be a lot happier and he deserves that."

"The dog?" Jill asked.

I nodded.

"Okay, go on," Jill said. "I just wanted to make sure I knew who you were talking about."

I smiled. "I guess, we'd be putting down roots."

"Which is hard to do in the city," Kelsey said. "Expensive but feasible."

"Didn't Aidan like, *just* expand his bar," Shay asked.

"He did. It's going well."

"What would he do Upstate?" She raised her eyebrows.

"I don't know," I admitted. "We didn't get that far into the discussion because I'd already shut it down. Well, not shut it down, exactly. I still listened to the idea. I just didn't care for it. I haven't talked about it with anyone but you guys, though."

"Why is that?" Jill asked.

"You guys have kids," I said in way of explanation. "You get the struggle."

"I don't plan on being here when Hannah is school age," Kelsey said.

"We're raising Blake in the city," Shay said.

I looked at Jill. "You're the tie breaker."

She grinned. "I'm undecided."

"Of course you are."

"It doesn't matter what we are going to do, though," Kelsey interjected. "You have to do what's best for you as a unit."

"Even if that means sacrificing what I want?" I asked quietly. "Because I know the best thing for us would be to move out of the city and live near Aidan's family."

"Sometimes we don't want change," Shay said. "And then it turns out to be exactly what we need."

I sighed. "I really need a beer."

After a few hours at the bar with my friends I walked home, lost in thought. They'd given me a lot to think about, but in true friend fashion, they didn't tell me what to do.

This would have to be my decision. Mine and Aidan's.

I let myself into the apartment and was greeted by the most precious sound I'd ever heard.

My children laughing.

Tiny, cute baby laughs.

They were on the living room carpet, on their backs while Jasper alternated between nosing one twin and then the other.

Aidan sat on the floor and watched them, a slight smile on his face. He looked up at me, heart in his eyes.

"Hey," he said, his smile widening into a grin.

I set my bag down onto the kitchen table and unwrapped the scarf from around my neck. "Hi."

Perching next to Aidan, I gave him a kiss. He slid his arm around me as we continued to gaze at our children.

"How long have you been watching this game?"

"About an hour. See? We don't need a nanny, we have Jasper."

I fell silent for a moment, reaching out to tweak Oliver's big toe. He kicked against my hand. Six months old and he was already packing a punch. He'd only grow bigger and stronger. His hair had finally started to sprout— blond fuzz. Completely unlike Sophie's wild, dark mane that was already covering her ears.

"We used the money from your grandmother to expand Veritas," I said quietly. "We could use my author nest egg."

He looked at me slowly. "Are you saying what I think you're saying?"

"There are a lot of things we have to discuss," I said. I reached up to stroke his cheek. "But yeah. I'm saying yes."

"We're leaving the city?"

"We're leaving the city," I repeated.

My heart broke and soared at the same time. I knew what I was giving up, but I thought about what Kelsey had asked. What was I going to gain?

Chapter 22

Mom Blog Entry:
The twins are sick again. I feel like I live at Urgent Care. Pretty sure parents keep them in business.

Mrs. Nowacki handed me her smart phone—yes, the woman had somehow been talked into getting a smart phone—and showed me the pictures of her newly purchased condo.

I swiped through the photos and nodded. "It looks really nice."

"It is five-minute walk from your *bubbe* and *zayde*."

"And this is really what you want?" I asked her. "No one is coercing you to do this?"

"No, Sibbila. This is my decision."

It was the middle of December and there had been a bitter snap of bad weather. It was currently snowing, coming down in massive flakes, which promised several inches by the time it was done. Mrs. Nowacki had only just returned to the city a few days ago and this had been her welcome home present.

"Jesse is moving to Atlanta with me," she said, standing up and heading to the kitchen to put on water for tea.

"He is?" I asked in surprise. "How did that come about?"

"I tell him I am moving before the first of the year. He offered to come with me. I say yes."

"Oh, wow. Congratulations. Does that mean you're getting married?"

She blinked. "Why would we get married?"

I frowned. "Aren't you Catholic?"

"Yes. So? He already been getting the goat milk for free. Why do we need the piece of paper?"

"Hey, do you, girl."

"Do me, what?" she asked.

"Never mind." I waved my hand away.

"I do have one tiny favor to ask of you."

"Anything."

"Jesse is allergic to cats. Will you take Aiko?"

Her eyes were so beseeching I couldn't possibly say no.

"Of course we'll take him." I smiled.

"Great. I bring him by tomorrow to get him comfortable and settled in."

"Er, wonderful." I pondered how I was going to break the news to Aidan, who was not a cat person. Not that I was a cat person. At least Jasper already got along with Aiko.

"When is your departure date?"

"December 27th. Are you having a Christmas get together here?"

"I hadn't planned on it," I admitted. "I wasn't sure when you were leaving, Annie is going to be in Montauk with her aunt and uncle. Caleb and Em are out of town. Zeb and Terry are spending the holidays with Terry's parents in Connecticut. And Stacy is going to be in London."

"London? Why?"

"Her boyfriend is taking her on vacation."

"Fancy."

I nodded.

"Does this mean you are going Upstate to spend time with Aidan's family?"

"No. Caleb is taking a few days off after Christmas with Em and extending their stay, so Aidan is sticking close to Veritas."

She shook her head. "Always so busy. Your *mąż*."

"Yep."

Mrs. Nowacki stared at me. "You do not seem like yourself."

"I'm myself. I'm just tired."

"Go lay down. If the *bubelas* wake up, I feed them."

I didn't have the heart to tell her my exhaustion wasn't just sleep deprivation. It was like another wave of post-partum had hit. Everything was good, but I just felt *blah*. And for the life of me, I couldn't figure out why.

Instead of taking a nap, I grabbed my laptop off my bedside table and flipped it open. I took my feelings to my mom blog and poured out all my thoughts and emotions—it was strange to feel completely stagnant and at the same time, my life was changing. It was difficult to reconcile, and I wasn't sure I knew how to do that.

I faintly heard the sounds of a baby crying, quickly followed by another. A few moments later, both of them stopped. Mrs. Nowacki had swooped in to save the day, just to give me a few more minutes to myself.

My mind wandered to the day Annie had come over and we'd both taken pregnancy tests. What would our life look like—mine and Aidan's—if I'd gotten pregnant again? That thought terrified me more than uprooting my life in the city and moving to the country.

I loved where his parents lived. It was serene and beautiful—and though I wasn't a nature lover, I did admit it had a nice sort of appeal.

But I was under no illusion that we were moving out of the city in order to save money. In the end, I knew we'd own something, but the idea of a thirty-year mortgage made me queasy. It was a commitment. And I had to be sure we found a house that I loved because I wasn't renting again. I'd already moved within the city too many times, and I did not want to have to move again.

Whatever home we decided to buy, it would be the house I was going to die in.

Dramatic?

Yes.

Aidan came home a few hours later, carrying bags of takeout. "Thai food. I have provided sustenance."

"You're my favorite, did you know that?" I asked, standing on my tiptoes to kiss his lips.

Aidan looked at Mrs. Nowacki and asked, "Are you staying? I got enough for four."

She shook her head. "No. Jesse and I go out for the date night."

Mrs. Nowacki set Sophie down on the carpet, underneath one of those contraptions with the dangling plastic pieces that rattled and swung when hit.

She walked over to Aidan and brushed her lips across his cheek and then clearly whispered something in his ear because he nodded and looked at me.

"Tomorrow, yes?" she asked me.

I nodded.

The front door shut and I went to the cabinets to pull out plates. "What did she whisper to you before she left?"

"She said I needed to be gentle with you tonight."

I raised my eyebrows.

He rolled his eyes. "She didn't mean it like *that*. Pretty sure she was referring to your feelings."

"Ah."

"What's going on, Sib?"

I set the plates down and then grabbed two paper napkins from the napkin holder on the table. "I don't really know. I just feel—well, how do you keep your daily life interesting when sometimes it's such a drudge."

"I have no idea, actually," he said. "And I love what I do."

"I love what I do, too."

"Do you?" Aidan asked.

I opened the box of Pad Thai. "I still love to write, but what I want to write has changed."

"Okay."

"I don't have any hobbies," I said. "I don't have an outlet."

"What about power walking with your mom group?"

"Not a hobby. Buddy system exercise. Sure, we get to

talk and be social, but again, not a hobby. I just, I think I'm having an identity crisis. I used to be this bumbling girl in her twenties trying to figure out life. Then things started to get good and my career started to do well. And now I'm a mother of twins trying to figure it out all over again. So when, *exactly*, do I figure out life?"

I took a pair of chopsticks, but didn't make a move to start eating.

Aidan watched me—carefully—like he was afraid that if he said the wrong thing, I was going to erupt. Finally, he spoke, "You don't want to move Upstate."

"This has nothing to do with that."

"I think it has more to do with that than you think."

"Or you think you know what you think you know, only to realize you know nothing."

"What?"

"Never mind. It really doesn't have anything to do with moving Upstate."

"Okay. So do you want to open a bottle of wine and look at real estate listings?" He scooped out some rice and then slathered it with red curry.

I took a deep breath and then walked over to the wall and gently started to bang my head against it.

"Guess that's a no, then."

"I need to go for a walk. Okay?" I asked.

He frowned. "Okay."

"The twins have eaten. They should be good for a while."

When I headed to the front door, Jasper followed me. I shook my head and said, "Stay."

He sat and whined.

I quickly bundled up, not wanting to feel one bit of the cold.

Aidan watched me, his brow furrowed in confusion.

"It's not you, okay?" I said to him. "I just need to clear my head."

"Okay. Take your time. No rush, really."

"And this is why you're perfect. You get me. Even when I don't get me."

I left the apartment and walked the streets of Greenpoint. I didn't want a drink, so I avoided bars and eventually found myself in front of Mother Shucker.

Almost every seat in the restaurant was taken, but there was a lone stool at the edge of the counter. I snagged the seat before someone else could.

Annie was at the stove, her back to me. I removed my coat and hung it up on the hook underneath the bar. Annie plated two orders of tacos and then turned to set them down at the customers sitting next to me.

She glanced at me and raised her eyebrows. "I didn't expect to see you sitting there. Where's Aidan?"

"Home with the babies."

Annie frowned and looked like she wanted to say something personal, but a quick glance at the people next to me had her shutting her mouth.

"Lobster roll please. With the wedge fries."

"Coming up. Anything to drink?"

"Water's good." I grabbed the bottle of tap water and poured myself a glass.

The people next to me finished their food just as I got mine and then they asked for the check. The server working the floor brought it to them and they left quickly.

"Dinner rush is over," Annie said. "We'll get some stragglers, but the crazy has passed."

I picked up a fry and took a bite. "Business looks good."

"It's very good."

"How was Thanksgiving?"

"Good. Yours?"

"Good."

She paused and peered at me. "Are you lying?"

"Are *you* lying?"

"What's going on, Sibby? You don't look like yourself."

"Why does everyone keep saying that?"

"Everyone who?"

"You. Mrs. Nowacki."

"That's it? That's only two of us."

"Yes, but you're two people who know me really, really well." I looked at my plate as I finished my fry. "I think my soul is sad."

"Is this you being a writer? A new mom? Or are you finally trying to be human?"

"Is this you trying not to be sensitive?"

"I'm habitually running on four hours of sleep a night. I don't think I have the bandwidth to be sensitive."

"I appreciate the honesty."

"No, you don't."

"No, I don't," I agreed. "But it'll have to do. You're my best friend."

A food ticket printed at Annie's station, but she crumbled it up. "Raw bar order." She gestured with her chin to the two guys shucking oysters. "Let's get back to you."

"I think I'm having an identity crisis," I said slowly.

"Go on."

"Nothing is making me happy. I sound like a complaining asshole. I'm very aware of this," I said. "I have a great career, amazing friends, a husband with dimples, healthy twins. Why, Annie? Why do I feel this way? Nothing is making me happy. Not the books I write. Not my relationships. I'm just...sad. And I don't know why."

"Have you talked to your doctor?" she asked gently.

"I talked to her a few weeks after the twins were born. I had postpartum. This doesn't feel like that. This feels different."

"What did postpartum feel like?" she asked. "And why didn't you tell me?"

"What could you have done?"

"I don't know. I would've tried to have been there for you, though."

"Stop." I reached across the counter to grab her hand. "You were busy with your restaurant opening and I wasn't even sure I knew what I was feeling. The only reason I even sought the counsel of my doctor was because of—"

I immediately fell silent, not wanting to burden Annie with any more guilt.

"Finish that statement."

"Em. She was the one who really brought it to my attention." I shook my head. "No. This isn't postpartum. This is something else. Something I can't put my finger on."

Annie withdrew her hand, but not her comfort. "I know what you're feeling. Like, every day you wake up and you're doing the same thing with the same people. And your life is good, but you're just kind of sick of it. But you're sick of it for no good reason because like you said, everything on the outside looks perfect. Great, in fact. But how you look on the outside is not indicative of what it feels like on the inside."

"You've felt this way before," I repeated as understanding dawned. "It's why you blew your life up and moved to Montauk. I get it now."

She nodded. "I just needed *different*. And now you need different, and no one can fault you for it. What you're feeling is completely normal. How you handle it…that's up to you."

"I'm not going to blow up my life."

"Aren't you? By wanting to write a children's novel? You're basically saying *screw you* to the foundation that brought you success. Look, I know what it's like to want to shake it up. But you're Sibby and I'm Annie, and my way was destructive."

"Was it? I mean, yeah, you were unkind to those who loved you, but look what you've done with the destruction." I gestured the to the successful restaurant she'd poured every moment of her time and emotion into.

"So what are you going to do, Sibby?" she asked. "How are you going to handle the unrest inside you?"

"I don't know. Scream into a pillow?"

She smiled. "That's a start, but what about long term?"

Now was the time to tell her. To tell my best friend that Aidan and I were making a plan to move Upstate, but something held me back. Maybe it was my own fear that if I said it out loud to my best friend, it would become real and I wouldn't be able to take it back.

Did I want to move Upstate? I'd had a few weeks to think about it. But I wasn't any more excited now than I had been when Aidan had broached the subject. I was scared of the unknown—and moving away from everything that was familiar still terrified me. Yet I knew it was the right thing to do. The right thing for our family.

"I think I need a hobby," I said. "Writing on a mom blog is not really a hobby. Exercise—well, we all know how I feel about that. I think I need something that's just for me, independent of my children, independent of my career, independent of being a wife."

"What hobby are you thinking about?"

"No idea, really. It used to be cocktail hour with you, but we're not those people anymore."

She shook her head and sighed. "Weird, isn't it?"

"What?"

"Holding yourself accountable."

"Why did we say we wanted to be adults again? I don't remember signing up for this."

"Too late. You've spawned. There's no going back."

Chapter 23

Mom Blog Entry:

Sophie cut her first tooth and I burst into tears. With the appearance of that first tooth, I flashed forward in my mind to the days when I would no longer be needed. I saw myself becoming obsolete, becoming her adversary over time as she progressed through adolescence. I'd have to fight for respect, and learn to speak modern teenager.

I called my mother and apologized for what I'd put her through.

I came home one evening, a week before Christmas, to a perfectly decorated and set up tree. Twinkly lights and red tinsel adorned the branches and I couldn't say I was disappointed to the pretty picture I'd walked into. Two sleeping babies, a cute pup wearing a reindeer sweater, and a husband rolling out dough on the kitchen counter while listening to Christmas carols.

I'm still Jewish, right?

"This is amazing," I said, removing the scarf from around my neck and placing it on the hook by the door. "You did all this?"

"I had some free time—and I wasn't going to let you fall into a holiday funk."

I went over to him and looped my arms around his neck. "Why are you the greatest?"

"Because I am." He pecked me on the nose.

"What are you baking?"

"We're not baking. We're making homemade ornaments for the tree. We're going to have the twins' handprints as ornaments to go with Jasper's paw print."

I felt my eyes prick with tears and then I was suddenly sobbing against his chest.

"Hey? What's wrong? Are you overwhelmed with happiness or sadness?"

"Both." I sniffed. "Why didn't I think of that?"

"Sibby—"

"Will I ever stop being such a mess?"

"Er—"

"Oh, hush." I laughed through my tears. I leaned over and scooped up Jasper into my arms and buried my nose against his fur. He smelled like cinnamon and pine.

"He's been drinking water from the Christmas tree stand, hasn't he?" I asked with a grin.

"But of course. It tastes better that way."

I put Jasper down and then rolled up my sleeves. "Do you need help?"

"Nah, the dough is done. The oven is ready to bake the ornaments. I'm just waiting for the twins to wake up, which should be any momen—"

Before he'd even finished his sentence, one of the twins let out a bellow. We marched to the nursery, wrangled the twins into clean diapers, and I nursed them in tandem.

"Are you doing okay?" Aidan asked.

"For once, I'd like not to talk about me."

He nodded. "Okay."

"How are you, Aidan?"

"I'm good."

We stared at one another.

"What is it you're not telling me?"

"I started looking at houses Upstate."

"Okay."

"I think I found a few. I'd really love to show them to you."

I nodded. "All right. How about tonight we open a bottle of wine, put the twins to bed, and look at houses?"

"Wow, we just became old, but that sounds kind of like the best night ever."

I forced a smile. "Sounds great."

"You know what? Let's not move Upstate."

"What?" I frowned. "What are you talking about?"

Oliver detached himself from my breast and Aidan took him and placed him at his shoulder to burp him.

"The idea of moving Upstate clearly has you grimacing. Which means your soul is grimacing. I'm not going to drag you away from your life and make you unhappy."

"I'm already unhappy, Upstate won't change that," I snapped.

He reared back like I'd hit him. "You're unhappy? With me?"

"No. Not with you. Just…with life. Overall, I guess." I looked down at Sophie whose eyes were closed.

"Talk to me, Sibby," Aidan said gently. "Let me help."

"I don't think you can," I said slowly. "It's not about you or the twins, or even my career. You know? I just feel…lost. And sad."

"A lot has changed in the past year," he said.

"Yeah."

"Maybe moving Upstate now isn't what you need. Maybe you need stability."

"I don't think so," I said. "My life is not really stable—I mean, aspects of it are. I can count on you. We're in love. Our children are healthy—when they're not getting pink eye. I don't think it's my location."

"Have you ever felt this way before?"

Sophie finished nursing and I laid her on my lap so I could tuck myself back into my bra.

"Do you ever feel like, you look at your life and who you are, and it doesn't line up with the person you thought you'd be at this age?"

"Well, sure. But who can ever know?"

"Is there anything about your life you wish you could change?"

"Yes."

"What?" I asked.

"Where we live."

We smiled at each other.

"I want something. I just don't know what it is. I feel stuck. Does that make sense?" I asked.

"Yeah. I get it, Sibby, I really do."

"Do you still love me? Even though I'm sort of insane?"

"You're not insane. You're human."

"I feel like a dingus, though. Complaining when nothing is really wrong."

"You can want more, you can want change. Just know that I'm here for you, always. And if you need to talk in the middle of the night, then wake me up. I'm here for you. Okay?"

"Okay," I whispered.

"Just promise me one thing," he said.

"What?"

"Don't let Stacy drag you to one of those retreats where you drop peyote and see your life's vision in the fire."

I blinked. "I'll promise no such thing. That sounds kind of great."

He laughed. "Come on, let's make the kids' handprint ornaments and then look at house listings."

New Year's came and Aidan and I spent the night at home with the twins. We drank champagne, had cheese fondue, and rang in the new year by looking at more real estate listings.

"You're shooting down everything I'm showing you,"

he said in exasperation.

"They're not our house," I said, reaching for my glass of bubbly.

He clam-shelled the laptop. "Do you think maybe you don't want to find a house?"

I waved my finger at him. "Don't do this. I promised you I was on board. I also promised you I wouldn't be passive aggressive about house hunting. If I don't like something, I'm telling you."

"You're right. You're not passive aggressive. More like regular aggressive. I find it kind of hot."

I arched a brow. "You clearly want to start the new year off with a bang."

"Maybe I do, yeah."

"You know I was talking about sex, right?"

"Yes, Sibby. I knew you meant sex."

"I've got a lot of rage lately. Do you mind if I take it out on you?"

"Be gentle."

"No promises."

January was colder than a witches' tit and only added to my irritability. While I was replying to comments on my latest blog post, I reached for my coffee cup. My fingers fumbled and managed to push the mug over…spilling coffee onto my keyboard.

"Shit balls!" I yelled, jumping up and reaching for a crumbled napkin, mopping up the spill.

The screen was still on and I breathed a sigh of relief. But then I heard a whirring noise and then the screen went black.

I pressed the restart button.

Nothing.

I picked up the laptop and placed it next to my ear. Not a sound could be heard.

Aidan came out of the bedroom, dressed for the day at the wine store. "What are you doing?"

"Did you know if you put a laptop up to your ear, you can't hear the sound of the ocean?"

"Did you put Bailey's in your coffee?" he asked in confusion.

"No, but I did spill coffee all over my keyboard and now Milton has gone dark."

He heard the panic in my voice because he came over and took the computer from me. He pressed the restart button and when nothing happened, he did a few other finagley things.

None of which made the computer turn on.

"I killed it. Here lies Milton. A moment of silence please," I said, placing my hand over my heart and bowing my head.

"Don't count Milton out yet. We'll take him to Mac Attack and let them work their magic." He looked at the clock on the stove. "Damn, I have to go. I'm going to be late for a wine rep meeting."

"I have to take Milton in now. What do we do with the twins?"

"Take them with you?"

"It's ten degrees outside. I do not want my babies out in ten-degree weather."

"Is Stacy back from London?"

"No."

"Is Annie—"

"Working."

"Em?"

"Wedding dress fitting."

Aidan hung his head. "We really should've made friends with our neighbors."

"So we can pawn our spawn off on them? This is Mrs. Nowacki's fault. If she hadn't left the city, she'd be here."

"Okay, blaming a Polish octogenarian for living her own life is below the belt, Sib."

I placed Milton into his computer bag and handed it to Aidan. "Just drop it off on your way and give them my number and tell them to call me."

"It's ten blocks in the wrong direction."

"I'm really trying not to freak out right this minute. My life is on this computer. Milton was only partly on the cloud. Do you know what will happen if I don't get Milton up and running again?"

Aidan slowly backed away from me out of self-preservation. "What will happen?"

"Complete and utter destruction of my sanity. I'm barely hanging on by a thread. I need this, Aidan."

Aidan grabbed Milton's carrying case. "Fine. I'll do it. I'll see you tonight."

"Thank you! I love you. Never change!"

"I love girls who have fun bachelorette parties," I said to Aidan as I set my cellphone into my bag.

"You promised not to get too crazy. Don't forget that, okay?" Aidan said with a wry grin.

"Too crazy? We're drinking beer and smashing plates."

"I worry, you know?" he said.

I went to the twins, who were on the rug, struggling to stay sitting up on their own.

Cue melting heart.

I looked to the ceiling so my tears wouldn't fall and ruin my makeup.

"Did I tell you that you look really hot?" Aidan asked after I had my moment and got myself under control.

"You did, but tell me again," I teased.

"You look really, really hot."

I went to my husband and kissed him. "I'll be home before midnight."

"Don't rush on my account. This is the closest thing to a girls' night you've had in ages."

"Yeah, I have a workaholic best friend, and my other closest friend is also work obsessed and deep in lust with her hot chef boyfriend."

"Boyfriend? She's calling him her boyfriend now?"

"No, she refuses to call him that. That's just what I call him because I feel stupid saying fuck buddy."

I wrapped myself up in winter garb, took one last look at my beautiful family, and then went out into the cold February night. I took a deep breath, loving the sting of cool, dry air in my lungs.

I was free tonight, but I knew what I was coming home to.

I trekked to Em and Caleb's apartment a few blocks away where we'd congregate, have a round of drinks, and then head off to the rage room.

Caleb was coming out of the building as I was reaching for the knob.

"Hey, Sib," he said with a grin and a hug.

"Escaping just in time, huh?"

"Yeah, they're already half a drink in. Listen, don't tell Em I asked you this, but will you make sure she doesn't drink too much? Keep her safe?"

I patted his shoulder. "On my honor as a mom, I promise not to let your fiancée get shitfaced."

He laughed. "You're the greatest."

"Sorry your guys' night includes chilling at my place with two babies."

"Nah, they're fun. Besides, if you promise me pizza and beer, then you can pretty much get me to do whatever you want."

"I'll remind Em of that," I said with a wink.

I went into the building and climbed the stairs. Laughter came through the closed door. I knocked and then let myself in.

Em was sitting on the couch, wearing black leggings and a red sweater, holding a mixed drink of some sort. Two young women who resembled Em with their brown hair and small statures, looked at me with smiles of greeting. Her younger sisters.

"Sibby!" Em got up and came to greet me. "Guys, this is Sibby. Sibby, meet my sisters, Evan and Ella. And Marigold is my best friend from when we were kids."

"Call me Mari," Marigold said. "Please God, call me Mari."

"I think I'm behind on the drinking," I commented, removing my scarf.

"I flew in yesterday," Mari said. "We've been drinking since then. So yeah, you're way far behind."

Em laughed, her cheeks flushed pink.

"I thought we were doing beer?"

"Vodka has less calories," Ella stated with a smirk. "And I plan to drink a lot—but I do have a bridesmaid dress I want to look good in."

"I like your style," I said with a grin. "Vodka it is."

Evan poured me a cocktail and then we all took seats around the living room. A cat came out of the bedroom and wrapped himself around Em's leg.

"You guys became fast friends," I said with a smile.

"He was the perfect gift," she said. "You sure Mrs. Nowacki doesn't mind that you gave him to us?"

I shook my head. "I talked to her the other day on Skype and she understands that our house was too crazy to add another living thing to it."

"Aiko gets under the covers on Caleb's side and curls up at his back," Em said. "It's the cutest thing I've ever seen."

"When did you guys fly in?" I asked Evan and Ella.

"This morning," Evan answered.

Em's sisters lived in Denver and shared an apartment together. I wondered if Em missed Colorado, but she seemed pretty happy in New York.

"Finish your drinks," Mari commanded. "And let's get going."

"Eh, I'm going to pace myself." I set my cup aside.

"Oh, right," Mari winked. "Em said you're breastfeeding. I don't miss those days, believe me."

I nodded. "I can't wait until I stop nursing. I've got a few more months of it at least."

"Ugh, can we stop the baby talk?" Ella asked.

She was the youngest of all of us and at twenty-three, wasn't yet thinking about babies.

We all slowly got our heavy coats and hats before trudging into the cold. Fifteen minutes of tromping through Greenpoint, then Mari announced, "Here we are."

She opened the door of the warehouse with large windows and let the rest of us go in first. Evan went up to the girl at the desk and gave her our party's name. We were led through the warehouse to a private room that was set up with ten tables designed to look like a hotel event.

"We have protective eyewear and mechanic's onesies and gloves, but we need you to sign a waiver releasing us of all responsibility for any possible injuries."

I took the pen she was holding, quickly skimmed the paper, and then signed my name. The others did the same.

"When you're finished, just come back out front where you can purchase a video of your time in the rage room. You're welcome to film with your own phones if you want to." She shut the door and the five of us looked at each other before we ran to the hooks on the wall and made a grab for the mechanic onesies.

When we were all protected, Mari handed each of us a bat.

I went to a corner table and stood behind a chair,

lamenting the fact that I was about to destroy beautiful china.

"Ready?" Mari asked. "Go!"

The noise of breaking dishes and girls yelling infiltrated my ears. They were having fun, enjoying the act of smashing plates and glassware.

"Come on, Sibby! Join in!" Em called out when she saw that I hadn't made a move.

I gripped the bat between my hands and lifted it. I took a step forward and saw my dim reflection in a goblet.

Something snapped inside of me.

Letting out my best Xena Warrior Princess war cry, I swung the bat, clearing most of the glasses from the table. The sound of crashing and breaking china was music to my ears. But it wasn't enough.

I went for the flowers in the glass vases, and then I let go of the bat completely so I could pick up two salad plates and throw them at a wall.

They shattered, pieces falling to the floor.

It took me a moment to realize the only sound I heard was the rapid beating of my own heart. I turned slowly, encountering four pairs of curious eyes on me.

"Sibby?" Em asked cautiously. "Are you okay?"

"Yeah. Why?"

"Because that was like, a lot of rage," Ella said.

"We're in a rage room."

Em looked at Evan and stage whispered, "How much vodka was in her cocktail?"

"As much as mine," Evan said defensively. "She looked like she could use it. Clearly I was right."

I lifted the bat and rested it on my shoulder. "I've got one table left."

Everyone instinctively took a step back.

I'd never felt more in control than I had when I lost my shit in that room.

There was definitely something to this rage room idea.

Chapter 24

Mom Blog Entry:

Why do my successes as a parent never occupy my mind as completely as my failures?

I'm giving my children everything I've got, and somehow it still doesn't feel like enough.

Em linked her arm through mine and held me back from the other three who were singing and skipping down Kent Street in Brooklyn. Evan had packed a flask of straight booze and the three of them had been imbibing steadily, but Em and I had made sure to pace ourselves.

"Are you doing okay?" Em asked.

I glanced at her. "I'm doing fine."

"What was that back there? In the rage room?"

"Me enjoying a night out with a friend of mine who's about to get married," I said, purposely evading her question. "Besides, I'm supposed to ask you how you're doing. Are you excited?"

"Excited for the wedding to be over," she said with a grin. "And go on our honeymoon."

"Ah, yes, the honeymoon. Have you guys already booked your hotel in Puerto Rico?"

"Yup. We're all booked and ready to rock. Why is it that even when you plan on having a small wedding, the event takes on a life of its own?"

"Let me guess. Your mother has made this bigger than you wanted it to be."

"How'd you know?"

"Because my mother did the same thing. Mothers think their daughters' weddings are about them."

"My mom got her wedding. Why does she need to have my wedding too?"

"Word to the wise. Just drink champagne and enjoy the marriage. The wedding itself is just one long, taffeta filled party."

Em groaned.

"I'm the honest friend, remember?" I said with a grin. "You'll be beautiful. Caleb will be handsome. You guys can sneak off and be alone."

"No, we won't be able to do that. My mother will be watching."

"I'll create a diversion."

"Would you really?"

"We'll come up with a signal and then I'll pretend to be choking or something."

"You'd do that for me?"

"We gals with crazy, wedding-obsessed mothers have to stick together."

She pressed her head to my shoulder. "I wish you were in my wedding party."

"Nah, you don't need me. I'll be the one making faces at you from the audience."

"We're here!" Ella called, holding open a heavy wooden door to a bar in Brooklyn that didn't have a sign on it.

It was dark, but not divey. It was very speakeasy, with old timey cocktails and a piano player. We grabbed a corner booth and I said, "First round is on me."

"I'll help bring the drinks back," Mari offered.

"Thanks." I smiled as the girls rattled off their drink orders after looking at the menus in the center of the table.

"The rage room was a genius idea for a bachelorette party," I said to Em's matron of honor.

She smiled. "She deserved something different, you know? She's like, my favorite person ever. I wanted her to have the best time tonight."

"Mission accomplished." I sidled up to the bar and waited for the bartender to see me. I flashed a grin to grab his attention.

He came over immediately and it had less to do with me attempting to be sweet and more to do with the fact that we recognized each other.

"Well, I'll be damned," Tracksuit said, leaning over the bar to give me a hug.

"I had no idea you worked here. You left Antonio's? When?" I demanded.

"About six months ago." His eyes darted to Mari. "Hey. I'm Tracksuit. I used to work with Sibby."

"Why do you call yourself Tracksuit?" Mari asked.

"Because he wears Tracksuits," I explained. "Like Tony Soprano."

"Oh." She frowned in confusion and then shrugged. "Must be a New York thing."

"What can I get you guys to drink?" Tracksuit asked.

I rattled off the five drinks of choice.

Tracksuit reached for a shaker. "Five drinks for two people? Is Aidan here?"

I shook my head. "Bachelorette party. A friend is getting married next month."

"Ah, then the drinks are on me."

"You don't have to do that—"

"Sure, I do. For old time's sake."

He quickly made the drinks and set them on the small tray in front of him.

"You want to see if I still have my mad waitressing skills?" I asked with a laugh.

"Mad skills? Please, you were a train wreck."

"Hey, I did okay."

"Not to break up this stroll down memory lane, but my buzz is wearing off. I need to keep drinking. Let me take the drinks to the table," Mari said.

"You sure?"

"Yeah. I used to do this in college. I got this."

"Cool, I'll be there in a second."

Mari nodded, swooped up the tray, and departed for the table.

"Does she need a job?" Tracksuit asked. "We're looking for a waitress."

"You are?"

He nodded. "Just two shifts a week. Swing shift. Nine

to eleven. Wednesdays and Thursdays. If you know of anyone—"

"Me," I blurted out.

"You?"

I nodded.

"Last I heard you were a full-time author."

"I am."

"And a new mom," he said.

"The twins are old enough to drink from bottles."

"I don't get it," he said. "Why would you want to work in a bar after having worked in a restaurant? Are you looking for that certain brand of torture only the hospitality industry can offer you?"

"Do you ever feel like your life doesn't fit you?" I asked.

"Oh no, don't do that."

"Don't do what?"

"Don't go all existential, fatalist, philosophical on me. If you want the job that badly, then it's yours."

I smiled. "Really?"

"Really. Boss is never here. The staff is cool. Uniform is black top and black pants or a skirt."

I snorted. "I'm not wearing a skirt. It's winter."

He shrugged. "Do what you want, Sibby. Come by next week for your first shift."

"Don't I have to train?" I asked in surprise.

"You're taking drink orders and serving cocktails. There's no food here. You've got to know table numbers and the cocktails, but that's it. You'll learn on the job."

"I don't know what it is about your tone, Tracksuit, but I have to say, I'm digging the show of power."

He grinned.

"I better get back to my friends." I leaned across the bar and hugged him. "It was good to see you."

I hopped down and went back to the table with a spring in my step.

"Who hit on you?" Evan asked.

I grinned. "No one. I just knew the bartender from my days of waitressing."

Em looked at me. "You look happier."

"Rage room," Mari stated. "Works like a charm."

"I want to take an art class," I said to Aidan the next night over a bowl of hot lentil soup with homemade bread, courtesy of Aidan.

"Yeah? I think that's a great idea," he said. "When is it?"

"It starts next week. Wednesday and Thursday nights. Nine to eleven."

He frowned. "That's a little late for an art class, don't you think?"

"Ah, it's taught by a real artist. You know how they are. Sleep during the day, create at night."

He nodded. "That's okay by me. The store closes at eight. I can come home and hang with the twins while you make art."

I smiled.

"What kind of art will you be making?"

"Still life paintings."

"Cool."

I felt a twinge of guilt.

More than a twinge, actually. I was outright lying to Aidan and I wasn't even sure why.

I wasn't even sure why I'd decided to take the cocktail waitressing job either.

"Aidan?" I said, with the intention of coming clean.

"Yeah?" His eyes were on the soup.

I paused and he looked up at me.

"This is really good," I said with a smile. "Thanks for making it."

"All hail the crock pot. Where would modern humans be without it?"

"Dead. Or living off Twinkies."

Jasper pawed at the front door and I shot up from my seat. "I'll take him out."

"No, let me do it, you've hardly touched your dinner."

"It's fine. I don't mind." I placed my hand on his shoulder and kissed him.

The following week, I stuck work clothes into a bag and then left for my shift. I kissed Aidan and the babies good-bye. "I should be home around eleven thirty."

"No worries," he said. "Have fun."

"I will."

I got to the bar and changed in the bathroom. I wore a black V-neck sweater that emphasized my cleavage and then went out onto the floor. I'd arrived a few minutes before my actual shift and Tracksuit gave me the rundown of the table numbers.

From the moment I clocked in, I was on the go. I was moving fast and serving drinks. I was laughing with customers and enjoying the piano music.

And when I crawled into bed next to Aidan close to midnight, I woke him up and made love to him.

"You must've really enjoyed your art class," he panted when I rolled off him.

I smiled. "I think it's a game changer."

The next night, the same thing happened.

And before I knew it, three weeks had passed, and I hadn't spilled any drinks on any customers. During the days when I was with the twins, I felt lighter, freer. I felt like something had been given back to me.

Milton was fixed, running like a brand-new computer, and I no longer looked at it with loathing. I found a rhythm with writing again and the words of the sequel of my cliffhanger novel poured out of me.

I had more energy, I had more focus, I had more enjoyment.

Annie noticed the change in me when I swung by Mother Shucker with the babies for a quick visit. My parents detected when we Face Timed. Mrs. Nowacki commented on it when she heard my voice on our weekly Skype call.

The only one who didn't seem to realize anything was different was Aidan.

Though he was reaping the rewards of my newfound enjoyment, he said nothing about it.

A Wednesday night rolled around and with a spring in my step, I gathered my belongings and headed for the door.

"You look nice," Aidan commented. "Are you wearing makeup?"

"Just a little lip gloss and mascara."

"Hmm. And the apology earrings I bought you? Are you sure you want to wear them to your art class? What if you get paint all over them?"

I frowned. "Paint washes off."

"So it does." He went back to looking at his phone.

"I'll see you in a few hours," I called as I reached down to pet Jasper's head.

"Yeah, see you."

I shut the door and mulled over why Aidan was acting weird.

Three and a half hours later, I finished my shift. I opened the bar door and went out into the night. Moving off the sidewalk, out of the way of foot traffic, I took the time to button my coat and wrap the scarf around my neck.

When I took a step toward home, I halted.

There was my husband, dressed in a beanie, a coat and gloves, waiting for me.

"What are you doing here?" I blurted out. "Where are the babies?"

"With Em and Caleb." He cocked his head to the side. "So. Is there something you want to tell me?"

I swallowed. "I'm not taking a painting class."

"You don't say."

"How did you know?"

"I didn't know. Well, let me rephrase. I didn't know you were working in a bar, but I damned sure knew you weren't taking a painting class."

"How?"

"You're Sibby. And you were coming home without paint on your face, clothes or hair." He gestured with his chin to the bar. "You started wearing more makeup. And jewelry on a regular basis."

"Oh. You thought that I was—"

"No. I didn't think that. I just couldn't figure out what you were actually doing."

"And so you followed me." My tone wasn't accusatory, just a statement.

"Yeah. I followed you."

"Why didn't you ask me what I was really doing if you knew I wasn't doing what I said I was doing?"

He blinked while he worked out what I'd just said. "Why didn't you tell me what you were really doing? *What* is it you're actually doing, Sibby? What the hell is going on?"

"I work here. Two nights a week."

"Why?"

"Because I want to."

"No, I mean, why didn't you tell me you were working here. Why the secrecy?"

I swallowed. "It's gonna sound selfish. And strange."

"You needed something that was just for you."

It was my turn to stare. "Yes."

"I never thought you'd go back to waitressing."

The front door opened and Tracksuit came out, holding an envelope. "Oh good, I caught you. You left your paycheck." His eyes darted to Aidan. "Hey, dude!"

"Hey," Aidan said in surprise. He held out his hand. "I didn't know you worked here."

Tracksuit shot me a look. "Sibby didn't tell you? She was here a few weeks ago with her friends. Bachelorette party. I told her I was looking for a waitress and she applied."

"Small world, isn't it?" Aidan said, his smile strained.

"Do you still see Jess?"

"Every now and again," Aidan said. "She's busy with her new place."

"Tell her I said hi when you see her, would you?"

"I will."

"And hey, you both should come in one night that Sibby isn't working. Have some drinks. We can catch up."

"Sounds good."

They shook hands again and then Tracksuit gave me my check before going back inside.

I looked at Aidan. "Buy you a cup of coffee?"

"Okay."

We walked side by side up the street and went into a Polish bakery with a few tables. It was empty save for the people behind the counter. We ordered coffees and a pastry to split and then sat down at a corner table.

"Are you mad?" I asked.

"Yup."

I grimaced. "Are you going to yell?"

"No. Though I probably should," he stated. "This is how it starts, Sibby. You start lying like this on the regular basis and the next thing you know, you *are* cheating."

"I've never wanted anyone else," I said.

"It's okay if you did, so long as you don't act on it. We're human, you know?"

"Yes. Human." I frowned. "But no, I haven't been tempted by anyone else. I don't want anyone else. I just wanted *something* else."

"Why did you lie about it being an art class? Did you not think I'd understand?"

"I felt guilty, okay? I felt guilty that you and the babies and my career weren't enough. I felt guilty that I wanted to be out of the house and not have to check in with you. If I told you what I was really doing…I don't know. I guess I felt like it wouldn't be for me anymore."

"Did you tell Annie the truth?"

I shook my head.

"You can't lie to me, Sib. If you need something, you have to tell me. We don't keep secrets from each other."

I nodded glumly.

"Can you try and explain to me the waitressing appeal?"

"When I saw Tracksuit a couple of weeks ago, and he said he was looking for a waitress, I just knew I wanted the job. I can't explain it, but when I was waitressing at Antonio's—that was a fortifying time in my life. I was confused about everything. I had no idea what I wanted. I was reeling. Licking my wounds from Matt's betrayal. Waitressing…I don't know. It reminded me of the girl I used to be. The girl who wasn't sure about her dreams, but who was still youthful and determined enough to find them."

I held on to my cup of coffee while I stared into it. "It made me hungry again. It threw me back into a time in my life when possibilities were endless, all I had to do was decide what I wanted. It was good to feel that again."

I paused and then said, "I've started writing again. A romance. A sequel to the book I just finished. I have joy, Aidan. Joy I wasn't sure I was going to find."

He reached across the table and took my free hand. "I wish you'd told me what you were doing. I get why you didn't, but I wish I'd been in the know. I hate feeling like an outsider when it comes to you. We're a team, and if we're not a team my life doesn't make sense. I know I'm not responsible for your happiness, but anything I can ever do to help you find it, I want to help."

"I'm a selfish asshole."

"Yeah." He grinned. "But you're my selfish asshole."

"Gross." I wrinkled my nose. "Do you forgive me?"

"Are you truly happy?"

"Yeah."

"Then I forgive you."

I looked down at the twins who were in their double stroller, both of them snacking away on their bottles of breast milk. They were doted on by everyone who passed them on the way to the bathroom.

Couldn't say I blamed them. My children were adorable. Well, Oliver was a cute baby. Sophie, not so much. She had a unibrow. If there had ever been any doubt about her parentage, the fact that my daughter had my brow line spoke volumes.

"If you wanted a serving job, I could've given you one here," Annie said as she placed fried fish tacos in front of me.

"I didn't know I wanted a serving job until Tracksuit told me he was looking for a server. I feel like a grade A asshole, though. Lying to Aidan about it."

"It wasn't like you were having an affair," she pointed out. "But yeah, the lying is not okay. Especially not to your husband."

"Yeah, I have the best spouse in the history of spouses and I would be all kinds of idiot if I fucked that up."

"Was he mad?"

"Aidan's version of mad. It was more hurt than anything else."

"Weren't you going home and screwing his brains out every night you worked?"

"Yeah, so?"

"So, I thought sex fixed all the problems in a marriage."

"You really don't believe that, do you?"

She paused. "No. I guess I don't. I'm just trying to make you feel better."

"It was selfish."

"Doing something for yourself isn't selfish," she said. "Lying about it was selfish. And unkind. And I've got to say, I don't understand why you felt like you had to lie to him. He would've given it to you. He would've understood. Because he's Aidan."

"Yes, he's Aidan," I said in exasperation. I picked up a lime wedge and squeezed it over my fish. "He's perfect Aidan who buys me gifts when he messes up, which by the way is like, so rare. He actually wants to take care of my feelings. I mean, he's better with my feelings than I am. Is there ever going to be a time when I don't suck at this marriage thing?"

"You have to want not to suck at it before you can do something about sucking at it."

I gasped. "You think I suck at it?"

She rolled her eyes. "No. I just think you sometimes revert back to old patterns of behavior, like we all do. Now hush up and eat your fish before it gets cold."

Grumbling, I picked up one of the tacos and dug in.

"Hey, Annie, I'm going to roll silverware in the back while there's a lull in customers," Tanya said.

"Sure, I'll call you if people come in," Annie said.

Tanya nodded and then headed to the back kitchen, leaving us alone again.

"There's no way you would've given me a shift or two. Not with a server like Tanya."

"Super waitress," she said. "I'd be lost without her. Anyway. You're looking really good."

"Power walking."

"Ah."

"If only I could burn calories by crying, I'd already look like a Scandinavian nanny."

"And you'd have to dye your hair blond and go by the name Inga."

"Sacrifices," I said. "To look good in a dress."

She swallowed. "When are your parents flying in?"

"A few days from now. They're renting a car and will meet us up there."

"Caleb and Em," she murmured. "Getting married."

"Yeah." I cleared my throat. "Mills?"

"Finally over. Finally, finally." She smiled. "I'm fine, Sibby."

"I didn't say you weren't."

"Your scrunched nose said otherwise. I really am fine. Everything is good. Perfect, in fact."

"Okay."

"Have a good time while you're up there," she said.

"We will."

The twins finished their bottles and I picked up Sophie first to burp her. While I was attempting not to get spit up on, Stacy walked in. Marched more like.

"Why does she look like a storm trooper?" Annie asked.

"Got me," I said with a frown.

"You-you," she sputtered at me.

"Use your words," I said.

"It's all your fault!"

"What's all my fault?"

Sophie let out a milky belch, which I managed to catch with a napkin.

"My boyfriend wants a baby and it's all your fault!"

"Dude, I haven't seen in you in over a month," I said calmly. "And I didn't think he was your boyfriend."

"Oh, who are you kidding," she glared, "of course Gregory is my boyfriend. There is no way I'd let some random fuck buddy do what he's done to me."

Annie raised her eyebrows. "This just got way more interesting. Can we kill the baby talk and go back to this other topic?"

Stacy threw up her hands. "I'm not ready for a baby. I'm not even ready to make Gregory a key."

"Again, how is this my fault?"

"Gregory ran into Aidan and Caleb at The Brandy Room the night of Caleb's bachelor party and apparently, Aidan couldn't stop showing Gregory photos of the twins."

Sophie was done belching, so I thrust her at Stacy.

"Hold this. I need to burp the other one." I reached down and scooped up Oliver.

Stacy held Sophie away from her like she had the plague.

"What's wrong with me?" Stacy wailed.

"You want me to go down the list?" Annie asked in amusement.

Stacy glared at her. "I'm serious. What's wrong with me? First, I date a musician who was good at pretending he wanted monogamy and stability, but that was a lie. And the next guy—the guy I was supposed to be using for his hot, sexy body—actually made me catch feelings for him and now he wants to procreate with me."

"Gregory Roubideaux is a world-famous chef, who just went through a divorce and actually knows what he wants the second time around and who still isn't marriage shy, baby shy, or relationship shy, who lives in a Manhattan high rise in a penthouse overlooking Central Park and who took you to Europe after only a few months of dating," Annie paused. "What's the problem, exactly?"

"The problem is she's young and in her twenties, and her career is booming. If she has kids, all that goes out the window." I looked at Stacy. "Right? Or did I just totally project everything I felt onto you?"

"Did your career really die, Sibby? Because from where I'm standing, you're more successful than ever. Mom blog, romance author, social media influencer."

"Take it back," I warned.

"Take what back?"

"You just called me a social media influencer. I've never been more offended in my entire life."

"She's right, though," Annie said. "You talk about a diaper bag on your channel—a channel that has followed you through one public SNAFU after another and they love you for it—and the diaper bag you mention sells out within minutes. That's a big deal."

"Yeah, you have like, serious power," Stacy said. Her gaze strayed to Sophie who was tugging on a lock of Stacy's purple hair.

She looked down at my daughter and touched her nose to Sophie's.

And then she sighed.

I exchanged a look with Annie.

"What's that noise?" I asked, looking around, under the counter, behind my barstool.

"What noise?" Stacy asked.

"It sounded like the gates of your uterus opening for business," I teased.

"Oh stop." She rolled her eyes. "I'm not ready."

"Newsflash. You're never ready," I said.

"I like things the way they are," she said. "I don't want them to change."

"That's life, kid," Annie added.

Stacy looked back at Sophie and her gaze softened. "She is awful cute."

Sophie opened her mouth, made a gurgle, and then effectively projectile vomited all over Stacy.

"Yeah," Stacy said after a stunned moment of silence, "I'm definitely not ready for a baby."

Stacy left to wash the baby vomit off her, and no doubt to ponder the idea of ever having a kid.

I took Sophie to the bathroom and got her cleaned up as best I could, but she needed a bath.

"So, when do you think she'll cave and lock that man's ass down?" Annie asked when I came back from the bathroom.

I set Sophie in the stroller next to Oliver, who looked passive, and not at all considering vomiting the way his sister had.

For that I was grateful.

"I don't know if she will," I said. "It might be the classic case of right guy, wrong time."

"Based on Gregory's career success and his determination to succeed, I have a feeling he might make it the right time."

"You think he'll wait around until she's ready?" I asked. "They were supposed to be each other's rebound. A fling."

"And we all know how men get with their rebound," she said pointedly. "It happened in *When Harry Met Sally* and it happens in real life all the time."

I snorted. "Name one instance in real life that a guy married his rebound girl."

"Well, you married your rebound guy," she pointed out. "And Caleb is marrying his rebound girl."

"Em isn't his rebound girl," I protested. "Gemma was his rebound girl. So, your theory is incorrect."

"She's basically his rebound girl," Annie muttered. "Doesn't matter that she's great or his perfect match, in my eyes, she's still his rebound girl."

"Why do you care? You guys broke up over a year ago."

"Because he was my first great love, Sibby. You don't forget that or get over it fast."

"You do know she's involved in your business now. I mean, on the periphery."

"Yeah, which you said you'd handle for me."

I took a deep breath and then pulled off the Band-Aid. "I don't know how long that will be feasible."

"What do you mean?"

"Aidan and I are buying a house Upstate. Near his parents and his sisters."

She gripped the counter, her knuckles turning white. "When?"

"I don't know. Soonish. Whenever we find the right house. The mom blog and the sponsorships are generating a decent income. Between my nest egg and the growth of the blog, we have enough for a considerable down payment."

"You didn't just arrive at this conclusion." It came out like an accusation.

"We've been talking about it for weeks."

"Weeks," she repeated. "And you didn't tell me."

"Did you tell me when you fled the city and moved to Montauk?"

"That's not the same thing and you know it."

"It's exactly the same thing," I said, feeling anger rise

in my belly. "Why are you upset? Because I didn't tell you? Because I didn't include you in a thought process that affects me and my family?"

"I'm not your family?" she asked, an expression of hurt flashing across her face.

"Of course you're my family," I softened my tone, "but you keep saying we're not the girls we were ten years ago. We're not those girls who met in college. We're adults now."

"And being *adults* means buying houses and raising families?"

"It means doing what's best for the collective unit, even when you want to be selfish. I want to stay in the city, Annie. But I can't."

"Can't? Or won't?" She shook her head. "You're living Aidan's vision of what life is supposed to look like, not yours."

"That's not fair."

"It's not?" she said. "Am I wrong?"

"Yes. You're wrong."

"Did you want children? Or did you have them because your husband wanted them?"

"Do not bring my children into this."

"You've said it a dozen times, Sibby. You've said you're not sure this was the right path for you and if you could do it over again, you would've made a different choice."

I looked down at my sleeping babies while their godmother spewed her anger at me.

"You write a mom blog. You hang out with other moms. Face it, we have nothing left in common anymore. We only have history."

"What are you saying to me right now? Because it sounds like you're breaking up with me. After all the shit we've been through together? After all the crap and heartache?"

"Like you said, Sibby. We're not those girls from college anymore. Maybe we should stop pretending that this friendship hasn't been broken for a long time and we've both been too chicken shit to end it."

I slowly rose from the barstool. "Why do you do this?"

"Do what? I'm not doing anything you haven't already thought about."

I shook my head. "No. Let's be very clear. You're the one doing this to us. I'm still here. You're still my best friend. Do I hate the time Mother Shucker has taken from us by keeping you so busy? Yeah, because I'm selfish and I miss my friend. But I'd never make you feel bad about going for your dreams. Why are you making me feel bad for doing what's best for me?"

"Because I'm not sure leaving the city is the best thing for *you*."

"And I suppose you know what the best thing for me is?"

"Sibby, *you* don't even know what the best thing for you is. You haven't been stable since the twins were born."

"Stable?" I repeated. "Why? Because I've suffered post-partum and an overwhelming feeling of sadness and dissatisfaction? Wow. I never thought you'd be the one to throw my weaknesses in my face. Call me when you get your head out of your ass." I gripped the stroller and started for the front door, but I turned back at the last second. "Oh, and for the sake of honesty? I know you're still in love with Caleb, but you're too much of a coward to tell him."

I stomped out of the restaurant, past the few customers that had come in while we'd been having the worst argument of our friendship.

An argument that I was afraid might have changed us forever.

Chapter 26

Mom Blog Entry:
   Life is a series of milestones. Marriage. Babies. Mortgages. That first gray hair you find in your hoo-ha region.

I looked out the passenger window of the car as we drove Upstate for Caleb and Em's wedding. The trees were bare, but we weren't due for inclement weather, which was a blessing.

"You're quiet," Aidan said, his hand sliding off the wheel to rest on my thigh.

"Hmmm."

"Annie?"

"Yeah."

"You guys have fought before."

"Not like this," I said. "Not even when we fought over her treatment of Caleb and her blowing up her own life after it all went to shit."

After a moment he asked, "Is she right?"

"You're going to have to be more specific about that. Right about what?"

"Are you only friends because of history?"

"Partly, I guess. She's still my favorite person on this planet."

"Hey."

"Next to you, of course," I said. "But seriously, she's a close second. She was there before you. You know? We met *because* of her. If she hadn't dragged me to a bar on the Upper East Side and gotten me good and drunk, I never would've gone home with you."

"You would've gone home with me," he negated. "I was charming. Even then."

"Yeah, you were." I smiled at him. "She's afraid of being left behind, I think."

"Like someone else I know."

I snorted. "I told her we were leaving the city and I saw it; that moment when she realized we couldn't go on pretending everything was the same even though she knows it's not." I swallowed and then admitted. "I called her a coward."

He inhaled sharply. "That's not good. Why did you do that?"

"I told her she was still in love with Caleb and she was too much of a coward to tell him."

"You didn't."

"I did."

"Caleb is getting married this weekend," Aidan said. "What did you think that would do? Telling Annie something she already knows?"

"She picked a fight with me over something that isn't even about me. She and I are very similar in that regard. We think we're upset about something, but when you do some digging, you realize it's not about that at all. Is she upset we're moving Upstate? Sure, but it's not like we're moving to Europe. No. She's upset because Caleb is getting married and that door is closing forever."

"Can I ask you something? And I want you to be honest."

"I'm worried. But okay. Go ahead. Ask."

"Was she right? About you living my vision of our life together?"

"Sort of. I guess. But you're not responsible for me wanting to write my mom blog or a children's book. That was just a natural evolution because of the twins."

"Yeah."

"I need to say something, and just, let me get it out, okay?" When he nodded, I went on, "I don't resent you. Or our life. Or the twins. But I resent the change. Okay? I resent that my new normal is never really normal. I resent that my time isn't my own. But this life we've built together, it brings me so much more joy than misery. And yeah, I think I'm like most people. I don't like change. I like knowing what I'm getting into. And having babies proves that you know absolutely nothing about most things. It's a learn-on-the-job kind of deal. You know?

"You were ready to get married before I was. And you

know what? Marrying you was the best thing I did. Taking that leap of faith that you weren't another Matt who was going to screw me over was the best thing I could've done.

"Accidentally getting pregnant when I wasn't ready turned out pretty well, too. I'm better for it. And I know that when we do find the house of our dreams Upstate, I know it will be the right thing for us."

He took my hand and brought it to his lips. "I'm glad you don't resent me or our life together."

"Me too. It would make marriage a lot less fun."

A few hours later, we pulled into the parking lot of the mountain lodge where Em and Caleb had blocked off rooms for their wedding guests. It was picturesque, nestled among the hills and mountains.

"Why don't you run and check us in," Aidan said. "I'll unload the bags and the kids."

The twins were cranky and antsy. They'd been asleep for most of the drive up, but now they were itching to get out of their car seats. They had started crawling a few days prior, and now, when they were restricted from moving, they made their unhappiness known.

Thankfully, my parents were arriving the next night to give us a much-needed break and then they'd babysit the evening of the rehearsal dinner and again while we were at the actual wedding.

I went to the front desk and got checked in before heading out to the front of the lodge. Aidan stood at the curb with the twins who were shrieking in their stroller.

"Hungry, hungry hippos," I muttered, taking the stroller and wheeling it toward the lobby. A bellman brought out a cart and loaded up our bags as Aidan handed off the keys for valet parking.

The crying of the twins reverberated through the

elevator and by the time we found our floor, I had a slight headache. The bellman wheeled the cart into our room and quickly unloaded our five pieces of luggage, our hanging clothing bags, the package of diapers, and the portable crib before scurrying out into the hallway.

As soon as we had privacy, I whipped open my shirt. Thankfully, as soon as I shoved my nipples into mouths, it was silent once again.

"Did their lungs get stronger?" Aidan asked as he set up the portable crib in the corner.

"During the drive up here? Probably."

When the twins were done nursing, we each took one to burp and then let them down onto the carpet to crawl around and explore. Sophie was doing her version of an army crawl, but Oliver made haste and was booking it across the floor.

We hung up our dress clothes and unpacked.

"Stellar idea coming up a few days early," I said to Aidan as I unzipped one of the twins' luggage. It was all clothing.

"One of my better ones," he agreed.

"Did you call Caleb and tell him we arrived?"

"I shot him a text while you were checking in." He grinned. "He asked if we wanted to meet him and Em in the reception area for a drink."

"Let me guess; the tone of his text was stressed."

"You know it."

I laughed. "Let me freshen up a bit, take a moment to myself, and then we can go down there."

Twenty minutes later we had the twins in their stroller, much happier now that they'd been fed and put into clean diapers. We met Em and Caleb in the bar area of the lobby and took seats near the gas burning fireplace.

"What does everyone want?" Caleb asked after giving me a hug in greeting.

"Glass of red, please," Em said.

"Same," I replied.

"Scotch," Aidan said.

Caleb slapped Aidan on the back. "Come help me with these drinks."

Aidan went with Caleb to the bar, leaving Em and I alone. I ensured the twins had toys to keep them entertained, but most of the time the two of them occupied each other. Having two the same age was hectic, but oddly easier sometimes.

"So, on a scale of one to stressed, how are you?" I asked her.

She ran a hand through her brown hair, her engagement ring twinkling. "Caleb and I have to stay in separate rooms," she said. "My mother's edict."

"You and Caleb are paying for your own wedding," I reminded her. "Why are you letting her dictate?"

"Because sometimes it's just easier to go along with what she wants than it is to fight her."

"Oh. Preach. My mother is just like that," I said with a nod.

"You're looking really good, Sibby. Happy."

I smiled. "Thanks. I'm feeling good. I lost all the weight I wanted except for those last five pounds, but I figure it's all in my boobs."

The boys took that moment to return. Aidan handed me my drink and took the spot on the couch next to me.

Caleb swooped in to sit next to Em and placed her glass of wine on a coaster on the table in front of us. "I wonder when the day will come that I don't accidentally walk into a conversation about Sibby's boobs."

"You and every server in Greenpoint." I grinned and raised my glass of wine. "Cheers. To you guys."

"To surviving our families," Em muttered.

"To crab puffs at the rehearsal dinner," Caleb said.

"To awkward dancing at your wedding," Aidan added.

We all clinked our glasses and took sips.

"Wedding weekends are marathons, not sprints," I said. "And just remember, champagne makes your plastered-on smile hurt less."

"We should've just eloped," Em muttered. "But no. My mother would've disowned me."

The sound of heels across the lobby floor drew my attention. I turned my head and grinned at the sight of bright purple hair. Stacy's photography and video crew trailed behind her.

"Well, isn't this a cozy picture," Stacy said with a wide smile. She whipped out her phone and snapped four photos before we'd even managed to get ourselves together for a picture.

Caleb looked at Em and grinned. "And so it begins."

"Pierogis!" Mama Goldstein shrieked, moving past me into our hotel room.

My father shot me an amused look. "Hiya, Wapa."

"Hi, Dad," I said, embracing him, feeling my throat tighten and my eyes sting with tears. "You look good."

"I feel good."

I pulled back. "Retirement treating you right?"

"I thought I'd be bored, but your mother keeps me busy. Sexually."

"Ew."

He laughed. "Where's Aidan?"

"With Caleb. Best man duties or whatever." I looked over my shoulder at my mother who was cooing at both her grandchildren. "Hi, Ma."

"Hi." She waved absently, refusing to take her eyes off Sophie and Oliver.

Well, at least I knew she wasn't put out about babysitting them for the next couple of days.

I wheeled the cooler bag to my father. "Breast milk is in here."

"Er—great."

"We brought a ton of diapers, two suitcases full of clothing, and we'll fold up the playpen and stick the kids in the stroller for you."

My dad blinked, looking shell-shocked. Clearly, he was along for the ride. My mother was driving this train.

I called for a bellman and a cart and before I knew it, I was twin and parent free. We were going to have dinner later that evening to catch up, but it felt good to be alone.

After closing the door, I flopped onto my back, nestling my arms underneath the hotel pillows.

The sound of the key in the door alerted me that Aidan was back, but I made no move to get up.

He came in carrying a paper bag and set it down on the chair in the corner. "You look comfortable," he said with a grin, immediately kicking off his shoes. "Guess that means your parents arrived and already took the twins."

"Shhhh, do you hear that?" I asked, pretending to listen.

"What is it?"

"Utter silence."

He laughed and settled down next to me and wrapped an arm around me.

"How's Caleb?"

"Happy. Calm."

"That's Caleb. Three days before his wedding, cool as a cucumber."

"Do you want to take a nap before dinner with your folks tonight?" Aidan asked, opening his blue eyes wide, attempting to look innocent.

I slithered out of his arms but only so I could roll on top of him. "Naked nap time, you mean?"

He smiled, his hands going to my hips. "Is there any other kind of nap?"

Aidan fell asleep after our interlude, but I was wide-awake and reading, curled up on my side.

There was a slight rap on the door.

I got up, made sure my T-shirt was covering my chest, and then went to answer it. It was Stacy.

"Bad time?" she asked, her voice low.

I shook my head. "Aidan is down for a nap and the twins are with my parents. What's up?"

"Can we grab a cup of coffee in the lobby?"

"Sure. I'll meet you down there in a few?"

"Okay."

"Is everything all right?" I pressed.

"Yeah, I think so."

I frowned. "It's not about Caleb or Em, is it?"

She vehemently shook her head.

I left Aidan a quick note on the hotel note pad, slid on a sweater and my shoes, not bothering to change out of my yoga pants.

Stacy was already sitting by the fire when I made it down. I ordered a cappuccino from a passing server and then took the chair across from Stacy.

"What's up? Everything okay?"

"How did you know Aidan was the one?" she blurted out.

"You thought coffee was a better idea than booze for this conversation?" I asked with a wry grin.

"I have to be sober this entire weekend," she said with a sigh. "Since I'm in charge of capturing all the perfect moments. Can't be puking in a potted plant and miss something."

"Makes sense." I nodded. "How did I know Aidan was the one? Well, I didn't. Not right away. He knew, though. About me."

"Why didn't you know? Isn't that bad?" She leaned forward and rested her elbows on her thighs as she waited for me to answer.

"I was screwed up from my previous relationship. I

wasn't looking for something serious. I didn't know I wanted something serious. Actually, I think I tried to break up with Aidan several times. But he stuck with me—because he knew I was the right one for him. Even though I wasn't ready. He waited for me to be ready."

The server came by with my cappuccino and set down a bowl of sugar cubes, but I didn't touch them.

"Is Gregory pressuring you?" I asked gently.

She shook her head. "Not at all, but he has been vocal about what he wants."

"Why didn't he have kids with his wife?" I asked. "They were together for a decade."

"She was a ballet dancer," Stacy explained. "She was at the height of her career and by some miracle hadn't gotten injured like so many of them do. Having kids would've ended her career. She chose the career."

"Ah, I see."

"It's worse than that. She was having an affair with the company director she danced for," Stacy said. "She got pregnant—and when she found out she didn't seem to care that carrying *his* baby would end her career."

"Cruel," I said softly. "That's so cruel."

She nodded. "Gregory is…well, he's amazing. A brilliant chef. Successful. He says he's over it. Over her. But I just don't know if I believe him. How do you get over that kind of betrayal?"

"How did I get over Matt's betrayal?" I asked. "I didn't get over it. Not until Aidan proved to me that no matter what I did, whatever crazy I showed him, he wasn't going to leave. He was worth the risk."

She swallowed. "I'm not sure I'm ready for that risk— and all that comes with it."

"Can I tell you a secret? You're never really ready, but that's life. And think about all the amazing things you'd be getting if you just took one more leap of faith and trusted that Gregory wasn't full of shit."

"He's twenty years older than I am."

"So what?"

She paused. "My parents will shit a brick when they find out."

I grinned. "Even better."

Chapter 27

Mom Blog Entry:

I've spent my life struggling to bear the weight of my parent's expectations. As I hold my babies and feed and nurture them, all I can think of is how happy and healthy I want them to be, and that I'll be proud of them no matter what.

But, I am going to encourage them not become basement dwelling neck beards.

The next night, I managed to catch a quick cat nap,

but before I knew it, Aidan was kissing me awake so I could get ready for Caleb and Em's rehearsal dinner.

I reached for my phone, wanting to check in with my parents to see how the twins were doing.

They'd slept the night with my parents, and I thought I'd be able to fall into a dreamless sleep, but it wasn't to be. Now that I was a mother, I entered a sort of doze, never really resting, always keeping an ear cocked for the tiniest noise.

I had a few messages from my mother. Photos of Oliver and Sophie taking bottles and looking quite content in my parents' arms. Clearly, they weren't missing me nearly as much as I was missing them.

After I pumped and put the fresh breast milk in the mini fridge, I went to shower. Aidan had left the water on for me and was currently standing at the counter, a towel wrapped around his waist.

I took a moment to admire the sight.

"It's not fair," I said, finally climbing into the shower.

"What's not?"

"Men get to turn into silver foxes. Women turn into white-haired crones."

"Nature's wicked sense of humor," he said. "Wait, do you already think I'm a silver fox? I'm not even silver yet."

"Figure of speech, love," I teased.

I took time with my hair and makeup and when I stood back to admire the results, I smiled at my reflection. I still had to wear a nursing bra that was thicker than thick, but I was happy with my appearance.

Sure, I didn't look like my old self—I never would again—but I'd taken the control back. I'd made a concerted effort to get my body in the best shape that I could, and it felt like a real triumph.

Plus, Aidan's amorous attention earlier that afternoon had done wonders for my ego and put a sparkle in my eyes.

Aidan whistled when I came out of the bathroom. "Foxy," he said with a grin and a kiss to my cheek.

"Thank you," I said, taking him in. He was wearing a three-piece gray suit and his dark hair was combed off his forehead.

"You look like a better version of Don Draper."

"You love Don Draper."

My grin widened. "Exactly." I grabbed my small clutch and my long peacoat. "Ready?"

Aidan winked. "Let's ride."

Em and Caleb had rented out a vineyard to hold their rehearsal dinner. The room was classy and beautiful. When we stepped inside, I immediately noticed Stacy flitting around the room, instructing her team to start snapping photos and taking videos.

She waved to me with an absent smile. I waved back. My curiosity was completely piqued about what she'd do about Gregory. Time would tell.

A server glided toward us, holding a tray of champagne flutes. I plucked a glass from the tray and handed it to Aidan and then took one for myself.

Aidan looked at the champagne. "There's a blueberry at the bottom."

"No, it's a huckleberry."

"How do you know that?" Aidan asked, taking a sip of his drink.

"Because we discussed the food and drink menu at the bachelorette party." I glanced at him. "What did you guys discuss at the bachelor party?"

"Not food."

I wrinkled my nose. "Charming."

"Prince Charming," Aidan said with a roguish grin.

"I like this version of you." I pressed into his side and reached up to kiss his cheek.

"What version is that?"

"The Aidan who is oh so good at seducing me."

"I seduced you this afternoon."

"Technically. Though, to be fair, it didn't take a lot to get me naked."

"As your husband, I appreciate that you're not hard work."

Chuckling, we moved through the room. The happy couple was surrounded by family, including Em's sisters.

Caleb looked dapper in his dark suit. Em looked like a fairy pixie in her black cocktail dress that flared into a ballerina skirt.

"Oh, thank god," Em muttered. To her grandfather, she said, "Excuse me a second. I need to talk to Sibby."

"What do you need to talk to me about?" I asked when we got away from her family and into a corner of the room.

She didn't reply; instead she took my champagne flute and downed half the thing in one swallow.

"Er—maybe you should pace yourself?" I said with a small smile.

"Everything is going wrong tonight."

I looked around. People were laughing and enjoying the puff appetizers being served. The tables were set with cream tablecloths and pristine china.

"Everything looks pretty good to me," I said. "What's going on?"

"My mother has a critical eye."

"Ah."

"Nothing is good enough for her." Em looked over my shoulder and smiled at someone and then turned her attention back to me. "She's watching me like a hawk, ensuring I don't drink too much or eat something that could get stuck in my teeth."

"What could get stuck in your teeth?"

"The spanakopita." She shook her head. "She wanted to know why I decided to serve a food with spinach in it."

"Just think, in two days, you'll be on a plane bound for Puerto Rico. You'll come home after ten days of fun in the sun, tan and in love, married, and most importantly, your mother will be long gone."

She squeezed my hand. "Sorry I took your drink."

"Well, it looked like you needed it more than me. Why aren't your bridesmaids supplying you with booze behind your mother's back? Isn't that their job?"

"My sisters are scared of my mother. And Mari is running interference."

"Interference?"

"She's just making sure everything goes right. So she's not glued to my side."

"I'll stay by your side," I said. "I'll hold champagne glasses and every now and again, you take a sip from it."

"What would I do without you?"

I flashed a grin. "I really have no idea."

An hour later, we all sat down to dinner. We were at Caleb and Em's table since Aidan was Caleb's best man. That meant I got to make polite conversation with the parents of the bride and groom.

I instantly disliked Em's mother and it had nothing to do with Em already telling me about her. She was cold and unapproachable. Unlikable even. Her father was a quiet man, who clearly had been brow beaten for years.

How had they managed to raise three genuine, affable daughters?

Caleb's parents were the exact opposite. They were like Aidan's parents—welcoming, laughed easily, and fawned over Em.

"What are you thinking about?" Aidan asked, brushing his hand across my shoulder while we waited for the soup course to be served.

"I was just thinking about how good it will be for Em to be part of Caleb's family."

"Noticed that, did you?" he asked with a slight smile.

"So, Sibby," Caleb's mom said, cutting off my private

conversation with Aidan. "When is your next book coming out? I want to tell my book club."

I smiled. "You're kind of amazing, did you know that?"

Mrs. Macy laughed. "Flattery will not distract me. Tell me."

"Well," I said, "I'll tell you if you can keep a secret."

"Lips are sealed."

"I wrote another book, but it ends on a cliffhanger."

"You beast," she said.

I nodded. "I know. So, I'm writing the sequel as fast as humanly possible so I can do a joint release. Drop both books at once so readers can binge read."

She sighed. "So, I'll have to wait then."

"It'll be worth it, trust me." I winked.

Mr. Macy changed the subject, not that I blamed him. He wasn't my target audience.

"Aidan said your parents came up and are watching the twins?"

I nodded. "Yep, we're baby free."

"Babies," Mrs. Macy sighed. "Can I see some photos?"

"Let the girl eat her dinner," Mr. Macy said.

"I don't mind." I dabbed my lips with my napkin and then reached for my clutch. I pulled out my cell phone and saw I had a few texts.

"From my mom," I said to Aidan.

"Anything to be worried about?"

"I don't think so. She just asked me to call her when I had a second." I looked at Mr. and Mrs. Macy "Excuse me just a second?"

"I still want baby photos," Mrs. Macy commanded.

I laughed and nodded. I headed out of the main room to the front reception area. I went to stand by one of the large glass windows, shocked to see that it was snowing.

"Hey, is everything okay?" I asked when I had my mom on the phone.

"Yes, everything is fine. Well, except, the twins have already gone through the breast milk."

"I pumped before I left. There are a few more ounces in our room."

"I'll send your father. That should get us through tonight. I think they're going through a collective growth spurt."

"Eating everything not nailed down, huh?"

"Pretty much. Sophie isn't into the mashed bananas, but really likes avocados. Oliver is partial to sweet potatoes."

"That will all change by tomorrow morning, I'm sure. If that's all do you mind if I hop off?"

"I wanted to tell you and Aidan to drive carefully. A storm blew in."

"Ah, yeah, I see that. I'm standing by a window."

"It started about an hour ago. We've already gotten an inch of snow."

"We'll be safe. That's why we bought a Subaru."

I briefly thought of Jasper back in Brooklyn. Zeb and Terry were dog sitting at our place. He loved the snow. I let out a sigh when I had a vision of winter next year. The kids on a sled. Jasper playing in the snow.

"Sibby?" Mom asked.

I shook off the dream that seemed so real—that would be real. And soon.

"I'm good. Kiss the babies for me." I felt a pang for my children, but I forced myself to hang up and not demand every accounting of their diaper changes.

Before I headed back into the dining room, I beelined it for the bathroom. I turned the corner. Em and her mother were facing off, and Em had tears streaking down her face as her mother scolded her like an errant child.

I immediately ducked out of their line of sight, but I could still see them clearly. I wasn't sure what I was supposed to do…except I really did have to pee.

"You're making a mistake," Mrs. Canton stated.

"I'm not," Em said, her voice surprisingly strong despite the fact that emotion was pouring out of her eyes. "I love Caleb. Why are you doing this now? The night before my wedding?"

"Because after you're married it will be too late. You don't realize it yet. You're young. Idealistic. But Caleb isn't in love with you. You don't see it because you don't want to see it. You have to trust me, Emmeline."

"Trust you," she repeated, sounding like she was in a daze. "Because you made really good decisions for me when I was a kid."

Mrs. Canton sniffed. "I did the best I could, but that's not what this conversation is about."

"I'm done with this conversation." Em snapped her spine straight. "You don't get to destroy my happiness. I won't let you."

Em whirled and marched into the women's public bathroom, the door closing softly behind her. It was only a matter of time before Mrs. Canton came around the bend and saw me lurking, so I pulled out my phone and pretended to be checking messages while I forced myself to move forward.

Mrs. Canton brushed past me without a word of greeting, and I breathed a sigh of relief as I went into the bathroom.

I heard the faintest sounds of crying coming from one of the stalls and my heart broke.

"Don't take this the wrong way," I said, "but your mother could give Maleficent a run for her money."

There was a brief pause, followed by a low chuckle. "You heard?"

"Yeah."

The stall door opened and Em came out, her mascara dripping underneath her eyes.

"Wash your face," I told her gently. "I'm going to use the bathroom. And then we're finding a bottle of champagne and a closet."

"Why a closet?"

"You need to hide for a few minutes, get your composure, and you need to get a little drunk."

Mom Blog Entry:
   Every moment, is worth it.

We found a coat closet. I told Em to stay while I went to the bar to grab us a bottle of champagne and to tell Aidan what was going down.

Servers were clearing away dinner plates and getting ready to serve dessert. If anyone needed empty calories at the moment, it was the bride-to-be.

"Are the kids okay?" Aidan asked after I waved him over to the bar.

I nodded. "Kids are fine. It's Em." I told him what I'd overheard and about my game plan to make Em feel better.

He blanched. "How is Caleb supposed to explain his absent fiancée at their rehearsal dinner?"

"Better an absent fiancée than an absent bride tomorrow because she's curled up in the fetal position sobbing her eyes out."

"Good point." He looked over his shoulder at Caleb. "I'll tell him. We'll get Mari to help us spin a story, but try and hurry back. Okay?"

"I'll do my best." I took the bottle of champagne from the bartender. Before I went back to the closet to hang out with Em, I swung by the kitchen and grabbed a plate of huckleberry cobbler.

Em was sitting on the floor at the back of the closet. Her heels were off, her face was devoid of makeup, and for the first time since I'd met her, she looked young and vulnerable. She looked…less than perfect.

I shoved the huckleberry cobbler at her so I could open the champagne bottle.

"You forgot forks," Em said.

"How about, 'Thanks, Sibby? You're so thoughtful for bringing me booze and sugar to ease my pain.'"

Her smile was small, but it was there.

I popped the champagne, managed not to hurt anyone, or spill it, and then I was taking a seat next to her. I offered her the champagne bottle and she took a sip from it.

"Oh sure, you complain about no forks, but you have no issue drinking out of the bottle," I teased.

"It would piss my mother off to know I'm drinking like a heathen." She drank again.

"So, she really is something else, isn't she?"

"You know what's awful about it?" she asked.

"What?"

"Not what she said or her timing of anything. Just the fact that she gets into my head. She's always been able to get into my head." She paused. "It's exhausting. Trying to be perfect all the time."

"Why do you do it? Striving for perfection is the easiest way to feel like a failure."

She laughed. "Yeah, no shit."

I fell silent for a moment. "Are you going to tell Caleb?"

"About what she said?"

She shook her head. "I don't think it would do any good. I texted him, while you were getting the champagne. I told him I had a fight with my mother about something stupid and needed some time to compose myself."

"Aidan, Mari, and Caleb will figure out a way to explain your absence. I wouldn't worry about it. Most people looked pretty drunk anyway. I doubt they'll notice you're gone."

"Thanks," she huffed out a laugh.

"I didn't mean it the way it sounded."

"I know. Why aren't you drinking?"

"I had a glass of wine at dinner. And I have to pump when we get back to the lodge."

Her eyes went to my cleavage and she shook her head. "Champion. You're a champion."

"Me? You went head to head with the woman who gave birth to you. That's powerful in my book."

"Do you think she's right? About Caleb not loving me the way he says he does?"

"How does he treat you?" I asked, putting the ball back in her court.

"Like I'm the most special thing in the world."

"Then I think your mom is jealous."

Em cackled.

"I'm serious. There are some people in this world who are innately unhappy. And they're not happy unless they can spread the misery around."

She paused thoughtfully. "You know, it's weird."

"What is?"

"I never thought I'd be sitting in a coat closet the night before my wedding. You might not be a bridesmaid, Sibby, but you might as well be."

"Aw, shucks." I gestured to the huckleberry cobbler. "If you don't eat that I will. Fork be damned."

"You did what?" I asked in shock.

Aidan didn't take his eyes off the road when he replied. "I didn't do anything. It was Mari's idea to tell people Em wasn't feeling well."

We were only a ten-minute drive from the lodge and we were both stone cold sober, but the snow was coming down in rapid sheets.

"I don't understand the problem."

"Em already wasn't drinking at dinner because her

mother would've berated her for it. Combined with telling people she wasn't feeling well, people are going to assume she's pregnant."

"What? No."

"*Yes*. You have no idea how these things work, Aidan Kincaid."

"What's it matter if people think she's pregnant? They're getting married."

The road was icy, and it took all of Aidan's concentration, so we didn't speak again until we were pulling up in front of the lodge.

The bellman and lodge attendants were out front, shoveling the walkways and roads. A valet took our car and parked it. I shivered as we walked inside. "That's a late spring storm for you."

"I was thinking," he said. "The day after the wedding, we should take the kids and find a snowy hill and go sledding."

"You read minds, don't you?" I asked, pushing the elevator button. "I was just thinking about Jasper back in the city. He's lonely now, but next winter we'll hopefully be in our new home and enjoying our first winter Upstate where he has space to run and play with the kids."

"I love the sound of that."

We got to our room and I immediately stripped out of my dress, moaning in relief when I got comfortable.

"Legit question for you," I asked as I attached the breast pump to my body.

"I'm listening." Aidan shrugged out of his suit coat and hung it up.

"How do you still want to have sex with me after you've watched me use a breast pump?"

"Suspension of disbelief. And is that really what you want to be talking about right now?"

"You didn't tell Caleb, right? About what Em's mom said to her?"

"No. I didn't tell him. I didn't need to fuck with his head the night before his wedding."

"Do you think she's right? Em's mom?"

Aidan removed his cufflinks and set them in their box on his bedside table. "I think you can, at some point in your life, love two very different people."

I frowned. "You think that? You think you can be in love with two people at the same time?"

"I didn't say that. I said love two people very differently. The way Caleb loved Annie...it was fierce and volatile. It was open with everything he had. Raw. You know? It was just...raw.

"But with Em, it's quieter. It's not dramatic. It's not hard for him to love her."

"You're not really answering my question."

"It doesn't matter what I think. Only what Caleb thinks, and he wouldn't have proposed to Em if he wasn't sure he wanted to spend his life with her."

"He proposed to Annie. Several times. He was sure he wanted to spend his life with her, too. You know? How can you want to spend your life with two very different people?"

"Falling in love with Annie changed Caleb. Breaking up with her changed him, too. Relationships don't have to be hard for them to be deep or epic."

I snorted. "You're so not a writer."

He laughed and unbuttoned his dress shirt. "And you're clearly from Russian peasant stock. You like the suffering, admit it."

"No. I don't like the suffering, but I do think a little bit of angst goes a long way. And as a writer, I'm a firm believer that you become better when you triumph over adversity."

I looked down at the bottles that were almost full. "My milk runneth over."

"You really are the land of milk and honey."

"And you're done."

I woke up the next morning to the phone alarm. I sent my mom a text, letting her know there was more breast milk in our mini fridge. And then I sent a text to Em to see how she was feeling.

She sent me a quick text back with a selfie of her already in full makeup.

"Morning." Aidan's voice was raspy with sleep.

His chest was bare, and he looked delicious. If we didn't have a wedding to get to, I'd suggest staying in bed.

"Hi," I leaned over and kissed him briefly, not wanting to kill him with my morning breath.

I got up and went over to the curtains and pulled them back. The snow had stopped, but at least a foot covered everything. "Oh, man."

"Is it bad out there?"

"Well, define bad. Prime day for snowman making, for sure. But it's going to take us forever to get up to the barn."

"Better get moving then."

We were out of the hotel room an hour later. I was dressed for the wedding, but Aidan didn't want his tux to wrinkle, so he hung up the garment bag in the back of the car.

"One last chance to make sure you have everything," Aidan said, helping me across the sidewalk by holding me and keeping me from falling. It wasn't slick, but I was in heels and he was a gentleman.

"I've got everything."

"Phone charger?"

"Yup."

"Gum."

"Yup."

"Bobby pins?"

I looked at him. "Why do I need bobby pins?"

"I don't know, it just seems like something you'd need." He leaned over to kiss me, his minty breath steaming in a cloud in front of his face. "You look really pretty, by the way."

I grinned. "I know."

"Hey, luck must be on our side," Aidan said a few minutes later once we were on our way. "The streets have been plowed."

"It's a good omen." I smiled. "It's a beautiful day for a wedding, isn't it?"

The sun was already out and it looked like a winter wonderland.

We got there twenty minutes later and parked the car behind the house where the wedding party was getting ready. Even though I wasn't in the bridal party, I still walked inside with Aidan and went to find Em. If anything, I could say hello and offer her reassurance, and maybe sneak her a glass of champagne.

But she didn't need it. She was calm, happy, a bright smile across her face. She wore a robe over her undergarments because she hadn't yet gotten into her dress, but her hair and makeup were done.

"Caleb came to my room last night," she whispered when she hugged me hello. "He kind of calmed me down."

I chuckled. "I bet he did."

The next hour flew by. Em got into her wedding dress. It had a demure neckline, but an open back, the lace sleeves stopping at her wrists. There was no train and instead of a veil, she wore a crystal headband.

I felt tears prick my eyes and I instantly reached for the tissues in my purse.

"What's wrong?" Em asked, when she saw me crying.

"You're so pretty!" I sniffled, causing her sisters to chuckle.

"She's right," her best friend said. "You're gorgeous. Caleb isn't going to know what hit him!"

One of Stacy's team members had been snapping photos since before I'd even arrived. She took one now, no doubt committing to film my ugly cry face. Somehow, I managed to get it under control, and I wiped underneath my eyes, just in case.

The wedding coordinator burst through the door. "Show time, ladies!"

"I'm going to go find my seat," I told Em. "The next time I see you, you're going to be married."

"I can't wait."

I squeezed her hand and then left the room. I made my way to the barn where the ceremony would be held. A platform and a wedding pagoda were decorated with white flowers. Candles in mason jars were scattered about the room. A string quartet played background music as guests slowly found their seats and made conversation with each other. I walked down the aisle and took a seat on the bride's side so that I could have a clear view of Aidan when he stood next to Caleb.

The string quartet struck a note signaling the start of the ceremony, and everyone fell silent.

Caleb walked down the aisle first, looking handsome in his tuxedo. His smile was sure, his stride confident as his parents flanked him. He kissed his mother's cheek, shook his father's hand, and then took his place on the platform.

Next came Aidan with Mari on his arm. He caught my eye and winked and damn if I didn't feel butterflies erupt in my belly. I still thought he was the most handsome man I'd ever seen.

He moved to stand next to Caleb.

Evan walked down the aisle with Caleb's cousin, and Ella was escorted by Caleb's friend from college.

A change in the music signaled for us to stand. And then Em appeared, chin raised, a radiant smile on her face as her parents accompanied her down the aisle.

When she got to Caleb, he held out his hand and she took it. They kept their fingers clasped as they stared at one another.

The minister stood between them and gestured for us to take our seats.

"We are gathered here today on this most glorious winter day, to celebrate the union of Emmeline and Caleb."

I felt tears prick my eyes again, but I tuned out everything the minister was saying, choosing instead to focus on the expressions on the bride and groom's faces and the look on my own husband's face.

Aidan caught my eye and sent me a smile; *everything* was

in that smile. It was private and intimate. It reminded me of the day when I'd stood up with him before our friends and family and we'd united our lives as one.

Neither Em nor Caleb decided to write their own vows, instead choosing to let tradition dictate their ceremony. The minister smiled at them.

"Emmeline, repeat after me. I, Emmeline, take thee Caleb."

"I, Emmeline," she parroted. "Take thee Caleb…"

Caleb's smile widened when she got to the word husband and I saw him squeeze her hand when she finished.

"Now, Caleb," the minister said. "Repeat after me. I, Caleb, take thee Emmeline…"

"I, Caleb, take thee Emmeline—"

I heard the heavy thud of barn doors as they flew open and hit the walls. A cold draft of air filled the room, and everyone turned to see what had caused the disruption.

Annie stood in the doorway, wearing a royal blue North Face bubble coat and a black beanie. She paused a moment and then marched down the aisle.

Her face was as white as the snow she'd tracked in, her eyes riveted to the scene at the altar.

She approached Caleb and Em, and then ground to a halt.

Annie swallowed. "Caleb," she croaked.

I turned my attention back to the couple in the middle of saying their wedding vows. Em looked stunned. Caleb's expression was blank, like he'd been sleeping for a hundred years. He finally came out of his stupor. He looked at Em, and then back to Annie, and back to Em once more.

He dropped his fiancée's hand.

"I'm sorry," he said, his voice sounding strangled.

And then he jogged down the steps of the platform toward Annie. He linked his fingers with hers without saying a word, and escaped through the open doors of the barn, disappearing into the snow that had started to fall again and drift into the room.

A moment of bemused silence filled the barn, and then Em's mother jumped up from her seat and yelled, "Music. Music, now!"

Em's bridal party crowded around her and tugged her off the platform, forming a protective bubble around her and whisking her from the ceremony.

The commotion finally started, and everyone spoke at once. I stood, looking at Aidan who was still up on the platform.

Our eyes locked. His gaze was as wide as mine.

I wanted to go to him, but guests were clogging the aisle.

"Excuse me!" Caleb's mother said, moving to stand on the platform. "Excuse me!"

Guests quieted down and turned their attention to the mother of the groom.

"Well, this is…unexpected," she let out a nervous laugh, "but we've got food and drinks and it's all been paid for in advance. So let's not let it go to waste, hmm?"

Mrs. Canton moved to stand next to Mrs. Macy and stated, "Absolutely not! We are not going to celebrate my daughter's humiliation by eating crab puffs!"

"They're bacon wrapped scallops," Mrs. Macy corrected, hands to hips. "It was crab puffs last night. Maybe if you hadn't had that last cocktail, you would've known what you were eating."

"You're a classless philistine!" Mrs. Canton bellowed.

"A you're a cold-blooded snob!" Mrs. Macy fired back.

Before I knew what was happening, the mother of the

jilted bride and the mother of the errant groom went down in a frenzy of tulle and flowers.

Aidan and I were the only two people left in the barn —everyone else had gone to the reception. Even Mrs. Canton and Mrs. Macy—both of whom were sporting scratches and torn dresses. But apparently all could be solved over a vodka cocktail after a good brawl.

"Oh my God," I said for what had to be the fiftieth time.

"I know," Aidan replied. "Did you know Annie was going to do that?"

I shook my head. "No, of course not. We haven't spoken since we got into that fight. Oh God."

"What?"

"Poor Em. This is all my fault. I told Annie she was a coward. That was like waving a red flag in front of an angry bull." I paused. "Like waving a donut in front of me."

"Her mother was right," Aidan said, still sounding like he was in a daze. "She's going to have to live with that on top of this humiliation."

"Caleb is a complete asshole."

"So is Annie."

We fell silent.

"Can I be a total dick for a second?" I asked.

"Sure. Thanks for asking permission, by the way." He smiled and grasped my hand.

"I'm really happy for them."

"Can I be a total dick for a second? Me too."

"Not at the cost of Em, but man."

"Did you text her?"

I shook my head. "I don't even know what to say. Are you okay? Sorry my best friend ruined your wedding and your life? Want to grab coffee and talk it out?"

"Yeah, I see your point."

"Caleb hasn't called you?"

He shook his head.

"I don't think I can, in good conscience, go to the reception," I said.

"Me either. I know I'm the best man and I should be schmoozing or whatever, but I think the parents can handle that."

"Speaking of parents…you want to go back to the lodge and relieve my parents of babysitting duty? I miss the twins."

He stood and then helped me stand. "I miss them too. Let's go."

When we got to the barn door, my phone rang. My heart picked up speed, but it quickly plummeted when I realized it wasn't Annie.

It was a number I didn't recognize—a New York number. Frowning, I answered it when usually I'd have let it go to voicemail, but so much was going on I had to find out who it was.

"Hello?"

"Hello. May I please speak to Sibby?" a female voice asked.

"This is Sibby."

"Hi, this is Jolie Kingston."

"Ha, ha, very funny."

"Excuse me?"

"This is a prank, right? Did Nat put you up to this? Or Zeb? Oh wait, they're in on it together."

"I don't know a Nat or a Zeb. I'm really Jolie Kingston."

I paused. "*The* Jolie Kingston?"

She laughed. "I don't really think of myself that way. That would be kind of arrogant, don't you think?"

"Yeah, arrogant. Sure."

Aidan looked at me in surprise and I made a face and shrugged.

"I was in LA last weekend having dinner with Famous Actor. Your name came up in conversation."

"Did he tell you I spilled wine all over him when I was a waitress?"

"He might've said that." Her voice was filled with humor. "But he also mentioned you were a writer with a very distinct voice. I checked you out and then read one of your books."

"Which book?"

"The one with all the terrible reviews."

"Ah."

"I think it's brilliant."

"You do? Now who's about to get a big head? *The* Jolie Kingston thinks I'm brilliant!"

She laughed. "I want to talk to you about adapting it for the big screen."

I blinked. "I'm sorry. Can you repeat that, please?"

"I want to talk to you about adapting it for the big screen."

"This is a joke, right? Famous Actor is paying me back for ruining one of his favorite cashmere sweaters. This is his revenge? Dangle the shiny red apple in front of me, hoping I take a bite and then I fall to the floor writhing in pain from the poison."

"He said you were dramatic."

"I was a theater major."

"Of course you were. Listen, I've got a magazine shoot to get to, but save this number. It's my cell phone. My schedule is pretty open next week, but then I fly out to Milan the week after that. I really do want to get together with you. You live in Brooklyn?"

"Yes."

"Cool. Text me your schedule. I mean it, Sibby. I'm not blowing smoke up your ass. I really loved your book and I loved that it didn't get a great reception. I do love a good underdog story, don't you?"

"Yeah." I looked at Aidan, a smile spreading across my face. "I love a good underdog story, too."

"Gotta run. Chat soon."

Jolie hung up and I stared at my phone.

"What. Was. That?" Aidan asked, his own face a mirror of shock.

"I think," I paused, emotion constricting my throat, "I think all of my dreams are about to come true."

"Yeah?" He took my hand and kissed it. "You know what that means, don't you?"

I shook my head.

"It means, you're going to have to change it from Sibby's Law to Sibby's Luck."

"Sibby's Luck. I like that."

He held my hand as we walked out of the barn. My

heel slipped on a patch of compact snow. I lost my footing and went down. But because we were on a slight hill, I managed to slide down it.

When I came to a stop, I looked over my shoulder and grinned at Aidan who couldn't contain his laughter.

"Yeah. That was the universe's way of telling me to remain humble. Sibby's Law it was. Sibby's Law it will remain. Forever and ever."

Epilogue
ANNIE

Five minutes later…

The snow came down, resting on the shoulders of my blue North Face coat. For a brief moment, I turned my face up to the sky and felt cold flakes as they melted against my skin, but Caleb's hand, linked with mine, continued to pull me away.

Away from the barn.

Away from the wedding.

His wedding.

"Oh god," I whispered. "I just ruined your wedding." I looked at the man I loved…who must've loved me too, because why else would he have left his bride—an amazing woman—at the altar?

"Did you drive here?" he asked, clearly not replying to my statement.

"Drive?" I repeated. "Yeah. I drove." I gestured with my chin to the black Subaru Forester that I'd parked haphazardly at an odd angle in the closest spot to the barn I could find. I hadn't been concerned about my parking job; instead I'd been worried that I was already too late to stop the wedding.

I hit the clicker and Caleb opened the passenger side door for me, gesturing for me to get in.

"What do you think you're doing?" I asked.

He frowned. "I'm driving."

"No, you're not. I'm driving. My car, my rules."

"Your car? You rented it, didn't you?"

I shook my head. "No. I bought it three days ago."

He looked at me for a long moment and then glanced back at the barn. I swallowed while I watched emotions play across his face. Finally, he nodded and got into the car.

I gingerly made my way to the driver's side. The car was still warmed up and it took no time getting the Subaru out of the snow.

My heart was hammering in my ears.

What now? I'd stopped a wedding. The groom had left. And now we were driving who knew where with all this *stuff* between us.

An unresolved mess.

"Where are we going?" I asked Caleb.

He paused for a moment. "There's an outlet mall about fifteen minutes from here. We can sit in the parking lot and talk."

I swallowed. "Talk. Okay." I paused. "Caleb, I—"

"Not yet, Annie. Don't talk yet."

Fifteen minutes later we arrived at the outlet mall. It was deserted and the shops were closed, no doubt due to the snowstorm that had decided to make a sudden appearance.

I left the car running and the heat on full blast. My

hands were cold, but I quickly over heated, shrugging out of my coat and throwing it in the back seat.

"Why did you stop my wedding?" Caleb asked, his expression curious.

"Why did you leave your wedding?" I asked back.

He smiled slightly. He looked at his lap and absently ran his finger along his tuxedo pant leg.

"I fought with Sibby. A few weeks ago," I said slowly. "I picked a stupid fight with her, but she had the last words. She said I was still in love with you, and that I was a coward because I didn't have the courage to tell you."

"You've got to be fucking kidding me," he growled, leaning his head back against the seat rest.

"What?"

"We've been broken up for how long? You waited until my wedding day to tell me your true feelings? I was just about to marry another woman, Annie! God, I feel like an utter shit bag." He looked at me. "You hurt me. No, you more than hurt me when we broke up. You fucking annihilated me. I didn't think I'd ever be happy again. And I was, Annie. I was really happy with Em."

I swallowed. "Then why did you leave her at the altar?"

"Because it's *you*."

Before I knew what was happening Caleb leaned over, took my face between his hands, and kissed me.

My body came alive and the rightness of his lips on mine settled in my bones. It hadn't been like this with Mills. It hadn't been like this with anyone.

Only Caleb.

Only ever with Caleb.

I sighed into his mouth and tried to get closer to him.

"Wait," he muttered against my lips and then pulled away.

"No. Don't wait. Let's keep going."

He smiled down at me and stroked the side of my face. "There are some things we need to get out of the way before I touch you again. Because once I touch you again, I won't be able to stop."

I shivered from the promise in his voice. "What do we need to get out of the way?"

"You came up here to stop my wedding. Did you have an idea of what would happen if I'd left with you?"

"Honestly? No." I bit my lip. "I thought you'd tell me I was too late and that you were going to marry Em."

"Fuck," he growled. "Em. I humiliated her. I promised her I was over my ex, and then left her at the altar. It's the single worst thing you can do to someone. I mean, it doesn't get worse than that."

"We're assholes," I said. "Giant assholes. But maybe… assholes who deserve each other? And deserve to be happy together?"

"What does that look like for you, Annie. Because I know what that looks like for me."

"Marriage, babies, eventually a house Upstate. Right?"

"Right. My wants haven't changed. We broke up because you didn't want those things."

"Truth time?"

"If you can't be honest with me in an empty parking lot at an outlet mall after I just left my fiancée at the altar for you, then when can you be truthful?" he asked.

"I was scared, of all the things that you wanted. I thought I didn't want those things because I saw what happened with my parents' marriage and I wasn't—I didn't want to fail at that too. Okay? I'd never been in love before you, Caleb, and I couldn't stomach the idea of twenty years down the road blowing it all up."

"So you blew it up on your terms. Yeah, I get all that. That wasn't a shock. But what's changed?"

"Me. I've changed. I needed time on my own to figure out what I wanted."

"You figured that out by dating another guy."

"You don't get to be mad at me for that. You proposed to someone else—which made me question whether your feelings for me were genuine at all."

He glared. "What does that mean?"

"It means, I didn't know if you really wanted a life with *me* or if you wanted a life with *someone*."

He didn't respond.

"I don't want to sit in the car and rehash all our old problems. I didn't make a giant fool of myself by stopping your wedding to talk out all our past grievances and spin in circles."

"We have to talk about them if we want to move forward. If you want us to have a future. Do you want a future with me?"

"Yes," I said without hesitation. "Do you want one with me?"

"I don't know," he said slowly, stroking his clean-shaven jaw. "I'm not sure I trust your intentions."

"How can I make you trust me?"

"I'm open to ideas," he said. "Lay them on me."

I thought for a moment. "How about I be the one to call your mother and father and apologize for breaking your heart?"

"That's a start. What else you got?"

"What about marriage?"

"What about marriage?"

"Yours and mine. We can drive to Niagara Falls tonight."

"You want to drive to Niagara Falls tonight just so you

can, what? Ease your conscience? Make an honest man out of me and protect my reputation?"

"No," I said, not smiling at his jests. "I want to drive to Niagara Falls tonight and marry you because I love you and I can't imagine spending another minute of my life without you."

He stared at me for the longest moment and then he took my cell from the phone mount on the dash.

"Same password?" he asked.

I nodded.

Caleb typed the four-digit passcode and my screen flared to life. I watched him scroll to my favorites list and then hit Sibby's number.

After a few seconds, she answered. "Hello? Annie? What the hell? Are you with Caleb? Where are you? What's—

"You're on speaker," Caleb said.

"So are you," Sibby said.

"Hey, dude," Aidan greeted.

"Hey," Caleb replied.

"I know I'm the theater major," Sibby said. "But you guys might have collectively taken the drama award."

"How bad?" Annie asked.

"Very bad," Sibby said.

"What are you guys doing?" Caleb asked.

"Avoiding your reception," Aidan stated. "Your mom got into a brawl with Em's mom over letting guests enjoy your wedding reception…you know, the one you're *not* at? Hi, Annie."

"Hey, Aidan," I said with a smile.

"We were just calling to tell you guys that we're headed up to Niagara Falls. We're going to get married in the morning."

There was a pause on the other end of the phone and then Sibby let it rip. "Like hell you are!"

"Sibby," Aidan began.

"Don't Sibby me! Our best friends are eloping and they didn't even invite us. Annie," she barked, "I was just about to forgive you for our stupid fight and now you're getting married without me and I was supposed to be your matron of honor!"

"Hey, Sibby," I interrupted. "Do you and Aidan want to meet us at Niagara Falls and be our witnesses?"

"What about our spawn?" Sibby asked. "They're still attached to my breasts."

"Right now?" Caleb asked.

"No, dingus. Not right now," Sibby said in exasperation. "They're at the lodge with my parents who have bottles of breast milk."

"Of course, your spawn are welcome at my wedding. I am their godmother. And Caleb is their godfather."

I looked at Caleb and we grinned at each other.

"Hello? Stop looking at each other all moony-eyed," Sibby said.

"How did you know we were doing that?" Caleb demanded.

"Uh, hello, I write romance for a living. I know things."

"So, where do we stand on this Niagara Falls watching the marriage thing happen?" Caleb asked.

"You think I'm going to miss my best friends getting married?" Sibby asked. "Count us in!"

"Second that," Aidan said. "I'm happy for you guys."

"Just, don't tell my parents you're invited and they aren't," Caleb said.

"You want to give them another reason to be angry right now?" I asked.

"When they see how happy we are, they're not going to

care. Especially if we promise them a grandkid in the next year."

"Are you telling me I've got to get knocked up in order to please your parents?" I demanded.

"Consider it a gesture of goodwill," Caleb said.

"Right-o, signing off," Sibby said. "Text Aidan an address. We're going to get the twins back from my parents and we'll see you in six to eight hours depending on traffic and bathroom breaks."

"Sibby?" I asked.

"Yeah?"

"Are we okay?"

"Of course we're okay. You're Annie and I'm Sibby. We're always going to be okay."

The call ended and then Caleb and I sat in silence.

"Wow," he said after a long while. "We're really doing this."

"We're really doing this."

"Are you ready?"

I grinned. "For our happily ever after?" I took his hand and laced his fingers through mine and brought our clasped hands to my lips. "You bet."

I've inherited a house in Gator Springs, Florida.

Ever hear of Gator Springs?

Yeah, me neither.

I head down to the beach for a little R & R, but of course nothing goes to plan…

Chapter 1

"You will never defeat me, heathen!" I yelled.

Sophie brandished her mock sword. "The kingdom will never be yours! I will never surrender!"

"En guard!" I pulled my own matching rapier from its sheath at my waist and posed to attack.

Sophie lunged for me, our wooden blades clacking against one another.

"You, evil queen, have done your last dirty deed!"

I held back a grin.

We whirled and twisted, fencing and dueling. She charged.

I feigned to the left.

"Mom, you were supposed to die," she admonished.

"Oops. Sorry. Go again?"

She nodded. Sophie lunged once more, her mock sword sliding between my armpit and my side. I dropped my rapier and collapsed to my knees.

"You have struck me," I moaned. "The better queen has won."

I dramatically fell onto my back and began to twitch, pretending I was dying the most horrible of deaths.

Through half-mast lids, I watched Sophie creep closer. When she was within arm's reach, I grabbed her and pulled her down to the ground and began to tickle her.

Her peals of laughter rang through the backyard.

"No fair," she gasped when I ceased my ticklish attack.

"All's fair in true love and make believe, kiddo," I teased. "How was my death?"

"Ten out of ten, two thumbs up."

We sat next to each other, cross-legged on the lawn. She leaned her head against my shoulder. "You're the best mom ever."

"How do you know?" I asked. "You've only had one mom."

"I know," she informed me, in her lofty seven-year-old worldly voice.

The back door slid open, and Jasper ran out to greet us, his entire butt wagging in happiness to see us. Aidan came out behind him.

The dog went to Sophie first, bathing her face with his tongue. Laughing, she pushed him away. Jasper came to me next and flopped down onto his back. I rubbed his belly for a few moments, and when he'd had enough, he bounded over to Aidan.

The man looked positively delectable in a pair of ratty khaki shorts, an old gray T-shirt, and a backwards Mets cap.

Jeepers, he was hot.

"Who won the sword fight?" he asked.

"Sophie, of course," I said. "She puts Arya Stark to shame. I didn't stand a chance."

"Who's Arya Stark?" Sophie asked.

"A character who's an expert with the sword," I told her.

My daughter had gone as Robin Hood last year for Halloween and even after she'd physically outgrown the costume, she hadn't been willing to let it go. So, I'd sewn her a new one, with room to grow.

She wore the costume four days a week, at least. And when she wasn't in her Robin Hood costume, she preferred overalls.

"Where's Ollie?" Aidan asked.

"Upstairs, making sure he's packed everything."

Aidan walked to me and reached down to help me off the grass. He then began brushing off my backside.

"I think I'm good," I said in amusement.

"Nah, you're covered in dirt," he said with a wink.

I arched a brow.

"Soph, why don't you go and tell Oliver that your grandparents are on their way," Aidan said.

"M'kay," she said, running toward the house, black braids flying behind her head. Jasper trotted after her.

"Seriously? I can't still be dirty," I said to Aidan.

"You're Sibby. You're always dirty."

"You made that sound sexual."

He pulled me into his arms and stared down at me. "Hello."

"Hello."

Aidan kissed me.

"You know you look like a college frat guy with the backwards cap, don't you?"

"Oh, definitely." He smiled, making his dimples pop up and say hello.

"God, were you this hot when we met?"

"Yes, I was irresistible even then."

"It was the flannel shirt," I assured him. "The dimples were just the icing on the lumbersnack cake."

We headed into the house which was nothing short of a wreck. I winced. "Yikes. I forgot that we destroyed this place last night."

"Don't look at it," Aidan suggested. "When the kids leave, we'll divide and conquer the clean-up."

"Or we could keep the living room fort we made with the kids and watch cartoons," I suggested. "And eat ice cream for dinner."

"We did that with the kids last night," he reminded me. He lifted his T-shirt to show off a six pack. "If I want to keep this and not have a dad bod, then ice cream for dinner two nights in a row isn't the best idea."

I reached around and grabbed my *tuchus*. "Probably right. But it's a hell of a lot of fun. I do suppose we could increase our cardio workout."

"We could."

"I was referring to sex."

He laughed. "Yeah, I gathered as much. And I fully support that endeavor."

"Excellent. Glad to have you aboard, sailor." I saluted him and then with a sigh, I went to the sink and began loading the dishes into the dishwasher.

The twins came down the stairs, arguing. "Ollie, please," Sophie begged.

"No," he said. "I don't want to."

She'd changed out of her costume and put on a pair of her favorite overalls. She pushed back a curl that had escaped one of her braids and glared at her brother.

They were best friends and worst enemies. And so completely different.

Oliver was currently wearing a clip-on red bowtie and a pair of Chinos. His dark hair was parted and combed.

He was as serious as an accountant during tax season. Looked like one too. I had to stop myself from squeezing the stuffing out of him because he was so cute.

"What's going on?" Aidan asked as he went to the fridge.

"I asked Ollie if he'd be the Sheriff of Nottingham to my Robin Hood while we're on our road trip, and he said he wouldn't."

"Then that's his choice," I said.

Aidan tossed me a loaf of bread. "Grilled cheese?"

"Heck yes," I said. "Oh, I guess we're standing firm at not eating like garbage?"

"It's gourmet cheese," he said. "From France. It makes a difference."

I wrinkled my nose at him.

"Can I have a tomato on mine?" Ollie asked.

"Absolutely." I pulled out a cutting board and washed a beefsteak tomato that Annie had grown in her garden.

I made two extra sandwiches in case Bud and Nancy hadn't eaten lunch and left them on the counter.

Sophie finished her sandwich first, all but inhaling it like a wolverine. She got up from the table and brought her plate to the dishwasher.

"Can I wait out front for Grandma and Grandpa?" she asked.

"Let's all go," Aidan suggested, polishing off the last bite of his sandwich.

The four of us went out front. Oliver sat on the porch swing with Sophie, but Sophie couldn't sit still. She launched herself off the swing and decided to do cartwheels across the front lawn.

"Hey, Soph, maybe give your belly some time to digest," Aidan said.

"Rats," she muttered, plopping down onto the grass. She tilted her face up to the sunshine.

"I'll have to count your new freckles when you get home in a few weeks," I said.

"I hope my face is covered in them," she said.

"You need to wear sunscreen," Oliver informed her. "You don't want to burn."

She stuck her tongue out at her brother and he returned in kind.

"Let's go over the rules again for when you're in a national park," I said looking from Sophie to Oliver and then back to her.

"No feeding the animals," she recited. "No touching the animals. No wandering near smelly water. Listen to Grandma and Grandpa."

I grinned. "Yup. You got it."

Sophie flipped her body around and did a head stand. "I'm going to miss you so much!"

"Sophie," I warned. "Do I need to clean out your ears? Your father said you need time to digest."

She lowered her legs to the ground.

"I like it when you're stern," Aidan whispered.

"Hush."

"Are you going to miss me?" Sophie asked me.

"Absolutely."

"Are you going to miss Ollie?" she inquired.

"Without a doubt. I'm so jealous you get to go to Yellowstone and see Old Faithful. It's going to be lonely around here without you guys."

"But you've got Dad to keep you company," Oliver pointed out.

I looked at my husband, who was lookin' at me like he couldn't wait to chase me naked around the kitchen.

"Too true." I glanced at Oliver. "You sure you don't want to change? Aren't you hot?"

He shook his head.

I tried another avenue. "You're going to be sitting for a long time. You don't want to wrinkle your clothes."

"I want to look nice for Grandma and Grandpa," he said.

"Well, you look very handsome," I commented.

"Just like his father, right?" Aidan asked.

"Right."

Bud and Nancy would be here any minute to scoop up the kids and then they were gone for six weeks on an epic road trip adventure.

Six weeks during the summer, and for the first time in a long while Aidan and I would be kid free.

Aidan's phone chimed with a text. He checked the screen. "They're turning onto our street."

"They're coming!" Sophie shrieked and then hopped up.

A few minutes later, Bud and Nancy parked a giant motorhome at the curb.

"That thing is a beast," Aidan muttered.

"Not a beast. A tank. I don't remember it looking that big," I said.

"That's what she said," he quipped.

"We're still saying that? After all these years?"

"I don't think it'll ever go out of style."

Bud cut the engine of the motorhome and then he and Nancy climbed out.

"Grandpa!" Sophie screamed as she ran to her grandfather. She wrapped her arms around his legs and he pretended she almost knocked him over.

"What? No Robin Hood costume?" he asked.

"I packed it."

Bud tugged on her left braid and then looked at his grandson. He held out his hand to him. "You're a mighty smart dresser, Oliver."

Oliver beamed and took his hand, giving it a hearty shake. "Thanks, Grandpa."

"Let's load up your suitcases," Bud said. "We've got a long way to go."

"Are you guys hungry?" I asked. "We made grilled cheese sandwiches for you."

"Sounds good, thanks," Bud said.

Nancy placed her hands on her hips and pretended to be upset. "Don't I get a hug and a kiss?"

"Hey, Mom," Aidan said with a grin.

"Don't *hey mom* me." She embraced her son and then stepped back to look at him. "You look tired."

"Mom." Aidan rolled his eyes.

"Are you sleeping enough? Eating enough? Or are you and Caleb burning the candle at both ends?"

"Have to make sure everything is ready to go for the craft brew festival," Aidan said.

Nancy's gaze slid to me. "And you?"

"And me what?" I asked.

"When am I getting another romance novel from you?"

I groaned. "You sound like my agent. Her emails have been in all caps lately. I'll tell you what I told her. I'm enjoying writing children's books under a pen name, but when I have a stellar idea for a romance novel, I'll write it."

The front door opened, and Bud strolled out, carting both Oliver and Sophie's suitcases. The kids trailed behind him with the grilled cheese sandwiches.

"Okay, say goodbye to your parents," Bud commanded

as he loaded the suitcases in one of the outdoor storage compartments.

Oliver hugged me first. "Do me a favor," I whispered in his ear. "Look out for Sophie. Trouble follows her."

He grinned. "I'll watch out for her."

"Good boy," I said, giving him one last squeeze.

Aidan scooped Sophie up and turned her upside down. "Promise you won't order pepperoni pizza without me," Sophie said in between bouts of laughter.

"Promise," I lied.

We stood on the porch steps and waved to them as they drove away.

I sighed and leaned my head against his shoulder. "Are you thinking what I'm thinking?" I asked.

"We just had grilled cheese."

"Appetizer," I stated. "I could easily crush a medium-sized Pepperoni pizza with extra cheese."

"You're trying to make me fat," he quipped.

"Yup. If you're fat, you can't run fast enough to get away from me."

"There's never any danger of that happening." He kissed the top of my head. "Besides, you're not one for running."

I grinned up at him. "You know me so well."

About the Author

Wall Street Journal & *USA Today* bestselling author Emma Slate writes romance with heart and heat.

Called "the dialogue queen" by her college playwriting professor, Emma writes love stories that range from romance-for-your-pants to action-flicks-for-chicks.

When she isn't writing, she's usually curled up under a heating blanket with a steamy romance novel and her two beagles—unless her outdoorsy husband can convince her to go on a hike.

Emma also writes rom-com and contemporary romance as E. Slate.

Additional Works

<u>Writing as E. Slate</u>

The Sibby Series

Queen of Klutz (Book 1)
Sibby Slicker (Book 2)
Mother Shucker (Book 3)
Sibby's Spawn (Book 4)
Hot Mess Express (Book 5)

Others:

From Stardust to Stardust

<u>Writing as Emma Slate</u>

The Tarnished Angels Motorcycle Club Series:

Wreck & Ruin (Tarnished Angels Book 1)
Crash & Carnage (Tarnished Angels Book 2)

Madness & Mayhem (Tarnished Angels Book 3)
Thrust & Throttle (Tarnished Angels Book 4)
Venom & Vengeance (Tarnished Angels Book 5)
Fire & Frenzy (Tarnished Angels Book 6)
Leather & Lies (Tarnished Angels Book 7)
Heartbeats & Highways (Tarnished Angels Book 8)

SINS Series:

Sins of a King (Book 1)
Birth of a Queen (Book 2)
Rise of a Dynasty (Book 3)
Dawn of an Empire (Book 4)
Ember (Book 5)
Burn (Book 6)
Ashes (Book 7)
Fall of a Kingdom (Book 8)

Others:

Peasants and Kings